The Dragon & The Book of Blessings

Tales Told by a Tinker Volume III

H.D. Bobb Jr.

Kindle

This Trilogy would not be possible without the help of my editor Donna Sheppard Bobb and my Illustrator and cartographer Andrea Bobb. Thanks to both of them for their patience and support in helping put together this series!

Contents

The Dragon
&
The Book of
Blessings
Tales Told by a Tinker
Volume III

By
H.D. Bobb Jr.

Winter Holiday with Pawpaw

Tizzy, Odin, and Alex were on their way to Pawpaw's. They were out of school for winter solstice. It was also Alex's birthday. They always got to spend a week in the country with Pawpaw every winter holiday. Their parents had enjoyed the same experience when they were growing up and felt blessed that these three cousins were lucky enough to continue the tradition.

Plus, they always had the best of times there. Pawpaw, as the whole family referred to him, was a storyteller. The generations of family members that visited the country estate over the years still carried fond memories of their vacations spent with Pawpaw.

There really weren't that many forests around anymore. Now days people lived in the cities where there were more choices. But not Pawpaw, he lived smack dab in the middle of the most beautiful and remote setting. There was a small pond nearby, behind the barn that had an assortment of ducks and geese running around. Over the years Pawpaw had carved dead tree stumps around the property to resemble animals. Rabbits, owls, squirrels you name it, he was quite talented at it. One of Alex's favorite things to do when he came to visit was to find the newest addition to Pawpaw's collection of animal carvings. It made being around the eighty acres he lived on, extra fun to play make believe.

On top of the fun to be had playing in the woods, were the songs and stories he sang and told after supper each night. They would all sit around a fire ring and sing and play music. Then, if he were in the mood, Pawpaw would tell one of his tales. The kids all thought his tales were the best. They were always about exotic places and had magic creatures, or heroes or sometimes even heroines. Tizzy was hoping to hear more about Swan, the heroine of the last story.

Her mom, Adria, was taking the three cousins to the compound. Adria never got tired of seeing the beautiful spot her grandfather had, away from the city. She had a lot of sweet memories from the place where she spent her school breaks with Pawpaw. He had opened her eyes to the exotic beauty all around us, that we miss for some reason. He also kindled her imagination with his tales of faraway places. There was a fresh layer of snow on the ground, and she couldn't wait to hit Alex with a snowball.

The first full day Pawpaw loaded them into a sleigh with padded red leather seats and hitched two solid black horses to it. He took them for a ride all around the property. They saw two bunnies chasing each other in the snow jumping over each other playing. A big beaver was looking out of his hut near the lake, and they saw a red fox chasing a mouse. They stopped to sled down a big hill that led out onto a small stream frozen over. Alex loved it! It was wicked fast going down that hill. Pawpaw had a rope you could hold onto, and it would tow you back up the hill so you could go again. It took all day, but the three cousins agreed they had no idea the property was this pretty in the winter. After dinner and some hot chocolate, they all sat around the fire ring for some music. Pawpaw played several tunes on his mandolin, and they sang along enjoying the music and the warmth of the fire.

Pawpaw put down his mandolin and lit his pipe The cousins knew when the pipe got lit, that was their que to ask for a story. The cousins pleaded with the old man to tell them one of his tales.

"Please Pawpaw, tell us more about Swan! I'm dying to know if she is alive!" Tizzy pleaded with excitement. "Last time you ended the story with her dying after fighting the ArchMage."

2

"No, make it a boy hero, please Pawpaw," Alex pleaded. You promised a boy hero last time." Alex always loved a boy hero saving the day. "Tell us about Jason the giant blacksmith and Jade his companion!"

Pawpaw smiled at the children's interest in his tales. He was old, but still spry. He reached over to a nearby chest and pulled out the large map. He unfolded it and spread it out on Tizzy's lap.

Pawpaw was comfortable in his padded chair by the fire and so were the three teenagers. He leaned forward over the map and said, "This tale might take all week to tell young ones, so settle in. It takes place in the same three kingdoms you already know about, and some new ones, and it goes like this." Pointing to the map, he began his tale......

The Granite River flowed from the Blackthorn Mountains in the east to the Emerald Sea in the west. It formed the boundary between Sulan in the north and Autry to the south. It was said the south slope of the Granite River had the best vineyards in the world. The mountain water was clean and pure. Fishing flourished along its banks, and it provided transport to the Port of Bar Harbor where sea going vessels could be found. It had steep slopes along the river which meant only a few bridge crossings between the two kingdoms existed. The many vineyards on both slopes of the river connected aqueducts to the vineyards for controlled watering from the river.

To the north, the Sky Mountains separated the kingdom of Sulan from the Kingdom of Balzar. Balzar had a huge coastal area that had originally been controlled by pirates raiding shipping of trading partners. In fact, the former King, Gregory, was a direct descendant of a pirate captain, he even had an eye patch. He inherited the crown from his father after he died of syphilis. Balzar was a very lawless nation. What had started as a base for pirates had grown to a full-blown port with a navy. During the recent war, their navy had been decimated by the Sky Rock Clan's aerial attacks in retaliation for Gregory's raids on their villages. Commerce between Sulan and Balzar was mostly through overseas shipping and since the war ended badly for Balzar it had practically ceased to exist. This left only two mountain passes that allowed passage between the two kingdoms, and that depended on the season and weather.

The mountains were dangerous because they were inhabited by trolls, ogres, and giants. The local mountain folk were mostly left to their own lives and defenses. The Sky Rock Clan provided protection from the trolls and ogres to the mountain tribes.

Magic was still widespread but had weakened through the generations. Each of the three kingdoms had their own opinions of magic.

In Balzar any kind of magic was encouraged, and chaos ruled.

In Sulan, magic was tolerated.

In Autry magic had been banned with a bounty on all magic users, but that law had been rescinded, since the marriage of King Ferdinand to Queen Jennifer. After helping to end the war, magic users had been pardoned. Most were still getting used to the idea of openly using magic.

We begin our story in Autry, at the Royal Castle in Tandor.

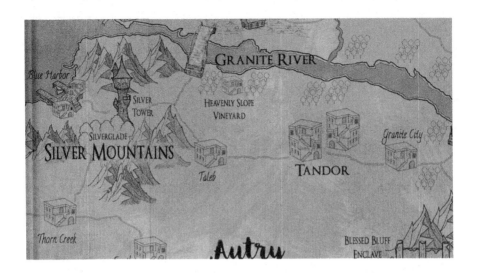

After the Silver Tower

Chancellor Graves was explaining to King Ferdinand and Queen Jennifer that the harvest of the fall crops was going to be small, due to the ash from Jordan's Bane that had fallen on the fields in the spring, after the eruption. He advised trying to buy more grain from Sulan to avoid hunger or worse yet starvation this winter. Word from Sulan indicated they had a bumper crop this year. Queen Jennifer assured them both that her father would help when asked. She would send a letter to him right away with the request.

Another problem that needed to be delt with involved the prisoners who had surrendered when the Silver Tower fell. Many of the magic users that had been jailed claimed the ArchMage was behind the rebellion. Silverglade and the area surrounding the Tower had suffered severe damage during the attacks. There had been reports of bombs being dropped. Some said they were dropped by a giant bird others claimed it was a dragon.

The King believed the story made it sound like Swan was responsible for the Tower's destruction. Others swore the devil himself came for ArchMage Ibis, consuming him in fire. One of Ibis' lieutenants swore he had been using black magic to steal other's lifeforces, extending his own life for years. That same mage claimed that Ibis was over four-hundred years old. He explained Ibis had found an ancient artifact, he called it the Reaper Wand. With that wand he could call black lightning, draining the lifeforce of whatever lifeform it struck. Whoever it struck died because their lifeforce had been transferred to Ibis. Ibis had killed Gretchen's husband, Henrick and his team, using the Reaper after having them ambushed as they were attacking the Tower.

The wand was not found when the Order of the Chalice searched the area, but many other artifacts were. Many of them had been stolen from the Blessed Bluff Enclave in Autry. Those items were being examined and catalogued by the Order. The elves that King Ferdinand had pardoned for their cooperation with Autry were also working on that dangerous task.

The most pressing news Chancellor Graves delivered was the expansion of lava tubes from Jordan's Bane rapidly growing towards the Granite River. There was serious concern about the lava flow fouling the water that Autry's cities used for drinking. There also was a lot of commercial fishing on the Granite River that would be totally ruined for who knows how long. The owners of the wineries pointed out the Granite River was also used for irrigation of the vineyards. Overall, not good news.

Queen Jennifer tried to soothe Ferdinand by reminding him of the narrow victory they had just accomplished over the Silver Tower. Thanks to Swan and the Sky Rock Clan, they had taken King Gregory of Balzar out of the equation. The war was over, and what was left of the Balzarian Navy had been recalled home, broken, and defeated.

From all the reports King Gregory was dead, but his body had, as yet been found. Queen Jennifer was most concerned with the fact that there had been no news of Swan and her condor, now that the fighting was done. One report said she had been struck down by Ibis and the Reaper Wand but there had been no confirmation of that. Although it broke the Queen's heart, it didn't surprise her that Swan may have given her life to save them!

After the Tower fell, Gretchen had reported her husband's death in the fight to the Royal couple. In addition to that, Gretchen reported that she assumed both Swan and Prism were dead, but so far, they hadn't found their bodies as proof. There had been many fires that day so they could have perished in any of them. Also, during the search, they had found a large stone pyre that appeared to have been stone melted by dragon fire.

Gretchen finished her report with, "After I saw a lightning bolt from her trident strike Ibis, she continued dropping bombs on the compound. At that point I thought Ibis was finished. Swan had burnt a hole clear through him, I saw it. Somehow on her next pass over the tower Ibis fired that black wand at her, striking first the condor and then Swan. They dropped from the sky, leaving a trail of smoke." Gretchen said through her tears.

"In the next instant a gold dragon appeared out of nowhere. I watched as it breathed dragon fire right into Ibis's face. It melted what was left of the Tower leaving only a smoldering pile. I have no idea where it came from. I thought all the dragons had been gone for centuries. The dragon, Swan and her condor disappeared and have not been seen since. May their spirits rest in peace." Gretchen began to sob, again.

Queen Jennifer hugged her and joined her in crying over the losses they had both endured. Jennifer was having trouble believing the female warrior that had saved Jennifer from being raped as a young girl, rescued her when she was kidnapped, and saved her kingdom from defeat, was gone.

Jennifer was as broken hearted as Gretchen. Swan would be severely missed!

Later that night, as the king and queen retired to their bedchambers, Jennifer's thoughts turned to the movement she felt in her belly. Reminding her of the life that would start soon. She knew the sadness of losing her friend Swan, would soon be replaced with the joy of a new life. That new life began because of Swan returning her to her husband after the kidnapping. A kick from the baby again reminded her of that coming life. She then felt more pressure, and then more yet. She thought she needed to urinate and got up from the bed just as her water broke, splashing across the floor.

Queen Jennifer called to Ferdinand as another contraction hit her. "My love, it is time to call the midwife to attend me. The baby is coming!"

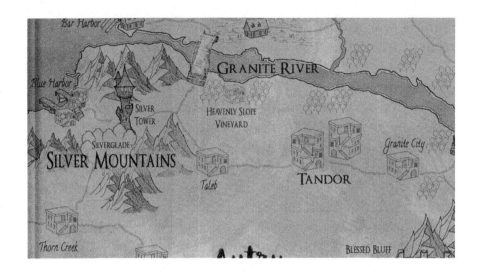

Dragon

Galad examined the injuries the giant condor had suffered. A long burn had cut the birds torso from its neck to under its left wing. The magnificent bird was barely breathing. Galad had not known of any flying creatures of its size other than dragons and some smaller creatures like flying squirrels and monkeys. None large enough for a human to sit on, let alone get airborne.

His attention then moved to the young female. She was dressed in form fitting leathers and carried a trident and recurve bow as weapons. Very unusual, he thought, especially for a female. Galad had a curiosity about this female, she was one of a very few that knew the exhilaration of flight as he did. Her breathing was labored and shallow and she had a blackened burn all around the gold necklace she wore. Galad detected there was magic protection in the necklace that had probably saved her from sudden death.

Swan was falling, after being hit by the black lightning, she saw visions of her life flash before her eyes. There was the day of the contest when she saved Marcus from falling into the ravine. How her heart had beat after pulling him up to safety. Then flash, the morning she woke to find her condor egg had hatched. Then flash, graduation and her first assignment at the Eastern Aerie. Then flash, flying formation on a troll raid. Flash again, the day Sydney, the apprentice alchemist, first showed her he had a recipe for a bomb using a gourd and some reagents. Then flash, a gourd on a tree stump exploded, knocking down a stand of trees and startling her awake.

Swan slowly opened her eyes; she couldn't believe what she saw staring back at her. She unstrapped herself from her saddle but found her right leg was pinned under Prism, so it was difficult to dismount. She had little strength left as she reached for her trident in case she needed to somehow fight the Golden Dragon towering over her. Swan could feel Prism's spirit slowly drifting away from her but could do nothing about it. Tears came to her eyes as she patted Prism's neck where she could feel the burnt feathers around the wound. Swan suddenly remembered the heal spell contained in a ring she wore. The spell would transfer some of her health to Prism. As she started to say the magic word, while touching Prism's wound the word "Stop!" came to her so sharply it shocked her. Had the dragon reached out to her mentally?

She then heard the words in her head, "You are too weak to link with your steed, giving him any of what little strength you have left will kill you. I am much stronger, let me try to help you. I am afraid he is beyond our help. We had a common enemy in Ibis and your aid in killing him put you and your giant bird at risk. It was a brave and honorable thing to do! Rare qualities among humans in my experience"

The Golden Dragon placed his fore paws on Swan and a gold light was exchanged between them. The dragon lifted Prism, removing the obstruction from Swan's leg. Dismounting Prism with her trident in her right hand she went to the bird that she had raised from a chick. Stroking his facial feathers and sobbing uncontrollably at her loss. she hugged Prism one last time. All she could think of now was how would she live without the majestic bird that had stood with her through thick and thin? The loss was a huge hole in her heart and the ache hurt badly. It was a pain she knew would never heal.

Finally getting a grip on her grief she looked up at the huge Golden Dragon watching her. Brushing herself off and wiping away her tears she approached the Golden Dragon who had been watching her intently.

"Thank you for your assistance, Sir Dragon. My name is Swan, and I am in your debt. I thought I had finished Ibis off, but he surprised me. Swan commented as she bowed to the dragon.

In mind speak the dragon responded, "Pleased to have assisted you Swan. At least we know Ibis will not be a bother to anyone now. I owed him the fiery death he received. He kept me a prisoner for many years. Since we both evidently had reason to terminate the ArchMage let it begin a new friendship between us."

"My name is Galad. I am deeply sorry Swan for your loss. I wish I could have saved your companion but too much of his life force had already been stolen by Ibis and that nasty wand. That wand almost killed you as well. Your bird looked to be a noble flyer. I was not aware of the breed existing or their ability to carry a rider. I have only known of dragons that allowed a rider. Perhaps we can start with you filling me in on what has happened while I have slept all these many years."

They spent the next few hours exchanging information. She explained the conflict in the three kingdoms and how much havoc the ArchMage had created. They compared flying in different conditions and the view they enjoyed that few had the pleasure of experiencing. Swan could hardly believe what she was hearing. There really were dragons and dragon riders. She also told the dragon about how she and Prism had been bonded since his birth.

The two talked long into the night, taking her mind off her loss for a short time. Swan also took some solstice in knowing that Prism and Firefly had a large clutch of eggs during their last mating season. Their offspring were beautiful birds with similar colors as their parents and were going to be quite striking when they matured.

Scarlet Desert

More of the Sundown Tribe were arriving at the area around the new river and lake every day. They were calling the area Mystery Waters. The water in the lake was crystal clear, with a sandy bottom that had been dry desert just weeks before. What had been colorless desert for centuries had sprung to life and was now a lush oasis. The desert people had moved above ground bringing their multicolored tents and lavish furnishings with them. All the desert people were overjoyed to have this new water source. It was the first discovery of water in the Great Scarlett Desert in centuries.

The news of the transformation of the land in the southern desert, around the new water source had reached all the Sundown Tribe cities and villages. Mikiel and Amara were currently using Swift, to ferry settlers to the Mystery Waters region, and had been for several weeks now. Swift, their family sand schooner, was outfitted with a small amount of magic. It rode on six skis that allowed the ship to skim along the sand driven by the wind.

Mikiel was a striking example of the dark-skinned Sundown Tribe. He was young, well-built, tall, and broad through the shoulders, a strong looking man. The symbol on his white turban warned he was a sorcerer.

The old legends spoke of two desert tribes inhabiting the desert, but the Sundown Tribe was the only tribe in existence now. Centuries ago, the Da Nang had lived in the northern Scarlet Desert, in an area known as the Drifting Sands. No one lives there now due to perpetual sandstorms. In more recent times the Sundown Tribe primarily lived underground in cool underground caverns and oases.

Mikiel's sister Amara was the darkest skinned of the four siblings. She was shorter than her brothers, with a cute curvy figure. She had very thin, sharp features and short curly black hair with violet eyes that folks sometimes thought were hard to quit staring at. She was an unusual looking mage. She had more the looks of a warrior than mage. Her dark magics and offensive abilities were off putting to most people. The fourth sibling was her twin, Dylan. Dylan had been the real fighter of the four. When they had been young, he would challenge Mikiel and Amara to battle at the same time and would usually win. He and Amara were very close, they told each other everything. Earlier in the year he was leading a caravan when the giant sand worms attacked. He had managed to kill one of the monsters but had been killed in the fight. Amara missed him terribly. They had confided everything to each other, their secrets, and joys. Lately, ever since Dylan's death, Amara had been having strange dreams.

Growing up, Mikiel always competed with their older brother, Willem. This competition, as such, led them to be very close to each other. Willem was now the Sultan of the Sundown Tribe with many responsibilities. While Mikiel and Amara would rather be riding Swift across the desert than deal with governing the Tribe.

As a young girl she had been given an amulet that had belonged to her now departed grandmother. Before her death, Amara's grandmother explained to her that the stone was a rare shade amulet. It would protect her when she communicated with the dead. When Amara's mother learned Amara had the ability to speak with the dead it had really creeped her out. After her mother was given some time to get used to the idea, she confessed her grandmother had the same ability but never really spoke about it with her.

Swift was currently anchored outside Vardo, the largest above ground city of the Sundown Tribe. Mikiel was spending the night in town with a woman he had a crush on. Amara had some supper and sat above deck looking at the stars twinkle above her. It was a cool evening for the desert and a nice breeze made for an enjoyable evening alone. She had always been a bit of a loner, but after Dylan's sudden death she found the silence of being alone to be a comfort. She took no sweetheart and had no close friends to speak of now that Dylan gone. After finishing off a bottle of wine, she called it a night and went below deck to her quarters and her bed.

Amara found herself wandering the desert and she sensed a terrible sandstorm was headed her way. Where was she? Why did she not have a waterskin or a weapon? Why would she leave Swift without any provisions? The blowing sand became more intense as the wind increased. Deciding on a direction, she headed that way one step after another. To where she didn't know. She wrapped her scarf around her face, covering everything but her eyes. The sand got so bad she tried to turn around and walk with her back into the storm, but it seemed no matter what direction she turned, the sand was whipping her face. She trudged along until her legs were wobbly and unsteady.

Reaching the top of a large sand dune she stood looking over the desert. All she could see was sand in all directions. Deciding it was less windy lower down on the dune Amara continued to head down the other side of the dune. The blowing sand had become so intense that she didn't see where the dune sloped sharply downward, causing her to fall, head over heels down the dune. When she came to a stop it took her a moment to check that her fingers and toes still worked, and nothing was broken. After taking a full inventory of her parts she realized she was unharmed. Then it suddenly occurred to her she was out of the sandstorm.

Looking up at the cloudless sky above her, Amara thought she was hallucinating. Clearing the sand from her eyes she still couldn't believe what she was seeing. She was witnessing a city, floating in the sky, directly above her. She watched as it rotated, almost as if it sat on a giant dish, slowly turning. As it turned above Amara, she saw a giant pyramid with a tall spire come into view. The white spire reflected the sun as it struck it, almost hurting her eyes with its brilliance. She continued to watch with fascination as the huge city revolved.

She could see nothing holding the city up in the air. She could find no obvious stairways or roads to gain entry to the city. She was in the shade of the city, contemplating how to get into it when she heard a mighty grinding noise coming from above. The floating city started to slow, its revolving getting slower, and slower. Amara was shocked to see the spinning come to a complete stop, and then appeared to be getting closer to her. The city was falling out of the sky, it looked like it was going to drop on top of her. As it reached her, the city landed with a crash, shocking Amara awake with a jolt.

Amara was sweating and her heart was racing. The city had seemed so real! What a bizarre dream. It wasn't uncommon for her to have vivid dreams and even occasional foretelling's but this time it didn't feel that way. For some reason it felt like the dream was something that happened long ago.

Amara knew, after what she experienced sleep would evade her, so she dressed and went above deck. When she got topside she took a deep breath of the dry desert night air. The stars shining above, and a half moon lit the desert beautifully. Amara felt a deep connection to the desert, but she yearned to find her soulmate. Someone she could confide in. Someone that she could talk to about her strange abilities and magics. Other than her mother's mother her family had always tried to ignore her darker magics and rarely ever talked about them. Her own mother, Freya, had reacted poorly the first time Amara had entered the mist and talked to her grandmother's spirit. Freya would not speak to her about her abilities, preferring to ignore the whole idea. Dylan had always been her confidant and since his death she felt she had no one to confide in.

Amara, and Dylan had required a lot of time and patience from their mother and father. When their father died suddenly from a snake bite, it was Amara that contacted his spirit to find out who he wanted to succeed him as Sultan of the Sundown Tribe. Her father's spirit explained that since Willem was four years older than Mikiel, he preferred Willem be named Sultan. He also wanted her to relay to the family that he was sorry he wouldn't be there for her and her brothers.

After Dylan's death she had tried to contact his spirit too, but without success. She missed talking to him daily and could not understand why she could not contact him in the underworld. It saddened her that she hadn't been able to say good-bye to his spirit.

The next day, when Mikiel returned to the schooner, Amara tried talking to him about her dream. She stressed to him that she thought it meant something because it was the third night in a row that she had dreamt of the city in the sky. Mikiel was in a good mood after spending the night with his girl in Vardo, so he humored her and asked her to tell him about it before they got underway for Palm Village.

Amara sat down at the table and began, "I was wandering in the desert and a sandstorm caught me. I stumbled through the storm not knowing where I was or which direction I was headed. After stumbling down a huge sand dune I was out of the storm and above me was a rotating floating city. I watched it turn from beneath it for some time, enjoying the shade it provided when I heard a loud grinding noise. After that the rotation slowed and it came to a stop. It then crashed to the ground, landing on top of me. Mikiel, it felt so real! Even now in the retelling I have goosebumps! Look!" Amara held her arm in front of her brother to show him.

Mikiel patted Amara's arm and said, "Don't you remember father telling you that story? You are recalling an old nursery rhyme about the Da Nang, the floating city of old. It was a fable that spoke of a northern desert tribe that lived in the drifting sands part of the northern Scarlet Desert. If I recall correctly, I remember father telling me and Willem the fable when we were young. From the way father rolled his eyes in the telling I don't think he believed the Da Nang ever really existed. He told it as if it was a fairy tale, not real history. That is what you are describing now, a fairy tale." Seeing how dismayed Amara was with that answer he decided to humor her. "With your magic, maybe you are tapping into an old spirit memory that lived there?"

Amara shook her head, "That may be it, but usually I have to initiate the contact, so I am aware when my magic is working. No, this seems different somehow. This seems important, I just don't know why yet. I will let you know if I have any more similar dreams."

Mikiel looked closely at Amara. It was obvious to him something was going on, so Mikiel resolved to pay closer attention to his sister. "I will ask Willem if he remembers any more details of the fable, maybe he has something to add to the tale. Amara I want you to feel free to tell me about any more of these dreams. Who knows, they may be part of the puzzle of where the Mystery Waters came from." Mikiel reassured her. "If you would like we can go by Blue Spring and talk to Willem before we head on to Palm Village!"

Breathing a sigh of relief that Mikiel seemed to be taking her dreams seriously, she responded, "Thank you for understanding Mikiel. You're right, I would feel better talking to Willem about it right away!"

South Town

Autry Hickory

RUBY ENCLAVE

SHADOW MOUNTAIN

Torevir

FANG MOOR

CHANNEL MOUNTAINS

STRONGHEIM

Jason and the Dwarves

Jason had been in Strongheim, the dwarf citadel, collaborating with Grand Master Bluthe for the past two months. He had even assisted the dwarves in building some amazing, and complicated devices. What Master Bluthe called his workshop was the size of half of Coal Valley and Jason felt fortunate to learn so much from him in such a brief period of time. Bluthe was a gruff old dwarf, short, round and used to having his orders followed precisely. Bluthe barked orders at his apprentices left and right, but he was very patient when teaching something to Jason. Over the last few weeks, he had shown Jason their system for supplying water to the homes in their underground city, as well as waste disposal. Grand Master Bluthe had engineered the system himself and it was extremely complicated and well-done engineering. Jason had never imagined pipes bringing running water to individual homes. Since the water came from snow melt in the mountains above them, gravity carried it in aqueducts to cisterns that then fed the homes. It was a brilliant system and according to Bluthe they had been doing it for decades now.

Master Bluthe and Jason were working on a plan to "put out" the volcano known as Jordan's Bane. Their plan used the same principles as the dwarf's water system. The two men were currently building a working model, to see if their plan might work. The idea was to take the runoff of snow melt and divert it from above, directly into the volcano's cone. They were hoping the icy mountain water would decrease the volcano's temperature, stopping the lava flows that were disrupting the sand worms and the cave spiders. They had killed many people since the lava flows spread to their underground nesting areas and drove them to the surface.

The model consisted of a variety of gears, levers and massive gates that would direct the water, much like they used to transport water to their homes. Jason was amazed at their inventiveness. Who would have thought dwarves could build such complex machinery. His work with Master Bluthe had given Jason many ideas of his own. The master had shown him an example of how you could combine many pieces of machinery to perform a specific action. They even had large boring machines mounted on rails. Ten men would run it by turning large cranks that ground away at the rock surface. Dumping the spalled rock into empty carts waiting on the rails to carry the rock away.

After watching the model work, Jason followed Master Bluthe over to a table with a large map on it. The map was of the existing tunnels under the Channel Mountains. It appeared to Jason that several of the tunnels could get them close to the volcano.

Bluthe went on to explain, as he pointed at the map. "There are tunnels above these lava tubes. I believe their floors could be drilled, then flooded with the cold mountain snow melt. Gravity should then drain the icy water into the lava tubes, cooling the molten rock. The plan calls for large gates to be installed, that will control the flow of the water through the tunnels. You have seen the massive reservoir up in the mountains that feeds the cisterns in the city. We will be diverting that water, using the large gates I designed. The reservoir is a result of damming two mountain streams that drained into the Great Ocean. My early ancestors built that wonder generations ago. We can send water to a variety of locations using the existing levers, gates, iron pipes and gravity. What do you think Jason? Do you see any flaws in the plan?"

Shaking his head, Jason responded, "Seeing the model of the plan has helped me make more sense of it. It looks doable to me."

Jason's part in the plan was to install the gate system in the tunnels. It would allow them to funnel the cold water directly down the mountain into the volcano. They would use the large ore carts to move the large pieces of the gates through the existing tunnels to the assembly sites. Jason, being half giant, was the only person with enough strength to be able to lift some of the larger pieces into position. His ability to do that would save them a fair amount of time, since they wouldn't have to build the lifting mechanisms needed to lift the heavy gates into alignment.

Jason smiled as he straightened to his full height of seven feet. He was a massive man, with broad chest, bulging arms and a rock-hard jaw line that made him look like a statue of a God. "I like the plan Master Bluthe, with your permission I will get to work on the gates right away."

Jason would have a group of dwarves helping him with the project. No one really knew what would happen when the ice-cold water met with the lava coming out of the volcano. Master Bluthe's theory was that the snow melt would both smother it and lower the temperature of the lava, at least to a level that would not melt rock.

They had tested Bluthe's theory on one of the smaller lava flows. The water had cooled the lava quickly turning it back to rock. The smell of sulfur and the steam given off when the cold water hit the lava caused several dwarves that were too close to pass out from the gas that was liberated.

Master Bluthe had given Jason the assignment to install the first of the gates at the reservoir near Fangmoor. Fangmoor was in Clan Dupre's territory in the mountains. Jason was to meet with their Clan Chief, Olax, and get their assistance with the installation, before returning to install the other components, on the way to the volcano. Master Bluthe would have his team working on forging all the remaining components that were required. Master Bluthe told Jason that when he met with Olax he was to inform him there could be a day or two without water, so they should stock up before they changed the flow.

The equipment that would be installed above Fangmoor, would take a slower tunnel route to get there.This was due to the fact that some of the more direct tunnels did not have the tracks to move the materials on. Chief Brackus had sent his assistant Grantis, as well as Gordo and Gadna to accompany him to Fangmoor, as well as be his guides. Jason was looking forward to seeing another dwarf city, he found the mountains and their occupants fascinating.

Jason was also amazed at the tunnel systems that ran through these mountains; they were like paved roads. As they traveled to Fangmoor they remained on a wide roadway with a high ceiling for several hours. When they reached a fork in the road, Grantis pointed to the right, so they turned onto the narrower road.

As they traveled Grantis turned to Jason and asked, "Would you like to hear a tale about that huge shield your friend the Tinker returned to Brackus? The one with our clan sigil on the upper half. I read about it in our archives."

Jason shrugged, "Sure, why not? A good tale will help the miles pass while we walk." Jason slowed his pace a bit when he noticed the dwarfs had to take three steps for every one of his.

Grantis began his explanation, "The legend says that

many generations ago, a giant came to the aid of the dwarfs and the elves. The legend doesn't speak of what this aid was, but the two peoples felt so grateful that they devised a gift for the giant. The tale tells of a dwarven Grand Master Blacksmith that was commissioned to smith the huge shield. It is made from the legendary metal known as mithril. The smith then emblazed the Clan Krakus sigil on the upper half. When he was done, he turned it over to the elves who then enchanted the shield with strong protective magic. Then they added the eye of a green dragon on the lower portion of the shield to watch over the bearer. When the giant was presented with this wonderful gift from the two nations he was overcome with humility. With his magic spiked club and the Shield of Torevir, he was invulnerable. The gods took notice of the extraordinary giant and asked his assistance. The Gods opened a portal that the giant gladly stepped into. It transported him to a remote island, where the gods commanded him to guard an ancient artifact of great power known as the Divinity stone. The Divinity Stone had been used to create the land, and as such, in the wrong hands, could doom the world they had created with it. Legend claims he may still be guarding it." Grantis took a sip from his waterskin.

Gordo, who was following the conversation said, "Sounds like poppycock to me!" before catching his toe on a rock and missing a step.

"Me too!" Gadna added.

Grantis glared at the two dwarfs. "Pay no attention to them Jason. Among the more educated of us it is commonly believed that when the Shield of Torevir has been found the Divinity Stone is also in play."

Jason chuckled to himself at the interaction of the dwarfs, they always seemed to be needling each other over something. The story sounded like fable or legend to him, but until meeting Swan he never believed there were birds large enough for a person to fly on their backs. Maybe there was something to Grantis' tale.

Late in the day the group entered a large cavern that held not one but two Inns. Grantis called them "way stations" and said there were many throughout the Channel Mountain Range. He claimed they made travel so much more comfortable. Grantis led them into Pali's Inn. Inside it was much nicer than Jason had expected to find under a mountain.

The foursome sat down in the common room, ready for some stew and ale. Jason sat on the floor, so the table was at a good height for him. None of the dwarf furniture was kind to a giant's frame. Jason felt bad anytime he sat on something that broke under his weight. Their server was a short, broad female with a small tuft of a red beard. Gadna tried to get her to sit on his lap, but she smiled at him as she threatened to castrate him if he tried anything. He laughed at the idea and called her a flirt. Jason also got a lot of stares from the dwarfs in the common room, before climbing the stairs and ducking his head under the rafters to go to bed. The bed was so small he decided to sleep on the floor.

The next morning, after a hearty breakfast, they were off again. Grantis explained they would reach Fangmoor later that day. He apologized to Jason for the poor conditions at the Inn. Jason had been a little stiff after sleeping on the floor, but that was not new to him. Since his arrival in the dwarf lands none of the beds fit him.

Along the route Gordo pointed out several small caves off the path that contained massive crystal formations made from the salt dripping from the ceilings. The light sparkled off them a million ways, making them almost painful to look at.

When they could see daylight at the end of the tunnel road, they knew they were getting close to their destination.

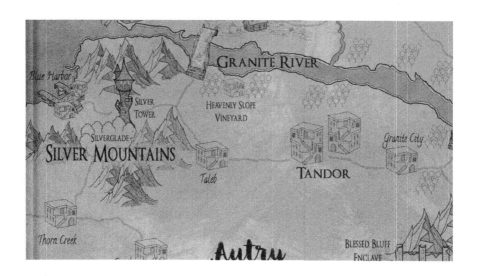

Dragon Claw Isle

The loss of Prism shook Swan to her core. She felt as if another part of her soul had been torn away from her. If Galad had not saved her she would have met the same fate as Prism. Initially she resented Galad for saving her, but as time passed, and as she healed, those thoughts came less frequently. She knew the dragon had done everything he could to heal Prism, but the lightning bolt Ibis hit them with had drained too much of Prism's life force, damaging the giant condor's heart beyond repair.

Swan found Galad's company fascinating. His stories of different lands and the different people he had met expanded Swan's view of the world. She also came to the realization that she and Prism had only seen a small portion of the world. She would miss flying with Prism for the rest of her life. It saddened her to think of the views and freedoms she had lost. They would be hard to replace. She spent a fair amount of time wondering what would become of her. She was a warrior in exile from her clan and worse yet, a flyer without a condor. She wished Marcus were there to comfort her. It was at times like this that she really missed his presence. Thinking of him reminded her of the days they stayed at the new estate King Ferdinand of Autry had gifted her when he named her a Duchess. Those days alone with Marcus were some of the best days of her life. Maybe she would make her way there soon.

Swan was totally exhausted and fell asleep in the wheat field where the dragon had placed her. That night she dreamed of Marcus on Firefly and her on Prism flying just for the pleasure of it. When she awoke, she was up against one of Galad's forepaws and he had covered her with a wing for warmth.

Galad had fallen asleep thinking about things he thought would never happen. Would she accept him as a partner? More importantly, was this female warrior worthy of being a dragon rider? Galad knew what it felt like to not be able to fly. Ibis imprisoned him for many years and all he could do was dream about flying. He knew her loss had to be unimaginable to anyone that had never experienced the joy and freedom of flight. He felt a pain deep in his core for this poor girl that no longer had a way to experience flight. He had been alone most of his life, even before Ibis trapped him, but yes, he might consider having her for a companion on his adventures.

Galad had not had much previous experience with humans and the few interactions he had, never felt like this. When most humans came across a dragon they turned into screaming fools, not this girl. She didn't see him as some kind of monster.

As they built a stone cairn over Prism the next morning, as a burial tribute, Swan explained how she had raised Prism from an egg and that they were bonded for life. As she spoke, Galad could sense her feelings of loss and much pain in the female. When they finished the cairn Galad breathed dragon fire on it, melting the rock into a proper memorial for Prism.

He had the sense that Prism had been a proud and powerful flyer that Galad would have respected. The dragon wished he could have known him.

After saying a prayer for Prism over his cairn, Swan decided she would head for Gretchen's house in Tandor. She needed to figure out where Nathan was and see if she could partner up with him again. She owed him so much. Her time with him in his tinker coach was the most peaceful time in her life, and she needed that right now.

Swan's thoughts were interrupted by Galad's mind link. He said, "Swan I would like you to come sit down here by me. I am considering a proposition and need your full attention." Unsure of what to think, she sat on the ground in front of him.

"I have been considering allowing you to join me in flight." Swan's mouth fell open, not sure what he was saying. The dragon went on to explain, "After my extended confinement I know how much you will miss flying. I have the ability to ease that pain for you."

The offer had been a rash decision on Galad's part. On impulse he had offered this female a chance to fly again, hoping it was the right thing for them both. Galad had been alone in that cave for so long he yearned for company and her company suited him quite well.

Swan was stunned at the offer. She had only just met this dragon! Until yesterday she hadn't thought dragons really existed, let alone learning that they could communicate and were highly intelligent. She found his offer very tempting. Marcus, the love of her life was dead, killed by a Silver Tower assassin, Prism was dead, and her clan had disowned her for disobeying them by exacting revenge on Ibis and the Silver Tower. Nathan had Gunter and Azrador to adventure with while seeking the tinker homeland. Did they really need her around? Does anyone need her around? She doubted anyone would even notice she was gone.

Swan felt guilty even considering his offer so soon after losing Prism. They had been together for over fifteen years, she felt like she was betraying him, but Swan doubted she would get an offer to fly from anywhere else.

After considering the pros and cons for most of the day she went to Galad with an answer. "Galad, after much consideration I would like to accept your offer, with one qualification. We do this on a temporary basis. If either one of us decides we have made a mistake they have the right to end our arrangement."

Galad was surprised at how happy her answer made him, "I think that is a good arrangement Swan. It's a deal! OK let's do it! Climb on my front leg and I'll lift you up onto my back, you can hang onto my spikes."

At first Swan thought he was kidding her. Then she saw he was serious, "Are you crazy? I need more than a spike to hang onto."

Puzzled by her response he explained, "Before being locked up by Ibis I had seen dragon riders. They were hanging onto their dragons' spikes while sitting between them. I don't understand why you would want to do it differently, but if you feel you must I'm willing to go along."

Galad watched as Swan spent the next morning adapting Prism's saddle to the spikes along the Golden Dragons spine. After several failed attempts at securing the saddle, she was finally happy with the fit. Galad was getting impatient with her fussing over how secure she would be. But by midday she was ready for their first flight. She hoped the dragon couldn't sense how apprehensive she was about it. Galad tried to reassure her that riding on a dragon's back would be much smoother and more comfortable than any condor. Still, Swan was anxious to find out.

Once Swan was strapped in, she gave Galad the OK and he took flight. She had to admit it was an exceptionally smooth take off. The strength of the dragons down strokes were a smooth rhythm. In fact, Swan hated to admit, it was smoother than riding in Nathan's coach. Swan became quiet for a long time. Tears ran down her face as she was overcome with the emotions brought on by flying again after believing it would never happen again. Sensing Swan's state of mind Galad turned and flew west, out over the Emerald Sea, where she could see the schools of fish as they changed direction.

After just a few moments of flight Swan felt Galad relax as he coasted over the very green, Emerald Sea. After a time, he gently banked, turning south past the Channel Mountains. He skirted the coastline as the terrain changed to dark green forests that ran down to the beaches. As he flew over the tree line, Swan could see all kinds of wildlife running through the forest. She also saw several large cats lounging in the taller trees in the heat of the day.

Swan asked Galad, through mind speaking, "Do you know where we are?

He replied, "Yes, of course I know where we are. I have flown over this area in the past, but I have only landed here once, long enough to eat and drink, many years ago. It seemed like a nice spot and there were few humans living in the area, nothing personal Swan. Once, while I drank at a lake near here, I saw some tiny fairy like creatures flying around. They reminded me of hummingbirds. As with most creatures they appeared to be frightened by me and kept their distance." Galad projected an image of the fairy's he had seen to her.

She thought they were the cutest thing she had ever seen and said so to Galad. "They are adorable! Are they friendly? Do they make good pets?

Galad raised an eyebrow as he answered her, "They might as well be cute, they're too small to eat." He responded with a snort. As they flew on, Swan thought about what Galad had said about the fairies and decided that was Galad's attempt at humor.

Late in the afternoon they passed a beautiful waterfall emptying into a small lake. Galad thought it a suitable time for a drink and a break for his rider. As Galad landed near the lake Swan gladly dismounted, stretching her legs. The lake looked very inviting since she hadn't bathed since the battle. So, while

Galad wadded out into the lake to get a drink Swan slipped out of her leathers and dove into the water. The water was brisk and felt exhilarating on her naked flesh. She swam over to Galad and stood up in the shallow water.

Galad lifted his head from the water and mind spoke to her, "You are a beautiful human female Swan. Perhaps you will find a mate on one of our adventures."

Thinking of Marcus, she sadly answered, "I don't think so Galad. There is no person on this planet that will ever replace Marcus. I'm afraid he took that part of me with him when he died. What about you Galad? Where are all the female dragons? You have been alone a long time. Maybe we should find you a mate?" Swan suggested.

Galad responded in an unusually quiet tone. "I wish I knew myself. I have been asleep for over a hundred years and before that the only female I knew of was my mother. My brother, also a gold dragon, was slain by a Wizard many years before I met Ibis. My Father was an ancient Gold Dragon and did not hang around for my mother to raise us. I have never encountered him in my travels." Tiring of the subject Galad suggested, "Let us go. We still have a distance to travel yet."

Getting dressed and climbing back on the dragon she asked, "Where are we going Galad? You have been sort of vague as to our destination."

She could detect his excitement in their link when he responded, "You shall see soon enough Swan. I believe you will love it!"

They were off again in an instant and Galad turned south. After some time, they passed over the Great Ocean. Hours later a small island became visible on the horizon. Galad turned toward it and they were soon flying over it. As they circled the island Swan could see mountains lining the shoreline, forming what looked like a dragon's claw. As Galad flew over the tallest mountain, Swan could see a wide opening in the top of the mountain. To Swan's surprise Galad glided into the cavern's mouth and gracefully landed a short distance inside.

Turning back to look at Swan he mind spoke, "Welcome to my home Swan." as she felt a warm comforting feeling pass over her.

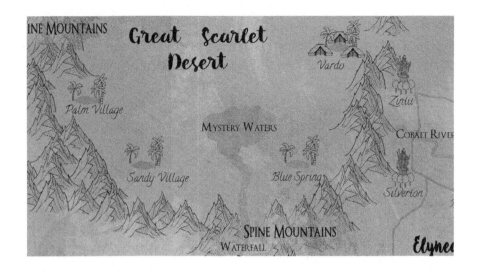

The Fable

When Mikiel and Amara arrived at Blue Spring, they disembarked into the underground bunker that was the Sundown village. They went straight to Willem's quarters where Willem's wife, Eve, greeted them both with a hug. She offered them some refreshments while they waited for Willem to get home. Eve caught them up on what the couple's three children had been doing. Although calling them children hardly applied now. All three were teenagers and each of them was showing some magical abilities already.

When Willem arrived, he was surprised by their visit, but happy to see them. Things had been so hectic since the new water had shown up in their desert, so he hadn't had much time for his siblings. He was concerned that his people were leaving the underground city and flocking to the new area. Most of his tribe was happy to be living above ground.

Willem was glad to see Mikiel, his brother made a good

sounding board for him. He gave Amara a kiss before sitting down at the table. "I'm glad to see you two are here. Eve and I find we are in a bit of a dilemma and could use your input. Half the tribe that lived here at Blue Spring have packed up and moved above ground, to Mystery Waters. Eve and I plan to move there soon, so I can be where the tribe needs me most. Our children are against it. They believe the sand worm attacks will continue and by moving above ground we will increase our risk of attack. So, as you can see, we have some strife in our tent." Willem explained as Eve served him some hot tea and biscuits

Mikiel took a sip of his tea before responding. "I've seen enough to know the responsibilities of ruling are not always pleasant."

Changing the subject, away from ruling, Mikiel asked. "Willem do you remember the fable father used to tell of a floating city in the northern desert? I believe he called it Da Nang. The reason I ask is that Amara has recently had some disturbing dreams about a revolving, floating city in the drifting sands. Her description of it sounds a lot like the tall tale father told us." Mikiel took a third honey biscuit and took a sip of tea before complimenting Eve on her baking skills.

Willem chuckled as he thought of their father telling them the tale of the floating city. "You were pretty young so you may not remember, when father told us that tale, he would roll his eyes like he didn't believe a word of it. Let me think on it for a minute, maybe I can remember the story." Willem took a bite of his biscuit and thought about it for a moment. "I seem to recall the story went like this. When the Sundown Tribe arrived in the desert, they had a tough time adapting to the harsh conditions. At one point the tribe's leader sent a group of ten men north. They were to look for a more temperate climate, but they only found the sandstorms in the north to be unrelenting. The group had lost two men in one of the sandstorms but still held out hope of finding them. While searching for them they stumbled on the floating city of

Bantez."

Taking a sip of his tea he continued, "As the fable went, the Da Nang Tribe had many wizards and they had somehow harnessed the sandstorms energy and used it to float the city above the storms. It was said a perpetual storm took place around Bantez, isolating it from any other tribes. The people of Bantez liked their isolation and refused to trade with any outsiders. No one from the outside world was allowed admittance to their city. Their leaders believed the tribe's magic had beaten the storm god and harnessed the storm's energy. The story goes that their isolation in the end led to their downfall and deaths. Eventually their magic failed, and the city came crashing down. Father would then point out the moral of the story, be careful what you wish for, you may get it. I don't think the tale was based on any truth. It was meant to be a lesson fable." Willem thanked Eve for refilling his teacup before taking a sip of the hot tea.

Amara, captivated by the story asked. "How could their magic accomplish such a feat? Who could be that powerful?"

Trying to be patient with his younger sister Willem replied, "No one is saying they were. The fable said something about a magic medallion, mounted in the spire of a pyramid made of solid gold, powering the magic that kept the city afloat. Amara I am sure it never really happened. It was just a fable, and I can't recall anyone else ever mentioning it, do you?" Willem asked.

Trying to make her brother understand, she answered him, "Well, it seemed very real the three different nights I have dreamt of it. The city I saw is as you described it. Including the pyramid!" Amara paused as she tried to calm herself. "It felt real Willem. It was like I was really there. In my dreams I get lost in a sandstorm that surrounds the floating city. Above me I see the gold pyramid and the spire. The part that worries me is that it stops turning and crashes into the desert. That's when I wake up."

Mikiel patted her hand and said, "Don't worry Amara, I

am sure you will figure it out. Your magic works in a different way than ours, I don't understand it, but I believe it will connect you with an answer soon enough."

Giving both her brothers a hug, "Thank you for listening and being so understanding. It helps me to talk about some of my stranger magic abilities, not many people understand them." Amara said to the two brothers. "I used to rely on Dylan for that understanding. I miss him daily."

Eve refilled Amara's teacup and asked, "Did you see any sign of worm attacks on your way here?"

Mikiel stood and stretched, "There was word of a worm attack on a caravan that was headed to mystery waters yesterday. Reports said only scraps of wagons were left. We are headed to Palm Village from here, so when we leave, we will run the schooner by there and check for survivors. Mikiel explained.

Willem stood and shook his brother's hand. He then gave Amara a kiss on the cheek. "Let me know if these dreams continue. While you are gone, I will check with our historians to see if they have any other information on the Da Nang Tribe. You two be careful on your way to Palm Village. I don't want to see any scratches on Swift when you return! It sounds like the worm activity must have picked up between here and there." Willem said with a chuckle before saying good-bye to his brother and sister.

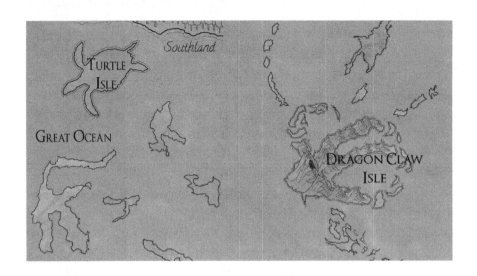

The Lair

Looking around the cavern Swan was shocked by the size of it. It was huge, the walls were lined with shelves overflowing with books and scrolls. The room was furnished with human sized chairs and a large sitting area was positioned off to one side. There were also several doorways that led elsewhere out of the main chamber. Swan took in the view behind her, looking out of the opening they had just flown through, all she could see was the Great Ocean, in all directions. Realizing there was no way off this island unless Galad allowed it, was making her a bit nervous. So far, he had given her no reason to worry. Just looking out over the water as the sun set gave her a real sense of peace, somewhat easing her sense of concern.

When she turned back from the view, she came face to face with the most handsome man she had ever seen. He was well over six feet tall, broad shouldered, with golden hair past his shoulders. Swan was so startled she briefly considered calling for Galad at the top of her lungs but thought better of it. She had no idea who this man was, but she didn't want the dragon to hurt him.

A bright white smile enhanced his golden eyes as this gorgeous man spoke to her, "I am sorry for the surprise, Swan," The man said apologetically. "I guess I should have warned you. Sometimes I forget people know nothing of dragons. I am able to shape shift into human form. In fact, as you can tell from my home, I prefer my human form at times." Wiggling his fingers he said, "You humans take it for granted, fingers and hands can be very helpful." Galad said chuckling at his own pun. "As you can see, in my previous solitude I read a lot. As a young dragon I tried to educate myself on humans and their history. Unfortunately, I underestimated and trusted Ibis. That mistake has cost me many years of my life. So, you can see why I am still a little mistrustful of most humans."

Swan turned back to the view of the sea crashing on the coast, trying to gather her thoughts and hormones. "It is a beautiful home Galad, but this is a lot for me to take in over this very short period of time. I am glad you shared this ability with me, but your human form has surprised me, and I am confused on how that is possible. It will take time for me to adjust to all of this."

The two of them stayed at the dragon's lair for many days. As the days passed Swan discovered, whenever she was close to Galad in his human form she was physically attracted to him, unlike when he was a dragon. She spent the mornings training with her trident while Galad left in the early hours, returning later with game for dinner. There were always plenty of vegetables in the kitchen. Galad explained that was because he kept them in stasis chambers deeper in the cavern that kept food fresh forever. Swan also found several kinds of fish in the stasis chambers.

They took turns cooking different meals. Galad liked his food spicy hot. He explained as a dragon he didn't enjoy the flavors of different foods that his human form enjoyed. Dragons don't have taste buds and can't tell the difference between an elk or a rabbit. Galad also had quite a wine cellar, full of a variety of wines that he had collected over the years. The entire wine cellar was a stasis chamber. Galad loved wine and he enjoyed telling her where each vintage had come from and for what wine that region was famous. One evening he served her frog legs with a nice red wine. Swan was surprised at how much she enjoyed them with the mushrooms that Galad had added. Explaining he had been given the recipe when he had purchased several cases of the wine from a merchant across the Great Ocean. It was Galad's turn to be surprised when he learned Swan was the owner of one of Autry's most prized vineyards.

Swan had really appreciated the break and distraction Galad had given her. He had quizzed her about her life before the wars. He had been fascinated at the tale of Nathan finding her injured. And then nursing her back to health over the two years required. Galad didn't say anything to Swan, but the story seemed similar to how he had rescued her. He tucked that thought away to ponder at another time.

Swan then went on to explain how she had saved Princess Jennifer of Sulan, twice. The first time was in Sulan, before Jennifer was promised to King Ferdinand. The two girls had decided to go for a ride, unaccompanied, and were accosted by outlaws. Swan had to kill all three of them to protect the Princess. The second time Swan rescued the Princess from Mone', an evil enchantress that had captured, collared, and leashed the Princess, renaming the girl Missy. Her intent was to give "Missy", as a gift, to curry favor for herself and the Silver Tower with her clan leader, Janus. Galad's eyes got quite large at the description of Missy's scanty clothing and the unspeakable things Mone' had forced her to do. As a way to show his gratitude after Swan returned Princess Jennifer to the King, he granted her a Duchy in northern Autry, along the south bank of the Granite River. The estate was named The

Heavenly Slope. It was a beautiful estate and Swan loved it there. Swan briefly went on to explain the poisoning death of Marcus, not wanting to dwell on the pains of her recent past. When she got to her attack on King Gregory of Balzar, Galad had to chuckle at her tenacity. He had only known her a short time but after hearing the tale, Galad was sure she had the ability to destroy the pirate King and his navy.

When he complimented Swan on her ingenuity, she gave credit to Sydney, the Master Alchemist of The Sky Rock Clan for coming up with the Dragon Eggs. She and a Flight of Clan members dropped Dragon Eggs on King Gregory's castle and Manchester Harbor destroying his navy. Galad could hear the anger in her voice when she told him how The Council of Elders had forbidden her from attacking Ibis and the Silver Tower. It was soon after, that she left the Clan in the dark of night, vowing revenge for the death of Marcus and Firefly, his condor. Galad's admiration for this feisty human woman only increased when he heard her talk about how she attacked the most powerful mage in over one-hundred years. They both knew the only reason she had survived that attack was thanks to Galad.

After this lengthy conversation Galad, still in human form, bowed in front of her and said, "Excuse my lack of manners Duchess! Should I address you as Lady Swan?" There was a slight chuckle at the end of the question, so Swan punched him in the arm.

"That won't be necessary, as long as you behave properly!" Swan replied, a devilish grin on her face. When he looked directly at her, Swan felt like she could fall into those golden eyes. He reeked of pheromones, and she was feeling their effect.

∞∞∞

Several evenings later, after Swan and Galad had finished dinner and were seated at the table enjoying a glass of wine with desert, she tried to avoid looking into Galad's golden eyes. Swan could feel the sexual tension in the room increasing as the meal went on and she feared he would see the lustful thoughts she was having about him in her eyes.

Galad looked deeply into Swans eyes, "Swan I feel I should warn you that I have not had sex for many years, in fact not since before Ibis imprisoned me. I can feel myself giving off pheromones that you might not be able to resist. Some of what you are feeling is part of the process of bonding. For a dragon and its rider to be physically attracted to one another is a natural part of the process. The final act that completes the dragon/rider bond is for me to have sex with my rider, as a human of course. It will become more and more difficult for you to resist me. You will need to decide if you wish to be my bonded rider soon. Before long you will not be able to resist the urges my pheromones have induced in you." Galad walked over and stood looking out over The Great Ocean, "Swan, if this is not what you wish to happen, we will say our goodbyes and I will take you wherever you wish to go. You should know I will always cherish these days spent getting to know each other. My only hope is that you have enjoyed them as much as I have. It has been a wonderful time for me, and I would hate to see it end."

Without saying a word Swan got up and walked over and turned Galad to face her. She looked deeply into his eyes before kissing him with a heat and passion she didn't know she still had. Between kisses she whispered, "Yes, yes, yes."

Many hours later they lay in each other's arms, naked and spent. They were both relaxing, enjoying the peace of the moment. Galad had been very enthusiastic in his love making and Swan was feeling the aftereffects with some sore parts. She lay there wondering what life would be like in her new role as a dragon rider. She imagined riding a dragon was going to be a lot different than riding Prism had been. She found Galad to be amazing. Just when things were darkest, he had shown up to save the day. This new beginning was starting to feel right to her. At times she found this new life to be a bit scary, but she thought she was ready to fully commit to this new paramour. She was now his rider, exclusively, and he was her dragon. Swan could hardly wait until they could adventure together.

Fangmoor

Once outside, in the mountain air, the road widened, and was paved. It led the way to a massive structure in the distance. Jason found his first look at Fangmoor distressing. The entrance to the city was carved into the face of the mountain, in the form of a massive Ogre. The ogre's eyes, nose, and mouth were windows, with huge fangs hanging down from the mouth, the gate was between the ogres legs and appeared to be made of iron. He found the view of the outside of Fangmoor frightening, but when he turned and looked behind them, the view looking out from there to the west was an expansive view of the western Channel Mountains, all the way to the Great Ocean. It was a stunning sight.

When Grantis saw the look on Jason's face as he scanned the exterior of the city he commented, "Our ancestors tried to make Fangmoor look terrifying to invaders, I suppose. Come, we are almost there."

Jason turned back from the view and looked at Fangmoor again, "They succeeded, it is fearsome looking." Once inside the city gates, the architecture was much different than the exterior. Everywhere Jason looked he saw graceful, delicate architecture, instead of menacing. He was so enamored of the sights that he didn't even notice that once again his size was causing a lot of staring and pointing as they made their way to the city center. They were soon greeted by an old dwarf with a short light red beard and short red and grey hair. He introduced himself as Bendri and said he would escort their group to Clan Chief Olax. Jason was excited to meet the Fangmoor Clan Chief and told Bendri they were ready to go. He led them to Clan Chief Olax's receiving room, where a fierce looking dwarf was reading an old scroll.

Olax rose to welcome them, "Welcome Grantis, it has been a while since we have seen you here in Fangmoor. Have you had word of our troubles here? As leader of Clan Dupre, I hope your visit is to offer your help. We currently have a problem with giant cave spiders in the mines, as well as trouble with a rogue giant. We have lost many men to the two problems."

When Grantis heard that news, he explained his clan's plan to cool the lava and quiet the volcano using water from the reservoir above Fangmoor.

Upon hearing that, Clan Chief Olax burst into laughter. "What a bold plan Clan Krackus has come up with. Why would we agree to such a ridiculous idea? You must think us all daft!" the Clan Chief replied with disdain.

Grantis let the comment pass and answered Olax, "With respect Lord Olax, the water shortage will be brief, a day or two at most. We believe the cave spider attacks are a result of the lava flows that are getting into their egg chambers. If we can put an end to the flows and extinguish the volcano, the spiders should return to the deep caverns. The volcano has already destroyed Clan Brunswick and as long as it is active it is a threat to all of us. We have heard from the dark skins of the desert. They are also suffering from attacks by the spiders, but they also are being attacked by large numbers of the giant sand worms that have lost their eggs to the lava flows." Grantis looked to Jason and then back at Olax.

"Grandmaster Bluthe, along with Jason, our giant friend, have come up with a working model that shows this plan will work. That is if we can install all of the gates and machinery needed to accomplish it. The equipment is now being transported through the tunnels, on rails from Strongheim. Our crews should arrive in two days with the needed items and begin assembly. After the gates and flow control mechanisms are installed here and along the path to the volcano, we should be able to direct the reservoir water to the volcano. No water interruptions would occur till then, and when it does it will be brief. This is for everyone's benefit Lord Olax!" Grantis pleaded. Neither Brackus nor Grantis had anticipated the Clan leader not accepting their plan.

Olax shook his head, not liking the sound of Brackus' plan at all. "I shall sleep on it and inform you of my decision in the morning. Bendri will see you to the dining hall for food and refreshments and then to your sleeping quarters. You are dismissed!" Olax then went back to reading the scroll on the table.

Grantis couldn't hide his disappointment and moped through dinner. "I sure hope he changes his mind. I don't want to have to go back to Strongheim and tell Master Bluthe no."

After dinner Jason saw Gordo go off with another fellow as Grantis and Gadna were walking to their sleeping quarters. "Where is Gordo off to with that fella?" Jason asked.

Gadna laughed and said, "That's not a fella Jason. That is Moria, Gordo's girlfriend. He stays with her whenever we are in Fangmoor. Gordo says she makes his heart go pity pat!"

Grantis mumbled something under his breath Jason didn't hear clearly but thought it was something about Gordo being crazy. Jason would have sworn the girl named Moria had a significant red beard and was quite broad. He had to acknowledge these dwarfs had much different tastes in what they found attractive in a female.

Thoughts of an attractive women brought Jason to thinking of the exotic mage Jade and their exploits in the Sky Mountains. He imagined the dragon tattoo on her chest and the ink serpent descending her abdomen. He could not help but recall her hypnotic green eyes. Jason found himself missing her for the first time since his arrival at Strongheim. Yes, they had much different taste in women.

It saddened him to think of how drastically things had changed since their first meeting back in Coal Valley. She had seduced him that first night, but he had been a willing participant after that. Jade was very present in his thoughts and dreams that night.

The next morning at breakfast in the dining hall, the group was eating hot porridge and biscuits when Lord Olax and his entourage greeted them. "I have decided to allow this diversion of our water, under one condition. We have a problem needing to be solved that we have been unable to solve. If you want our water you will have to dispose of a rogue giant that has claimed Mt. Clainous and the valley below the reservoir. My chief engineer pointed out that is the route you are most likely going to be bringing your equipment through. We have lost ten of my best warriors fighting this monster. Reports say he is twice as big as your giant friend here." Olax said as he pointed at Jason. I will not waste anymore of my men on the task. Clan Dupre grants you use of our reservoir, but you will have to take care of the giant to do it or return to Brackus empty handed. The decision is yours Grantis!"

Grantis stood scratching his chin whiskers, considering his response. "This is a strange development Lord Olax and an even stranger request on your part. Lord Brackus won't be pleased if you don't agree to send some of your own clan with us to defend your own land against this monster. Surely you wouldn't want it said that Clan Krackus came to the rescue of Clan Dupre and rid their land of this giant while you drank ale at the inn with the women. If we must clear this giant from our path alone, we will, but goodwill between our clans would suffer. After all, if we succeed your lands will be free of your giant spider problem too." Grantis replied.

Jason stood up and asked, "Chief Olax can you tell me more about this giant? How long has he been a problem? How did he come to be in this valley you speak of? Where are his people?"

Eyeing Jason's size again, Olax answered him. "Reports say he showed up just two weeks ago. He has made camp and warned off our clan, claiming the valley as his now. Our scouts reported he does not wear the beads of any known tribes so he must be a renegade, or worse. More than a week ago I sent a messenger to the closest entrance to the giant lands, deep in the Channel Mountains. He was carrying a request for their help in relocating or defeating the rogue, but my messenger was not heard from again." Olax took a deep drink from his mug, thinking about Grantis's request for Dupre Clansmen assistance. Slamming his mug on the table Olax looked at the group from Strongheim. "I have decided! There are four of you, so I agree to send four warriors to guide you as well as provide transportation. They will help if a battle breaks out that you can't manage on your own. Bendri, show these dwarfs to the armory. Now get going before I change my mind."

After being dismissed by the Clan Chief, the group was escorted to the armory where they were to equip themselves for battle with a giant. It wasn't long before the three dwarfs had chosen armor and several weapons each.

Bendri looked Jason up and down. "I am sorry big man, but I have no equipment to offer one your size."

Jason smiled at Bendri as he watched, stunned, as Jason pulled his armor from his magic bag. After dressing in the adamantine chain mail tunic, helm, and shield, he pulled out Night Star, his massive, enchanted mace. Bendri let out a gasp when he caught sight of the black weapon.

Jason turned to face him and said, "Made it, and my

armor myself. Do you like it?"

Bendri's voice carried a new respect when he answered Jason. "Like it? Are you nuts? It's amazing! I've never seen anything like it!" "What is it made of that gives it that black color?"

Jason answered as he offered Bendri the mace, "The metal is called adamantine, it is made from combining iberium and palladium in a very specific way. Both metals are exceedingly rare. They are very difficult to combine and forge, but worth it if you succeed. Night Star never needs sharpening and is enchanted to boot!" All the dwarfs Jason had met seemed to be entranced by the weapon. All dwarfs, male and female had to have rudimentary blacksmithing when growing up before they chose a path or specialty later. So, they knew how special the weapon was.

Bendri took the mace from Jason, pleased to have an opportunity for a closer inspection. Bendri only came to Jason's belt but was strongly built and looked like he was not new to combat. Jason watched as he took a few practice swings with the mace.

Bendri whistled after a few swings of Night Star. "She's a beauty Jason. I can't wait to see you use it on this rogue giant!" He reluctantly gave Night Star back to its owner.

Jason took the mace and hung it from his belt. "I hope it doesn't come to that Bendri. If possible, I intend to talk to this giant before I fight him. I won't turn away from a fight, but I also have no problem if it can be avoided. My hope is to convince the giant to either move on to another valley, or better yet convince him to live with you dwarves in peace. Having a friendly giant around for the heavy lifting can come in very handy you know." Jason added as they left the armory.

When they stepped outside there were two large wagons pulled by mules waiting for them to load up. The tunnel road to Mt. Clainous was wide and smoothly paved. The four Dupre Clansmen rode in the lead wagon while Jason and his crew took the second.

Later that day, they were near the Mt. Clainous exit when the Dupre dwarfs suggested Jason's team scout the valley for signs of the rogue giant while they unloaded the wagons and set up camp. The sun was getting low on the horizon, but the view of the valley was impressive, with the reservoir in the distance. The lush foliage and pine trees, filling the valley with that fresh pine smell reminded him of home.

As he scanned the valley Jason thought to himself, "I couldn't blame someone for claiming this valley. It would make a fine home, plenty of water and game to hunt." Maybe that was all the rogue giant wanted, or maybe it wanted to just be left alone.

The group made camp in the tunnel for the night, back where the giant would not detect their campfire. There was no sense announcing their presence before they were ready. After eating camp rations Grantis proposed they attack as a group in the morning after dawn. Bendri advocated a sneak attack, before dawn, hoping to catch the giant unaware or better yet asleep. Jason listened to the two arguments and varying opinions being voiced for longer than he should have before standing and voicing his own, "I have met several giants in my adventures, and all have been good folk. Who knows, this rogue may be what you have painted him to be. However, I intend to try speaking with it before making a judgement. We greatly outnumber him and if it is required, we will kill him. But I am going to try negotiating first. I will go alone, at first light to confront him. Then we will see if a fight is necessary!"

Grantis still disagreed shaking his head as he laid down on his bedroll with a huff. It wasn't long before everyone followed suit, tired from the days travel.

When sunlight came through the tunnel entrance and woke dwarfs, they found Jason was already gone.

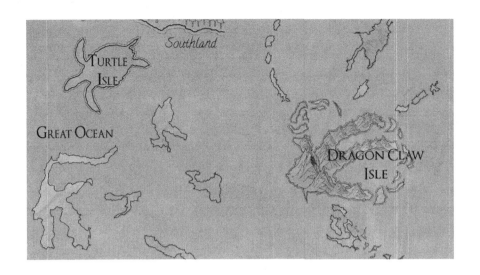

Riding the Dragon

Swan and Galad had been enjoying the benefits of the dragon lair for several weeks now, with little contact with the outside world. At times it had been overwhelming to Swan, but she had grown to like the solitude. One of the many benefits of the dragon lair was the fabulous hot bubbling springs. The grotto was surrounded by that same purple rock that surrounded the pool she had bathed in as a Junior Flyer back in the Sky mountains. Shaman Quesa had said bathing in the waters made your hide stronger and added to each flyer's magic ability. As she lay in the soothing, bubbling waters she let her mind wander. She had to admit it was really relaxing. Soon Galad joined her in the grotto, it always invigorated the gold dragon in his human form. It wasn't long before the relaxing turned into something more, as was usual. The dragon's ability to read her mind made him the most attentive, loving mate a woman could ask for.

Enjoying the afterglow of a wonderful joining, Swan thought back through the many challenges she had faced to get here and decided they had all been worth it.

∞∞∞

Galad had made Swan a special saddle in his workshop. He bragged he had customized the padding to fit her bottom perfectly, and much to Swans surprise, it did. To practice her riding skills Galad and Swan had been going on daily flights, always to unusual places. Prior to her flights on Galad she had not known many of the places they flew too even existed. She was learning the world was much bigger than she had thought growing up in a small village in the mountains.

Her new saddle was much more comfortable and allowed easy access to her recurve bow and trident. On their daily excursions they hunted a variety of game for their dinners. Galad was pleasantly surprised by how quickly Swan became proficient at shooting game with her bow from his back. Swan explained it was actually easier because dragon flight was much smoother than the flight of a giant condor. She found it was much easier to aim from Galad's back than it had been from Prism's. On one of their most recent excursions Galad spotted a large herd of elk and turned to follow them. He knew Swan would enjoy this unique elk, from one of the southern islands. Galad said the elk on these islands ate a wild mushroom that only grew there. It gave the game a delicious taste that could only be gotten there.

It didn't take long for Swan to find out that Galad was also a fabulous cook that enjoyed uncorking a good bottle of wine from his wine cellar every evening. She was beginning to enjoy the pampering, after such a hard life. They seemed to enjoy each other's company more each passing week. Even before being trapped by Ibis, Galad had been alone most of his adult life. Dragons were becoming scarcer, and it had been so long since he had seen another dragon that Galad was not sure if there were any dragons left. Dragon parents were not big on parenting, like humans. When a youngling reached fifty years old, they were encouraged to go find a part of the world to live in, away from its parents. Most dragons were raised on Dragon Isle, far across The Great Ocean. Because of the stasis spell Ibis had cast on him he had been asleep for over a hundred years, so he had no idea what might have happened to dragon kind.

The schools of fish changing direction as they watched from above always amazed Swan. One day after they had been on a long flight over the eastern Coral Sea, Swan saw her first pod of whales. She was fascinated at how long they could hold their breath before surfacing for more air, so Galad followed them as they hugged the coastline of the Green Folk, avoiding being seen by any of the elves that lived there.

Some of the Green Folk could mind speak and would want to converse with a Gold Dragon if they saw him. Galad methodically flew inland over the immense trees of the forest with little effort as Swan enjoyed the beauty of the forest land. As they flew over it Swan wondered if this was what the Tinker Homeland would look like if Nathan were to find it. Swan briefly thought that this could be the land Nathan was looking for, but then thought better of the idea.

They had been flying over the southern forest, when Galad suddenly tensed up. In mind speak he said, "Something bad has happened Swan, I feel there has been a drop in available magic! I have never felt anything like this! We must find the source of this disturbance!"

Swan could feel the sudden tension in his wing strokes as he banked turning west. Soon they could see the trees that had been magnificent, were now shortened and most had died, along with most of the vegetation in the area. As the land became more barren, they started spotting some type of large lizard creatures. It appeared they were crawling out of cracks in the ground.

Swan mind spoke. "Galad what would cause this?"

"The elves have a special relationship with nature and this forest has always been enhanced by their woodland magic. They have always taken care of the forest and its creatures. What we're seeing must be what happens when the forest has been denied the magic that has kept it flourishing. I think I see the source of this evil in the distance."

As they flew closer Galad mind sent, "It's a Temporal Rift! It is sucking the life and magic from the area, much like Ibis's wand did to you and Prism. I can feel it has noticed us! We must leave immediately; I can feel it leeching my strength and magic."

Abruptly Galad changed direction and headed northwest toward the mountains. Just as they reached the Spine Mountain range Swan could feel Galad falter. He was barely able to land in a small glen high up in the mountain chain.

"I don't understand." Galad whispered in her mind. "My strength has been drained and so has my magic! Don't you feel it Swan?"

Swan grabbed her bow and trident as she dismounted. "No Galad, I don't feel any different." She felt very anxious. They were in unfamiliar territory and Swan's instincts kicked in as she scanned the area for threats. Swan had not seen Galad get so agitated before, it was something unusual to have him so bothered. Galad had landed just above the tree line so they were close to the mountaintop, if they were lucky, they could find a trail over it.

Fortunately, Galad only needed a trickle of magic to shapeshift to his human form. After doing just that he turned to her and said, "This is serious Swan! Magic is being sucked up by something or somebody, near that temporal rift. Unfortunately, I can't risk getting any closer to it. In fact, we should be trying to put some distance between it and us, as soon as possible. Hopefully we can get far enough from it that my mana will return so I can fly us back to the lair."

Swan suddenly realized that Galad was very concerned about the loss of his abilities. It occurred to her that he was feeling more vulnerable than the gold dragon ever had. She patted him on the back, trying to comfort him. "Don't worry I'll protect you until you get your magic back!"

After grabbing her pack and weapons she started searching for a trail. Her skill in tracking came in handy when she found a deer trail leading higher up the mountain. Swan led the way up the trail. She told Galad it saddened her to have to leave her saddle behind, but Galad promised to replace it if she got him home. They followed the trail until it led to a cave in the side of the mountain. Stepping into the cave Galad grabbed Swan by the arm and whispered," I smell Trolls! Come, we should find another path. I carry no weapons and have no magic to offer, and you can't possibly defend us both against trolls."

Swan stiffened upon hearing Galad didn't think she could handle herself and offered, "Galad I have been in many such caves, and I have killed hundreds of trolls and ogres in my past." Swan spun her trident like a baton as she led the way into the dark cave. After passing through several connecting chambers Swan mind spoke to Galad, "Be silent, and whatever you do, don't disturb the spiders." Galad looked up and saw hundreds of red eyes looking on from the many ledges surrounding the walls of the chamber. They moved slowly and silently as they made their way across the chamber, to a tunnel on the opposite side of the room. They both breathed a huge sigh of relief as they exited the spider cave. It reminded Swan of the adventure she, Nathan, and Gunter had experienced on Jordan's Peak. The three had gone to the volcano to dispose of the cursed Tinker weapons. Little did they know dumping the cursed weapons would cause the volcano to erupt. Who knew what adventure they might be on now? Afterall, last she heard they had new clues to the Eye of Illusion. She hoped they were both safe and well.

The tunnel they were following was leading down and to the west according to Swan's compass. That was fine, the more distance they could put between themselves and the

Rift the better. They had been making satisfactory progress when the smell of trolls hit them. Three of the filthy long-haired creatures rounded the corner and were met with two quick shots from Swans bow. One of the creatures went down immediately but the other two charged directly at Swan. The lead troll swung a two-handed axe at her head, and she easily evaded the blow by ducking. She dropped her bow and grabbed her trident, spearing the seven-foot troll holding an axe in the throat with her trident. Quickly retracting her trident, she was able to barely block an attack by the remaining troll. He was using a pole arm weapon with multiple blades that allowed for a long reach by the smelly ugly creature. The length of the troll's weapon was effective at blocking her initial attacks, so Swan decided she'd had enough hand to hand with the troll and commanded lightning to shoot, but nothing happened. She apparently was without magic after all. Her lack of magic distracted her momentarily, allowing an attack by the troll to get past her defenses. It struck a glancing blow to her left shoulder. Without magic, her ring and necklace failed to protect her as she felt the stinging bite of the troll's weapon. Recovering her concentration, she began to spin the trident despite the blood running down her arm. As she slowly closed on the troll, he attempted to fend off her attack but failed to block it. The three tines of the trident embedded in its chest, ended the fight.

Galad quickly retrieved a bandage from his pack and tended Swan's injury. Once the bleeding in her shoulder stopped, they moved on down the tunnel, trying to get away from the smell as much as the sight of the bloody mess. Swan knew the smell would attract the spiders and more trolls, so they kept moving down and west.

Swan assumed since there were trolls and spiders in these mountains, just like home, there were probably ogres too. Ogres were smarter than trolls, they would set traps for their prey. She warned Galad that it would be best if they stayed alert. The pain in her shoulder reminded her she was without her usual magic protections and would have to be more cautious if they came across any more monsters. Swan's shoulder was also beginning to tighten up, and she could feel her heartbeat in it.

Galad felt terrible he had not been of any assistance to Swan. Especially since she had become injured protecting him. He was the Gold Dragon here; he was supposed to be invulnerable. At least he always had been before this. Galad was concerned his loss of magic could be permanent, but was trying not to let Swan see that, she had enough to worry about at the moment.

After several hours of hiking down the tunnel they saw a speck of daylight up ahead. Feeling like an exit was close they both picked up their pace. When they got closer to the light source, they could see several large boulders were blocking the exit but allowing sunlight to pass through. As Galad inspected the boulders it became obvious they were not from this cave because they were not geologically similar to the surrounding rock. Something didn't feel right to him, but he couldn't put his finger on what.

With Swan's help Galad was able to get one of the boulders to rock back and forth. Just as they rolled that rock out of the way Swan was struck by a boulder from above. The large rock merely bounced off of her injured shoulder. Evidently her shield was back. She immediately checked her trident to find her lightning was back. Aiming the trident at the ogre that had hit her with the boulder she called lightning. This time her magic responded at full force. She burned a hole straight through the huge monster with the tusks. Another ogre farther up the mountain threw a huge spear at Galad. His magic stopped the spear in midair, reversing the spears course. It buried itself in the chest of the ogre that had thrown it.

Galad flicked his wrist at the remaining boulders, scattering them ahead of the two of them like marbles. When they exited the tunnel, they found themselves in the Scarlet Desert, looking at red sand as far as they could see. They had finally placed enough space between themselves and the Temporal Rift to regain their magic. Galad was extremely relieved that he could feel his strength returning, as he took in the hot, dry desert air. Galad was quick to heal Swan's wound as soon as his strength returned. As he watched the tissue knit back together, he again apologized for not being able to protect her. He also thanked her for protecting him from the creatures. He admitted to her that he had never felt so defenseless and didn't ever want to experience that again.

Hugging Swan tightly Galad said, "I will try to better protect you in the future, this I promise you. I am quite fond of you human and do not wish to lose you. I don't want to be alone again. I also don't want to do without my magic ever again. The world looks much different when I don't have my magic. I have never feared any creatures before. Let me tell you I did not like it!"

Swan had to confess, "I have never thought of myself as a magical being, but without my enhanced reflexes and increased strength I was barely able to defeat those trolls. I also discovered that without lightning my trident is mostly just a big stick!" Swan said sadly. "I had to revert back to my basic training to defeat those trolls."

Galad kissed her and gave her another big hug before transforming back into the magnificent Gold Dragon. Swan would have to rough it, riding on his back between the spines without her comfortable saddle, but the freedom of flight and the view it gave was worth it.

Dragons like it hot, so Galad chose a route to home that flew over the southern desert. They flew in silence while they were both contemplating the experience they had just had together. They were both considering what was happening to their world. What would the world be like without magic? Swan had a thought that maybe King Ferdinand had been right after all. Maybe it was best to govern his kingdom without magic interfering.

As they were about to pass over the Spine Mountains

Swan spotted a beautiful waterfall pouring out of the mountain. The water was spilling out into the desert and collecting in what looked like a newly formed lake. The flowing water looked out of place in the sandy desert. It didn't look like the water had been there long. Swan could see plants just beginning to grow along the edges of the small river leading to the lake. Galad made one more pass over this newly discovered water source before he turned south, flying over the mountain range and out over the Great Ocean. It wasn't long before they landed on the island sanctuary that was Dragon Claw Ilse.

New Dreams

Early the next day Mikiel and Amara boarded Swift and got under way. They headed out across the open desert towards Palm Village to the west. A strong easterly wind aided their trip, so Mikiel had all the sails up on the Schooner as she sailed across the sand. Late that afternoon they passed a caravan headed to Mystery Waters and waved as they sailed by. Mikiel had to cast a wind spell to keep smooth sailing. They lowered some sail and slowed when they started to see debris from the Sand Worm attack reported the day before. Mikiel stopped Swift near one of the largest worm holes and Amara disembarked. She had to touch the sand to feel for tremors from the large beasts. The two of them searched the area, flipping over debris, searching for survivors. A few melons were still intact but nothing else was found. Disappointed at finding no survivors they returned to the ship.

After boarding the schooner, Mikiel raised sail and Swift

continued on to Palm Village. They anchored outside the entrance to the underground village and were greeted by several distant cousins and friends. Mikiel and Amara were invited to the evening meal with the cousins and brought them news of the new Mystery Waters and how quickly a city was developing around the river and lake. They were deeply saddened to hear there were no survivors from the caravan that had left from their village three days before. After dinner and conversation with the cousins, Mikiel gave his sister a hug before he said good night and departed. He had briefly mentioned he was going to drop by an old friend of his. He told Amara he wouldn't be far since the lady friend's quarters were nearby. Amara always preferred sleeping on Swift so she also said her good nights and went back to the ship.

Sitting above deck with a glass of brandy, watching the stars come out, felt so relaxing. While she sat there, she watched two shooting stars race east, across the sky. After a short time enjoying the solitude of the desert, she thought she might as well turn in. Going below deck to her quarters she changed into her sleepwear and stretched out in her big bed. As much as she liked her time alone, she hoped someday she would share it with someone special. Thoughts of a cute boy she saw in their last trip to Vardo occupied her mind as she drifted off to sleep.

∞ ∞ ∞

The full moon came into her view as the city slowly revolved. The stars were bright when she looked away from the brightness of the moon. Below her, at the base of the pyramid, there was a ceremony of some kind taking place. She was dressed in ceremonial attire, Hundreds of her people below were singing a hymn as they were looking up to her as she placed the Sacred Sun Medallion into its holder in the shining white spire. Three large mana stones lay at her feet, depleted of any magic they once held. Those three stones, along with her own magic, had recharged the Sacred Sun Medallion, which allowed the city to hover over the desert as it rotated above the sandstorms below.

All attending were overjoyed. She had done her duty

as High Priestess. All would be well for another season. The crowd below cheered as the radiance of the Sun Medallion began to glow again. As the other priestesses looked on, Amara floated down to the dais below. When she gently landed, she turned to address the throng.

But instead of the roaring crowd she came face to face with her dead brother Dylan. It shocked her so much she instantly woke up. Oh my, another bizarre dream and this time Dylan shows up! She lay in her bed as she pondered what it meant. It had felt so real, again, she could even recall the texture of the blue gown she had been wearing.

She knew from past experience there was no way she was going back to sleep, so she thought she would make another attempt to reach Dylan's spirit again. She thought that since he had appeared in her dream, he was trying to send her a message. Sitting up and assuming a lotus position in the middle of her bed she focused on the shade amulet in her hand. The shade amulet allowed her to enter the underworld without risk or harm. It was the same amulet that had belonged to her grandmother. She also could speak to the dead. Amara focused her memory on Dylan's image. Her vision began to blur as she reached through the veil of death. Soon she was in the mist. As she continued to concentrate on Dylan's image, he gradually took shape in front of her.

Dylan didn't say anything, but he motioned for her to follow him. He then stepped out of sight and into the mist. She hurried to follow him as he went deeper into the mist. Suddenly the mist began to clear, revealing the remnants of buildings that began to appear out of the mist. There were also huge sand dunes scattered around the area. She followed Dylan's shade as it led her to climb a massive sand dune. As they neared the peak of the dune, she could see something sticking out of the sand. The shade led her on, moving toward the object sticking out of the sand. When Dylan's shade reached the object, he motioned his hands over the item. As the shade cast the wind spell the sand around the object was rapidly blown away, showing the remains of what looked to be a broken spire. Dylan's shade turned to Amara and smiled. The contact was abruptly over, and Amara found herself sitting on her bed. Thinking of the smile on Dylan's face made her heart break. She missed him now more than ever. Taking a deep breath, she tried to quit feeling sorry for herself and focus on her dream, and what Dylan's spirit was trying to tell her. Why had Dylan's shade smiled at Amara finding the broken spire?

The dream was pointing her towards an area in the northern desert known as the Drifting Sands. It was named that because of the violent sandstorms that unceasingly moved the sand around. Could the floating city be more than just legend or fable? Were there the ruins of the ancient city buried in the sand that might prove the fable true? What did it all mean? Is that what Dylan's shade was trying to tell her?

When Mikiel rejoined the ship the next morning, he noticed how red Amara eyes were. "Amara, what's wrong? Have you been crying?"

Having regained her composure she asked, "Mikiel when was the last time you were in the northern desert region? Have you ever ventured into the Drifting Sands?"

Not happy that she had ignored his questions, he responded, a little too sternly. "I am not going to answer any of your questions until you answer me. I know you are not a cry baby, but I can see you have been crying. What has you so upset?

Looking Mikiel in the eye she replied, "Yes you are correct, I have been crying. You see, I was finally able to contact

Dylan's spirit last night. I have been trying to contact him ever since he left us. It didn't last long, and he didn't say anything, but he motioned for me follow him. I think he may have led me into the Drifting Sands, I'm not sure. Have you ever been there?"

Mikiel was stunned to hear his sister had contacted Dylan. Up until this moment he had not realized just how much he missed his brother. Mikiel turned away from Amara, not wanting her to see his pain. "Yes, I have. It was many years ago. Dylan and I were young and foolish enough to venture into the area in spite of the fact that Father had made it quite clear we were not to venture near there. But I let Dylan convince me to do it anyway. He had heard the alchemist in Blue Spring was paying quite well for the venom of the mega scorpions that live in the region, unbelievably well. Plus, their stinger works as an aphrodisiac, how could I resist? We told father we wanted to go visit friends in Vardo so he let us take Swift. We didn't see a whole lot while we were there. The sandstorms we encountered were very sudden and violent. They would come at us out of nowhere. The landscape was continually changing so we had no real point of reference, making it impossible to map the area. Since then, I have been told, some of those storms are said to last for years. After seeing it for ourselves we weren't surprised that no known tribes live there, we found no oasis anywhere we went. During a break in one of the sandstorms we managed to bag three of the scorpions before heading home. We sold all three to the alchemist and got a surprisingly good reward for them. We didn't tell Father where we went on that trip. He heard about our little excursion from one of the other alchemists in town when he asked father if he knew exactly where we found the mega scorpions. He was furious with both of us when he found out. As punishment he wouldn't let us board Swift for a month. That was enough for both of us. I never had any reason to return, and I don't think Dylan did either. There was one other thing that was strange about the area. For some reason compasses don't work there, making it awful easy to get disoriented and lost, especially in the storms. Why the sudden interest in the Drifting Sands? Are you sure you contacted Dylan's shade? Maybe you were just dreaming?" Mikiel asked as poured them both some tea and sat down.

Amara sat quietly as she drank her tea. Thinking about just how much she wanted to tell Mikiel. She eventually decided to confide in Mikiel and tell him all about her experience the night before. After explaining the whole episode to him, Mikiel was inclined to believe that she had made a connection with their brother. He was as baffled as she was at what Dylan's appearance meant. What was their brother's connection with the Drifting Sands? It gave Amara some comfort that Mikiel believed her. He always seemed to sense her emotions and comfort her when needed.

After breakfast they loaded the schooner with passengers and cargo and got underway, headed for Mystery Waters. The trip was tense but uneventful. Amara had sensed a group of Sand Worms, but they veered away from Swift, on their way to the new desert water supply. After arriving at Mystery Waters, they disembarked the passengers and unloaded the crates of cargo. By the time they got all the work done it was late and the stars were out. Mikiel and Amara had been invited to a friend's tent for food and drinks, but Amara was tired, so she stayed alone on the ship. Grabbing a quick bite to eat she thought she would turn in early, since she had not slept much the night before.

∞∞∞

The dream began the same as before. She stood atop a massive gold pyramid, holding the Sacred Sun Medallion aloft for the assembled crowd of hundreds below her. She placed the medallion inside its holder, atop the shining spire. In moments the medallion started to glow like the sun. The large mana stones again lay nearby where she had used them to recharge the ancient artifact. She was again dressed in a royal blue robe, tied with a white silk sash and she was wearing the elaborate gold headdress adorned with jewels. She again floated down to the dais joining the other priestesses that had observed the ceremony. She had successfully performed the Ceremony of Renewal. Ensuring the floating city of Bantez would continue to float and spin for another season.

After the ceremony was complete and speeches given, she turned and walked through double doors into the pyramid and down a large hallway richly decorated. She made her way down the hallway to the High Priestess quarters. Standing guard outside her suite of rooms were two large minotaur guards. The minotaur were fierce warriors and would protect her while she was vulnerable, recovering her mana. Her powers were always greatly diminished after the ceremony. Her magic and mana plus the mana the stones stored were necessary to recharge the ancient artifact. She would have to rest and meditate for the next two days to recover. Walking to a wall sconce in her living quarters she passed her ring under it. The wall opened revealing an ornate marble altar. On the altar lay the Book of Blessings. The book contained the spell required to recharge the Sacred Sun Medallion as well as many other powerful spells. She opened the book, as she had many times before. She quickly discovered she could not read it. The text was foreign, it was in a language she did not even recognize. The shock of not being able to read the book startled her awake.

Damn! She wished she could have read what was in the book in her dream, before waking up! It had felt like she was there! The Minotaur's were intimidating, they must have been over seven feet tall and carrying two headed axes. How could the High Priestess float down to the others? Did she have some unique magic? Amara had stayed in the dream a little longer this time. It was the first time she had seen the Minotaurs.

Since it was still too early for breakfast, she chose to stay in her quarters while it was quiet and ponder on recent events. There were so many mysteries going on these last couple of months. A volcano that seemed to be causing trouble with the sand worms and cave spiders. The appearance of the Mystery Waters. The dwarfs suddenly being helpful and strangers from a strange land in the north. She wondered if they were all somehow related.

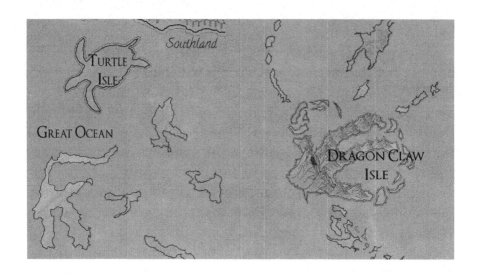

Library

Upon landing at the lair, Galad shapeshifted and immediately went to search his library for clues, hoping to find an answer to the Temporal Rift. Hopefully, his extensive library contained some clues to this phenomenon. He was afraid the Rift would cause a disruption in the ley lines that renewed mana for magic users. If it continued to spread who knew what havoc it could cause in the world.

Swan was enjoying the view from the lairs entrance when a large hawk swept past her, landing on the dining table. Unsure of what to do and not wanting to scare the bird off, she mind spoke to Galad. "We seem to have a visitor Galad, I need you here, now."

Galad reluctantly left the library to see what Swan was so adamant about. Seeing the golden hawk on the table he approached it and began stroking its head and shoulder feathers. This went on for several minutes, until the hawk screeched and flew out the lairs entrance.

Turning to Swan he explained, "That was a golden hawk named Dawnwind. She is a recent acquaintance of mine; she was bringing news. It appears the Temporal Rift is growing. She is going to spread the word to the elves, those of them that can hear her. The area should be avoided but needs to be watched from afar. After hearing from Dawnwind, the Green Folk will take notice and watch for any further changes. It is just too difficult for me to explore the area without my dragon magic. Instead, I will go back to the library and continue to search for answers. Perhaps I can discover a prophesy written about such a thing." Galad turned and headed down the plush hallway back to the huge room he called the library.

Swan decided after fighting trolls and ogres a bath was in order, and she was right. The hot water felt good, since she was bruised and sore everywhere after the fighting. She let her mind wander as she relaxed in the bubbling waters of the grotto. It wasn't long before she thought back on her time with Nathan the Tinker. She recalled that Nathan wasn't affected by most magic. That made her wonder if he might be able to explore the area close to the Rift without being affected by it, or maybe he is somehow connected to it. That made Swan wonder more what he and Gunter were up to currently. She had a feeling that she would meet up with them sometime in this adventure! She hoped that was so.

After Dawnwind left, Galad had made his way back to his massive library. He thought he knew the section of the library that may contain some clues to what was happening in southern Elyneas. He also hoped to find some information about any similar disturbances in magic in the past. This part of the library was very dusty, mostly due to the fact that Galad had not looked at its contents in more than a century. With a flick of his wrist the dust disappeared. He was confident that he would eventually figure out what was happening, but something in his gut told him time was a real issue. If Dawnwind's report was correct the spread of the anomaly would cause crop failure, poison the local water source, and cause innumerable deaths due to disease and famine. It made him wonder if there were Temporal Rifts opening elsewhere in the world. He approached a large cabinet in the back of the room, unlocking it with a magic word. It was filled with incredibly old scrolls, brittle and yellow with age. Carefully reaching inside he removed several of the scrolls, taking them to a large nearby table. Using small chunks of gold he found on a shelf in the same cabinet as paper weights, he laid out the first scroll. It was written in old elvish, which most scholars found to be very tedious to read. Fortunately, Galad had been able to translate old elvish since he was a youngling. When he finished that scroll, he moved on to the next, and then the next.

After many hours of reading old scrolls about things like "How to Create a Unicorn" and "How to Make Friends with Fairies" he finally came across a mention of a similar anomaly. According to the scroll, like the current Rift, it took place in Elyneas, more than two hundred years ago. The scroll described the anomaly swallowing a large elven city on the southern coast of the Great Ocean. It had developed slowly, and initially they didn't detect the loss of magic. According to the scroll, reports began to come in of the landscape changing from a beautiful lush green land to a barren waste, from the Spine Mountains in the west and had spread east, destroying everything in its path. All of their water sources dried up and the land cracked open. Initially the elves blamed the cycles of the moon. There were reports of it being weird colors during its cycle. It was about the same time that a crevice appeared that the pace of the Rifts expansion sped up. The scroll went on to describe lizard like creatures from another world emerging from the cracked ground.

Having completed reading that scroll he set it aside and moved on to the next. After reading several scrolls and books on "How to Make a King Love You" and "How to Make a Mountain Out of a Mole Hill" and a "A Guide to Traveling," he found another relevant document. This scroll described in more detail the destruction the Temporal Rift had caused before a remedy was found. Galad continued to read the scroll late into the night.

The next morning when Swan woke, she discovered the other side of the bed untouched. Galad had not come to bed all night. She dressed and brushed her short red hair, before searching him out. After a search of the huge complex, she concluded he must be out flying, maybe he was getting her a surprise for breakfast.

To pass some time Swan decided to make some biscuits. Just as she was taking the biscuits out of the oven Galad arrived, stirring dust as he settled his wings.

Swan hollered at the golden dragon, half-jokingly "If there is dirt in my biscuits it is your fault Galad!".

Transforming into his human form he gave Swan a kiss before sitting down at the table. "Sorry Swan, I needed to clear my head after reading all night."

Swan asked expectantly, "Did you find an answer Galad?"

Trying to calm Swan's excitement he answered, "I read several ancient scrolls written in old elvish that described something similar to our Temporal Rift. All of the scrolls on the subject predict lots of doom and gloom if someone doesn't stop this thing. The author of the one of the scrolls called it the Dead Zone Rift. That was two hundred years ago. I was a youngling at the time, but I don't recall mention of it from any of my tutors." Galad said as he spread jam on one of the dusty biscuits.

Swan eyed Galad suspiciously. "Are you trying to tell me you are over two hundred years old?" She asked in disbelief.

Proud that his handsome looks didn't betray his actual age he responded "Actually, I am just under three hundred years old. Dragons are considered younglings until they reach the age of one hundred. I have been considering not counting the hundred years that Ibis nicked me for, during the stasis spell. Technically you don't age in those damn spells." Galad buttered another dusty biscuit with honey and took a large bite. Chuckling to himself he thought, Swan was right they did taste like dirt, but there was no way he would admit that to her. He'd never hear the end of it if he did.

Steering the conversation back to the main topic she asked, "So, did you learn anything else, like how to stop it?" Swan reached over and wiped some of the jam off Galad's cheek. "Is there some kind of spell or magic that will stop it?"

Picking up a third biscuit he responded, "I had to read a lot of gibberish about the chaos such a rift can create, but eventually I found some clues as to how to eliminate the thing." In between bites of biscuit Galad explained, "The last scroll I read describes a sort of scavenger hunt of ancient artifacts that are needed in the final battle in closing the Rift. The scroll describes how the artifacts are to be used to defeat the Rift. When the artifacts are used correctly the Rift will be destroyed and the artifacts will be redistributed across our world, to be found again the next time a rift appears. My conclusion is that it worked two hundred years ago, so why not now? All we need to do is find the artifacts again."

Swan grabbed a second biscuit, drenched the top with honey and took a bite. Looking at Galad as she spit out the bite of biscuit she asked, "How many of these have you eaten? They are awful! They taste like the Scarlett Desert." Shaking her head, she walked to the cave entrance and tossed the remaining biscuits out for the birds. Returning to the table she asked Galad, "What kind of scavenger hunt? I don't suppose it's easy to find stuff available at your local magic store?" Knowing the answer to that question before she asked it, she continued, "Don't answer that, I can see by the look on your face these artifacts, as you call them are the kind protected by monsters."

Shaking his head he replied, "I wish, we could easily handle monsters. I'm afraid there's more to it than that. These are all rare magical artifacts. They will be difficult to collect. In the meantime, the Temporal Rift will continue to grow, sucking magic and life from the people and the land. I believe we have no time to waste."

Reaching into his pocket Galad retrieved a scroll and handed it to Swan. "That is a list of what is needed to complete what I call the quest of a lifetime. I think the most difficult part may be getting an item called the Celestial Rod. It is a superior adamantine rod that is to be forged each time a rift occurs. It is to be made from the two rarest ores on the planet, you have probably never heard of them, iberium and palladium. We will also have to find the Eye of Illusion, the Dragon's Tear, the Sacred Sun Medallion, and the Moon Stone. Those items must then be mounted on something it calls a Celestial Rod. The last item on the list is a legendary dwarven shield known as the Defender of Torevir. It is to be used to protect the person that has to throw the Celestial Rod into the Rift. I found a detailed drawing of each item, but no clues as to where to find these items."

Trying to ignore Galad's comment that she wouldn't know what adamantine was. She asked eagerly, "Did you say the Eye of Illusion?"

"Yes, it is one of the five essential items," Galad replied distractedly, only half paying attention, he was thinking about the description of the Sacred Sun Medallion.

Swan stepped in front of Galad to get his full attention. "I think my friend Nathan, the tinker, may have the Eye. He is on a quest to find his lost homeland. He had a scroll that said he would need the Eye of Illusion to accomplish his goal. We should go find Nathan, it shouldn't be too difficult, all we have to do is look for his large multi-colored coach; it should be easy to spot from the air. I can't wait for you to meet him. You and he have one thing in common already. You both have saved my life. I know he would be of help; I am sure of it!" Swan said really warming up to the idea.

Galad asked with curiosity, "Don't you think it a strange coincidence that a friend of yours would have one of the five required pieces from the scavenger list?"

Swan thought about it for a minute and then shrugged

her shoulders, "Maybe it was meant to be? Who knows?"

Getting up from the table he motioned for Swan to follow. Galad took her hand as they walked down a long hallway that led deeper into his lair. After several turns, some left and some right, they stood facing a blank wall. Galad said a magic word under his breath and the blank wall swung away, revealing a huge room filled with gold objects. The gold was piled to the ceiling. The room looked to contain everything from candlesticks to statues, crowns, all solid gold. Swan also saw large piles of coins from many lands.

Looking around in awe Swan asked, "So, the myths of dragons hoarding gold is true!" she squeaked. She was stunned, looking over the huge hoard of gold. She doubted any ruler in the kingdoms had anywhere near this much gold. It practically hurt her eyes to look directly at the glittering piles.

Galad started rooting around in the pile. After several minutes he pulled a gold medallion the size of his hand from the pile. Galad held up the solid gold medallion. "What do you think? Could this be the Sacred Sun Medallion?"

Taking the medallion in her hand she examined it closely. "I don't know Galad, it looks to be of foreign design and incredibly old, but it isn't nearly large enough to fit the description you gave me."

Galad, with much disappointment in his voice conceded, "Darn! I thought I might already have the Sacred Sun Medallion, but you're right, this medallion is too small to be the one we need. It is an exceptional piece though and has been enchanted with a spell that extends life. Why don't you keep it Swan? It almost shines as brightly as you do." Galad said as he placed the necklace around her neck. Swan felt a shiver up her spine and wasn't sure if it was the closeness of Galad putting the necklace around her neck or the enchantment he mentioned it had.

Swan admired the medallion as she questioned Galad. "Why do you have all this stuff Galad? You don't need it. You'll never spend any of it! You really are a hoarder, aren't you?"

Galad didn't like the way she said the word hoarder, like it was a bad thing. "You don't understand my dear. Dragons must collect and hoard treasure. It is how our magic mana is replenished. You see I am a Gold Dragon so I must collect gold for my hoard. The larger my hoard is, the more magic I have available. Without my hoard I would have very little magic. I would not even have enough magic to transform to human form without it. So, you see a dragon's hoard is a necessary part of being a dragon. To your point about me not spending any of it, I have furnished my lair with only the finest of furnishings and I paid for most of them." Galad chuckled.

Seeing Galad in a new light Swan asked with a certain amount of relief, "So, it's not greed after all?"

Grinning slyly, he responded, "Well maybe a little greed, it's hard to take the greed out of a dragon entirely. Come, let us collect the supplies needed for our journey to find your friend the tinker. I am going to the workshop to make you another saddle. This trip is going to be to long for you to ride bareback. Why don't you outfit us with supplies while I do that?" Galad closed the wall to the treasure room, and they hustled down the hallway, in a hurry to get started.

Swan busied herself with packing supplies. Galad was right, they may be gone for some time, so travel rations worked best. They did not spoil quickly so they were essential when traveling, and plenty of drinking water. She then filled her quiver with arrows and packed a cloak for each of them.

As she packed items into the bottomless bag, she thought of Gunter. He had gifted her the magic bag years ago. When they were at Blessed Bluff, he had also given her the Trident Ring she now wore. The Trident Ring contained three spells, healing, protection, and a fire spell. That quest seemed so long ago. She hoped Nathan and Gunter were well and that she would see them soon. The last she heard they were headed for the New Pass from Autry to the Scarlet Desert. That sounded like a good place to start looking!

Mystery Waters

Nathan and his companions, Azrador and Gunter, had been enjoying the new desert community. They saw no reason to be in a hurry to leave the Mystery Waters area. With more people arriving each day there were sales to be made and gossip to hear. Customers in the north always recognized the huge colorful tinker coach coming down the road and knew it was Nathan, the tinker, when they spotted his bright purple hat with the ostrich plume in the band. His tailored vest and matching high-top boots were also part of his daily uniform. He had never married, but was still open to the idea, if he were to find the right woman. Clara, the dressmaker, from King's Cross had been flirting with him for some time, but Nathan had kept it all business to this point. Freda, the head cook for King Rudolf, always cooked him his favorite foods, when he was in town. Even inviting him for the night hoping he would take the hint and propose.

The giant tinker coach he lived in, was pulled by two extremely large horned oxen, and contained many cupboards, drawers, and cabinets that were built into it. Nathan had inherited the coach from his father, and his father before him, both tinkers themselves. The coach was a rainbow of colors inside and out. It was made of live wood and was semi sentient, a leftover of their homeland. As the coach was magic itself, it was bigger on the inside than the outside.

As Nathan traveled, he was always looking for clues to the tinker homeland. For many years he spent most evenings at a campfire listening to local children telling tales and singing songs, hoping for a missing clue. Nathan hoped that some new clues might be found in the songs of these desert people. The desert people seemed to have many things in common with the tinkers, and their code.

Gunter was a longtime friend of Nathan's and they had been on several successful adventures together. Gunter, a mage/enchanter, was always dressed in forest green leathers and boots. He was very fit for his forty-five years. He did wear an odd hat though; it wasn't pointed like most mage hats. Gunter wore a flat green cap with an eagle feather in it.

Since coming to the Great Scarlett Desert he had been busy collecting samples of all the new plants that had emerged near the new river. He had excitedly told Nathan and Azrador that he had collected two new species of mushrooms, claiming they were unique. Gunter said he was going to come up with a good name for them since he had discovered them. In his excitement it hadn't occurred to him the Sundown Tribe might already have a name for them.

Azrador, who had also accompanied Nathan on adventures, was a full-blooded elf and would brag to anyone who would be willing to listen of his heritage. He was a Ranger/Mage, and looked the part, with his long ash blonde hair, tied back with a green leather strap. He had an exceptionally light complexion, slightly pointed ears, and an air of arrogance. He fit most people's idea of an elf. He was quite a contrast to the dark-skinned desert people they had met here. He was also an accomplished bowman and was also quite able with a rapier as well. Since they would be here for a while, Azrador had decided to explore the headwaters of this new Mystery River the Sundown Tribe was flocking to.

After breakfast with Nathan and Gunter, Azrador headed south along the river. He could feel nature sighing with relief from the nourishing waters. Somehow there were already fish swimming in the new river. The families with their colorful tents that were settling along the river began to thin out as he progressed further south, toward the mountains. Finally, around mid-day, he saw the last of the settlers behind him as he hiked along the fast-moving water.

This was when Azrador was most at peace when it was just him and nature, alone. The sound of water flowing was medicine that soothed his soul. He also heard the songs of a couple of birds he did not recognize, as he strolled along the riverbank.

He heard the waterfall long before he could see it. Once he could see the waterfall feeding the river, he saw it was cascading from an opening high, up the mountain. The size of the waterfall seemed to increase as he got closer. Before long the roar of the water became deafening. Nathan had told Azrador that he was convinced he had seen a cave entrance behind the waterfall when they first arrived. Azrador also recalled a nursery rhyme Nathan had told him years earlier. Nathan said the nursery rhyme had described the entrance to the lost land being behind a glittering waterfall. Azrador was determined to find out.

It was very slippery all around the foot of the waterfall and he almost fell into the icy cold water a couple of times. The mist created at the base of the waterfall was enough to chill Azrador to the point he was shivering. Climbing the rock wall, he found the stones slick from the mist. When he reached a third of the way to the top of the waterfall he could see the opening of a cave. Slowly working his way on the slick stones, he found himself sliding behind the falls and into the cave.

Looking outward from the entrance, all he could see was water and sky. The only sound he could hear was the roar of the falls, far below. He wasn't sure how Nathan had known there would be a cave here, but it seemed like a great time to explore what was here. Azrador cast a ball of light so he could check out his surroundings. He was in a gigantic cave, with extremely lofty ceilings, and it went on for a long way. As he walked, the long wide cave, it started to remind him more of a road than a cave with no tunnels leading off it. About half-way down the cave, Azrador began to see paintings on the walls. The images on the walls continued until he reached a large marble arch at the end of the hall. Azrador was glad he had thought to bring the Eye of Illusion with him, in case he found something strange, just like this.

Using the Eye, he looked at the arch. The Eye revealed pictures that looked like a dragon with a rider. The rider looked like a female, dressed in leather armor. Another was of a giant, holding a staff and shield. Both appeared to be carved in the altar, but without the Eye he saw nothing but the marble altar. He thought it odd that there was no script anywhere, no written words of any language. Azrador hoped Nathan might know what that meant. As he turned to walk back down the long cave, he examined the artwork on the walls more carefully. It seemed like they were telling a story, one of mass migration.

On the wall to his left, he saw the story of the tinker exile, the pictures depicted their large coaches, being pulled by oxen, leaving what appeared to be their homeland, one after another. The painting reminded Azrador of one of the covered paintings in Nathan's coach, the one he claimed was of his homeland. On the wall to his right was a painting of the exile of the desert people, and their great sailing ships.

Azrador's heart skipped a beat when he realized he was looking at two of the biggest clues he had ever seen. These wall paintings told the story of the exile of both groups.

Everyone knew the Tinkers had been exiled as punishment for the cursed weapons they had created. Nathan had been trying to find and destroy those cursed weapons his whole life. Somehow, these two peoples, the Tinkers, and the desert tribes, were connected. Azrador was so excited he couldn't wait to tell Nathan what he had discovered in the cave. He was sure it had to be part of the Tinker puzzle.

Azrador was almost back to the cave entrance and the waterfall when a great shaking of the ground occurred. The quake was so severe that rocks fell all around Azrador, one knocked him to the ground when it hit his shoulder. When the quake subsided, and the dust settled Azrador could no longer see or hear the waterfall. The path back to the waterfall was blocked by a pile of huge boulders. It quickly became obvious to Azrador he wasn't getting out the way he came in, so he searched the entire cave, this time using the Eye of Illusion. He found no hidden paths and no way out. Azrador was trapped. The blow from the rocks dropping on him had dislocated his shoulder and bruised his back so he knew he wasn't up to moving boulders.

Finding a flat spot, not far from the altar, he sat down, in a lotus position. Folding his arms in front of him, he began humming as he reached out to nature for a solution. He reassured himself "No reason to panic!"

Jason and the Rogue

The hike down the mountain to the valley in the crisp morning air gave Jason time to think. Would he have to fight another of his kind? He hoped not, could he defeat a full-blooded giant? His long legs ate the ground up quickly, so it wasn't long before he found himself standing at the edge of the rogue giant's campsite.

Jason got a good look at the creature as it exited his large tent. The giant was a good foot taller than Jason's seven feet and much broader in the chest and neck. The rogue was bald with a large scar over one eye, that still looked angry. When he scanned the camp and caught sight of Jason he angrily demanded, "Who you? What you want? I not return with you yet! You will kill me first!" The rogue giant picked up a huge, spiked club and grabbed his shield.

Instead of grabbing his weapon Jason extended his hands, palms up, "I am Jason Carron, son of Garth of the mountain. I am not here to fight you. I am not here to bother you. I have come to help the dwarfs install gates on the reservoir over there." Jason said as he pointed at the vast body of water between two huge mountains. "Once we have all the equipment installed, we plan to douse the volcano to the east, with enough water to put it out. We have no quarrel with you unless you want one!"

The giant rested the club on the ground and contemplated Jason for several minutes before speaking, "I be called Hutch the disgraced, this place is my new home. You leave now!"

Trying to keep the rogue giant calm, Jason evenly stated, "I mean you no harm Hutch. Where are your people? Why are you disgraced?"

Hutch scratched his head as he looked Jason up and down. "Your beads say you from Caretaker Tribe, but you a tiny giant. I sent to kill bad creature, but animal surprise me, so I fail, so now disgraced. The chief orders me go home, even disgraced." He then pointed at the scar over his eye, "is reminder of my disgrace. My hunt to prove adulthood was capture or kill creature named Mangler. It moves like cat and is big, it has claws and two large teeth sticking out from its jaws. Mangler can change color and hide in trees or rocks. My chief say I was to bring back pelt as proof. I am failed on both. Mangler not natural to this place and was freed as a test for me. I cannot return with honor without it. I see mangler in this valley three times, I killed no dwarfs, so far! I saw it kill dwarfs but could not help in time. Then it gone again." Hutch hung his head, ashamed of his failure.

Jason was beginning to feel bad for the giant. "Where are your beads Hutch? The dwarfs think you're a rogue giant since you're not wearing any. They believe you are on the prowl, looking to claim this valley for your own. They also believe that you killed the dwarfs that were sent to spy on what you were up to." Jason thought he was making good progress in the conversation.

Hutch thumped his chest as he explained, "I not get beads until I kill Mangler. I not adult until I win my test. My tribe is the Watch, our beads are blue and yellow, if you earn them."

Jason had heard enough to decide. "Hutch, could my friends and I assist you in tracking this beast? With our help maybe you can still complete your quest and return home with honor. I have much equipment and many more dwarfs arriving here in the next couple of days. What else can you tell me about the creature, while we wait for them to arrive?" Jason inquired.

Hutch nodded at Jason, happy to have help. "It stink, like muskrat when close. I sure I injured it with my club when it clawed my face, but I find no blood. I hit it real hard, but cat is as big as you are! Then it disappeared, gone." Hutch pulled out two cups and filled them with grog and held one out to Jason.

Jason accepted the invitation and the drink, excited as he thought to himself, "I learned something new, I am of the Caretaker Tribe."

Hutch sat on one of two large tree stumps and asked Jason, "Come, sit, I will not harm you little giant"

The two giants sat there drinking and continuing their conversation, until Jason noticed the dwarfs sneaking up on the campsite. Jason stood and waved the dwarfs out of the brush they were hiding behind. They gradually stood up exposing where they were but did not approach any closer.

Jason spoke to the dwarfs, "Stay where you are for now, Hutch and I are still talking. Who among you is most talented at tracking?" Jason asked.

Without hesitation Grantis spoke up, "That would be Gordo, he can track anything! Eh Gordo?"

Gordo grinned at Jason as he responded. "Always found what I was tracking, so far!"

Under his breath but still noticeable Gadna mumbled "Mostly women folk!".

Turning back to the giant, Jason asked, "Perhaps if we lend aid in tracking the creature you can kill or trap it. What say you Hutch?"

Hutch thought about the offer for a few moments before he responded, "I be the one to trap or kill or it!" He said as he looked at the dwarfs.

Jason proceeded to fill the dwarfs in on the situation. After hearing Hutch's story, they agreed to help the giant return home. Everyone agreed that helping him was a better solution than fighting the giant, especially if it was a large cat that had killed their fellow dwarfs and not the giant.

Hutch led them to the clearing where he had battled the Mangler. He then pointed to some nearby broken brush that the cat knocked down with its exit. Gordo examined the broken brush closely, after sniffing the leaves and stems he found some of the creature's blood. Even its blood had camouflaged itself, but Gordo's big flat nose had the scent of the creature now and was headed through the brush, following it. Jason and Hutch were right behind him as he started to follow a path up the mountain. The terrain got rockier as they climbed, and it wasn't long before there was no path at all. At one point Gordo lost the Mangler's, scent until he realized the cat had lept across a crevice. It took them a short time to cross the crevasse and pick the scent back up on the other side.

By mid-day they were high above the valley and were doing more climbing than walking. Gordo pushed on up the mountain like a blood hound. When he reached a short switchback, his nose started twitching. Jason watched as Gordo reached out and pulled back a small scrub tree, to reveal a narrow crevice that led to a small cave entrance.

Gordo grinned again as he pointed at the cave entrance and stated, "I would bet that is where your injured cat is waiting. If you injured it badly, it could be dead or it might be laid up in the cave, resting. Good luck Hutch!"

Jason put his hand on Hutch's back to reassure him, "I'll be right behind you, in case it gets by you. I will try to block its escape."

Hutch readied his spiked club, and Jason readied his

mace and shield, "I go in now, Thank you little Gordo for your help!" Hutch then turned and entered the cave.

When they entered the cave the scent of the Mangler was strong. It reminded Jason of mink or otter rather than cat. It was dark inside the cave, but giants have good vision in the dark, so Hutch moved on slowly and deliberately, searching for any clue to where the big cat was hiding. It wasn't long before the cave opened to a large cavern with many ledges. They both knew that the Mangler could blend into any type of surrounding, making it ridiculously hard to find, until it strikes.

While not moving and listening closely, they heard a slight drip from one of the ledges. Jason pointed at where he thought the sound came from and Hutch nodded. The cat's previous injury had given away its location. Jason moved to block the exit while Hutch removed a large net from his pack. It was an unusual looking net, with small balls attached to the ends of the net. Hutch began swinging the net in a circle over his head, as the big cat let out an ear-piercing growl. The cat leapt at Hutch from the ledge in a blur of colors as Hutch released the net. The net caught the large animal in midflight and the balls wrapped tightly around the four-hundred-pound animal, holding it snug as it landed at Hutch's feet. The big cat thrashed about, and Jason worried Hutch might get caught by one of the protruding fangs. After a few moments of that, the animal became calm and to Jason's surprise, more relaxed.

Hutch chuckled as he explained, "Net do sleep spell that lets me carry animal. Much honor if cat alive, not just a pelt." Hutch was smiling a toothy grin at the success of the capture. "I get beads now!"

Jason and Hutch carried the massive animal down the mountain, to Hutch's campsite. When the dwarfs saw the monster, they couldn't believe it's size. Asleep, and undisguised, it had deep blue skin with tan stripes, except around the eyes. Orange spots covered the face of the animal. Its eyes were closed in sleep, but Hutch claimed the cat's eyes were a deep blue color. The group celebrated Hutch's success that evening. Everyone had more than their fill of grog, and a few dwarfs were passed out in the brush still the next morning.

When the carts of materials started arriving the next day, Hutch offered his assistance as repayment for their help capturing the Manger. With Jason and Hutch lifting the heavy gates, installation went much faster than planned. Since they did not have to install all the levers and pulleys needed for the heavy lifting. By the end of the third day the work at the reservoir was complete.

Once done they returned to Hutch's campsite, where he again thanked Jason and the dwarves for their help. Picking the cat up and swinging it around his neck and shoulders, he began hiking Mt. Clainous, heading for his home portal, deep in the mountain.

Azrador Missing?

Nathan looked out on the new mystery waters, toward the waterfall in the distance, wondering if he really had seen a cave behind it when they first arrived. He had driven the tinker coach past the waterfall and then along the river to where the large multi-colored tents were pitched like a fair. It made him think of an evening around the fire ring in King's Cross. Peter, a young cobbler, sang a verse to a lullaby that spoke of the road to a new land. It would lay in a cave, behind a glittering waterfall. The lullaby went like this.

"An ancient people wielded strong magic, some for good, some for evil. They lived in a paradise forest that could only be reached by the pure of heart. A cave entrance behind a waterfall that glistened in the sun like a gem would be the road."

Nathan was looking forward with anticipation to Azrador's return. He really wanted to hear his report on the waterfall.

As he looked over the many-colored tents of the Tribe, he thought it odd that the Sundown Tribe dressed all in white, but their tents and the furnishings inside them were every color of the rainbow. A great many of the Tribe were moving from their underground sanctuaries to this new fertile land. Who could blame them? The water was creating a whole new environment for the desert people.

Mikiel and Amara had visited often in the last couple of weeks, as they carried word of the new mystery waters to the other villages and towns. They were shuttling settlers from other parts of the desert to this new community on their sand schooner. Swift was certainly a sight to see, sailing across the desert, just like a ship on the high seas. Nathan enjoyed watching Swift sailing across the sand, she certainly was a graceful ship to watch.

On this trip, Mikiel also brought word from his brother Willem, the Sultan. The Green Folk were seeking the Tribe's aid in eliminating a magic anomaly. It was the first time in their history the elves had asked for assistance from outsiders. In fact, they still typically did not allow foreign visitors in their lands.

Mikiel had invited Nathan to dinner on the Swift that evening to discuss the recent events. As Nathan passed the huge multi-colored tents and shade stands, as they called them, it was apparent their love of colors was displayed everywhere. Thick colorful carpets lined the floors in their tents. Large stuffed pillows scattered about were used to sit on around low tables. The interiors were lit with colorful glass globes. They made very intricate glass shapes as decoration in every color and shape. The desert supplied the needed sand for glass blowing and it was an art form among the tribe.

Everyone Nathan met seemed extremely friendly and welcoming to him and his fellow travelers. Swift was docked where the desert met the new oasis. The oasis area was growing daily, and since the schooners could only travel on sand, it was a bit of a hike for Nathan to reach Mikiel's schooner.

As Nathan touched the railing to the ship, he was reminded that it was made of the rare live wood that his coach was made of. He wondered, not for the first time, if the two forms of transport were connected? The legends said live wood grew in the world's original forests. They also say the tinkers were allowed to harvest the live wood, but only if it was used to create a means to travel to their exile. Nathan wondered how the Sundowners came by enough live wood in the Scarlet Desert to create a vessel the size of Swift. Perhaps he would ask Mikiel, it could make good dinner conversation.

The interior quarters of Swift were plush and comfortable and very colorful, much like their tents. Nathan was seated on a plush red cushion at the dinner table. He immediately took notice that the interior of the cabin was larger than the exterior. Swift and his coach had more in common than it appeared. Mikiel was again dressed from head to toe in white, but today he was dressed more formally. He was wearing gold accents on his turban and belt, with a curved dagger in its jeweled sheath. Nathan, in contrast was dressed in his typical black tunic under a purple vest and black, turned down boots. And as always, he wore his purple hat with the ostrich plume.

After a delicious pheasant dinner with desert greens, Mikiel offered a sweet dessert wine as the dishes were cleared by a servant.

Once they were alone again Mikiel explained, "Willem feels that if the elves were asking for help, the situation must indeed be dire. He is considering whether to send help or not as we speak. He is not sure if the elves should be trusted since they have kept all visitors out of Elyneas for generations and only allowed commerce between us and them on a very limited basis. King Alwin, as a rule, does not allow any social interactions between our peoples. So, Willem is unsure whether we would be welcomed if we went to their aid? Before he decides, he'd like more information about the magic anomaly and why it is causing such concern?" Mikiel respected his brother and his judgement, and he would abide by Willem's decision, whatever that would be.

Mikiel went on to briefly describe the dreams Amara had been having to Nathan, and how they had him concerned. He explained Amara's ability to communicate with the dead and that she seemed to be in contact with a long dead high priestess of the Da Nang tribe. Amara had confided how real the dreams seemed. The conversation ended when the sun was starting to set, and Nathan said his goodnights.

Nathan had been surprised to hear the Sundown Tribe followed the same basic tenets that the tinker path preached. The tinkers believed if you have done wrong you must pay for those past transgressions, whatever they may be, by helping your fellow man in any way possible. That is the main reason why the tinker's travel. They supply whatever is needed, wherever they travel. Always listening for clues to the path home.

Nathan, for the first time, felt in his bones that recent developments must be leading him to the answer. Swan and Gunter had helped him destroy the cursed weapons, and when they did all hell broke loose. First a volcano explodes, and a new land opens up. He then meets a clan of dwarfs, after spending his life thinking that dwarfs were a myth. Next, he finds a dark-skinned desert tribe that was totally unknown in the three kingdoms. Not to mention learning of the elves and Elyneas. So many facts were stacking up that somehow the desert tribes were linked to the tinkers. There were just too many coincidences for them not to be pieces of the same puzzle.

As Nathan walked back to the tinker coach, he experienced a huge quake that shook the ground violently and knocked him from his feet. He saw several tents collapse as the ground pitched and rolled. When it was over, Nathan got up and brushed himself off. He would have sworn the waterfall had stopped for a second or two. Nathan rubbed his eyes and looked again to see the waterfall just as it had been. Did he imagine the waterfall stopping or had the quake caused the water to stop flowing?

When Nathan stepped into the coach Gunter greeted him with a wave.

Gunter asked, "Did you feel that one, wow, it was a doozy? It had the coach jumping around I'll tell you! How was supper with Mikiel and Amara? I just love that girl's violet eyes."

Nathan wondered if Gunter might have a crush on Amara, but decided not to ask, "Amara wasn't there, it was just Mikiel and me. Dinner was good. He somehow came up with pheasant cooked with minty greens of some kind. It was quite delicious. He also served an exceptionally good dessert wine that you would have appreciated Gunter." Nathan sat down at the table and filled his pipe, "He told me about some dreams Amara had been having. Did you know she has the foretelling ability?"

Tamping a load into his pipe and taking a couple puffs to get it going Nathan thought of something else to tell Gunter. "Another thing, did you know Amara has some darker magic and speaks with the dead. He told me she was able to communicate with a long dead High Priestess of this pyramid in the northern desert. She told Amara that her people were called the Da Nang. She claimed that her tribe lived above the desert sands, in a floating city. It's a pretty remarkable story, considering Mikiel says his father used to tell them a fable about a floating city of wizards."

Gunter sputtered, "I am not surprised that she has the foretelling ability, but you say she can speak with the dead? That explains the air of mystery that accompanies her. I find her to be a very interesting individual."

Nathan lit his pipe again and took a few puffs to get it going before asking, "Have you seen anything of Azrador? He went to investigate the waterfall and the headwaters of the river this morning and I haven't heard from him since. I'm a little surprised not to find him here, ready to tell us all about his great discoveries."

Gunter chuckled at Nathans comment, "If he had discovered anything great, we would have heard about it by now, you know how he loves to brag. I haven't seen him all day, but I'm not too worried about him. He is able to fend for himself, and he would be the first to tell you that, by the way!" Gunter exclaimed as he unwrapped a muffin, he had made the day before. "All I had for dinner was mushroom soup, not some gourmet meal like you, so I'm still hungry."

"Mikiel had news from the Green Folk. He says the elves have never allowed non elves to travel their lands but have asked for the Sundowner's help. They have invited the Sundowners to assist with destroying a magic anomaly in the southern part of their country. Mikiel is waiting on a decision by his brother, Willem, as to whether to render assistance or not. The elves claim an anomaly is draining all life and magic from their lands. According to Willem their lush forest landscape is changing because of it. Plant life in the area has died and the ground has cracked open. The reports also state magic does not work there; many elves have died trying to stop it." Nathan relit his pipe enjoying a few puffs while considering what to do next.

Gunter asked, with a mouth full of muffin, "So why haven't they just sent an army of non-magic users to investigate it?"

Nathan shook his head as he answered, "Mikiel said that King Alwin had sent several squads of soldiers to investigate, but they met up with some large lizard creatures that came out of the cracked ground. Sounds like they had a tough time defeating them. Reports state that they are awfully difficult to kill since they are not much affected by magic. Plus, the lizards actually ate many of the elves! Doesn't sound like a good place to travel to does it?" Nathan asked as he tamped his pipe out in the crystal ashtray.

Gunter grunted. "It certainly doesn't, but I am sure you have a good reason why we are going anyway?"

Nathan snickered as he responded, "To be honest I haven't decided yet! Mikiel's schooner will only travel on sand so he will have to transfer to horses at the border town of Vardo, a much less comfortable way to travel. The coach offers much more comfort on a long journey like that. Who knows, maybe this route will lead to the path of the lost homeland?" Nathan said while gazing at the covered painting hanging on the wall. He believed the painting was of his homeland, but it could hypnotize you if looked at it too long, so he kept it covered. It and a couple of others had come from the ruins at Ruby Falls Enclave and were magical. "I think it best I sleep on the idea." Nathan said after several minutes.

Bantez and Drifting Sands

Willem had set up his own tents at Mystery Waters now that more people were relocating there. When Willem heard the latest tale of Amara's dreams, he thought it best if they were to go investigate the area. There were too many clues to ignore, especially if Dylan were pointing that way. He cautioned them of the dangers of the Drifting Sands after Dylan and Mikiel's trip for scorpions. Willem warned them to be careful on the journey but to report back as soon as they learned anything.

Mikiel and Amara left on Swift the following morning, heading for the northern desert. The schooner sailed over the sand with a good southerly wind pushing its five sails. They passed by two large sand crabs eating what was left of a camel carcass. Mikiel wondered if the large sand crabs ate the sand worms or vice versa. He hadn't seen any evidence of it so far. Amara reported she could feel several groups of sand worms moving under them, but none bothered them.

Two days later it became obvious fairly quickly that they had reached the Drifting Sands. The wind speed had picked up and Swift's compass quit working. The further north they traveled the taller the sand dunes became.

Mikiel laughed as the ship rolled and bobbed up one dune and down the next. "I wonder if this is like sailing on the ocean waves?" The wind kept increasing so Mikiel lowered some of the sails to slow the ship as the terrain became steeper. Navigation became difficult when the sun disappeared. Clouds moved in and the sand really started to blow around. As the wind increased so did the sands movement. Finally, they had no choice but to drop sail and batten down the hatches before the sandstorm they saw coming on the horizon overtook them. Black clouds swirled above them as sand particles blasted anything in its path. Once everything was locked down above deck they went below. They could feel the Swift being tossed about in the sea of sand. The anchor didn't hold for long, so the rest of the night the ship was thrown first one way then another. Neither Mikiel nor Amara got much sleep during the storm.

Late into the night they fell asleep due to exhaustion. When they woke the next morning, they could feel the ship was leaning heavily to one side. Due to the slant of the vessel, it was difficult to walk inside the cabin. As he made his way to the hatch Mikiel commented, "I am surprised Swift hasn't righted herself. There must be something wrong." He was eager to get topside and see where they were. Amara was right behind him climbing out of the hatch. A quick look around told Mikiel what he needed to know. Swift's deck was buried in sand. Mikiel and Amara both cast wind spells, quickly clearing the deck.

As the two of them surveyed their surroundings they were both surprised at the view. The ship had come to rest against the roof of an ancient building or ruin. They could also see the peaks of roofs of several nearby buildings above the sand. Amara's attention was drawn to something pointed sticking out of the top of a tall sand dune. The sight made her feel vindicated. Her dreams seemed to be correct. Yes indeed, there had been a city here sometime in the past. It may or may not have floated, as in her dream. Not far off, in the distance, she could see the top of the pyramid of which she had dreamt. No spire was visible but who knew how much more of the city lay under the sand. The scene was quite a strange site to view.

After lowering the plank and disembarking Mikiel found the sand was quite loose. His boot sank into the sand covering it to the top of his ankle, making walking slow and sluggish. Mikiel cast a small dust devil ahead of him. He watched it blow the loose sand away leaving the packed sand after that. It was immediately easier to walk so he continued to expose more of the surrounding structures.

After watching Mikiel use his wind spell, Amara did the same, as she worked in the direction of the pyramid. Mikiel used a stronger wind spell to unbury and level Swift before hurrying after Amara.

Amara was so eager she could hardly contain her excitement. She was anxious to see if the mezzanine level she floated down to in the dream really existed. If it was there, it would prove to everyone that her dreams were more than just dreams. When they were a short distance from what appeared to be the front of the exposed pyramid, Mikiel cast a large whirlwind spell. It quickly blew away thirty feet of sand. That exposed not only the mezzanine level but also a lower-level entrance, with large double doors. Amara felt like her dream had leapt to life.

Mikiel smiled at her and asked, "It's your dream, would you like to show me this pyramid of yours?"

Amara actually giggled before replying, "I would be delighted to lead the way! Who knows what treasure we may discover!" Amara replied leading the way to the newly exposed entrance.

The entrance had two large double doors that stood over

ten feet high. They appeared to be made of some type of gold metal that she was not familiar with. Neither pushing nor pulling had any effect on the doors. Mikiel tried several unlock and open spells with no effect. The exterior of the pyramid was a golden color but made of a marble neither of them had ever seen. After examining its walls, they could detect no seams at all. They had no way to know how much more of the pyramid was buried under the sand.

After watching Mikiel attempt to open the doors using his magic, Amara decided to try something different. She had been communicating with this high priestess in her dreams, perhaps she had the ability to open the doors. Amara closed her eyes and placed a hand on each door. Taking a deep breath, she visualized the moment she placed the Sacred Sun Medallion into the spire atop the pyramid. As she imagined the moment the Medallion had started to glow, she heard a loud click and the doors swung inward.

Strongheim

Grantis felt like the installation had been a tremendous success and Bendri said Olax would be happy with the speedy outcome. Work would continue in other parts of the mountain chain blocking off the side tunnels to contain the water flow, but thanks to Jason and his band of dwarves, the first major step in their task had been accomplished.

When Jason and his group returned to Strongheim he was invited to dinner with Master Bluthe, so he went to his quarters immediately, got cleaned up and hurried to Bluthe's dining room. Master Bluthe greeted him warmly when he arrived, and then introduced him to an incredibly old dwarf named Throdon. Master Throdon's grey hair and beard were past his waist and Jason found it hard not to stare at his large protruding nose. The conversation during dinner revolved around their plan for the volcano and how successful they had been in the installation of the reservoir gates.

Throdon had stayed mostly quiet during dinner, but once the table had been cleared by a short, round, red headed dwarf that Jason thought was female, Bluthe refilled their mugs as Throdon cleared his throat and extended his hand to Jason. "I will see it now!" Throdon demanded in a gravelly voice more powerful than Jason expected from the frail looking dwarf.

Master Bluthe explained in a somber tone. "Jason, if you wouldn't mind, please show our esteemed Grandmaster Mage the staff of power you built. If he believes you and the staff are worthy, he has agreed to complete the last step in activating the magic contained in the stone."

Jason was hesitant to just hand this stranger the staff, but he trusted Master Bluthe, so he did as Bluthe requested.

Jason removed the staff from his pack, placing it on the table, where they had just eaten dinner. He was surprised to hear a loud gasp from the old dwarf. Throdon stared at the staff and its workmanship with awe. The gold lining the joints and prongs where the stone met the crown was perfect. Lifting it for balance, he inspected it from its tapered base that was black as night, to the gold lined crown that held the blue stone.

Slowly the old dwarf smiled a toothy smile, showing he had all his teeth even at his age. "Jason, do you know what you have here? This is the Divinity Stone! Where in Bloodhammers name did you get this? In the old texts there are numerous mentions of its immense powers, and how it was used at the forming of our world. That's an exceedingly rare artifact that you have added to an already powerful tool!" Throdon exclaimed.

Jason nodded as he told his tale. "ArchMage Ibis sent a mage named Jade to my hometown of Coal Valley. She carried the stone, and her task was to find a Master Blacksmith that could create an adamantine staff and include the stone you call the Divinity Stone. She held my foster parent's hostage, so I could not refuse her. She promised she would kill them both if I failed to create the staff. After I did her bidding, she was supposed to return to Autry and give Ibis the staff, unused. For some unknown reason Jade decided not to do that. She chose to keep the staff. That choice eventually cost her life." Jason said in a quiet voice.

The ancient dwarf looked at Bluthe and then at Jason, trying to decide how much of his story to believe. "The fact you created this at such a youthful age is astounding to me Jason. You were right about this young giant Master Bluthe. Yes, his giant heritage and having a good teacher could make a good smith, for sure! This tinker you speak of, the one that gave you the lost recipe for adamantine, is he still alive?" Throdon asked.

Jason replied, "Yes he is. In fact, he was just here a brief time ago, meeting with Clan Chief Brackus. He left with the dark-skinned desert people, the Sundowners, to investigate a new water source that was recently discovered in their southern desert."

Throdon directed the conversation back to the staff. "Very interesting! You say this enchanter was able to enchant the staff and your mace. Was she powerful with it?"

Jason recalled watching Jade use her magic and smiled. "Yes, Master Throdon she was very powerful, in fact she was scary powerful when using her magic. Once I watched as she froze a troll solid. Another time I saw her blast an ogre off a mountain using it. I also saw her throw lightning and fire. I still believe if she hadn't depleted her mana that day in the mountains, she would still be alive." Jason said with sadness in his voice.

Ignoring the pain in Jason's voice Throdon continued to examine the staff. "Yes, yes I can feel the enchantments. Not too bad an effort either." Taking a closer look at the Divinity Stone he went on, "She must not have known how to activate the stone, or she had not been powerful enough to accomplish the task. The ArchMage must have thought there was no risk of her being able to activate the Divinity Stone to entrust her with it. His distrust of her sounds well deserved since she did not return it to him. That is something we can all be thankful for."

Throdon looked Jason up and down, for a third time before speaking, "But are you worthy to be the wielder of such a weapon? That I do not yet know! If I were to find you worthy, I do know how to activate this ancient artifact!" The old mage took the staff in his hands placing the base on the stone floor smiling. "I can feel its power just waiting for the right person to tap it."

Jason took Night Star from his pack, dropping it on the table with a loud thud. "Excuse me Master Throdon, I am not a mage. This is the weapon I wield; Night Star and I fight as one! It is for a mage to wield that staff."

Throdon picked up the mace and whistled, "My, my, she is indeed a beauty. Also enchanted, with increased battle damage and a boost to your stamina, all while weighing less than a normal mace. Very impressive work for any Master Smith, or Grand Master for that matter wouldn't you say Grand Master Bluthe?"

Master Bluthe had already looked Night Star over quite closely. "I doubt I could duplicate either one of them! Magnificent workmanship on both and made of metals not seen in hundreds of years, with enchantments that are worth a fortune." Master Bluthe said with respect in his voice.

Still holding the mace in his hands Throdon nodded, "This is indeed a very lethal weapon and with your physique and strength added to it, more than adequate for a fight. But compared to what the staff could do when activated, it is but a stick!"

Jason stated in no uncertain terms, "Well then perhaps you can wield it, you said it yourself, a mage should be the one to do some good with it!"

Throdon put Night Star back on the table and focused his attention back on the staff. "Yes, a mage could wield this staff and maybe even command some of its magic. There is an odd tendency with created magical objects like this one. These objects are always more powerful when their creator is using them. And so, as you can see, since you created it, you are the staff's one true master. It can be lent to others, for a time. But it will always have a stronger response to the commands of its creator." Throdon explained to Jason. "The stone you set in the crown is no ordinary blue rock, Jason. The Divinity Stone is mentioned numerous times in the legends about the beginning of the world. When I was younger, the mage I apprenticed under, would seek out any information he could find about it in the old texts and scrolls. My master was convinced that the giants had been given the Divinity Stone for safe keeping, until it was needed again. How the ArchMage of your land obtained it I do not know. I do know we must be thankful he didn't end up with it because of what it is capable of."

Jason was starting to get more than a little frustrated with the old mage when he snapped at him, "How can you be sure this blue rock is any better than any other blue rock? I keep telling you I have no magic, dwarf; I am a blacksmith not a mage. I am a warrior that fights with a mace and shield, not a staff!"

Throdon continued to calmly explain, "Master Bluthe recognized your magic Jason, the first time he saw your mace. It requires magic to forge adamantine from those two metals. It is also a high art of craftmanship as well, to accomplish that weapon. Bluthe knew no ordinary smith could make such a thing. No one in centuries has made them! Not since the dawn of ages have these types of weapons been forged. Master Bluthe himself, who has accomplished much in his several centuries, said he did not have the ability to forge them. According to your own story, you have made three such weapons. And as proof you carry two of them. Do you need more proof? How about the fact that you pull these weapons from a magic bag, that only magic users may use. The fact that you are unaware of all your abilities is another clue that you may indeed be worthy of wielding the magic in that stone."

Jason turned to Master Bluthe and said, "Will you talk sense to him please, I am no mage!"

Master Bluthe merely smiled and said, "We believe your destiny lies down a different path than you planned."

Master Bluthe added, "Jason you have not reached full adulthood for giants. Your abilities and size will continue to grow over the next several years, including your magic. You don't know where your magic comes from, but it is obvious you have it. Perhaps, your mother? Was she a witch or a mage perhaps?"

Jason answered, "I know very little about my mother, she died in childbirth. I was raised by the midwife that delivered me and her husband, Olaf the blacksmith. While Jade and I were prospecting in the Sky mountains I met my father, Garth the giant. He and the giants rescued us after Jade had been injured. They took us to their village deep in the mountains. Garth explained to me that he had found my mother, Rose Carron, disoriented and freezing in the mountains. She explained to him she was a traveler and that she had been thrown through the wrong portal by an adversary. Garth told me that she was dressed in foreign clothing, made of silk, not dressed for the harsh mountain climate. Garth took Rose back to his village, where she recovered, and they eventually made a life together, until her pregnancy forced her to seek help. Garth brought her to a farmer's place in the foot of the Sky Mountains. Farmer Jones took one look at her and knew she needed help fast, so he brought her to Zella the local midwife in the town of Coal Valley."

Throdon asked with curiosity, "Are you saying you met your father, the giant, and he took you to their village? And they rendered aid to your companion as well. This is very unusual according to the stories I have read. It is said the giants never let anyone that enters their villages leave, for fear of their villages being found"

Jason continued his story, "Well, the mage that enchanted this weapon was injured by a rock to the head, thrown by a troll. She was unconscious and I was near exhaustion when the giants showed up. They carried Jade down the mountain and through several tunnels to their homeland and city. Their healers worked on Jade for several weeks, until she recovered. That gave me some time to get to know Garth and their city. The architecture was beautiful, similar to the dwarves but much larger. I have never seen any landscape that matches it. Huge trees and flowers of every color. The necklace and ring that I wear are all my mother had with her the day I was born. Garth identified the ring as his. As long as I wear them, I will be welcomed at any giant village wearing the beads of their tribe." Jason said showing the ring and beads to the old mage.

Throdon was shocked at Jason's latest tale and demanded to know. "They let you leave just like that. The legends say they never let anyone that is not a giant leave, forcing them to live out their days in the giant's home!"

Jason shrugged as he went on, "Garth offered to let me stay, and I was tempted. It was the most beautiful place I have ever seen. But I decided not to. If I had stayed, I would be the runt giant there, here I am the giant that towers over most folks. Plus, I am blessed with good friends here. I have also discovered I like adventure and travel. Garth told me I was welcome to return whenever I wished but to keep their location a secret. He also said there are multiple paths to reach his land." Jason added while reminiscing of the beauty of the place.

Master Bluthe interjected, "Throdon it sounds to me like Jason's mother may have been a powerful traveler. As far as I know stepping out of a portal was only possible in the old legends. But who knows, the aura that envelops the boy grows stronger each day. Maybe his is strong in whatever magic his mother had."

Throdon scratched his beard as he considered Bluthe's words. "The legends described travelers as being from another world, able to step from one to another. Some ancient texts even claimed travelers are who originally created this world. That would be powerful magic to inherit Jason!" Throdon got up from his chair and straightened his robes.

Throdon spent the next several minutes staring at the staff before turning to face Jason. "I have decided! Jason, give me your oath, on your father's grave, that you will pledge to only help this world with the magic contained in the Divinity Stone and I will agree to complete the last step in its creation." Throdon said with reverence in his voice.

"I pledge on my father's grave and my honor to only help the world with this staff! " Jason said humbly.

Throdon turned and headed out of the room, "It is decided then! We do this!" he exclaimed. "Follow me Jason, my workshop is just down the hall. You and I shall complete the process of waking the Divinity Stone!"

Jason had to scramble to catch up with the old mage, shocked he could move faster than Jason would have thought possible with such short legs. Throdon had hoped he lived for a higher purpose all these years, even if he had thought the story of the Divinity Stone a fable before seeing it.

Master Bluthe patted Jason on the back as they grabbed the two weapons off the table and chased after the short old mage. "Come along Jason, this should be interesting. I haven't seen the old coot this excited since an apprentice caught his beard on fire!"

Golden Pyramid

When Amara opened her eyes, she was facing a wide, long hallway that extended into the interior of the giant pyramid. When she turned around to face Mikiel, his mouth was hanging open in astonishment.

Mikiel shook his head as he motioned his sister forward. "Lead the way, you are the one who has been here before. The pyramid evidently recognizes you!" Mikiel said laughing. The walls were lined with torches and with a flick of her wrist they flamed to life, lighting the great hallway. Amara was surprised there was not a heavy layer of sand or dust as they made their way inside. The hallway was littered with skeletons that were wearing luxurious fabrics, still visible after all these centuries. There were even a few minotaur guard skeletons.

The great hallway had many branches off of it, but Amara didn't deviate from her path. She continued to lead straight ahead, to a chamber that contained a large altar on a platform raised several steps above the floor. Without hesitation Amara walked straight up the steps to the altar. There on the alter in front of her were the blue mana stones of which she had dreamt.

Rushing to the alter she explained, "Mikiel these are the mana stones that were used in my dream! They were used to recharge the medallion that kept the city afloat and turning. No one I have ever known has seen mana stones. They are the magic of myths and legends, until now! We have to take them with us!" Amara cried as she placed them in her pack.

Mikiel had never seen his sister so wound up. "Amara this is an amazing discovery! What else was in your dreams? Do you have any idea where the medallion you keep speaking of might be?" Mikiel asked as he looked around the assembly hall. It was lined with full size marble sculptures. There was also what looked like a marble fountain with fairies carved into it. It no longer spewed water but at one time must have been quite beautiful. He could imagine large groups of citizens meeting and praying here.

Amara thought for a moment before responding, "I already had the Sun Medallion it in my possession in the dream, I placed it in the highest point of the spire on the peak of the pyramid. I looked for the spire outside, but it appears to be gone I suppose it could be buried somewhere out there."

Amara gave it more thought as she examined the large hall. A thought suddenly struck her. "Another possibility is the city fell from the sky because someone removed the medallion. Why don't we see if we can find stairs up to the mezzanine level? That's where I entered in my dream. I think from there I will be able to find my way to that room. In the dream I returned to my quarters after the ceremony, that is where I found the Book of Blessings that I couldn't read. I woke up right after that." Amara explained as she descended the stairs from the altar. "Let's backtrack to the intersections we passed in the hallway. We need to find some stairs going up."

They soon found themselves in a confusing maze of

hallways and rooms. One of the smaller rooms they passed through had a small stash of unusual weapons. Mikiel sorted through the stash and found a curved sword he took a liking. It was made from a red metal he had never seen before, and its sheath was decorated with fine enamel artwork. The words "Fire tongue" were etched into the swords blade. Mikiel gave the sword a couple of good swings before returning it to its sheath. Mikiel pointed out a bow that was partially covered by a large piece of chest armor. Amara tossed the armor away, revealing the bow. Amara could feel it calling her. Picking up the bow she could feel the magic in it right away. The bow was made of a very dark wood and was the most beautiful weapon Amara had ever seen. Engraved in the bow was the name "Surefire." What a find! Two fine weapons to add to their loot and they had barely explored the pyramid. Amara wondered how much Dylan's shade had to do with the find.

After a couple of dead ends and stepping over a lot of skeletons, they found a stairway up. The stairs were littered with skeletons, much of their clothing still showing bright colors. When they reached the next level, the skeletons were even more numerous. Some in uniforms, some in formal robes, their deaths must have come all at once. It was very creepy. The pyramid felt more like a mausoleum than somewhere people had worshiped and lived. This hallway was not as wide as the lower floor. It displayed many wall carvings and statues, but none as extravagant as those on the altar level. Amara judged that this was not the mezzanine level, so they continued to search rooms and hallways for another stairway up.

When they estimated they were in the center of the pyramid they found another stairway up. Amara recognized this level as the mezzanine from her dream. She thought if they turned right, they would find an exit out of the pyramid. In her dream she had entered the pyramid from that direction. She decided to retrace her steps, hoping to recognize where in the pyramid she was. They followed the hallway to the right, and it did indeed lead to two large double doors, similar to the doors they used to enter the pyramid. Amara tried to open them but to no avail. Amara thought she knew her way from here and could find the High Priestess quarters.

Doing an about face she led the way back into the pyramid. Taking a right when they reached the intersection of hallways, they made their way down that hallway until they began to hear hissing noises ahead of them. The pyramid had been incredibly quiet up until now with no signs of life so far. At the next intersection of hallways, they found a stairway down and the source of the hissing. The stairs were covered in slithering snakes, hissing, and tasting the air, with their forked tongues. Mikiel tapped Amara on the shoulder and put his fingers to his lips, indicating silence as they passed by the stairwell. Amara nodded and led on straight ahead.

Amara pointed down the hall at another set of doors as she whispered to Mikiel, "The High Priestess's quarters are this way, behind those doors."

Mikiel placed his ear against one of the doors, listening for any sounds on the other side, before attempting to open them. He didn't hear any sounds and he wasn't able to open the doors. Turning to Amara he bowed and swept his arm towards the doors as he said, "It's all yours High Priestess," Choosing not to respond to Mikiel's comment Amara closed her eyes and again placed a hand on each door as she replayed the dream in her head. Focusing her mind on the room beyond the doors she recalled the interior of the chamber. After a brief moment she heard a loud click and the doors slowly swept open.

As she entered the chamber she heard a deep male voice say, "Welcome High Priestess." The voice surprised her and Mikiel enough that they both drew their weapons.

Searching the chamber, they found no clue as to where the voice had come from, but Mikiel did find what looked like a headdress. He picked it up and found it must weigh at least twenty pounds. He had never seen so many gemstones in one place in his life. After finding no one in the room, Amara went on ahead and searched two more chambers. They found nothing explaining who, or what they had heard. Proceeding deeper into the rooms, Amara entered what looked to be a bedchamber. Lying on a large bed in the center of the room was a skeleton. It was dressed in a royal blue gown that was tied at the waist with a white silk belt. She was wearing a circlet of gold in her hair. Amara immediately recognized the skeleton as the High Priestess. Upon examining the skeleton further, she found a large knife buried in her chest.

She called out to Mikiel, unable to take her eyes off the corpse. "Mikiel come here quick! I have found the High Priestess! She must have been murdered in her bed. Who would do such a thing?" Amara examined the large knife closely and detected the knife was spelled with dark magic.

She decided to try contacting the spirit of the High Priestess. "I am going to try and reach the spirit of the High Priestess, Mikiel."

Mikiel rushed into the room, still carrying the High Priestess headdress. "Do you think that would be wise? Who knows what you may run into? I don't like the idea at all."

Amara disagreed strongly, "I am doing it, whether you like it or not. You can stay and protect me, while I'm gone and if I'm gone too long you will have to awaken me!" Amara said as she made herself comfortable on the bed. In preparation she sat lotus style at the feet of the skeleton. Placing one hand on the skeleton's leg and the other on her Shade amulet she began by concentrating on how she felt in her dreams. She tried to focus on when she was holding the Sacred Sun Medallion. She slowly drifted into the mist of the afterlife as Mikiel unhappily stood watch over her.

Amara was shocked to feel danger in the mist right away. Her grandmother had warned her there was danger in the mists, but it was rare, unless you remained in them for too long. Staying too long could draw the attention of dark spirits. That could lead to dreadful things happening. She thought she could feel the presence of many such dark spirits already. Caution would be required when calling the High Priestess.

Abruptly the temperature around her dropped and she could see her breath as she exhaled. Slowly a hooded figure dressed in black from head to toe materialized before her. The figure was holding a staff as tall as it was and had no face. "Begone or perish!" the figure shouted menacingly in her face. Unintimidated by the spirit with a single word and the flick of her wrist, she cast a dispel and the figure disappeared in a puff of black smoke. This was not the first time Amara had been in danger in this realm. Her grandmother had taught her many defenses she could rely on, as well as a few offensive spells she could use, if necessary.

Amara went back to focusing on the High Priestess. Under her hand, instead of skeletal bone, she began to feel the flesh steadily warm. She opened her eyes to see what a skeleton had been moments ago was now flesh. Looking back at her from the bed was the dead High Priestess.

In an angry raspy voice, the corpse asked, "Who are you, that has awakened me, the High Priestess Danica, of the Da Nang tribe, from my slumber?"

Surprised at the anger in the spirits voice she answered, "I am Amara of the Sundown Tribe; I am sister to Sultan Willem." Amara answered proudly. "High Priestess what has happened to your beautiful city? That is why we are here, to find out what happened, how did your death come about?"

The Priestess's shade rose from her bed and approached Amara, "I am honored to meet one such as you, I knew many dark skins in my lifetime. In my time there were many powerful shamans in the desert tribes, maybe too many. What happened to my city was due to wizard arrogance and pride. You see some among us wanted to trade and travel to the other lands and peoples, but the wizard's guild wanted to keep our people pure and our magic strong, by avoiding the other races. The wizards thought our people too good to comingle with the other races."

The shade of the High Priestess walked around Amara taking stock of her before continuing, "After many years of discussion, the wizards convinced the people that isolation was the safest, best way to preserve life as we knew it. The sandstorms helped to keep things that way. Unfortunately, the storms also caused much destruction over the years. Early on, the wizards understood that magic was extraordinarily strong here and didn't want to give up its power, so they devised the magic spell that kept the city floating above the massive sandstorms. It was the High Priestess' magic though that kept the city spinning by using mana stones to recharge the Sacred Sun Medallion each season. The Medallion was an ancient artifact from the past, the wizards were not even sure who had created it or where it came from. But they recognized the power it contained. The Sacred Sun Medallion required a magical infusion, using the mana stones, to power the rotation of the city. The spell of transfer was a very taxing magic to perform, and it left the High Priestess drained of her magic for days afterwards. While the High Priestess recovered, for her protection, guards were stationed outside her doors. There had been a delicate balance struck between the wizards and the priestesses that lasted for many generations." Danica's shade paused for a moment to collect her thoughts.

Looking back at her corpse the shade stated, "I know not whom stabbed me in my sleep after the last Renewal Ceremony, but I am sure that whoever did it was astounded when the city fell from the sky when the next season came. You see, we Priestess' had a secret the wizards did not know. The Book of Blessings is where the spell of Renewal is recorded and it can only be read by a person wearing the Circlet of Knowledge. I assume that since I am still wearing the Circlet, no one learned the spell after my murder. Those foolish wizards were the undoing of my beautiful city."

The mist began to thicken, and the High Priestess was gone. Amara again felt bone under her hand. Mikiel was calling her name and shaking her, trying desperately to awaken her. The mist cleared and she was back in the sleeping quarters of the High Priestess Danica, sitting on her bed.

Mikiel, breathing a huge sigh of relief asked, "Are you ok? You have been gone for hours! I have been trying to wake you for some time." Mikiel said with more than a little concern in his voice.

Amara rose from the bed, stiff and achy from staying in one position for so long, answered her brother. "Yes, I'm fine, thank you Mikiel. It didn't seem like I was gone for long to me. I was able to speak with the High Priestess' shade. Her name was Danica of the Da Nang people. She explained that after recharging the medallion, using the mana stones, her own magic would be sapped and for days afterward, she would be defenseless, so guards were provided for her safety after the ceremony. Someone apparently got past the guards and killed her while she was asleep, but she didn't know who did it." Amara explained, while examining the hilt of the blade that had killed Danica. On impulse she grabbed the knife after dispelling the dark magic attached to it and pulled it out of the skeleton's chest. Without saying a word, she turned and handed the blade to Mikiel. He stuck the blade in his belt, but not before looking the fine blade and jeweled hilt over closely.

Amara thought removing it was the least they could do for the High Priestess and then turned back to the body and started to examine the circlet still on the head of the corpse. It consisted of a fine gold band with a large crystal that hung suspended over the forehead of the wearer. Taking out her belt knife Amara started to cut the circlet from the dead woman's hair. The Priestess' curls had grown around the thin gold circlet and seemed to refuse to let go of it.

Mikiel asked, bewildered at his sisters' actions. "What are you doing Amara? If you want a treasure, you should take the headdress I came across in the last room. It's three times the size and has hundreds of gems in it. I'll go get it."

While he did that, Amara went back to her task at hand. It was only a few seconds before Mikiel returned carrying the Headdress. Amara's eyes opened wide at the sight of the High Priestess' ceremonial headdress. In an awed voice she explained, "That is the Headdress High Priestess Danica wore when she performed the Renewal Ceremony. I don't think we should take that. It should be left here with Danica."

Returning to freeing the circlet from Danica's hair, she at last cut it free. As she held it out for Mikiel to inspect, she explained, "This is called the Circlet of Knowledge and it enables the wearer to read the Book of Blessings. The Book of Blessings contains the spell of Transfer that is used in the Renewal Ceremony and, according to Danica's spirit, the Book also contains many other powerful spells. Danica's shade told me that without the spell of Transfer, used in the Renewal Ceremony, the city would not continue to be powered by the Sacred Sun Medallion. If that happened it would cause the magic to fail, ensuring the city would fall. Their wizard's guild had discovered the magic that allowed them to suspend the city above the sandstorms but failed to recognize that only the High Priestess could perform the ceremony that transferred the power of the mana stones to the Sun Medallion. Evidently the fools thought they didn't have to share power with them any longer. We saw that someone had obviously murdered the High Priestess, my guess would be a wizard or one of his minions. Her death meant there was no one to perform the transfer."

To Mikiel's shock Amara placed the Circlet of Knowledge on her own head. His sister's impulsiveness again catching him off guard. He was also stunned by the fact that the old fable of the floating city his father had told him was true.

He watched as Amara placed the gold Circlet on her black curly hair. The crystal rested mid-way on her forehead. Amara felt a little funny and dizzy for a moment, as flashing colors paraded in front of her eyes. Mikiel reached out to steady her but after a few seconds the feeling passed, and so did the colors. As she looked around the bed chamber, she saw no sign of the Book of Blessings. She walked to a closet and opened it. Hanging inside was a row of several formal gowns that must have belonged to the departed high priestess.

Amara, feeling that something in the closet was pulling her in, moved the clothing to look behind them. In the back wall of the closet, she noticed a brick that was a slightly different color than the rest. She reached forward and pushed on the brick with her right hand. A small panel above the brick opened and there in front of her was a drawer containing an assortment of jewelry.

Taking the drawer out of the closet she set it on a table near the light. The Circlet of Knowledge informed her that the light blue topaz necklace was an amulet of frost, a very delicate ruby ring carried a dragon fire spell and a pair of diamond earrings she picked up contained a strong shield of protection spell. Shaking her head she thought, what a shame Danica wasn't wearing them when she was murdered.

Mikiel was looking over her shoulder as she put the jewelry on. The Ruby ring fit her left ring finger perfectly, almost like it had been made for her. She sorted through an assortment of other fine jewelry but found no other magic artifacts. Knowing the value of the non-magic items, she placed them in her pack for future sale.

Once they were satisfied nothing of value remained in the bed chamber, they moved back to the room Mikiel had left the headdress in. Pointing at the headdress Mikiel asked, "Shall we take this too? I don't detect any magic in it, but it must be worth a fortune in gemstones."

Amara considered the headdress for a moment before responding, "No, I don't think so. If you don't mind, I feel it should be left with Danica. If anyone else were to find her it would tell them just how important she had been in life."

Seeing how much it meant to his sister, without a word, Mikiel picked up the headdress and placed it on the bed next to Danica's body.

Happy with that decision Amara and Mikiel returned to the ante room. As they passed through that room, she thought back to the dream and when she found the Book of Blessings. She recalled that she had passed a ring under one of the sconces in the anteroom and a wall opened, revealing an altar with the book lying open upon it.

Stopping dead in her tracks Amara exclaimed, "Mikiel, wait here a second, I want to check on something." Returning to the bed chamber she reexamined the corpse. Much to Amara's delight the ring was still on the corpses finger. It was the only piece of jewelry left on the body and it took little effort for Amara to remove the ring from the boney finger. She felt a cold chill run down her spine as she placed the ring on the opposite hand as the fire ring she had just picked. Once again, the ring was a perfect fit on her right ring finger. Once the ring was on, Amara began to feel stronger and full of energy.

Mikiel had to chuckle as he observed, "I'm beginning to think this is more an adventure to get you some nice new jewelry than an exploration!" Mikiel continued to chuckle to himself as he followed her back into the anteroom.

Walking to the wall sconce she remembered from the dream, she passed the ring under it. A loud grating sound occurred as the wall swung open like a door. Amara turned and looked back smiling at her brother before she stepped through the door. Mikiel watched as she climbed the three steps up, to an alabaster altar. On the altar, right in front of her, was the Book of Blessings. She had found it! Amara had no idea what it contained, other than the spell that had kept the city of Bantez afloat. She only knew it was important. She carefully examined the ancient tome. She could see it was incredibly old with a thick binding. The language on the front of the book was foreign. Wearing the Circlet of Knowledge allowed her to read it, but what she read made little sense to her. Amara knew she would have to study the book to reveal its secrets, so she carefully placed it in her pack for further scrutiny later. When she looked up from her pack Mikiel was smiling at her.

Taking his sister's shoulders in his hands he looked her in the eye, "You have done well with this foretelling Amara; I am proud of you! Where do you think we should look for this mysterious artifact, the Sun Medallion, you speak of?" Mikiel asked.

Recalling the details of her dreams she replied, "The last time I saw the Sacred Sun Medallion it was ablaze with magic, in the spire, atop the pyramid. I assume that is where it was when the city fell, so that would mean it is outside somewhere. I think it must be near the pyramid if it was still atop it when the city fell. If someone were trying to recharge it without the Book of Blessing it could still be in the pyramid somewhere. I have no idea where. We have barely scratched the surface of this mystery I think we must continue looking." Amara stated as she headed back out into the hallway.

Leading the way she told Mikiel, "I can feel the Circlet pulling me down this hallway. I hope the wizard quarters are this way, it's the most likely place for us to explore next." She retraced their steps, going back to the down stairway that was covered in snakes." Knowing that snakes were one the few things her brother Mikiel was truly afraid of she said, "I know you don't want to hear it, but I think this is the direction we must go. It is likely more magic artifacts are down there, but more danger as well. I would not be surprised to find magic traps along the way. The way I figure it, if the wizard guild removed the Sacred Sun Medallion, they would have hidden it in their quarters." Amara stared at the intersection with the stairs, and the snakes, lots of snakes.

The hissing got louder as the two of them approached the intersection. Crawling up the stairs and over the banisters were hundreds of spotted snakes, some small, most were not so small. To Mikiel they all looked to be eight to ten feet long and as thick as his thigh. It was all Mikiel could do to contain himself as he watched the snakes as they crawled and slithered over one another, flicking their forked tongues in the air. Without hesitation Amara pointed the ruby ring at them and said "Freta." As fast as she said it dragon fire leapt from the ring. She directed it at the banister and stairs. Within seconds the writhing creatures were on fire, the smaller snakes were turned to a greasy ash instantly. The smell of burnt snakes permeated the air and was most unpleasant.

Mikiel picked his chin up off his chest and exclaimed, "Wow, I have never seen you use fire before, that is some jewelry you found today!" While picking his way over the greasy ash on the stairs he commented, "It looks like you have cleared a path to the wizards' quarters. Shall we have a quick look before we return to the ship? It is getting late, and we still have to deal with a schooner that is still buried up to its decks in sand."

Letting Mikiel take the lead she retorted, "Sure, if we find more snakes, I have more fire!" as she followed him down the steps.

After tiptoeing around the snake corpses, they found themselves in a wide hallway at the bottom of the stairs. There were many elaborate tapestries lining the walls and you could still see some of the scenes that depicted the floating city woven in many colors in the faded fabric.

The first several rooms off the hallway contained skeletons wearing what must have once been very fine robes. Mikiel was starting to feel like a grave robber as he checked each corpse for any magic objects of value or items of interest. These people were powerful wizards and mages, so it was likely they were wearing magical artifacts when they died. There were many more skeletons on this floor than the others. Mikiel started to take notice of something odd about the corpses. All the bodies were clean of any flesh or tissue. No partial degrading of tissue like a typical corpse, they were all clean to the bone. He wasn't sure what to expect them to look like, after who knew how long, in this dry hot climate.

It wasn't long before they reached another intersection of hallways. This one had three choices. Amara charged ahead as she yelled, "I think I know where the Grand Wizard quarters are from here." As she turned down a hallway to the left.

Mikiel had to pick up his pace to follow closely behind her and was feeling suddenly uneasy. They came to an abrupt stop as the hallway ended at two large metal doors, just like the

High Priestess' quarters. Taking a deep breath Amara threw open the double doors.

There in front of Amara were thousands of black scarabs, crawling over the chamber and the many remains of what had once been wizards. She was stunned at the sight but luckily Mikiel quickly pulled her back to the hallway. He slammed the doors shut just as the creatures began making a loud clicking noise and moving, in mass, towards fresh food. He then cast a lock spell on the doors. Turning to Amara he asked, "Are you ready to get back to the ship now?"

Amara, still stunned at the site of the mass of melon sized, crawling flesh-eating bugs said, "Yes, I think I have seen enough for one day, let's go!" patting Mikiel on the shoulder for his quick assist she turned back the way they had come.

They both turned and headed down the hallway, toward the stairway where they had encountered the snakes before. As they got closer to the intersection they began to hear loud clicking sounds ahead. At the intersection, the hallways straight ahead and to their right were full of the crawling insects. The only path open to them was to the left, so they ran down that hall, away from the thousands of insects chasing them. A short way down the hallway Amara stopped and pointed her new ruby ring and shouted, "Freta!" Dragon fire consumed hundreds of the large flesh eaters. Mikiel then cast a whirlwind spell that carried hundreds of the bugs down the hallway and out of sight. They got to the end of the hallway where another large set of double doors barred their exit. Mikiel attempted to open them, but they refused to budge.

While Mikiel tried to open the doors, Amara turned to face the oncoming armored insects. She took a deep breath and placed her left hand over the Amulet of Frost and whispered, "Frezet," as she blew air down the hallway. Suddenly frost covered the walls, the ceiling, and the floor of the hallway as far down it as they could see. Scarabs are a desert creature so when her spell hit them, they froze in place. Much to Amara's relief the clicking had stopped. After use of so much magic in such a short amount of time Amara felt a little faint and leaned on the wall.

Mikiel steadied his sister when he saw her weakened condition. "Why don't you sit down and rest for a minute? We both have used a fair amount of magic. A short break won't hurt." Mikiel felt relieved after their victory, but the double doors remained stuck, and he knew their only recourse was to head back the way they had come.

Amara, as usual, was anxious to move on so after a short break they headed back down the hall. It only took a few steps before it became apparent how difficult walking on the frozen bugs was. Amara took some satisfaction as she heard the bugs crunch with their footsteps. There were thousands of the creatures, and it was now obvious why they had not seen any flesh on any of the bodies they had come across. A few of the snakes were still smoldering when they climbed the stairs, but they thankfully met no other obstacles on their way out of the pyramid.

When Mikiel and Amara got outside the hot dry desert air smelled fresh, after the stink of the burning snakes. Dark menacing clouds were swirling on the horizon, so they hustled back to the ship. Once aboard, it became clear another storm was headed their way, and it looked like a bad one. They cleared most of the accumulated sand from the ship and moved Swift away from the buildings in case they were thrown about by the storm. Once Mikiel thought Swift was a safe distance from the ruins, they battened everything down and found sanctuary in the cabin below deck. Amara wanted to stay close enough to the ruins for another excursion inside the pyramid or at least a search around the ruins in hopes of finding the Sacred Sun Medallion. As they were going below deck Mikiel commented on how the sky had turned a strange color. Amara shuddered when she looked and saw the sky was something between dark blue and black.

Before going below deck Mikiel had placed four of Swift's anchors at the compass points, hoping to diminish the ships movement during the storm, but it wasn't long before they felt the ship shudder as it broke loose and start drifting. They now had no choice but to ride it out and hope for the best.

They were both drained after their adventure, so they wolfed down some bread and cold jerky before they sought out their private quarters. The live wood schooner was very well built and almost immune to damage, but Mikiel worried about the ship being harmed by the storm. Amara was exhausted by the events of the day, but she thought she would try reading some of the Book of Blessings before trying to sleep.

Finding herself too tired to concentrate she decided to get some sleep. When she tried to remove the Circlet of Knowledge, she found the wind had tangled her black curly hair in the Circlet. After a halfhearted attempt to remove it, she gave up and climbed in her bunk. Amara fell asleep almost instantly, despite the ship being tossed about by the storm.

Soon after falling asleep, Amara found herself again in the mists. She wandered in the mist for some time before it started to clear. When it did, it quickly became apparent, she was back in the pyramid. High Priestess Danica's shade was sitting on her bed, facing Amara. She again was flesh and blood and quite beautiful. Amara hadn't noticed the last time she saw the High Priestess, but Danica had violet eyes, a similar shade to her own, a rare color in the Sundown Tribe.

The shade stood and approached Amara. The spirit walked around Amara as she looked her up and down. It looked to be measuring her up before it spoke, "I see you have helped yourself to some of my most prized possessions. Was it you that removed the blade from my breast after all these centuries?"

Amara was not sure how to answer, afraid the High Priestess would think her a thief. "Yes, High Priestess I took your jewels and yes I removed the dagger. It seemed like the thing to do at the time."

The shade bowed her head to Amara, "I would like to thank you. That knife has pained me for centuries. It pleases me that you found my jewels, although I thought I had hidden them where they could not be stumbled upon."

Amara nodded in response, "I did not stumble upon them, I could feel them call to me."

The High Priestess went back to sitting on the bed, "You must have been wearing the Circlet of Knowledge. It would have led you to the strong magic in the pieces. The pieces fit you well, I think you will do nicely. You may have found your hair is already threading itself around the Circlet. You see, it takes the Circlet time to join you completely. Thankfully it is light and thin, soon you will not even notice your wearing it."

The shades expression suddenly changed to one of seriousness, as she continued, "You must listen carefully to me. Something terrible is coming to your world, something dark and sinister. A demon in the underworld named Tassarion is lose and planning some kind of revenge on the elves. Tassarion is intent on connecting the underworld with your world. He wishes to drain the magic from your world and use it to form a new one. One of his own creation. You will need to gather as many allies as you can to fight this demon. He is very powerful, so you need to beware and be careful." The mist began to form again, and she could hear Danica's shade say, "If you are to defeat Tassarion and his minions you must find the Sacred Sun Medallion."

Leila

The Lady Leila was a beautiful elf, and she was a sorceress of some renown. Her grandfather, Lord Bretta, was an advisor to King Alwin of the Green Folk. King Alwin was an ancient elf and was known for being an exceedingly kind man. The Green Folk were a peaceful people. Quite pale of complexion, especially compared to the desert folk. They also had a natural gracefulness that could be seen in everything they did.

Leila had the long, pale, straight hair that was typical of the elves. Her eyes were a brilliant green and she had the pointed ears elves were known for. Leila was a graceful creature with a lithe strong body. She was also tremendously talented in nature magic and was able to mind speak to most animals.

For many generations King Alwin had not allowed foreigners to travel the elven kingdom. He thought that was the best way to keep the peace, and it had. Under Alwin's rule there was extensive trade with other parts of the world, through its seaports but foreign sailors were not allowed off their ships when in an elvish port.

As a general rule elves loved nature and as a result many of their villages were built up in the trees. A giant oak might contain multiple homes with many families living in it. The giant trees were connected by elevated walkways and hanging bridges through the treetops. The elves strength in nature magic is what allowed them to coax growth in trees and crops, far beyond their normal growth.

The apples, and other fruit in Elyneas grew to twice their normal size and were much sweeter. Wheat grew fifteen feet high and corn cobs were huge. This gave them plentiful food sources and very little crime. There legal system was fair, and everyone had an opportunity to excel. The head of the family was always male, and he made all decisions, including arranging marriages for the women. A female's choice was rarely considered when life decisions were involved. So far Leila had been able to avoid the marriage thing by being good at what she did. Magic! So far, her uncle had kept her close to home, knowing how valuable her skills were to the family.

Leila had recently been summoned from her home in Topaz City to King Alwin's court. She lived with her mother Brendal, and her uncle, Lord Ulric. She had gladly left Lord Ulrich's home after her uncle barged in on her while taking a bath. When he closed the door behind him, he was unbuckling his pants, making it clear what he was after. As the unmarried head of the household, it was his right to claim any unwed women in the household, but Leila disagreed with that premise and cast a sleep spell on him before he could get out of his pants. The thought of that old fat man climbing on top of her still gave her the willies. Leila and Brendal were sure there would be a penalty for her actions, so King Alwin's summons came at a perfect time. They both knew if she returned to Topaz City there would be a penalty to pay. She was hoping while at court to get a better offer than what had presented itself so far.

Leila arrived in Riverrun, the capitol of Elyneas, just as the sun was setting over the Spine Mountains. The sun shown on the sparkling river; the colors of the sunset reflected in the calm water. When she entered her grandfather's townhouse, Hanson the butler greeted her warmly. "It is no nice to see you again Lady Leila. I have been instructed to show you to your quarters. I also took the liberty of ordering you some refreshments to be brought to your rooms. Your grandfather has requested your presence in the library after you get settled." He then bowed and left her rooms.

After freshening up she entered the library, where her grandfather was deep in thought, looking at an old map on a large table. Simon, his valet, cleared his throat and said, "Lord Bretta, your granddaughter, Lady Leila has arrived sir." The ancient elf looked up from the map and smiled when he saw Leila.

Taking off his spectacles he approached his granddaughter, giving her a kiss on the cheek. "Aren't you a sight for these sore old eyes my dear! You look well. How was your trip here? No trouble, I hope. Come join me at the map table, I will explain what we know so far, of this strange anomaly in the south. Perhaps together we can figure out this mystery and come up with a plan." Lord Bretta pointed to the map in front of him.

Leila joined him at the map table. She was already familiar with the map of Elyneas, the Green Folk land. But it was the first time she had seen this map; it showed the Scarlet Desert and the known Dwarven Clans. In the southwest, east of the Spine Mountains and north of the Great Ocean there was a large red circle, marking the location of the anomaly. Silverton was the closest city to the anomaly and so far, most of the reporting had come from there. Her grandfather handed her a scroll, "This is the most recent report. It is from an expedition out of Silverton. I'm afraid there is not a lot of good in it."

Leila read the report immediately. It stated the area of influence around the anomaly had doubled in size, compared to the week before. Initially it was thought the anomaly only drained magic, but more recent evidence showed it is also draining life from anything living in its range, including animals and plant life. Several mages, after having their magic drained, decided to stay and explore the area. They all died while examining the anomalies range, not realizing what was happening before it was too late, they didn't have the strength to escape the area. The report went on to explain that after the vegetation died, the ground cracked open and large scaly creatures emerged. These creatures looked like lizards, but they walked upright, like men. They were reported as vicious fighters that could spit a paralyzing poison. The lizardmen were also proving to be exceedingly difficult to kill, due to their thick leathery hides and they were immune to many magics. Their numbers were reported to be growing rapidly. The end of the report read, "Send help immediately!"

Her grandfather looked at her seriously and said, "We have lost thirty guardsmen to those lizard-like creatures. We have lost two other expeditions that were sent to investigate the anomaly itself, but they haven't been able to get a good look at the center of it, because the lizard creatures seem to be guarding it. So far the lizardmen seem to be protecting the area that has been decimated and have not ranged any further." Lord Bretta paused as if unsure how to proceed, reluctant to scare Leila with all the doom and gloom.

As Leila poured her grandfather a cup of tea he continued, "King Alwin has instructed me to use any means necessary to stop this phenomenon. He has even given his permission to allow the Desert Tribes to travel our lands, hoping they can help us defeat this scourge. Willem, Sultan of the Sundown Tribe, has approved of this cooperative effort and is sending his brother Mikiel, and sister Amara to meet you in Vardo.   Hopefully their magics will be more effective on the anomaly than ours have been. We have reports that Amara has a most unusual type of magic, maybe she has a different idea on what to do to defeat this foe. Now that you understand the serious nature of what we face in the south I must ask you to be our eyes and ears!" Lord Bretta said in a sad voice. "It is dangerous, but I fear I must still ask you to be our lead and meet with the Sundowners."

Leila sat quietly for a few minutes, considering what she had just read and heard. Setting down her teacup she got up and started pacing the room. "I wonder if all this is connected to the Satin River, in the north, drying up overnight. When I was exploring the source of the river, hoping to find a reason for the loss, I felt many quakes shake the ground. The wildlife in the area was complaining of the changes in both their food and water sources. Changes in the geology might explain this anomaly opening, considering the cracked ground reported. They seem like similar kinds of problems." Leila added.

Lord Bretta considered Leilas thoughts before responding, "The first thing I want you to do, when you arrive at the site, is to set wards that can contain these lizard creatures. That should keep them from roaming around and getting into our cities. I would like those wards to create a perimeter all of the way around the anomaly region. Tomorrow you will have a formal escort of eight guardsmen and two mages to escort you to collect the Sundown Mages in Vardo. Your group should then head directly to the anomaly, others will join you as you progress. You are to send reports of your progress using the messengers I will provide. I am sorry I am too old to join but I want to keep close track of your progress, and I need to know whenever you have something new to report."

Looking up from his map and into her eyes Lord Bretta stated, "Leila I cannot stress this enough, you must try extra hard to get along with the dark skins, in spite of some of their most unusual customs." Changing to a more grandfatherly tone he stated, "More importantly Leila, please be careful my dear, your mother will skin me alive if something were to happen to you. If given a choice, I would not have sent you on this task, but King Alwin insisted upon you doing it. You are the strongest elf, in the use of nature magic, of our people. It is our hope that perhaps you will be able to communicate with the lizard creatures, if we are fortunate, they will listen to you! Above all else you must be very careful, protect yourself above all else." Lord Bretta hugged his granddaughter.

Leila smiled up at her grandfather, taking note of a few more creases in his much-loved face. "Be assured grandfather, I will be careful and not take any foolish chances. I will make our family proud. I swear to you, my team and I will solve this riddle!" Leila returned the hug and left her grandfather as he returned to his map.

Not long after the conversation with her grandfather Leila retired to her rooms for the night. As she lay on the large feather bed she wondered about the desert people, and what they would be like. Her grandfather had alluded to the fact that they were "different" than the elves. How different were they? Was their magic different from her own? She also wondered what would cause such unusual effects on the landscape. Why do these lizard creatures show up as everything else is dying? And where were they coming from? She had a restless night, full of dark-skinned mages and lizardmen.

DRIFTING SANDS

BROKEN
SPIRE

reat Scarlet
Desert

Vardo

Broken Spire

Amara awoke up to a loud crunching sound as the ship tilted before coming to a stop. Mikiel came to make sure she was unharmed before trying to see what had happened to the ship. It took some effort to open the hatch as it was covered in sand.

Surveying the damage was difficult because the schooner was buried in sand again. Only about a third of the ship was currently visible, but the wind from the storm was settling down. The two decided to have breakfast and let the storm retreat the rest of the way before trying to dig Swift out.

After having some morning nourishment, they both set about removing the sand from the ship. Both Mikiel and Amara were gifted in wind spells, so it didn't take them long to remove the sand from the deck and the area surrounding the ship. This revealed a broken spindle that connected one of the six skis to the ship's hull. After cleaning the break and adding a splint Amara poured an elixir over the break and said the magic word, "Helix." They could hear Swift sigh with relief as the repair took place. Much like bracing a broken bone, the live wood of the ship repaired itself, with the help of the elixir.

Mikiel was relieved the damage to the ship was not any worse. When he checked their compass, it still was not reading true, so he was sure they were still in the Drifting Sands. Swift had come to rest at the bottom of a large sand dune, so visibility was limited to a small surrounding area. After refitting a new sail and raising three others Swift got under way. Amara maneuvered the schooner to the top of the next large dune so they could survey where they were. She scanned the horizon with a looking glass. Searching for any objects or landmarks to get their bearings, all she could see were sand dunes.

Each dune was large enough to hide a small village behind it, so they slowly sailed the ship over one dune and then another, always watching for danger from the creatures that lived there. After they crested each sand dune, Amara would look at the horizon through the looking glass. Late in the afternoon she caught a glimpse of the sun reflecting off of something to their left. She pointed towards it so Mikiel would steer the ship near the object. Swift crested the next large sand dune and, in the valley below, was an object partially sticking out of the sand.

When the ship pulled alongside the object, Amara immediately recognized what she was looking at. It was the broken spire from the gold pyramid in the floating city of Bantez.

Amara turned to Mikiel and explained, "I had another dream last night. The High Priestess Danica visited me again. She said we need to find the Sacred Sun Medallion. The High Priestess commanded me to find it, or we might all perish. She insisted that we need the Medallion for a fight that is coming to us, soon. She spoke about a demon from the underworld named Tassarion, and that he is enormously powerful. The

High Priestess explained that he is trying to siphon off all the magic from this world, so he can create his own world in its place. She insisted we gather as many allies as possible for the coming fight, Mikiel." Amara cast a small dirt devil to clear loose sand from the deck.

"I had many more questions for her, but the mist came before I could ask them. I have no reason to not believe her, so I guess we search around here for the Medallion. What do you think Mikiel?" Amara asked as she lowered the plank to disembark.

Seeing how serious Amara was made his answer easy, "Yes, your right. I think we must look for it. Did she say what we are to do with it, if we're lucky enough to find it?"

Amara was fiddling with the Circlet of Knowledge as she answered him. "No, not exactly, just that it was a must for our worlds survival. Come on, let's go blow some sand!"

Amara and Mikiel disembarked Swift and immediately started using their magic to remove the sand from around the broken spire that was lying on its side. It appeared this was the lower portion of the spire, not the top piece that held the Sacred Sun Medallion. They continued to use their wind spells to gently sweep away the lose sand in the area. It was not long before another metal support was exposed. As Amara observed the metal support beams getting thinner and smaller, she hoped the medallion was close.

Mikiel abruptly grabbed her shoulder and while pointing said, "Three of the large sand crabs are headed this way we must hurry!"

Not ready to give up Amara tugged free of him, "Just a few more moments Mikiel. I know I'm close to finding it. I can feel it ahead. I think the Circlet is leading me to it! Just let me remove this sand here." Amara said as she cleared the last of the sand, exposing the upper half of the broken spire. As the sand around the upper half of the spire cleared, it exposed what they sought. The Sacred Sun Medallion was right where she had placed it in her dream. Amara reached out and grabbed the Medallion, removing it from its centuries old resting place. She instantly felt a warmth come from it, while placing it in her pack.

"Alright Mikiel, I've got it! Let's go, before those crabs catch up with us."

After boarding Swift, Mikiel could see the sand crabs cresting the closest sand dune. These were the largest crabs that Mikiel had ever seen! Each of the large, shelled beasts was as big as their ship. Their armored shells made them immune to most magics and weapons. While hoisting the sails Mikiel yelled, "Amara maybe your new dragon ring will harm them." The sun was on their right, so Amara turned the schooner in the direction she guessed was south, and out of the Drifting Sands. Mikiel finished raising all the sails and soon they were quickly sailing away from the sand crabs and any other visible dangers. At sunset, their compass returned to normal and confirmed they were going the right direction, south towards home. Next stop was Mystery Waters.

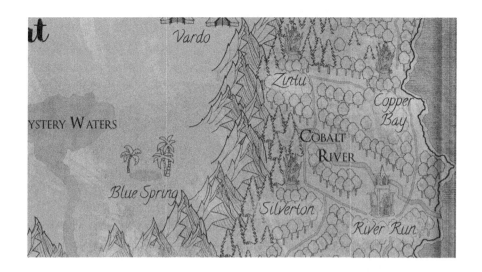

A Request for Help

The next morning Mikiel came knocking on the tinker's door. After Nathan welcomed him into the coach he had a seat at the breakfast table, where Gunter served him some hot, black coffee. Mikiel took a sip, "I have heard of coffee, but I have never tasted it. I find it a bit bitter. I have sampled many teas in my lifetime, but I find coffee intriguing." He downed his first cup and asked for a second.

Gunter grinned at Mikiel as he poured another cup, this time adding some milk and sugar. "Try that, it may be more to your taste."

Mikiel took a sip and smiled at Gunter, "that's much better, it almost tastes like chocolate, quite delicious." He finished the second cup and asked for a third before he put his cup down. "I bring news of Willem's decision. He has decided to send a delegation of magic users and warriors to aid the Green Folk. He has already sent a messenger to King Alwin in

River Run, informing him of our agreement to an alliance. He has asked Amara and me to lead the group. We are to meet up with the elves at Vardo and then, as a group, approach the anomaly. He explained the elves were not sure if all magic was useless or only elven magic, he still holds out hope the Sundowner's magic might prevail. We are to lend whatever aid we can to the elves, with the hope it helps to create a bond between the two peoples." Mikiel drank his third cup of coffee in one swallow, and then poured himself a fourth, emptying the coffee pot.

Gunter laughed as he slapped Mikiel on the back, "You might want to slow down on the coffee, you won't sleep for a couple days at the rate you're drinking it."

Mikiel had a sudden thought, "Nathan, do you think your coach can keep up with Swift? We would be thrilled to have you and Gunter join us. Your expertise could be very helpful."

Nathan considered the offer, and responded with some envy in his voice, "I really appreciate the offer; it sounds like quite the adventure. But we like it fine here at Mystery Waters, don't we Gunter? Besides we have to wait for Azrador. It wouldn't be right to go on to Elyneas without him."

Gunter chimed in with his unsolicited opinion, trying to be supportive of Nathan, "It sounds like a wild goose chase to me, and a long way to go, just to get killed."

Mikiel smiled when he replied, "I am like you, Gunter, happier here at Mystery Waters. The water is transforming the desert here into a livable place, for the first time in centuries. We have truly been blessed after so many years of hardship. It will indeed be hard for me to leave, but it is not the Sundown Tribe's way, to refuse to help those in need. Besides, I am curious what it is like to travel in a green forest, and to see another land. Like Willem said, we can hope it improves relations between our peoples."

Nathan nodded to himself, taking note of another similarity between the Tinkers and Sundown Tribes ways. "When do you leave Mikiel?" Nathan asked while attempting to refill his cup but finding the pot empty.

Mikiel finished his coffee and replied, "Amara is resupplying the Swift now, we will leave tomorrow. We will pick up additional members of our party along the way. The elves will be sending a delegation to meet us there. We have been told it is a six-or seven-day ride south from Vardo to the anomaly. From what I understand it is much further south than Mystery Waters, too bad Swift can't fly." Mikiel was chuckling to himself at the image of Swift flying as he exited the coach.

Nathan followed him out, "Safe journey Mikiel! We may catch up to you when Azrador shows back up. He went to explore the waterfall yesterday and has not yet returned."

Nathan was surprised at Gunter's hesitation to go on this adventure with Mikiel and Amara. Nathan knew deep down Gunter wanted to get to know Amara better. Gunter seemed more interested in the dark-skinned woman than any other Nathan had been aware of before. They seemed to have hit it off, when together. Her ability to talk to the dead was a little off putting to Nathan, but Gunter thought he could get past that. He had even commented to Nathan that he had never met anyone with such violet eyes before.

After waiting a couple of days, and no sign of Azrador, Nathan and Gunter decided to search for him. Nathan hitched up the oxen and the two men headed upriver, towards the waterfall. Once they arrived at the base of the falls Gunter went to work with his multicolored glass, looking for any signs of Azrador or magic. The roar of the falls was deafening, and Gunter had to yell to be heard, "I don't see anything strange Nathan. I find no sign of Azrador, or a cave, either. Maybe he headed up the mountain to see where the water starts. Sounds like something he would do!"

Nathan eyed a path up the mountain, "I want to examine behind the waterfall. I am sure I saw a cave there when we first arrived." Nathan stated as he carefully started picking his way up the slippery rock surfaces. He climbed a fair distance up the rocks alongside of the waterfall. He found a flat ledge to stand on as he peered behind the torrent of icy water. How disappointing, all he could see was rock. There was no cave entrance there, he must have just imagined it. It is said, hallucinations are common in the desert.

Nathan's hopes of Peter the cobbler's nursery rhyme leading to his homeland forest were dashed. He was heartbroken. He had been so sure he was on the path, but it was just fantasy, he supposed. He was afraid listening to the old stories and songs while looking for clues to the homeland may have been a waste of time. All the pieces seemed to fit, until now.

When the two men returned to the coach, they discussed their next move. They had found no sign of Azrador. They weren't even sure he had made it to the waterfall, let alone climbed it. After dinner they shared a brandy when Nathan reluctantly decided they would leave word of their departure with Willem and the Sundowners. He could tell Azrador where they went when he showed up. Nathan would also request Willem supply Azrador with transportation when he appeared.

If he showed up soon enough, he would be able to catch up with the tinker coach. Nathan chuckled at the thought of Azrador catching up on a camel. Their awkward gait looked uncomfortable to ride on. Azrador could speak to animals, so a camel may be a new best friend for him. He hoped Azrador caught up with them in a few days.

They would head to Vardo and from there into the elven land of the Green Folk. Perhaps Mikiel was right, they could lend a hand, and who knows, maybe tinker magic may still work around the anomaly. At least they would get to see an elven forest. According to the legends, elves use woodland magic to aid their trees to grow to enormous sizes.

After saying their good-byes to Willem, Nathan and Gunter headed north the next morning. Willem has estimated it could take several days for the coach to arrive at the border city of Vardo. Once they left the lake of Mystery Waters and reached the bleakness of the desert the heat began to rise. They had to stop and water the oxen frequently, but the animals didn't seem any more tired pulling the giant coach over sand versus dirt. Luckily, there were no incidents with giant worms or sand crabs during the journey, Nathan and Gunter were thankful for that.

The citizens of Vardo had traded with the elves and other members of their tribe but they had never seen a tinker's coach, or many of the goods it contained. Once word got out that the coach had rare items for sale, Nathan was mobbed by customers. A baker was thrilled to get buckwheat flour and new bread pans. A blacksmith needed a new hammer and nails. Nathan was so busy Gunter decided to lend a hand by helping a cute seamstress pick out some satin fabric. Along with the rash of sales came a lot of gossip and information.

The gossip from the seamstress Gunter was helping said the large magic anomaly was spreading and that many elven soldiers had died there. Another shop keeper told Nathan that large lizard men were crawling out of the cracked ground, spitting poison, and killing hundreds. A leather worker spoke of reports of magic failing all over the Green Folk land. Worse yet the streams and water sources were drying up forcing people to migrate to the cities. It all sounded chilling to Gunter, and he was having some reservations about continuing the journey, until he thought of Amara and her violet eyes.

The Meeting

Vardo was one of the largest cities of the Desert Tribes, and it was all above ground, unlike, most of the villages. Most of their communities were built under the desert sand, out of the sun and heat. Vardo had grown to its size because it was built on the site of a large oasis. The tribe's livestock and vegetation thrived there. The buildings were all painted bright colors that stood out dramatically against the dull desert in the distance.

The arrival of the group of elves stirred a lot of excitement as they rode through the city. Word of the elf's arrival had stirred a lot of interest and a large crowd had started to form outside of the Oasis Inn, where they were to meet their counterparts. As the group rode through town Leila made note of the colorful buildings. Unlike the elves, whose homes and clothing were created to blend with their surroundings, these people built using every color in the spectrum. She also noticed how plain the clothes they wore were. They looked like they could instantly disappear in the desert.

The crowd parted to allow the riders passage. After they dismounted Leila noticed a camel tied to a nearby post. As a child she had been told about these desert travelers but had never seen one. She almost laughed at the odd-looking animal as she approached it, with the hope of communicating with it. When she got within a few feet of the beast a young tribesman ran up and stopped her. "Excuse me my Lady, you don't want to get any closer. That particular camel is named "The Spitter". He holds the Scarlett Desert record for spitting distance. My pa won 5 gold pieces on him last week when he spit over one-hundred feet. Unfortunately, you never know when he's going to do it."

Leila took a step back from the camel, "Thank you, young man, I had no idea they did such a thing. Why do you think they spit at us?" she asked as she gave him a copper.

The boy grinned at the coin before answering her, "I have no idea, but pa says they are just a foul tempered beast that should be left in the desert." He then stuck the coin in a pocket before running off.

Leila had always had a problem with resisting her curiosity, and today was no different. Turning to face the camel she started to hum. Everyone in her party stopped to see what she was doing as she closed her eyes. After several minutes she stopped humming and opened her eyes. She looked the camel in the eye and slowly started to approach it. When she got close enough to touch it, she placed her hand on its snout. The crowd gasped when she used her hands to pry open its mouth. Taking a deep breath, she reached inside the camel's mouth. She then grabbed hold of its tongue and pulled it out where she could see it better. She could immediately see that the whole tongue was infected. Pulling Icicle, her short sword from its sheath she cut into the back right side of the camel's tongue. It let out a loud groan as she pulled her hand out of its mouth. The camel then gave a shake of its head and laid down at Leila's feet.

The Captain of the Guard cautiously approached Leila and asked, "What did you do to it? The people in the crowd were betting on whether he would stomp on you or spit at you. I don't think "laying down" was on their betting card."

Leila shrugged as she answered him, "It was quite simple really. When I asked him why he spit he explained that he had a large sliver in his tongue that had been there for as long as he could remember. So, I removed it." She stated as she held up a wooden sliver that was a couple of inches long.

The captain grasped Leilas elbow and guided her to the entrance to the Inn. "I think it best we get you inside. Leila gave him a puzzled look but let him guide her indoors. "I don't think you want to be around when that crowd realizes their money-making spitter no longer feels a need to spit."

Once inside she thanked the captain as she considered what had just transpired. She decided this was one of those instances her grandfather had warned her about. He was right, these people do have some odd customs. She wondered if he knew how much they loved to gamble. Elves rarely gambled and it made her wonder what kind of person bets on how an animal will act. She guessed she was about to find out

Looking around she saw the interior of the inn was elegant and plush. There were bright colored pillows and rugs around low tables and sprinkled around the room. Seeing this she assumed it was the desert dwellers custom. An older man introduced himself as the innkeeper before showing Leila and her team to a suite of rooms, strictly reserved for dignitaries. A bowl of fresh fruit awaited her with a brief welcome note, from the Sundown Tribes Sultan, Willem. There were several pieces of fruit in the bowl that she was not familiar with. One had a very prickly exterior but smelled like a lime. Another was star shaped and tasted a little tart, but she liked it. The group of elves were pleased with the comfortable rooms and with the respect they had been shown, so far.

The next morning, at breakfast, Mikiel and Amara introduced themselves to Leila and her Captain of the Guard. Amara approached her first, "It is an honor to meet you Lady Leila. I would like to introduce my youngest brother, Mikiel. We are the siblings of Sultan Willem and are his two most trusted advisors. He is who has asked us to lead members of the Sundown Tribe on this expedition to defeat the unknown."

As they ate breakfast Mikiel explained how many warriors they had brought, along with their strongest mages. He declared the Sundowner Tribe was pledging their help in any way they could. Amara explained that others were on the way and would join them near the site of the anomaly.

Leila observed the pair from the desert as they discussed travel arrangements and logistics. She found Mikiel to be a striking example of the dark-skinned desert tribes. He was well-built, muscular, tall, and strong looking. It was obvious to her that he was self-assured and was used to leading. She also felt a strong magic aura around him as well. The gold symbol, on his white turban, warned he was a sorcerer, and she didn't doubt his strength in magic. Amara had a magic aura of her own. She was an unusual looking mage, short haired and very intense, with more of the look of a warrior than a mage. Leila quickly took note of the circlet she wore woven into her hair. A clear crystal hung from it, resting on her forehead. Leila was sure the necklace Amara wore contained strong magic by the vibe she got off it. Perhaps this female elf was battle mage material? There was also something about her that Leila could not quite put her finger on. There was something not quite right, something a little creepy about her. Leila again wondered if this was another of the things Lord Bretta had warned her about.

Divinity

Throdon's workshop was another dwarven marvel. Shelves of glass jars containing a variety of objects including eyeballs, that Jason swore were staring at him. There were several apprentices working on different potions and enchantments in the room. Throdon went to several cabinets and retrieved numerous glass jugs of different colored fluids. Apprentices were setting up a long trough for the Grand Master mage. As Throdon gathered materials Jason took a moment to look around the workshop. One wall was lined with jars of plants and the raw materials for potions and other magic. One apprentice was working at a table on a delicate looking wand, while another mixed a smoking concoction of some sort. There was a large copper kettle with copper tubing connecting it to other copper objects he had no idea what they were for.

Soon, Throdon declared he was ready as he started

pouring the different colored fluids into the trough, mixing them with a large wooden spoon. The combination of fluids created a strong unpleasant smell. Throdon then walked over to a large metal chest. Taking out a key he wore on a chain around his neck, he unlocked the chest. Throdon removed several large pearls, the size of his fist, and handed them to his apprentice who proceeded to grind them in a mortar and pestle. He then added the ground pearls to the mixture, as an assistant continued stirring the mixture. Throdon also removed two dragon scales from the metal chest and instructed the apprentice to grind them in the mortice and pestle. They were also added to the mixture as the stirring continued. The brew was bubbling now, and the smell had grown stronger. Lastly Throdon took a small pouch from the metal chest, before he closed, and locked it.

Throdon approached Jason and instructed him, "I now ask you to place the staff in the trough, and then grasp both sides of it!"

Jason did as the old dwarf commanded him and placed the staff into the bubbling brew before taking his place holding the sides of the trough. The fluids were rapidly changing color now as Throdon opened the pouch and pulled a handful of sparkling powder out, sprinkling it into the bubbling brew. When Throdon whispered a magic word so quietly it couldn't be made out by Jason, the colors began changing even faster.

Throdon held a scroll in front of Jason and said, "You will say the following phrase while you continue to hold the sides of the vessel. The words must be precise, but more importantly you must mean them!"

Jason looked at the scroll in front of him and committed the phrase to memory. It seemed so familiar and yet he had never heard it before. He still wasn't sure he was the right person for this, despite Master Bluthe and Throdon's opinions.

Taking a deep breath, and a firm grip on the sides of the trough containing the staff and stone, Jason began the hymn.

"This Staff of Divinity I awaken to heal the land!"

"Let word go forth to not oppose it!"

"Peace be with those wise enough to be an ally!"

"Death and damnation to those foolish enough to threaten it!"

As Jason finished the chant the solution in the trough turned a brilliant blue, the foul smell disappeared as an explosion of brilliant light flashed through the workshop. After the air cleared, Jason saw Throdon was smiling a big toothy grin as he instructed Jason to remove the "Staff of Divinity" from the trough. As soon as Jason touched the base of the staff, he felt it. The staff was different, somehow. It felt like it welcomed his touch. Weird! Once it was removed from the trough the blue stone looked different too. Where a big blue stone had sat before was now a twenty-four faced, brilliant blue sapphire, the size of his fist. So bright, it was hard to look at when light passed through it. Jason could feel the pulsing raw power in his hand, waiting to be called upon, even though he had no idea how to use it, or how to tap its power.

Throdon handed Jason a piece of metal, "Oh my, Jason, the power coming off the Divinity stone is blinding, in the magic spectrum. Placing this lead cover over it will calm its brilliance down, until you have a call for it." Throdon watched as Jason put the cover over the Divinity stone. He then picked up a wand, waved it, and said, "The Divinity Stone has awakened, let the land be healed!" The sound of his voice was loud as it went out of the workshop. Throdon assured Jason that all dwarves will have heard the announcement.

As he stared at his new staff Jason asked, "How do I learn how to use this staff? I have no training in magic."

Throdon smiled at Jason's reluctance. "That is the beauty of the Divinity Stone. It isn't necessary for you to have formal mage training. In fact, it may be an advantage for you not to be formally trained. You have no idea what the staff can do, a trained mage would assume restrictions on what spells might or might not work. You, on the other hand, will have to trust the staff to decide which magic fits the situation. It will sense your thoughts and disposition and then decide on its own, which magic fits the moment best. It requires you to trust in the staff and its protection. Over time you and the staff will adjust to each other. Once you adjust to using it, you will find the staff more than helpful. The legends claim the Divinity Stone has only been used to heal the land in the direst of situations. In past centuries it has only appeared during catastrophic events, like the plague. Keep in mind, while holding the staff your thoughts must be pure in heart and purpose. Use it wisely Jason!" Throdon said as he bowed his head in respect.

Jason watched as Master Bluthe helped Throdon back to his seat, surprised at how much the spell had drained the old dwarf. He looked ten years older if that was possible and very pale.

After getting Throdon settled he turned to Jason, "Jason, you have had a long and wonderous day, but I think it's time you get some rest. You will need to be at your best before you attempt to tame that volcano tomorrow. Then we all can move on to healing the land." Master Bluthe slapped him again on the back and said, "Garth would indeed be proud of his son!"

Sleep came slowly to Jason that night as he thought back on where he came from and how he got here. His years as an apprentice to Olaf had been a nurturing place for an orphan to grow up and the skills Olaf had taught him had proven to be priceless. Zella had been a loving mother to him and had contributed greatly to his gentle touch, in spite of his size.

Due to the small size of the bed in his room Jason made a pallet of blankets and slept on the floor again that night. What sleep he got was restless and full of colorful dreams. He dreamt of his flight on the back of a giant condor, with the beautiful warrior named Swan. He could even recall how she was dressed in tight-fitting leathers that had a swan stitched over her heart. He would not have believed a female could fight using a trident like she could, until he saw it for himself. She would twirl it in one hand like a baton before she attacked with it. He found himself missing her smile, as well as her music.

When Jason woke, it was still dark, much too early to wake the others so he went back to his thoughts about his life. Who would have thought it all started when a tinker gave him a magic hammer as a child? Just for singing him a song. Jason always enjoyed his time with Nathan, and he hoped their paths would cross again.

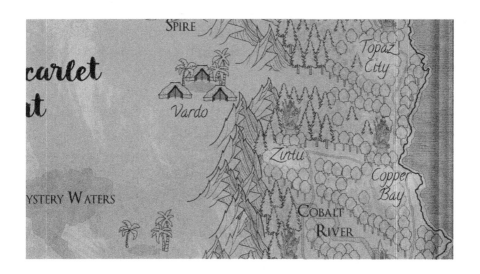

Traveling to Silverton

It took several days for the large party to travel from Vardo to Silverton. They had quite a wagon train of men and supplies as they wound their way through the forest of the elves. The Sundowners were enthralled by all the greenery and trees, some that grew to two-hundred feet high. The tallest had homes and villages built in them, and their foliage was made up of every color in the rainbow, reminding the Sundowners of their own homes. The fruit trees had apples and oranges the size of pumpkins, plus cherries and plums bigger than they had ever seen. It was all so colorful compared to the desert lands. The Sundowners were continuously looking around, admiring the scenery, and remarking at the plentiful streams and rivers. They also learned that on this side of the Spine Mountains, when the snow in the mountains melted it drained east, into the Cobalt Sea. None of the snow melt flowed west, to the desert side of the mountains. What a difference geography can make, Mikiel thought to himself. Depending on which side of the mountains you lived on would determine what kind of life and culture you would live with.

When the wagon train reached Silverton, they met up with the other elven guardsmen that had been sent by King Alwin. The guardsmen warned the group against setting up a home base any closer to the anomaly than Silverton. They were also warned to stay alert to conditions, the area of what is being known as the dead zone, had grown to four times the size of the previous week. Mikiel gave orders to set up their tents on the east side of town. Leila gave the captain orders to do the same while receiving an updated report from the area of the anomaly.

Later that day, towards evening, they met in Mikiel's large multi-colored tent. Amara began the conversation, "We need to plan the placing of wards, our hope is to get them in place by the end of day tomorrow." Lady Leila and Mikiel nodded in agreement. She went on to describe how they were trying to surround the zone with magic wards, in the hope of containing the large lizard like creatures.

Lady Leila rose to speak, "The lizardmen are lethal, they are deadly in combat and have killed many elves already. We have learned they are very difficult to kill. The latest report from the elven guard stated that crossbows were being used, with some effect on the lizards, but many times took three or four arrows to bring down one lizardman. The archers also need shields to protect them from the lizards spitting poison. The elven guardsmen had been hunting single lizards in groups, but the lizardmen seem to have adapted to that, now they are also hunting in groups of five or six. Amara, I have received some information that indicates you have the ability to speak with the dead. If that is so in the morning, I would like you to take ten tribesmen and see how close you can get to the anomaly. My hope is you might be able to learn something from the fallen near the perimeter of the anomalies reach."

Amara did not hesitate, "I would be pleased to lead

an expedition to retrieve any information that may prove helpful." She didn't say anything to Lady Leila, but she also had hopes she could learn more about the demon Danica had warned her about.

The next day Amara led the mages as they started putting up magic wards in places where the landscape was still lush. They gradually were able to surround the anomaly and the dead zone with several layers of protection. Hopefully that would contain the remaining lizard creatures, while others hunted down those that may still be outside of the wards, with any luck, preventing them from roaming into villages.

Lady Leila was impressed with the command of magic that Mikiel displayed, while installing the magic wards. After the wards were in place, he erected a wall of torches two-hundred paces inside the wards, they were to notify them if the magic free area continued to grow. There was no way to know if the wards would hold or if the anomaly would swallow them like all the other magic that had been tried. They hoped the shields they wove with both Sundowner magic and elven magic would hold.

As dusk approached Amara returned to Silverton to report from the void area. She returned with only five of the ten warriors she started with. She appeared to be having trouble using her right arm as she dismounted from her horse. She proceeded inside Mikiel's huge multi-colored tent. Inside Lady Leila was seated on a large red pillow next to two of her mages where Amara joined them.

When Mikiel saw her holding her arm with a bloody compress he yelled for a healer, "Sister, you are injured! I have sent for a healer, please sit down here by me."

Amara shrugged her shoulders, "I'm alright, I just got a little careless trying to read one of the dead soldiers near the anomaly. While I was investigating what he knew, one of the damn lizardmen snuck up behind me after slaying the two men watching my back. The damn things are human size, walk on two legs and have scales all over them. Long nasty teeth extend on both sides of their mouths. Powerful jaws that can snap a man in two. Real ugly fellows and they smell worse than they look. Crossbows were effective from a distance, but the beasts can move fast, and their scales can deflect arrows. They also use their tails to sweep your feet out from under you, so they can more easily kill you. I was lucky I sensed their attack, my protection spell allowed me to dodge the worst of the bite. My flying daggers spell was also effective, outside of the void, but as soon as I entered the dead zone, I could feel it draining my magic. I could feel it immediately. It starts to sap your strength in a brief time. The dead elf I talked to said that one of their mages had used a freeze spell on the creatures, with profound effect. He stated the anomaly appeared to sense the mages having success with the freeze spells and grew the magic free zone towards him. His magic was quickly depleted, and two lizards ate him." Amara sat down on a large green cushion, exhausted, while a healer tended her injury.

Leila added, "If crossbows are effective, we shouldn't have trouble outfitting enough men with them to get the lizardmen under control. What to do about the anomaly that seems to be creating the havoc, is another question."

Amara explained, "None of my magic had any effect inside the area where the ground is cracked, and it rapidly saps your mana and energy. At my furthest point in, I could see what appeared to be a colored spinning disc in the distance. I would guess that to be the center of the disturbance. Fortunately, within moments of leaving the area my mana returned, and my magic worked again. Our observers tell us that so far the wards do seem to be keeping the lizard creatures from roaming free."

Mikiel was nodding his head when he spoke, "Ok, so we know arrows and crossbow bolts work on the creatures. We also now know that casting cold can kill the creatures. Lady Leila is there a way for us to create bolts and arrows with cold spells on them?"

Lady Leila grinned at Mikiel, "What a great idea! I am not

sure we have the ability, but just think about how much help that would be. I will send word to Lord Bretta, asking him to research the idea."

Mikiel nodded in approval, "Good, in the meantime we can continue to learn as much as we can about the anomaly. Maybe we can find a weakness in it."

Leila turned to Amara "Tomorrow Mikiel, you and I will make another attempt to take a closer look at the anomaly. Our party will be outfitted with bows, crossbows, and ice wands. We will be accompanied by a large escort that will deal with the lizardmen while we try to learn something useful against this anomaly."

Amara responded, "I would suggest shield spells when we enter the void area. We can see how long they protect us and how quickly we feel our mana being drained."

Mikiel agreed, "We need to figure this out quickly. The more the void grows the harder it will be for us to get close enough to effect it. We will set out in the morning!" Mikiel said with enthusiasm. "Let's get some rest."

After the meeting broke up Amara and Mikiel were still sitting around the table, talking about viable solutions. "I've never seen anything like this brother. I am frightened by this aberration. It felt alive and I swear I could sense it noticing me. I felt it when it's attention started moving toward me. Danica was right, there is something evil and sinister about it." Amara said pouring a cup of hot tea. "The High Priestess warned me about a demon named Tassarion. She claimed he is behind it. I have no idea how she would know that, but I believe her."

Amara could see Mikiel was tired, his eyes were getting droopy, and he was starting to yawn. "There are so many odd things going on, all at once. Things like, the new pass in the north opens, because of a volcano exploding. Or a new river and lake appear in the Scarlet Desert where it has been dry for uncounted generations. Then there are the dwarves, who are now cooperating with us. We have also met a tinker from the north that travels in a sentient coach, similar to Swift. And to top it all off, the elves are asking for Sundowner assistance in defeating a bizarre magic phenomenon that no one has ever seen before, in their southern district. I am glad you are here with me to face this thing! I'm tired and I can see you are too. Let's call it a day." Amara remarked as she gave Mikiel a hug before they both turned in for the night.

The Search

Galad and Swan had decided they would search for Nathan's giant tinker coach from the air the next day. After dinner Galad offered to play some music on an instrument Swan had never seen before, he called it a harpsichord. It had moveable keys and played unique notes she had never heard before. It had white and black keys and each one each played a different note. Galad was quite accomplished on it and played some wonderful music that Swan had never heard before. It occurred to her that she should get her flute out and join him as a duet. When she did, Galad enjoyed the compliment her flute made to his harpsichord, and they played a beautiful duet together.

Following that tune, Galad got up from his seat to fill his cup with wine. As he did Swan started to play a lively solo on her flute. In the blink of an eye, she and Galad were flying over a desert and a lake came into view. Hundreds of people were gathered around the lake with colorful tents everywhere. They could see caravans arriving from all directions. It appeared there were more tents going up all around the lake. From the air they could see the area all around the lake and the river that led to it. The land was turning green as it came to life. There was a rebirth of growing plants and trees where before was only sand. As Galad circled the area he flew over the source of the river and new lake. A very tall waterfall flowed out of the southern mountains and down the rocks to the mystery waters. When Galad flew over the waterfall he thought he heard a voice mind speak to him, but it faded as he passed over it. Turning back the way they had come he listened closer, "Anyone who can hear me, my name is Azrador, I am trapped behind the waterfall. I entered a cave behind it, but a rockslide caused by a large quake has blocked my exit! I need help!"

Suddenly the music stopped, and the vision disappeared. Looking around Galad found that Swan had collapsed on the floor. He picked her up and carried her to their bed. He then placed a damp cloth on her forehead. Even with his magic it had been startling to find himself in a foretelling. It seemed so real!

Swan remained asleep until the next morning. Galad was more than a little surprised to find himself worrying about this human, a feeling he was not familiar with.

When Swan awoke in the morning it was with a start. She bolted upright in bed and exclaimed, "Galad, Azrador needs our help, he is in trouble! We must hurry!"

She was up, dressed, and gathering her things as she swept through the lair. Galad knew enough to stay out of her way while she prepared for departure. Shortly after that, they were air borne, and headed north over the Great Ocean.

Swan never got over the thrill she got when flying on Galad's back. Her golden dragon was a powerful flyer and was proving to be good company as well. As they flew over the coastline everything below them was a lush deep green, until they reached the Spine Mountains. The peaks were so high that nothing could grow there, but Galad easily flew over them, even though that's high enough for the air to be very thin and very cold. When Galad flew this high it made Swan thankful for her training with the Sky Rock Clan. Shaman Quesa, the clans leader, had trained his riders to tolerate thin air as well as freezing temperatures. Thoughts of her youth and training always brought bittersweet memories of Marcus, her love, and Prism, her condor. She doubted they could have flown high enough to get over these peaks.

The desert popped into view as they passed over the last of the mountains. Galad knew exactly where he was headed after Swans foretelling. As Galad put all he had into his flight Swan could feel the powerful downthrusts of his wings, trying to speed their arrival. Galad had no idea who Azrador was, but knew he must be important to Swan, by her immediate response to her vision.

As they turned to the east, the new lake and river came into view. Swan was stunned at how green it had become, all around the new water source the desert had receded. She was so happy for Willem's people. For the first time in recent memory the Sundown Tribe would have a good water source. Their colorful tents could be seen for as far as she could see. As Galad flew over the crowd she could see more people arriving via caravan. Galad circled the area before finding a place to land near the waterfall. Swan could see the gold dragon's landing had caused quite a panic among the desert people. They ran screaming, hiding away from them in their tents. Galad chucked to himself at how the desert people hid in their tents. Did they really think that would protect them if he wanted them?

Setting his mind back to the task at hand he tried mind speaking with the trapped elf but got no answer back.

Swan decided to climb the rocks, to get a look behind the roaring waterfall. Rock climbing on wet surfaces was another of the experiences she could draw on from her youth. As she neared the top of the waterfall she found a small narrow ledge, behind the ice-cold water so she inched her way across it. Looking at the wall of rock behind the waterfall she couldn't tell if the rocks fell there recently or had always been there.

She called out for Azrador, but her shouts were swallowed by the roar of the waterfall. Disappointed, Swan returned to Galad, who was still in dragon form. He tried again to mind speak to the elf but got no reply. Galad then mind spoke to Swan, "I know this is where the elf was trapped. I recognize it from your foretelling. Stand back and let me try to clear the rocks behind the waterfall. If it is solid rock with no entrance I should know quickly!"

Galad stepped into the river at the base of the waterfall and stuck his head and front legs through the sheet of ice-cold mountain water. The obstruction of his body caused water to spray everywhere, including on Swan. She watched as the dragon went to work on the rocks. His gold scales were almost blinding in the sunlight as he dug with his foreclaws. It wasn't long before he started pulling large boulders out from behind the waterfall, throwing them out of the way. Swan was amazed at the dragon's strength, some of the boulders were bigger than Nathan's tinker wagon, including the oxen. In a short amount of time, he had removed a small mountain of boulders.

Galad mind spoke to Swan, "I have cleared a small hole and I can see there is a cave behind the waterfall, just as we thought. It won't be long before I have it cleared."

Soon Galad signaled to Swan that the path was open, and she again climbed the slippery rocks adjacent to the roaring falls. This time when she got to the ledge, she was able to duck inside. The opening was dusty and the air thick, as she entered the cave.

Galad cast a sphere of light so she could see better as she advanced deeper into the dark cave. As she walked along the wide path, she noticed paintings on the cave walls. When she looked closely at them it appeared to be two different caravans, both pointed at the cave entrance. The drawings immediately made her think of Nathan and Gunter, and their search for the lost lands. He would be so excited to see them!

Swan was so enthralled with the dioramas on the cave walls she didn't see Azrador sitting in a lotus position, with his eyes closed, in front of an altar of some type, and almost tripped over him.

Galad chuckled to himself as he mind spoke to Swan, "Is he alive Swan?"

Swan replied, "I am not sure!" Placing her fingers on Azrador's neck, checking for a pulse she exhaled with a sigh of relief. "Yes, he is alive! But he is barely breathing, and his pulse is really slow. I see no injury and I don't see blood anywhere around. I'm not sure what to think."

Suddenly Azrador's eyes popped wide open. He then took a deep breath, as he grabbed Swan's fingers. He took three more very deep breaths before addressing her, "I am glad to see you, Swan! Give me a few minutes to orient myself, you see I was running out of air, so I had to place myself in a stasis spell, to survive longer. It will take my body a little while to wake up entirely."

When Azrador was able to stand up Swan gave him a hand, helping him keep his balance. Azrador was brushing all the dust and dirt off his leathers, when he became aware of the large gold dragon's face, sticking through the waterfall. It took him a second to collect his wits before he mind spoke to the dragon. Bowing to the golden dragon he addressed him directly, "Thank you Sir Dragon, for assisting in my rescue! It is indeed a pleasure to meet you! I see you have met my friend Swan! How did you come to know her?"

Looking the elf up and down Galad replied, "You are welcome elf, but don't thank me. Thank Swan, it was she who insisted on saving you. And if you are truly a friend of hers, you know she refuses to take no for an answer!"

Azrador laughed out loud at that, before mind speaking to the dragon, "Yes, as I recall, she can be quite persistent."

Swan interrupted their conversation when she exclaimed, "Come on Azrador, let's get you out of here! How did you get trapped in here anyway?" She inquired.

Azrador pointed at the first painting, "I was examining these extraordinary paintings when the whole cave started to shake. Before I knew it my exit was gone. I tried to dig my way out, but it quickly became obvious that was going nowhere. It was not long after that I put myself in stasis, hoping someone would notice my failure to return."

Swan had never seen the reserved elf so excited about anything as he grabbed her hand, dragging her closer to the pictures on the east wall of the tunnel.

"Look Swan, on the tunnel walls leading out. I studied these paintings for quite a while before going into stasis. I believe this one depicts the exile of the Sundowner people. It shows a long line of their desert schooners, but they are sailing on water, not sand!"

Dragging Swan to the west wall of the tunnel he pointed at it. "Look here! See, this one, it's of a long wagon train of tinker coaches, all going the same direction as the schooners, towards the cave exit. I am positive these show the legend of the tinker and desert tribe's exile from their homelands. Nathan and Gunter need to see this! I am sure it's a clue to finding the tinker homeland!"

Swan went back to the north end of the tunnel to reexamine the altar. She didn't see anything unusual about it. In fact, it was rather plain looking, until Azrador handed her the Eye of Illusion.

Looking at the ancient artifact in her hand, Swan grinned at him. She then put the Eye up to her own and looked at the altar, she saw a huge golden dragon carrying a rider carved into it. The dragon, just like the coaches, and ships appeared to be moving towards the waterfall.

Swan ran her hand over the carving of the dragon as she asked Azrador, "Is that what you think they mean? You think this is all about the Legend of the Exile?"

Azrador nodded at Swan as she handed the Eye of Illusion back to him. She was more than a little shocked at what she had seen on the altar. She was sure that it represented her and Galad flying together, but she didn't think anyone had ever seen her ride the golden dragon.

It was at about this time that Galad had transformed into his human form and joined them. Swan formally introduced the two men, even though they had already mind spoke with one another.

After the introduction Azrador went back to using the Eye of Illusion to examine the altar. Through it he could see the carvings in color. At first look, he thought the carving was Swan riding on Prism, her condor, but on closer inspection it was a golden dragon with a rider on its back. Was Swan now riding a golden dragon? If so, what happened to Prism? Letting his curiosity get the best of him he asked, "OK, where is Prism? And how did you manage to show up with a dragon? They haven't been seen in decades!"

Galad had seen Azrador looking through the Eye before he asked, "Would that be the Eye of Illusion your using? I once saw a drawing of that ancient artifact, in an old scroll of mine." If so, please tell me, how did you come to possess it?"

Azrador found he couldn't stop looking into Galad's eyes when he replied, "Yes this is the Eye of Illusion. Nathan, Gunter, and I ventured to the Ruby Falls Enclave northwest of the New Pass to obtain it. King Ferdinand of Autry had already ransacked the enclave in his effort to eliminate magic and its users. While searching the enclave, Gunter found a hidden hallway that went into the hillside that ended in an exceptionally large room.

When we entered the hallway, we could see footprints in the dust, indicating we might not be alone. The three of us prepared for a confrontation, but when we entered the large room all we found was several dead mages scattered around the room. It didn't take long before we figured out what happened to them. Turns out a stone golem was guarding the room from theft. We found a clue on how to disable the golem, so we gave it a try. It required a full-blooded elf, so I was able to disarm the golem." Azrador said as he proudly puffed up his chest. "Once past the golem we found a hidden vault that held many rare items. One of the rarest was a large dwarven shield. There was an eye painted on the lower half of the shield, and a dwarven sigil on the top half. The Eye of Illusion was attached to the back side of the shield." Even after finishing his explanation, Azrador found it hard not to stare into Galad's golden eyes.

Galad chuckled at the coincidence of finding the Eye of Illusion in the hands of a friend of Swan's. "That is the first good news I have heard in days my new friend Azrador! Swan and I must bring you up to date on all that is happening. The elves of Elyneas have a major problem with magic, that may threaten all of us. And you can relax Azrador, eventually you'll get used to my eyes!"

Swan proceeded to fill Azrador in on what they knew about the magic anomaly and how it was draining all magic and life from the land. She told him how this Temporal Rift was killing everything in the elven lands that it came into contact with. She then told him the story of how she and Galad, in dragon form, had lost their magic when flying in the rift's range and how they had almost been killed by trolls and ogres without their magic protections.

Swan went on to describe the rift to Azrador. "The anomaly appears as a multi-colored spinning disc. All life on the ground around it is dying. The area closest to it is devoid of any sign of life. The soil around it has turned brown and is so dry it has cracked open, allowing large green and yellow lizard looking men to come out of the cracks in the ground. These monsters are killing and eating everything they come across. It seems the anomaly can sense magic when in use. It will drain the magic from anyone within its range, and its range is growing rapidly. The lizardmen are dreadfully hard to kill and are extremely vicious.

In a search for an answer to the Rift Galad found an ancient scroll in his collection of old stuff that described an event similar to this happening in the past. The scroll was centuries old, but it described the same Temporal Rift, and it appeared in the same area." Swan explained.

Galad, on the spur of the moment, decided he was safe in confiding in the elf. "The solution in the scroll reads like a scavenger hunt for magic artifacts. The artifacts, once properly assembled, have to be thrown into the center of the Rift. According to the scroll, that alone will close the chasm that is the Temporal Rift. We hope!"

Azrador looked at his two rescuers with confusion, "Wait a minute! Are you two sober? The story you are telling me sounds like an old legend somebody wrote centuries ago."

Knowing how confused Azrador must be, Swan felt she needed to give him a full explanation of what had happened to her since she last saw him, but their time was limited. "It is a long story, and someday I will tell you the whole of it, but there is no time for it now. I can tell you that, to Galad's credit, Arch Mage Ibis is dead. Unfortunately, I made a foolish decision after Prism and I attacked Ibis, dropping Sydney's dragon eggs on him. We had destroyed his tower and I thought him dead when we made a pass over his tower, scouting the damage. That is when Ibis surprised us. He struck Prism with a bolt from the black magic wand he called the Wand of the Reaper. The blow knocked Prism out of the sky. As we were plummeting to the ground, Ibis hit me with a shot from the wand. It felt like my life was drained out of me before I lost consciousness, and everything went black. When I came to, a Golden Dragon was standing over us. Galad was able to save me, but not Prism. The Reaper had drained all his life force, transferring it to Ibis. That's how he had lived for so long!"

Swan continued, "It turns out, more than a century ago, Ibis betrayed and captured Galad. He used Galad's magic to power the protections around the Silver Tower. That was why no one could tear it down. One of the large quakes freed him from his bonds so the first thing he did was seek his own revenge on Ibis. That's when he showed up, just in time to fry Ibis and save me. Needless to say, our relationship has deepened over time. I think it has all worked out for the best. I like to say, he needed a rider, and I needed a ride!" Swan laughed as she made a face at Galad."

Galad indignantly stated, "I certainly did not need a rider! But you did seem pretty needy as you plummeted to the ground. You will eventually learn that I always have trouble refusing a pretty human lady." Galad said smugly.

Azrador was stunned by the tale, unable to imagine what Swan had been through. "Wow, that is a lot to digest. So, the Silver Tower is defeated, and King Ferdinand of Autry has legalized magic?" Azrador was still digesting all the information he had learned when he asked Swan. "All that as well as you are on a scavenger hunt, with a dragon, looking for artifacts that haven't been seen in centuries."

Galad gave Azrador a big slap on the back as he chuckled, "Glad you have a handle on it, elf. Now a bit of good news, the ancient scroll in my treasure room has a drawing of each item, and how to assemble them.

Azrador, in awe asked the dragon, "Are you telling me dragons really have a treasure room?" Shaking his head Azrador stated, "I guess I should not be surprised by that."

Swan interrupted their conversation stating, "You would not believe what a hoarder he is Azrador! I couldn't believe all the stuff I saw when he let me see it. Until you see it, it's hard to fathom that much gold in one place. Galad explained to me that the size of a dragon's treasure effects the strength of a dragon's magic, or so he claims." Swan said, taking the opportunity to rib Galad about his hoarding.

Trying to ignore the playful jab from Swan, he went on to explain, "Thanks to you we now have the Eye of Illusion. That leaves the Sacred Sun Medallion, the Dragon's Tear, the Moon Stone, and that dwarven shield you found."

Curious now Azrador asked, "What does the shield have to do with it?"

Galad answered, happy for the chance to show off his

knowledge to the elf, "The shield is known by historians as the Shield of Torevir. According to the scroll whoever throws the activated Celestial Rod, with the artifacts attached, into the Temporal Rift must be standing behind the shield for protection, or they won't survive."

By now, Azrador was totally caught up in the pair's tale, when he exclaimed, "Whoa, a lot has happened since I got trapped in here. I think the first thing we need to do is find Nathan; he may have one of those magic items. This Dragon's Tear, as you called it, might it be a tear shaped emerald with a dragon etched into the gem?"

It was Galad's turn to be excited, "Yes! That is the exact description in the scroll! Have you seen it?"

Azrador would never admit it to Galad or Swan, but he was pleased to know something that Galad didn't. "Yes, I've seen it. Nathan has it, or at least he did have it, the last time I saw him. We found it on a mist covered island in the northern seas. I also know where the Shield of Torevir is. Nathan, Gunter, and I just delivered it to the dwarves of Strongheim, in the Channel Mountains northwest of here." Azrador said as he headed for the exit. "Come on we need to find Nathan!"

Swan, Galad and Azrador climbed out of the cave and headed for Mystery Falls, the town that had sprung up around the new water source. Azrador was still stunned by the presence of the gold dragon, even in human form. All the elven legends spoke of dragons and their immense power, but common knowledge said they didn't exist. He was glad, even if it was bizarre, that Galad showed up just in time to kill Ibis and save Swan. To him their tale sounded like it was out of one of those legends that Nathan told around the fire ring. One that people made songs and poetry about.

When Swan, Galad and Azrador reached the colorful tents of Mystery Waters a dark-skinned man greeted Swan like they were old friends.

The white robed man that was wearing a white turban with a gold emblem on it approached Swan, giving her a kiss on each cheek. "Welcome back Swan, I am pleased but surprised to see you. My watchers didn't report seeing you and your giant condor arrive. That's very unlike them, they will have to be reprimanded. Your arrival must have been what the reports of a dragon landing were about. Can you imagine? They all must need their eyes examined. A dragon of all things! I guess people see what they want to, as if dragons ever existed." Willem shook his head, laughing at his young scouts.

When Galad joined the group, he glared at the white robed man. He didn't like the way the man spoke of his kind. What's worse was he saw the man kiss Swan. Seeing the glare directed at Willem, Swan quickly introduced Sultan Willem. Willem was startled by Galad's golden eyes, he had never seen eyes that color before.

After Swan introduced Azrador he greeted the Sultan with a proper bow before asking, "Where is the tinker coach parked, I don't see Nathan anywhere around? We need to speak with him right away."

Willem turned to Azrador and said, "Any friend of Swan's is a friend of the Tribe. I am pleased to meet both of you. Swan has come to my people's aid in the past, saving many lives from the giant sand worms. To answer your question Azrador, Nathan has left, following my brother Mikiel and my sister Amara. They are to lend aid to the Green Folk. They headed to Vardo to meet the elves and then onto Silverton, the closest town to the anomaly. He left word for you to follow, when you returned from whatever rock climbing you were doing. Come, join me in my tent, out of the midday sun. I offer some cool refreshments in exchange for any information you may have learned about the Rift." Willem motioned for them to join him in his tent.

Galad stepped past the Sultan as he entered the tent. "Yes, thank you for your hospitality! I wish to hear more about your tribe and how you came to live in the desert."

The Sultan chose to ignore the breach of protocol, assuming Galad of an overlarge ego the way he carried himself.

"Please follow me," Willem led the others into the cooler interior, where attendants brought them chilled wine and snacks. They joined the Sultan on large pillows surrounding a low table where the refreshments were served. Willem's wife, Eve joined them once she saw that everyone was served. Azrador looked around the plush interior of the tent and its wild colors made him think of Nathan's tinker coach and all its colored doors and drawers.

After the refreshments were brought and everyone had their fill, a lively conversation broke out. Galad peppered the Sultan with many questions. Willem told the legend of the Sundowners, the story of how his people had, at one time, been a sea faring people. Living on their ships and sailing the seas to far off ports. Centuries ago, the Sundowners committed an unknown sin that was bad enough to cause the tribe to be sent away from the sea, and the nourishment it provided.

Willem sat his teacup down and continued, "My people learned to scratch out an existence where there was little life or water. Once we discovered the underground deposits of water my people adapted to living underground. We grew our food and livestock in caverns that the sand worms created. We are a hardy people and have mostly thrived in these conditions." Willem took another drink of his tea. "That is the old legend repeated by my ancestors in song. My people have never seen enough water to sail on, until the Mystery Waters appeared. Our schooners travel on the desert sand not on an ocean."

Willem's wife, Eve, had sat quietly during the telling of the Sundowners history before she added, "If the legend is real, maybe the Mystery Waters mean our penance is served. The water will make life much easier for our people."

Willem reminded his wife, "That is if we can get the sand worm attacks under control. Until recently they had never attacked us, now they attack as a group." Willem took another sip of his tea. Privately, he wondered what sailing on a ship at sea would be like. When he was a young man, his grandfather had told him stories of sailing on the seas.

Azrador took the break in the conversation to suggest an expedition, "I believe you will probably be interested in a cave I just explored, it's behind the waterfall. It has paintings on the walls that seem to depict the exile of your people and the Tinkers. It seems your two peoples are somehow linked." Azrador explained.

Willem considered what he had just been told before declaring, "Perhaps the legends are more real than we realized. I will send someone to explore this cave right away. Do you realize this is the second legend that has recently become real? Strange times indeed."

BLESSED BLUFF ENCLAVE

Putting Out a Volcano

Jason's team of dwarfs had done an amazing job of getting the needed machinery into the tunnels that required restrictions or blocking. After the reservoir gates and the adjacent tunnel plumbing was installed, they had to work their way east, toward the volcano. Two new tunnels had to be drilled to connect the network of tunnels.. They were required to make the needed connections and to control the water flow. These tunnels had to keep a downward slope for water flow and yet remain above the mouth of the volcano, for the final release. The dwarf surveyors did a great job of planning. The other three gate systems they had installed would direct the ice melt and reservoir water through the maze of tunnels and pipes to just above Jordan's Bane. They had also installed similar gates on two small rivers, to be used to redirect their waters which typically led to the ocean. This redirection of river water would provide an additional stream of water that would merge with the reservoir water traveling through the tunnels and gates. The last gate, the largest, was located directly above the volcano and should allow some control of the water flowing down the mountain and into the volcano, if all went as planned.

Where they were working now, above the volcano, had the strong smell of sulfur and was very unpleasant to breathe. The exit of the last tunnel was just above the volcano in the southern Shadow Mountains and Jason's team had to fight two battles against roaming cave spiders the size of humans along the way. They lost one of his dwarves when he was dragged off, before they even knew they were under attack. The machinery that Jason and his team were currently installing was the last piece of Master Bluthe's puzzle. If Bluthe's plan worked, it would put an end to the quakes that were caused by the volcano and its lava flows.

Once the assembly work was complete Jason lifted the last huge gate into place, holding it until the dwarves locked it into position. The theory was, with proper signaling, the gates would control how much water was delivered. Master Bluthe was concerned if too much water was added and they cooled the volcano too quickly, they could trigger another eruption or explosion. He had composed a chart of numbers that would be followed by his apprentices. They would use the chart to determine the rate of flow into the volcano.

Grand Master Throdon had insisted Jason now use the Staff of Divinity as his primary weapon, so he was carrying it, trying to get used to using it. When the spiders attacked and Jason aimed the staff at them it froze several of them in place, with little to no effort on Jason's part. He was still not used to being without his mace and felt naked without it.

The water gates were the same size as the tunnel, to be effective at holding the water back or releasing it. The gates could gradually be lowered, controlling how much water was released at a time. The weak link in the project was the large iron pipes they had to use to get water over the New Pass and into this section of the mountain. Jason had been amazed at the dwarfs' skill at making such things, and how well everything fit together.

After the last bolt was tightened and the assembly was complete the team took a much-needed break. They retreated up the tunnel to get away from the sulfur smell and to eat and drink a little. Everyone had worked hard and needed the rest before they tested the plan. Jason had been leery of whether all these pieces would fit together. Now that they had, would it work as laid out. He and his team had been working on this for several grueling weeks. After the break and some travel rations, it was time to see if it was all worthwhile.

Jason climbed to the staging area where the controls for this last gate were located. From this perch Jason could observe the volcano and control the water passing through the last gate. Master Bluthe had advised them to go slow. He was afraid too much icy water would cool the lava too quickly, causing explosions. Signals to control water flow would be passed between the dwarfs stationed across their network of tunnels and gates. Even Master Bluthe admitted his plan was mostly theory, no one had ever undertaken such an enormous project. But he thought they were up to the task. The dwarfs were much more advanced in these engineering tasks than any people Jason had ever heard of. They had been diverting water to their homes for generations.

In their brief time together, Master Bluthe had opened Jason's eyes to so much. The mechanical wonders he had witnessed at Strongheim, like how they moved ore or water, were taken for granted. It made smithing alone look primitive. Jason had an immense amount of respect for Master Bluthe, but he still questioned Throdon's suggestion that he had his mother's magic, and it was growing in strength. Could his mother really have been a magical being? Garth said she was a traveler and could open portals. What else could she do? It was at times like these he really wished he knew more about her.

After much preparation and coordination, the signals

were given to open the west gates. That would divert the river water and reservoir into the tunnels. Instantly thousands of gallons of water changed direction and were rushing east toward the volcano. As the water passed tunnel junctions the closed side gates kept the water moving east. When the water reached the large iron pipes over the New Pass there was some mild leakage around a few of the pipe fittings, but nothing serious. The bulk of the water continued to flow east. Jason heard the water coming before he saw it. A huge roar from the sloshing water reached Jason just before it burst through the gates that were only a third open. The ice-cold water cascaded down the mountain taking any loose rocks or boulders with it. Soon smoke and mist filled the valley below them, making it difficult to see what effect the water was having on the volcano's lava flow. Several of the side tunnels above the lava tubes had the floor drilled with holes and were then flooded, so the water would spray down on the flowing lava. The thought was, if they could harden the lava, the flow would slow down or stop. Especially if Jason and company could put the volcano out.

Gadna, the dwarf that had been Jason's assistant through the assembly process, thought they could open the gate to halfway, now that they had let the water flow for a while. With all the smoke and steam created by the water on the volcano they could not see very far, but they could hear rumbling and felt several strong quakes, making them gnash their teeth as they hung on to their perch.

Jason turned the crank which opened the gates a bit further. If the water cooled the volcano too slowly it could form a hard cap and eventually cause the volcano to blow up again. When the gate opened further the water flow increased, creating a large waterfall that now flowed directly into the mouth of the volcano. The noise caused by the moving water was loud where Jason and Gadna were perched, but they suddenly heard a large boom, followed by a massive quake that knocked Jason and Gadna off their feet. Two other apprentices were thrown from their perch into the rushing water and down the mountain. Within minutes of the massive quake the water began to slow, until it was but a trickle.

As Jason got to his feet, he surveyed the valley below him. Smoke and the acrid smell of sulfur was thick in the air. A breeze cleared some of the smoke, and he could see several of the lava flows were no longer red or moving. Gadna turned to Jason and stated, "I fear the last quake may have broken something along the water route. I imagine that the pipes over the New Pass, our weak link, haven't held up to the big quake. I will signal down the network to close their gates."

Master Throdon was sure the Divinity Stone was fully activated and in Jason's control, whatever that meant. So, as he had promised the old dwarf, he was holding the Staff of Divinity in his right hand. Jason wished the steam would clear so he could get a better look at the volcano. He was anxious to see if they had been successful before the water stopped.

Suddenly a stiff wind came from the south blowing the smoke and clouds away. Within seconds Jason and Gadna had a clear view of the valley below them. It was disappointing to still see lava churning in the center of what was left of the volcano. At least the water had done a decent job of reducing the lava flows. Jason was disappointed, it would take days, if not weeks, to repair the plumbing that brought the water from the west.

Jason was discussing their next step with Gadna when another huge quake struck. Jason kept upright with the help of the staff, while Gadna ended up on his butt, again. They heard a loud growling sound, just as the tunnel below them collapsed, destroying one of the water gates they had installed. Jason and Gadna were standing just above it all when the dust settled, and they could see the water had not been enough to put the volcano out.

Jason tried to contain his disappointment. He and Master Bluthe were sure this plan would work. After examining what happened, he decided with time the gate could be rebuilt and they could try again.

Jason felt a light vibration in the staff, drawing his attention to it. Could it be responsible for the strong wind appearing and clearing his sight? Jason had an idea that he had to try.

Jason instructed Gadna as he started down the mountain toward the volcano. "Gadna, you stay here, if this fails you will need to send word of my failure back to your clan!" Using the Staff as a walking stick for support Jason made his way, climbing over fallen rocks and debris. The heat began to increase as he descended, toward the mouth of the volcano. He was forced to take several switchbacks and the smell of sulfur was getting stronger, making breathing more difficult, as he reached a small flat rock ledge, just above the cauldron. Jason removed the lead shield that covered the Divinity Stone. The brilliant blue twenty-four faced gem lit up as if it was the sun. Jason took a deep breath as he closed his eyes and cleared his head of any thoughts. He concentrated on the chant, "Heal the land" as he slammed the staff into the ground. He continued repeating the mantra "Heal the land" over and over.

An intense blue light emanated from the crown of the staff, bathing the valley in its brilliant light. Jason felt more at peace in the blue light than ever before and after several long moments Jason noticed he could no longer smell sulfur. Still reciting the mantra "Heal the land" he opened his eyes and looked around. The blue light was beginning to fade and in its place was clean fresh air. The smell of lilac flowers replaced the odor of smoke and sulfur that had been reaching Jason's nose. He could hardly believe his eyes as he glanced around a glen in full bloom. He was amazed when he saw a small clear blue lake now lay where the cauldron had been. Wildflowers were in bloom around the lake and were being tended by a flurry of bees and butterflies.

Jason rubbed his eyes, to make sure he was not hallucinating, after breathing all the bad gases. He could hear Gadna along with the remaining dwarfs whooping and hollering above him.

The volcano was gone, like it had never been there. Jason approached the newly created lake, picking several wildflowers on his way, smelling their scent. He was surprised when he saw the water was clear and already had fish swimming in it. He was stunned at what had happened and wasn't sure how! Throdon had been right. He had no magic training, but the Staff was immensely powerful and able to do amazing things. Placing the lead cover back in place over the Divinity Stone, Jason could feel his energy drain.

A slap on his back brought Jason out of deep thought as Gadna and six of the dwarfs joined him sitting on a rock near the lake.

Gadna could hardly contain his excitement when he spoke to Jason, "By the gods Jason, you have done it! It was an amazing thing to watch. It will be the stuff of legends for years to come. Clan Chief Brackus will be very pleased. It looks like Throdon was right, you were the right man to wield the Divinity Staff."

Jason could hardly believe it. The land had been healed, the volcano was no more, and the lava flows and quakes would be but a memory for the dwarven people. It was just starting to sink into Jason, what a huge thing they had just done. The threat of disaster to the dwarves was over and he had helped make it happen. Would the cave spiders return to the depths? Would the giant sand worms quit attacking the desert people? He certainly hoped so. He had to remind himself, one problem at a time.

As he returned to surveying the stunning glen that had replaced the nasty smelly volcano, Jason recognized a blessing had been placed on this land, and he had been part of making it happen. From now on Jordan's Bane would be known as Jordan's Blessing!

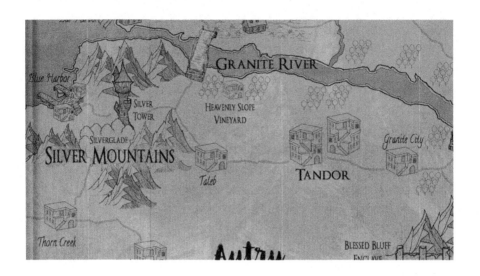

A Baby is Born

After Queen Jennifer's water broke, due to the weather, it took the midwife sometime to arrive. When, after being in labor all night the babe had still not been born by noon the following day, and the Queen was becoming concerned. The midwife tried to reassure her that many women had long labors, especially with their first born.

King Ferdinand was alone in his study. Impatient and on edge, he felt bad that he had yelled at the midwife the last time she had given him a progress report. After that he thought it best if he waited out of the way of the women. He was thankful that Queen Jennifer's older sister, Margaret, had arrived from Sulan. The Princess had been planning to spend a few of weeks with Jennifer before the baby's coming, but the little one was impatient, like it's father, and came a little early. Jennifer was thrilled to see Margaret and was relieved to have her sister present for the birth of their child.

Princess Margaret was able to soothe her sister when no one else could. Princess Margaret had birthed a son of her own, so she was able to help the Queen stay focused on her breathing, and not the contractions. Margaret also brought good news from their father, King Rudolf. Sulan had been blessed with bumper crops this fall and pledged to aid Autry with much needed food this winter.

A worried King Ferdinand was sitting down to a solitary dinner, when word came of the birth. The King tossed his napkin on the table, took a deep drink from his wineglass, and rushed to be at his wife's side. He couldn't wait to witness the magic that their love had made. When he arrived at the entry to her rooms he stopped and gathered himself before entering.

Ferdinand was quietly greeted by Princess Margaret, "Congratulations Ferdinand, you have a beautiful baby girl. It was a most difficult labor, and the Queen needs her rest."

The King thanked her and informed her that dinner was being held, waiting for him to return to the dining room, and that he would join her there soon. He proceeded to Jennifer's side, quickly giving her a hug, and kissing the baby on the forehead. He could see Jennifer was weak and exhausted after the long labor, but she made it quite clear, she wouldn't rest until they agreed on a name for the babe.

Turning to the midwife he thanked her and told her he would stay with the Queen while the midwife ate her dinner. After she left and Ferdinand and Jennifer were alone, he admitted, "I would prefer you get some rest, but I can see by the determined look in your eye you will not until this is done. I have a suggestion, we can name her Alexandrea, after my mother. We could call her Alex for short."

Jennifer looked into Ferdinand's eyes and smiled. "I think Alexandrea is a wonderful name, but I have known this babe's name since she came into being. If it is acceptable to you, she will be named Swan Alexandrea as a reminder of the person that has made my life possible. It is such a shame Swan will never get to meet her namesake." Jennifer sighed as a tear rolled down her cheek, and onto the babe's head.

Ferdinand didn't tell Jennifer, but he felt a little slighted about not being consulted on the child's name. But decided to leave well enough alone. He told Jennifer that he thought Swan was a great name, but it was now time for her to rest. He gave her another kiss, but she was already asleep.

The King then joined a very tired, but happy, Princess Margaret at the dinner table. After wine was poured Margaret proposed a toast to the Royal Princess Swan Alexandrea. As they ate dinner, they could hear bells ringing throughout Tandor, announcing the birth of a royal princess.

After dinner Margaret conveyed that her father, King Rudolf, had agreed to share the abundant crops of Sulan with Autry this winter, so no one would go hungry. With the defeat of the ArchMage Ibis, the destruction of the Silver Tower and the death of King Gregory of Balzar, peace and prosperity should quickly return to the two kingdoms. And the two kingdoms rejoiced, Sulan and Autry now had an heir to the two kingdoms. King Ferdinand and Princess Margaret both agreed, they should help each other in as many ways as possible.

As they were eating their dinner a messenger interrupted, "My King, I bring news from the South! I am pleased to report, a miracle has happened in the south of Autry. Jordan's Bane, the volcano that has been raining ash on the crops in the south is gone. No one claims to know how, but in its place is a clear lake, surrounded by wildflowers and butterflies. The people of Autry are taking the appearance of the lake and the birth of the new princess as a sign of the healing of the land!" King Ferdinand thanked and dismissed the messenger before he went to a window, where he watched as his people were dancing and singing in the streets!

Lizardmen

They got an early start the next day, anxious to figure this thing out. The party on horseback was met by numerous lizardmen that had gotten away from the area before the wards went up. The elven crossbows were effective, but many times it took three or four arrows to stop one of them. The ice wands were much more deadly. One cast brought down one of the lizardmen.

Leila was extremely interested in the lizard creature's anatomy. She thought that she could learn more about them if she could communicate with them. On close up examination they had very thick hides that were covered in green scales with yellow flakes or spots. They had a long jaw with exceptionally long teeth protruding under a long snout. Their front legs shorter and thinner than its thick muscular hind legs. They also had long sharp claws on both front and hind legs. Leila instructed several of her men to load one of the dead lizardmen on a horse and take the dead carcass back to camp for further study.

The party killed eight of the lizard creatures on their way to the warded area. They stayed close to the mountains, skirting the dead zone, in an attempt to get a better look at the multi-colored spinning object. From their viewing point, in the foothills above the anomaly, they could see the colors and speed of the spinning rift vary. There was a rhythm to the changes, almost like it was breathing.

Leila cast a floating light twenty feet ahead, "That should let us know if the anti-magic field is growing towards us while we observe that thing from a distance."

Mikiel decided to cast a weather spell. He wanted to see if it had any effect inside the void zone. Moving his hands in flurry he cast the whirlwind spell, causing a small tornado to spring up. He then directed it toward the spinning object. It picked up rocks and dirt as it passed over the broken landscape, swirling towards the multi-colored spinning anomaly. When the tornado reached the rift, it appeared to merely be sucked into it as it disappeared. When Mikiel cast the spell, he felt it decrease his mana supply a lot more than it should have. Looking up he noticed Leila's floating light had also disappeared. "That spell cost me substantially more mana than it should have. And the casting of the spells seems to have brought us to the attention of the anomaly. It feels to me like it is moving closer to us."

"Let me try something," Leila said as she folded her arms, closed her eyes, and started to hum, mentally reaching out to the nature around her for clues. Her face suddenly tightened up and her eyes snapped open. "We must move, now, quickly, you are right Mikiel, we have somehow drawn its attention!" Leila ran to mount Ebony, her horse, a short distance away. She then ordered her people to pull back. Mikiel and Amara brought up the rear, as the group retreated to a safer space.

Amara hung back to try and read one of the dead lizards for clues as to why they were here, thinking she was a safe distance from the vortex. When Mikiel looked back to see if she were following, he saw the ground under the anomaly open. He watched, helpless, as the Rift began to expand and move towards Amara. She was so focused on using her magic, trying to learn where the lizards came from that she wasn't aware of the danger. Mikiel yelled her name, but she didn't seem to hear him, so he turned his horse to run back to her just as the anomaly widened. Mikiel watched with horror as the ground under his sister opened. It looked like it was going to swallow her whole.

Instead, Amara hovered there, in midair, above the opening in the ground. She then placed one hand on her necklace and said the magic word, "Frezit." The ground all around her instantly froze, turning white. The opening under her vanished and the anomaly shrunk and moved away from her. Amara then mounted her horse and headed back to camp with the others.

When they got back to camp Leila followed Mikiel and Amara into his tent. "Amara, how did you keep the anomaly from swallowing you? It looked to us like the ground opened under you. How did you avoid being taken by it?"

Amara tried to reassure Leila and Mikiel, "I am sure we will find a solution to the Rift and the Demon that created it. I am now surer than ever that we are not defenseless. We all saw how it responded to cold, we must find a way to use that info to fight it."

Leila nodded in agreement, "I'm not yet sure what that solution will be, but we learned a lot today. Tomorrow we can all put our heads together and figure out what comes next. Goodnight to you both."

The Rift

When Nathan and Gunter arrived in Vardo they were stunned at the colorful buildings and shutters. Plants hung from the many awnings in front of the buildings, adding shade to the sunny streets. Gunter commented that it looked like a town the tinkers had taken over. They both chuckled at that thought.

Nathan's skills as a tinker were in high demand, once people knew he had goods for sale, as well as being able to repair almost anything. He and Gunter found it hard to believe when they were told Vardo had never seen a tinker's coach. Doing business with the dark-skinned people allowed them to learn about the desert people and their culture. They also were able to accumulate a fair amount of gossip. They quickly learned that they had missed Mikiel's group by just a few days. They also heard a rumor about a plan, developed by a giant blacksmith and the dwarfs, something about dousing the volcano, using snow melt from the mountains. They hoped, if the volcano and its lava flows were neutralized the large cave spiders and giant sand worms would return to their homes. That sounded like a crazy idea to them, but they both chose not to voice that opinion.

Once Nathan and Gunter were alone, they discussed the dwarves plan at length. Nathan confessed to Gunter "I feel a certain amount of responsibility for Jordon's Bane. I'm sure the way we destroyed the cursed weapons is what released the bad mojo that triggered its eruption."

Gunter was not surprised to hear Nathan's feelings, he felt much the same. "I agree Nathan, but it had to be done. We both know it was the only way to destroy all those horrendous, corrupt weapons. I give credit to the dwarves for devising such a bold plan. Unfortunately, I have my doubts about them having any success neutralizing it."

Nathan was more optimistic about the dwarven plan. "The legends of old spoke of the great engineering skill of the dwarves. The dwarves are the first people I have ever seen that had running water in all their buildings. In all my travels I have only seen such luxury in the homes of the most wealthy. Maybe they still have the engineering skills needed. Don't forget, I also heard they had some giants helping them. I wonder if one of them is Jason?" Nathan stated.

Gunter shook his head, "I doubt it. He seems more interested in smithing than engineering. Even if he is helping them, I still have my doubts as to whether such a feat can be accomplished. Strongheim's water system was pretty impressive though. Even using magic to move the amount of water required, it seems the distance involved would prove to be too difficult. I wish them luck though."

More disturbing were the reports they were getting of the lizard like creatures that seemed to somehow be tied to the rift. The stories being told of these lizardmen were horrendous. Tales of them eating people by the dozens and being extremely difficult to kill were alarming. It was a magic void, so the creatures could not be killed using magic. The weapons proving to be most effective were iron hand to hand weapons and crossbow bolts. The lizards were also rumored to spit a strong poison that paralyzed the victim until the lizard could shred them with its long claws and fangs.

Another of the rumors they collected was the story told by one of the city's bakers. He had sworn he had seen a dragon, carrying a rider, flying over the desert a few weeks before. When Nathan and Gunter heard this story they agreed, the baker must have seen Swan and Prism, when they did their flyover months before. That night they both went to bed thinking about how much they missed Swan and her spunky personality.

The next morning, after breakfast, Gunter hitched the oxen to the coach. They then followed the brick road leading to Vardo Pass. The pass entrance was not far from town and had a slight incline in elevation as they traveled through it. The pass went through the mountains and into the elven kingdom of Elyneas, where they would turn south and head to Silverton.

As they exited the pass, riding down a wide paved road, they entered a forest that reminded them both of the forests in the moving pictures they had taken from Ruby Falls. The trees were two-hundred feet high, and their foliage was made up of hundreds of colors. It was simply the most beautiful landscape either of them had ever seen. The air was fresh with the scents of pine and wildflowers and large colorful butterflies flitted over the flowers. Nathan could only smile at Gunter as he was continuously making the coach stop so he could take samples of this plant or that mushroom. Many of which he had never been seen before. At one point he stopped and picked each of them an apple off of one of the trees they had passed. They were the size of a melon and had the sweetest flavor in an apple that Nathan had ever tasted. Gunter even kept the seeds from his, as another sample.

As the tinker coach made its way south, they passed several villages built in the trees. The elves in these villages were very stand offish and never approached the coach. They mostly stayed in the trees that had adjoining bridges and walkways, some more than fifty feet off the ground, connecting the homes to each other. On the fourth day, as they continued south on the wide paved road, a large shadow passed over the coach. It didn't catch Nathan or Gunter's attention until the oxen stopped moving.

Nathan stepped down from the coach just in time to see a golden dragon land on the road ahead of them. Dismounting from its back to Nathan's amazement, was Azrador. More shocking yet was that dismounting behind Azrador was Swan! Nathan could not believe his eyes; it really was Swan!

Swan was dressed, as usual in her warrior leathers, her trident strapped to her back. She ran to Nathan, nearly knocking him over with her enthusiasm. She threw her arms around him, giving him a huge hug while Azrador was trying to get his land legs back, as he staggered over to the coach.

Nathan heard a low, quiet growl, but wasn't sure where, or who, it had come from.

Grabbing a rail on the coach to steady himself, Azrador exclaimed, "What a ride Nathan! You have to try it sometime. You cannot imagine how far you can see, and the sights you see from up there are breathtaking."

Gunter was just exiting the coach, after hearing the commotion, when he saw Nathan hugging Swan. He ran over to her, nearly knocking the unstable Azrador over in his hurry to get to her.

Azrador threw Gunter a dirty look, that he chose to ignore, as he gave Swan a kiss. Again, they heard a low quiet growl. "Swan it is so good to see you again, we sure have missed you on this adventure. Funny, just the other day Nathan and I were wondering what you were up to."

Swan threw Galad a scolding look, for the growl, as she grabbed both of them by the hand, excitedly leading them nearer the golden dragon. "I have missed you guys too. As you can see, many things have happened since I last saw you. We have much to tell you, but first let me introduce you to my new friend, Galad!" In the blink of an eye the golden dragon they had just seen transformed into his human form.

Nathan and Gunter both blinked several times, looking into Galad's golden eyes before believing what they had just seen.

Gunter was sure he had now seen everything as he nervously stated, "I guess witnessing a dragon landing and transforming are going to make it difficult to deny that dragons are real."

Nathan, no less nervous than Gunter, tore his gaze away from the golden eyes and greeted Galad. "Welcome Sir Dragon, we are blessed to meet you. My name is Nathan, and this is my friend Gunter. I see you have already met Azrador and Swan. Gunter and I have a few tales of our own to tell you. Please, join us inside the coach. We can enjoy some refreshments while we catch up with each other's journey."

As Galad entered the multi-colored coach he allowed a gasp of surprise to escape his lips, as he took in the posh interior and its generous size. Once all were inside the giant coach, Gunter served a large tray of cheeses as well as uncorking several bottles of wine and laying out bread and honey as well. Everyone got comfortable for an exchange of stories.

Galad nodded at Nathan and Gunter as he replied, "I am pleased to meet you Nathan, and you as well mage. Swan has told me much about your adventures. I find myself indebted to you tinker. If you had not saved Swan from certain death, I would not have found her! As I have gotten to know her, she has told me many tales of your adventures and what colorful people you tinkers are. I must say I had some doubt when she spoke of a coach that was larger inside than out, but I see it was not just a tale." Galad explained as he smiled at Swan.

Nathan turned to Azrador and asked, "How did you find Swan? Last we knew you were investigating the Mystery Waters waterfall. We even waited an extra couple of days before leaving, hoping you would be back."

Azrador laughed as he explained, "I didn't find Swan, she and Galad found me! I was trapped in a cave behind the Mystery Falls after a quake. It is her story to tell, and it's quite a story at that."

Swan proceeded to tell her tale to Nathan and Gunter, taking frequent sips of the wine Gunter was serving. She started with her trip home after leaving Nathan and Gunter. She found it difficult to not be emotional when she spoke of the loss of her love, Markus, his condor Firefly, and worst of all the death of Prism. But when she spoke of how they had destroyed Gregory, the Pirate King and ArchMage Ibis both, Nathan saw her fiery spirit return. He also saw a bitterness in her that he had never seen before. Who could fault her after all this young woman had been through?

Those present were not surprised to hear Swan was in the middle of an attack that had destroyed a kingdom and a centuries old mage. Most had seen her in action, more than once.

Galad interrupted Swan's narration, stating, "Fortunately, this is where I made my appearance! You see Ibis and I were old acquaintances many, many, years ago. I was young and naïve when it came to humans, and he trapped me in a stasis spell, and I was in isolation for a century. So, my first thought upon gaining my freedom was to find Ibis and make him pay for what he had been doing to me. I had just gotten to the Silver Tower when I saw Ibis on the roof. I swept in, shocking him with one-hundred years of dragon anger and fire, right in his face. That's when I saw Prism falling from the sky. I quickly grabbed the condor before he hit the ground. I was too late to save Prism, but I was able to help Swan."

Nathan, his voice full of sympathy exclaimed, "Oh Swan! I am so sorry for the loss of Prism. I know how much he meant to you! And poor Gretchen, loosing Henrick in the battle. I wouldn't be here without him!"

Swan gave Nathan a peck on the cheek and replied,

"Thank you, Nathan, it was quite a challenging time, afterwards. Galad helped me bury Prism, we built a cairn over his body to commemorate his valor. Galad then used dragon fire, melting the rocks into one solid slab, as a grave marker. He then carried me to his lair to help me recover from my injuries. Galad and I have found comfort in each other's company. He was recovering from one-hundred years of loneliness and pain, and I was a lost soul after losing both Prism and Markus. It is also because of Galad that I have not lost the joy of flight." Swan said as she gazed at Galad.

Azrador added, "You can keep flying Swan, but I am staying on the ground from now on! Don't get me wrong, I did enjoy my ride, but once was enough. Besides, it is as cold as ice and hard to breath up there."

Both Swan and Galad chuckled at that declaration. Swan went on to explain her recovery at Galad's lair and her surprise when he transformed into human form. Swan described how they found they had a lot in common.

Since then, they had flown to many parts of the world that Swan didn't even know existed. They were on one such flight when they flew over the magic anomaly. She spoke of Galad flying them back to his lair when their magic recovered. "Ever since then he has been searching in his library for clues. Yesterday he found something that he thinks might be helpful."

Galad took up the conversation from there, "I found a scroll in my library that describes a rift that occurred hundreds of years ago and how it scarred the ground as well as drained the world of life and magic. It described the level of destruction as enormous before action was finally taken. Thousands were killed and magic was almost extinguished completely. The many different people of the lands finally realized it would take a united effort if they were to stop the killing and close the rift. They crafted a special magical device that was made of several ancient magical artifacts. The scroll went on to list the objects needed to build the device, called the

Celestial Rod. The scroll goes on and describes in detail how the rod is to be assembled. Once this rod is created, by a Grand Master Blacksmith, it must be activated by an extremely high-level mage.

Once activated the rod is to be taken to the rift and thrown into it. I am unsure who can get that close to the rift. You heard Swan describe what happened to us when we got too close. It was only a matter of a few minutes before we found ourselves without magic. The scroll says if you accomplish this, the rift will close. It then goes on to explain there could be a backlash in its closing but does not go into what that "backlash" could be."

Holding up a scrap of paper Galad read them the list, "The Eye of Illusion is the first thing on the list, because it is needed to find the other artifacts. They are the Moon Stone, the Sacred Sun Medallion, and the Dragons Tear. The translation also mentioned an ancient dwarven shield called The Defender of Torevir. This shield is required for the protection of the one that carries the Celestial Rod. This object might be what allows the bearer of the Rod to get close enough to the rift, without it killing them. That is why the Shield of Torevir is so important. The scroll described a cataclysmic event that happened three to four-hundred years ago, in the same area, causing a similar effect. The scroll called it the Rift of Hell. The scroll described the rift as a doorway that leads to another world. I have no way to verify the truth in the scroll, but my instincts tell me it is telling the truth." Galad concluded.

Azrador took this opportunity to redirect the conversation, "Nathan you were right! There is a cave behind the waterfall. That is where Swan and Galad found me. I was exploring it when a quake struck and caused a rockslide that trapped me inside. I found the most marvelous wall art on the walls inside the cave. One of the drawings depicts a caravan of tinker wagons and on the opposite wall a stream of schooners following one another. It appeared like they were all headed towards the falls. There was also an altar of white marble at the far end of the cave. It was covered with carvings like the ones we saw on that misty island! The wall art brought to mind those paintings behind the canvas in your coach."

Nathan was excited and disappointed at the same time. He had been close to joining Azrador before deciding to help the elves defeat the rift. "What do you think it means Azrador?"

Azrador considered Nathans's question before answering the tinker. "It looked to my like the tinkers and the desert people came to these lands at the same time, perhaps for committing the same crimes."

Gunter poured some wine for Galad and asked, "So the war is over then, with both the Silver Tower and Autry?"

Galad answered proudly, "I would say yes, since there is no longer a Silver Tower. I saw many of its mages surrender to the troops, and the wards of protection that the mages could not bring down were powered by draining my magic. Once I broke free of my chains, those wards crumbled. Hopefully, without that evil wizard, your people will find peace has come to their lands." Galad sat down as he ended his tale.

Swan gave Gunter a hug, "Condolences Gunter, on the death of Henrick, I am sure it is a terrible blow to you and your sister. I know how close you were."

Nathan, who had been deep in thought while listening to the conversation, got up and walked over and opened a yellow drawer. Galad's golden eyes opened wide as Nathan showed him a large, tear shaped emerald with a dragon etched in silver into it. He grinned as he placed it in front of Galad as he inquired, "Would this qualify as a dragon's tear?"

All Galad could do was smile a toothy grin and say, "Yes indeed, that should qualify!"

Returning Heroes

When Jason, Gadna and their team of dwarfs returned to the mountain citadel of Clan Krackus they couldn't believe their eyes. The streets were decorated with flags, streamers and banners hanging everywhere they looked. They were greeted as heroes by the people lining the streets, throwing flower petals as the group passed, on their way to see Clan Chief Brackus.

As Jason waved at the rejoicing crowd he spoke to Gunter, "I had hoped we would be the ones to tell Clan Chief Brackus about our success, but it looks like word might have proceeded us." They both chuckled at that.

When the team passed through the gates of Strongheim a messenger was waiting for them. He carried a request that the team join Clan Chief Brackus in his meeting hall as soon as they arrived. As the group paraded into the meeting hall Clan Chief Brackus, Grand Master Bluthe, and

Grand Master Throdon were seated at a long table, with many other dignitaries. Jason nodded at Bluthe when they made eye contact. It was then that Jason noticed the wide grin hiding behind his beard. The large room was overly full of dwarves wanting to congratulate and thank the returning heroes. It was not until then that Jason realized what a big feat he and his team had accomplished.

When Clan Chief Brackus rose from his seat the crowd quieted. "I am pleased to announce that this team was able to do the impossible! They have not only saved us from Jordon's Bane's wrath, but first indications are that the giant spiders and worms are returning to their homes. In special recognition of this feat, we are here to honor the men involved."

At this point he called each of the team members forward. The Clan Chief then presented each of them with one of the highest honors he can bestow, The Medal of Horlick, as well as a pouch of gold for their bravery against the rogue giant, named Hutch.

When all had been honored Clan Chief Brackus got up and approached Jason. The half giant loomed over the short squat dwarf. "Jason, when I first met you, I knew someone incredibly special had arrived in Strongheim, but I didn't believe old Master Bluthe when he claimed you could save us. It was not long before Throdon added his two cents, blathering on about a Divinity Stone and the staff that held it. It didn't look that special to me when I saw it, back then. Now, if you don't keep the damn thing shielded, the glow will damn near blind a man! My Clan and I are in your debt, thanks to you there will be no more giant worms or cave spiders attacking our people. As Clan Chief I grant you any boon in my power to give, now or in the future!" The throng of dwarfs, led by Grand Master Bluthe, gave a cheer that was deafening.

Jason bowed to Brackus, "Lord Brackus, my team worked hard on the plumbing and engineering to move the massive amounts of water, redirecting what normally would have just flowed to the sea. Bluthe's plan worked well, until the quakes dismantled part of the system. My compliments to your smiths and engineers, without their work and planning, the complex machinery they created would not exist. I have watched as your forges and shops made some amazing components needed to complete the task. I had never seen some of your inventions, before coming here. Do you think we could use that same machinery to bring desperately needed water to the desert people? It would be a great act of cooperation and I am sure the Sundowners would appreciate the help! It would be a huge step in bringing the peoples of the lands together."

It was at this point that Jason rose, raised his cup, and toasted,

"To healing the land!" The chant was then picked up by Gadna and the team.

"To healing the land!"

By the third repeat of the chant every dwarf present tipped his cup and recited, **"To healing the land!"** It was not long before the chant could be heard on every street and every home in Strongheim.

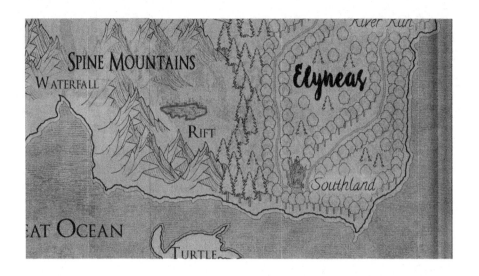

Within the image: SPINE MOUNTAINS, WATERFALL, RIFT, Elyneas, River Run, Southland, AT OCEAN, TURTLE

Leila Meets Azrador

The tinker coach had finally joined the camp that had sprung up near the elvish town of Silverton. Nathan parked the huge multi-colored coach next to the lavish tent that he recognized as Mikiel and Amara's. He was glad to see the elves were also camped a short distance away. Mikiel was pleased to see Nathan and his group had arrived and invited them into the tent, where he was meeting with Lady Leila of Elyneas. She was King Alwin's representative on this expedition. She was also in command of the elf mages and soldiers. After all the introductions were made they each took a seat on a bright colored pillow around a large low table.

Azrador was surprised when he felt an immediate attraction to the beautiful elven female. "Is this seat taken?" He asked as he sat down on an empty pillow next to her. "You will have to excuse my staring; I am from the land of Sulan and have met few full-blooded elves."

Lady Leila was shocked when she heard Azrador's claim that he was full-blooded elf and had never heard of Elyneas or the Green Folk. The two of them quickly found themselves deep in conversation, while the others were being briefed on the lizard like creatures that had been plaguing the area. Azrador and Leila soon discovered they had similar magic talents. Azrador was pleased when he discovered they both could mind speak with animals, one of his favorite forms of magic. Lady Leila bragged to Azrador she had even mind spoke with a gold dragon once, as it flew over her head.

A few weeks ago, he would have called her a liar, but Azrador laughed and said, "That same gold dragon saved me from a cave I was trapped in. His name is Galad, he and a friend of mine gave me a ride here! And let me tell you, it was the ride of my life!"

Lady Leila was beginning to think Azrador was making fun of her, and her mind speaking story, until she heard Galad mind speak to her, "He speaks the truth young one." On hearing the gold dragon in her head Leila was so startled her eyes grew wide. Azrador nodded at Galad, acknowledging the subject of their conversation. He then introduced her to the golden eyed Galad, once again in human form as the dragon.

Lady Leila turned to Galad, "It is my pleasure to meet you Galad. After our brief conversation I had hoped to meet again."

Azrador felt an unfamiliar twinge of jealousy as he watched Lady Leila and the dragon converse.

When her conversation with Galad ended Lady Leila turned and whispered in Azrador's ear, "Please tell me more Azrador, I find your story quite fascinating!"

Azrador felt a strange tickle in the pit of his stomach, when he felt her breath on his ear. He was having some trouble focusing on the plans the others were working on.

Nathan, Amara, and Mikiel were seated across from Galad and Gunter. Swan was grabbing some bread, grapes and cheese from a platter that had been laid out. The discussion had moved from the lizard like creatures, to how to deal with the Temporal Rift itself. Galad explained what they had learned from the ancient scroll from his library. He then explained they already had the Eye of Illusion, and the Dragon's tear in their possession, so all that remained was to find the Sacred Sun Medallion, the Moon Stone, and the Dwarven Shield. Galad then showed the group drawings of the required items.

When Nathan saw the drawing of the Shield of Torevir he recognized it instantly. "Gunter and I had that shield in our possession! We just turned it over to Lord Brackus of Clan Krackus. We found it and the Eye of Illusion on an excursion into what was left of Ruby Falls after King Ferdinand left it in ruins. That is how we acquired the Eye of Illusion. It was attached to a bracket on the inside of the Shield of Torevir. It was guarded by a stone golem that appeared unbeatable. The room was strewn with the bodies of a dozen mages that it had killed. If it hadn't been for Azrador, the thing would have killed both Gunter and me. He and Gunter figured out that only a full-blooded elf could command the golem. Turns out they were right. Azrador was able to disarm the golem, so we could continue our search.

Lady Leila suddenly became interested in their conversation. "Did you say Azrador disabled a stone golem?" Turning back to Azrador she asked, "How did you disarm a stone golem Azrador? That must have been frightening!"

Trying to focus on the task at hand, Azrador explained further, "Gunter and I had translated an old elvish inscription we found. It disclosed that only a full-blooded elf could disarm the golem guarding the magic artifacts in the room. After I did that, we were able to complete our search. Most of the people of Sulan and Autry don't realize that a large number of the magic artifacts we retrieved at Ruby Falls were used to defeat ArchMage Ibis and the Silver Tower. That is also where we found the Shield of Torevir and The Eye of Illusion. We also found an old scroll that described a series of tunnels that go under the Emerald Sea. We entered those tunnels at Ozgood's Lighthouse, an old lighthouse on the northern most point of Balzar. Those tunnels went under the water, in several directions. One of them led to an island, shrouded in mist. On Misty Island we found an old garden that contained several marble statues. At first, we didn't see anything unusual about them, but when we looked closer, we realized the some of the sculptures looked too familiar. There was a tinker, a male elf, a female elf, a sundowner, and a female warrior holding a trident, anyone care to guess who that was supposed to be. On the same island we discovered an underground chamber, where we found the Dragon's Tear. I also found this ring!" Azrador said, as he showed Leila the ring with the emerald stones that formed a tree. "Gunter is an enchanter and claims he recognizes it from some legends of old. He called it the Ring of the Forest. I haven't gotten a chance to try using it yet."

When Azrador sat back down Lady Leila picked up their conversation, "That is fascinating Azrador. It is such good fortune that your group has already obtained some of the items needed. Do you know any more about this Moon Stone, Galad, that you spoke of? What does it look like? How big is it? And what color is it"

Galad pointed to the picture drawn on the scroll. "From what I translated from the script, the Moon Stone is a huge pearl, half black, half white, looking somewhat like a half moon. It is said it can change the tides and the direction of the flow of waterways. I think Swan and I should scour the outer islands, to see if any of the primitives might have seen it, or better yet have it."

Leila got up from her pillow and walked around the table to get a better look at what the Moon Stone looked like. Her grandfather, Lord Bretta, would probably have heard of it. He was strong in water magic and as a younger man, had created most of the irrigation systems used on farms in Elyneas. He was also a historian and had lived a long time, even for an elf. Looking up from the scroll she states, "My

Grandfather, Lord Bretta, is a senior advisor to King Alwin, I will send a messenger, seeking any knowledge he may have of this Moon Stone, or anything else that may prove useful." Leila added.

Amara looked at Mikiel, wondering if it was time to reveal what she had learned of the situation after meeting the dead High Priestess, Danica.

She caught Mikiel's eye, wanting to know if he thought now was the right time. Instinctively Mikiel knew what his twin sister was asking and nodded yes.

Taking a deep breath Amara stood, "Not long-ago Mikiel and I boarded Swift, and ventured into the northern Scarlet Desert, searching for a place I had seen in a foretelling. In the foretelling I learned of an ancient, floating city, known as Bantez. It was located in the stormy area we know as The Drifting Sands, where it is known to have unending sandstorms. The people of the City of Bantez were known as the Da Nang. They were powerful wizards that had created magic powerful enough to keep the city floating and rotating, above the storms. That magic required recharging the artifact that powered the city, annually. To keep the balance, and not give the wizards full and total control, the cities High Priestess was the only one able to read the Book of Blessings, the book that contained the Spell of Renewal. Someone, probably a renegade mage that had no clue to what he was doing, stabbed the High Priestess, in her bed. Without her, there was no one that could recharge the magic artifact, so the city crashed to the ground killing them all. Bantez is now buried in the sand of The Drifting Sands."

Gunter, who had been listening intently to the exotic, volet eyed Amara stated. "Sounds like a bit of a legend, rather than real don't you think?" Gunter was surprised to find himself strangely attracted to the exotic looking woman from the desert.

Understanding the handsome mage's skepticism Amara smiled as she reached into her pack, pulling out an object and held it up for all to see. "This, my friends, is the Sacred Sun Medallion." She held up her other hand and explained, "these are mana stones. They are what must be used to power the Sacred Sun Medallions magic. Most importantly I have the Book of Blessings. I know I can power the Sacred Sun Stone because I have the ability to read it."

Gunter whistled at the beauty of the medallion, but he was even more interested in the mana stones. "What an amazing discovery and very timely don't you think? Have you communicated directly with this High Priestess's spirit?"

Amara was reluctant to reveal the truth to Gunter, afraid it might scare him off, like most others. Getting another reassuring nod from Mikiel she answered. "Yes, in fact she comes to me almost every night in my sleep. She says a Demon in the underworld named Tassarion is responsible for this Temporal Rift. He is draining magic and life from this world, to make a world of his own. Danica, the High Priestess, says he is getting more powerful by the day, and we must hurry! The Book of Blessing states when we find the Moon Stone, we are to power it with the mana stones, like Danica did with the Sun Medallion, before using it."

Gunter, who was finding this desert dweller more interesting by the minute, added, "Thanks to you and Mikiel, we have found another piece of this crazy puzzle, and you, with the ability to read the Book that prescribes the magic needed to power these powerful artifacts." Gunter didn't say it, but it felt like their meeting was destined.

Nathan who had mostly listened without commenting stood. "I would like to add that I believe we are destined to be on this path. Only destiny could propel these events and bring so many different people, from so many locations together. Each providing a piece of the puzzle."

The odd group that found itself working together debated well into the evening, trying to decide what their next step should be.

Galad made the offer that he and Swan would fly

to Strongheim and recover the Shield of Torevir from the dwarfs. "It is good to know where it is. Swan and I will get to Strongheim quicker that any of you can. Besides when a dragon makes a request it can be very difficult to say no. The sooner we can gather all the pieces the less the Rift will have grown."

Gunter warned Swan and Galad, "The dwarfs may not care to cooperate with our plan, since they just got the shield back! It really seemed to mean a lot to them." Gunter added. "They seemed awful happy to get it."

Nathan interjected, "I sure hope they will." Nathan then turned to address Galad, "How is this rod to be made? Once we have collected all the required items how are we to attach them to it?"

Galad looked at Nathan, a little surprised at the question, "It is the old recipe Nathan, you know it. It's the recipe that you shared with that young blacksmith friend of yours. I believe his name is Jason. That's the recipe he used to create Swan's trident. Surely Nathan, you must be capable of creating it!" Galad demanded.

Nathan shook his head, "No that's where you are wrong Galad; I gave him the recipe, but none other than he can forge the required metals together. Before Jason it had been centuries since anyone has seen, let alone made anything using that recipe. We will need him to complete the rod. We are in luck though, last I knew Jason was with the dwarfs in Strongheim, helping with some civil engineering project they had going on." Nathan explained.

Galad got up from the pillow he was seated on and concluded with, "It is settled then! Swan and I shall fly to the dwarven City of Strongheim and retrieve this half giant named Jason and the Shield of Torevir."

Everyone followed Swan and Galad outside where she gave Nathan and Gunter one last hug. She and Galad then walked hand in hand into a large field near the camp where Galad found the space he needed to transform into a full-grown golden dragon. They all watched, awestruck, as Swan climbed aboard, strapping herself into her saddle. In an instant hey took flight, leaving Silverton and all of Elyneas behind.

Leila and Azrador watched in awe as the dragon took flight, soaring over the valley outside of Silverton. The pair silently watched as the dragon disappeared over the horizon before Leila spoke. "A Gold Dragon and his rider, who would have believed it. I have heard tales all my life and thought they were just a legend."

Turning her attention back to Azrador she inquired, "Looks like we have some time on our hands. Would you like to see the Temporal Rift and maybe some of the lizardmen? I am to lead a scouting party today. I need to check the wards; they are what is keeping the lizardmen contained. The last time I was there I tried to communicate with them, both dead and alive, but had no luck. We also killed a few that had either slipped out of the wards or were outside of the range of the wards when implemented. "Who knows, maybe we will get a chance for you to test out that ring. You say it is called the Ring of the Forest? I wonder if it effects trees themselves?"

Flattered at Leila's invitation he quickly answered, "Sure! I would love to get a look at these foreign lizard creatures, and the Temporal Rift too for that matter. It all seems odd don't you think? If Amara is correct, a demon is responsible for creating this Temporal Rift and is transferring life and magic from here to somewhere else. Did a demon really create such a thing? You know Galad believes this whole thing has happened here before. He says that is why there is a scroll that instructs us on how to stop it."

Azrador grabbed Leilas hand and exclaimed, "Let's go! On our way to the wards, we can try using my ring on one of those small trees."

Leila smiled as she followed the arrogant, handsome elf to the stables to get their mounts.

Clan Krackus

Swan and Galad were pleased the flight over the desert, enroute to the dwarven stronghold of Strongheim, was uneventful. Along the way, Swan noticed the land was much greener than her first reconnaissance of the Scarlet Desert. Galad pointed out that they had seen no sign of the menacing sand worms that had been terrorizing the caravans of the Sundowner Tribe. Word had spread of the golden dragon and his rider, so when they flew over several caravans the travelers waved to them instead of cowering in fear.

Galad caused quite the commotion when he and Swan landed, just outside the gates of Strongheim. At first the guards were flustered, but they quickly recovered their composer when Galad mind spoke to them. He asked them strongly, "There is no need for you to be afraid. If you would, please announce our arrival to Clan Chief Brackus. We demand an audience with him, at once. We would also like to speak with the blacksmith called Jason!" Galad raised his chin and spewed dragon fire into the air as encouragement for a quick response.

Swan mind spoke to Galad, so no one heard her ask, as she dismounted, "Was that really necessary? I think most of them crapped their collective pants. They have never seen a dragon fly, much less land right in front of them!" Swan chuckled as she stated, "I do have to admit the looks on their faces was priceless."

Galad understood her concern but did not agree with her. "It probably was not necessary, but I want to leave a lasting impression, so they remember seeing one! Dragons are not known to be patient with humans, as you know. These dwarfs don't need to know that I happen to be the exception to that rule!" Galad said in mind speak.

Inside the Clan stronghold the dwarfs were still celebrating Jason and his team's victory in eliminating Jordan's Bane. They had been making toasts to the team that had stopped the volcano all night and by now everyone was quite drunk. When Grantis told Clan Chief Brackus about the demand for his and Jason's immediate attention he laughed and slapped Grantis on the back. "That's a good one Grantis! You must have had too much to drink if you are seeing dragons. Who gets credit for the joke?" Brackus asked, laughing in his cup of ale. "Sure, a dragon was knocking on their door!"

Brackus went back to drinking and the celebration until a second messenger, wearing a still smoking burnt cap was able to convince Brackus to go outside and see this so-called dragon. As they headed for the city gates Brackus asked Grantis, "who shall I thank for such surprising entertainment?" Grantis just shook his head, unsure what to say.

Everyone in the hall, that was not too drunk to walk followed, laughing at the joke. Staggering outside to the entrance, the drunk revelers could hardly believe their eyes! Standing in front of their citadel was a giant golden dragon.

Upon seeing this was no joke, many of the dwarfs hung back. Not Jason though, he easily pushed his way through the crowd and stood next to Brackus. When he got to the front of the crowd, the first thing he saw was Swan, standing next to the golden dragon. Jason stepped forward as Swan spotted him, running to give him a hug. Galad, as usual, growled at the affection Swan was giving Jason.

Swan turned to Galad, and mind spoke, "Stop that! This man is an old friend! He is the maker of my trident, and no threat to you, relax! I know I told you we have known each other a long time. He is one of only a few that have heard me play the flute and fly with me in a vision."

When Swan turned her attention back to Jason Galad took a hard look at the half man half giant that Jason had grown into. Galad could see the strong magic aura surrounding Jason, that no one else had seen. Galad saw he had a strong aura of blue from the magical spectrum. When Galad spotted the hooded staff Jason held, he became quite subdued. Swan proceeded to introduce Jason to Galad and then went on to explain their dilemma with the Temporal Rift in Elyneas. Knowing Jason had created the marvel that was Swan's trident and knowing that the Master Smith would be needed to create the Celestial Rod, forced Galad to take more stock of this young giant. Jason's abilities at such a youthful age were impressive, even to Galad. It was not long before Brackus came marching up behind Jason, guarded by fifty clansmen guards.

Feeling fairly confident he was safe for the moment Brackus approached the dragon, "Greetings Sir Dragon! What brings you to our door?" Brackus asked in a respectful tone of voice. After all, who knew what wrath a gold dragon could have? Of course, like everyone else, growing up he had been taught that all the dragons had been dead for centuries.

Galad, using mind speak replied, "Lord Brackus we have no time to waste. I need a certain shield that I believe you possess. A short time ago a tinker that goes by the name of Nathan, delivered the Shield of Torevir to you. I demand you deliver it to me immediately! A Temporal Rift in Elyneas is leeching magic and life from the land and its reach is growing, as it consumes all life around it. There are also large lizards exiting from the cracked ground the Rift is causing. These lizardmen are killing any living thing they come across. I anticipate if it is not stopped, it will eventually consume everyone's lands. The Shield of Torevir is essential to stopping the anomaly, as are several other items, including the Moon Stone. Perhaps you have heard of it also?"

Taken aback by the request Brackus responded, "The Shield is an ancient artifact of our clan, in fact it bears the Sigil of Clan Krackus. It was stolen from us long ago, and you are correct Nathan the tinker recently returned it to us. I shall not see it leave here again!" Brackus spoke with authority.

Hearing the strong denial by the Clan Chief, Swan turned to Jason and said, "We must have the shield, Jason! Nathan already has some of the artifacts we need. He, Gunter and Azrador have found the Eye of Illusion, and the Dragon's Tear. Amara, sister of Sultan Willem of the Sundown tribe, found the Sacred Sun Medallion in an ancient city in the north of the desert. All we are missing is the Shield of Torevir and the Moon Stone. The shield is necessary to protect the person who will close the Temporal Rift by throwing the Celestial Rod into the anomaly. Without its protection that person will be killed, or so the ancient scroll says."

Swan suddenly noticed Jason was holding a staff instead of his mace. "Jason where is Night Star? I have never known you to not have it close by. I know I have never seen you with a mages staff!"

Jason looked at the staff before answering Swan, "This is the staff I made for Jade. It holds the Divinity Stone provided by the dead ArchMage Ibis. Before Jade died, she enchanted the staff, which proved helpful when we battled trolls and ogres in the Sky Mountains, but she didn't know how to activate the Divinity Stone. When I arrived here, looking for Nathan, I met a Grand Master Smith and Armorer named Bluthe. He has been teaching me ever since. The mechanical marvels the dwarfs have is amazing. They have running water to every home! Something they call plumbing brings water to them and takes waste away. Sometime, when we have time to sit and visit, I will tell you more about it. Getting back to the staff, I was having dinner with an old dwarven wizard named Throdon. He was curious about Night Star and quizzed me about it quite thoroughly. When I explained I had created it he wanted to know if I had made any other weapons. When I showed him the staff, the old dwarf almost had a stroke. Throdon, who is quite wise and very skilled in magic knew how to activate the Divinity Stone that crowns the staff. Before he would activate the stone, I had to prove myself, in his words, worthy. He also made me promise to only use the staff to heal the land. Throdon believes I got my magic from my mother, who may have been what he called a "traveler"."

Galad had been listening intently to Jason as he spoke of his mother and now understood the blue aura he had observed around the half giant. He spoke in Jason's mind, "If your mother was a traveler, you may have indeed inherited her powerful magic. From tomes and scrolls I have read; travelers were known to grow stronger with age. A strong traveler could create portals to other worlds. I recognize the Divinity Stone in your staff because I am the one that obtained it for ArchMage Ibis, so many years ago. That is something I have been ashamed of ever since I realized the deception Ibis had used to obtain it. You see the stone was guarded by a giant that had pledged to protect the Divinity Stone with his life. It was a brutal battle, and I was seriously wounded, but in the end, I prevailed over the giant. Did you know the Divinity Stone was used in the very beginning to calm the land? According to the ancient legends it is one of the most powerful artifacts ever created. Jason, since you are the staff's creator and have awakened the stone, it will only fully respond to you. You may lend it to another magic user for some purpose, but they will not be able to command the Divinity Stone. They may access the enchantments that your mage friend added to the metal, but you are the only one that may draw the full power of the staff and stone. It is extremely powerful magic, and you must practice prudence when using it."

Lord Brackus stepped forward and addressed the Dragon. "Sir Dragon, I must deny your request. I cannot allow the Shield of Torevir to be taken, having just regained it. You will have to find another way!"

When Galad heard the Clan Chief's response he glanced at Swan, who gave him a slight nod of the head. Galad then raised his chin and breathed dragon fire into the air. Using his loudest mind speak voice he growled at Brackus, "Wrong Answer dwarf! How many of your kin shall I feast on first!" Showing his huge sharp teeth.

Jason could tell something was going wrong in the conversation between Galad and Brackus. He felt that the chance of violence was not far off. Galad had made it clear to Brackus that the shield was necessary for them to succeed in closing this Temporal Rift. He was not happy that Brackus was being obstinate by not agreeing.

Jason turned to Brackus, towering over the dwarf clan chief, "Lord Brackus, you offered me a boon, for our success in closing the volcano. I now ask that you grant that boon by allowing me the use of the Shield of Torevir. I swear by my giant blood the Shield of Torevir will be returned to Clan Krakus when the task of closing the Temporal Rift is done!"

Brackus frowned as he stood with his fists doubled up at his side, angry with Jason's request. After he stomped a circle around Jason he looked up at the giant and conceded, "Alright dag nab it, you got me between a rock and a hard space. Jason, I gave you a boon and as Chief of Clan Krakus I will honor that promise, on the condition that only you shall carry it! You alone will be responsible for our shield and its return. Do not return without it for you will not be welcome here without it!" Brackus turned and stomped back into the mountain citadel.

They all watched as the dwarf, accompanied by Gadna passed through the gates, back into Strongheim. Swan turned back to Jason. "Thank you for helping us, Jason, we need both you and the shield to accomplish the arduous task ahead of us! Our quest now moves to finding the Moon Stone." Swan said patting his shoulder.

Galad mind spoke to Swan, after looking over Jason's size and weight. "You really don't expect me to carry that giant, do you? He is huge and I presume heavy!" Swan chuckled knowing he would have to do just that.

Gadna returned shortly, carrying the huge shield, barely keeping it from dragging the ground. At one point his beard got caught in it and he looked like he would trip. Handing the shield to Jason he asked, "please be careful with-it Jason. I have never seen Brackus so angry. Losing the shield after just having it returned after all these years has upset today's celebration." Jason took the shield like it weighed nothing and strapped it to his back. Taking a long look at the gold dragon's size and girth he realized what an impressive beast he was. Jason's only flying experience was in a vision that Swan had shared with him. In the vision they were flying on the back of Swan's condor, Prism. Turning to Swan, Jason asked, "Where is Prism, Swan? How did you come to ride a dragon?"

Swan gave a deep sigh. "It's a long sad story Jason. I will tell it to you while we travel to Elyneas. Galad is happy to fly us there, aren't you Galad?" Swan asked in a syrupy sweet tone.

Galad growled at Swans question and then mind spoke to Jason, "I appreciate your help young giant. I will try to make it a smooth journey, but after we get airborne it may take me a few moments to get used to the additional weight of a second rider. There is but one saddle so you will have to sit between the spines on my back and hang on!"

Swan quickly climbed up the dragon's front legs onto her saddle, Jason followed slower, picking his way over the dragon's shoulder and up on its back. Eventually reaching an area where he thought he could fit between the large spikes on the dragon's spine. It was not comfortable, but Galad didn't give him much time to think about it before he jumped into the air. With a sharp bank to the right, that almost knocked Jason off, Galad turned toward the mountain. Jason had to admit it was much smoother than he remembered in Swan's vision and the view was just as impressive as he remembered, looking at the mountains they flew over, before the heat of the desert reached them. Soon all he could see was sand as Galad fell into a rhythmic wing beat. After several hours of flying south, they started to see green spaces in the desert. He could also see several caravans of desert travelers, all heading in the same direction. When they flew over the new Mystery Waters where the multi-colored tents surrounded the lake and river Jason smiled at all the bright colors. He also saw palm trees and tall grasses swaying in the breeze. The air was noticeably cooler as they flew over the lake. Before long they were flying over the mountains again. Jason felt a peace fall over him, as he thought of the giants and his father Garth. It seemed so long since he had seen him. So much had happened to the world in that time.

As they traveled, Swan explained what had happened to Prism. She then went on to describe how her love, Markus and Firefly, his condor and Prism's mate had been murdered by Ibis. She told the story of meeting the golden dragon and him flying her off to his lair before she knew he could transform to human form. She explained she would have died had Galad not healed her. Jason was stunned beyond words when he learned that Galad could assume human form.

Swan continued her story. She told Jason of the things she and Galad had in common, like their love of flying. She further explained how Ibis had captured Galad and used his magic for over one-hundred years.

Galad added to the story in mind speak, "From what I have read in the ancient scrolls in my library, I believe the cursed tinker weapons thrown into the volcano released a lot of black magic energy. That black energy had built up in those weapons over centuries of dastardly use from one generation to the next. Those weapons caused corruption in all that handled them. My breaking free of my bonds disconnected the magic drain Ibis used to power his magic wards protecting the Tower. This made him and the tower vulnerable. Ibis was not expecting me to arrive, in fact he had an incredibly surprised look on his face when I breathed dragon fire on him, melting him and the Silver Tower. I believe the black magic Ibis's death released and the cursed weapons dropped in the volcano may have somehow empowered a demon, named Tassarion, to open the Rift we are enroute to see." Galad gained an updraft after clearing the Spine Mountains and when he banked south the scenery changed to lush green forests. Jason was impressed as they flew over the beautiful scenery, of lakes and glens and more forest, until they were circling an area outside of a town. There were dozens of multi-colored tents around the small town. It was then that Jason spotted the familiar tinker coach. Jason couldn't wait to tell the tinker all he had seen and learned.

Nathan was waiting outside the coach when they landed. Jason and Swan quickly hopped down from Galad's back and made their way to Nathan, who was grinning from ear to ear. "Jason my boy, you have grown again since last I saw you!" Nathan reached out and shook the huge hand as it was extended in friendship. Galad had transformed to human form and joined the group outside the tinker coach.

Jason turned to Galad, surprised by the golden eyes. "Thank you Galad for the amazing ride. I know I must have made it more of a burden than just flying with Swan." Jason said still staring at the golden eyes.

Ignoring Jason's stares Galad stated, "Swan is the first person I allowed on my back. Then Azrador needed saving and now you are the third. You need to understand I am not an animal of burden, but I do make exceptions. Especially if Swan asks me nicely. But don't misunderstand, I never mind giving her a ride! She has a way of talking me into things even I am surprised at,"

It was not long before Nathan noticed Jason holding a staff with a hood over it. He had the Shield of Torevir strapped over one shoulder and the staff in the other hand. Nathan was shocked at how natural Jason looked holding the staff, rather than his mace, Night Star. Now he looked exactly like the statue on Misty Island. Swan couldn't wait to tell Nathan how Jason had healed Jordon's Bane and the land around it using the Staff. Nathan invited them all into the coach where Gunter was just putting out some snacks and tea. Swan gave Gunter a hug and then said, "Sit down Gunter you aren't going to believe what Jason did to our volcano!" A vigorous story telling ensued.

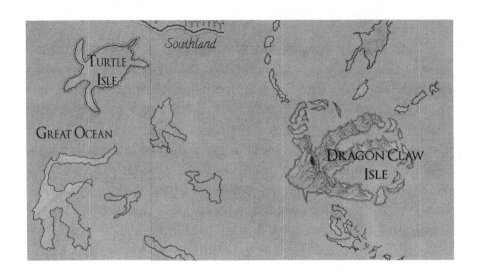

The Dragon's Tear

Swan and Galad had flown back to his lair on Dragon Claw Ilse so they could comb through his massive library again. He wanted to search for any information that might be helpful in fighting the lizard creatures as well as how to close the Temporal Rift. Digging in a chest full of old manuscripts Galad found an old text that talked about portals and how a traveler could open and close them. That made him consider if Amara was correct, and this was a Temporal Rift to the underworld or another world entirely. He began to wonder who was draining this lands magic, on purpose. He hoped this didn't mean the beginning of a war with other creatures. So far, the only creatures seen coming through the Temporal Rift were the large green lizards.

Swan was looking through some scrolls on elixirs and antidotes, hoping to find a cure for the poison the lizardmen spit, but hadn't come across anything useful yet. Swan pulled another scroll from the cubby and rolled it out. She felt a little guilty leaving Nathan, Jason, and Gunter behind, but she couldn't be of much use helping the blacksmith create the rod, or the placement of the artifacts. She thought it seemed farfetched that all these things had to be done to close the damn Temporal Rift. Before they left camp the last report stated the dead zone around the Rift had doubled in area, so it was still growing. She hoped Nathan, Jason and Gunter were safe. She and Galad had been hard at it, searching for clues for many hours when Swan walked over to Galad and kissed him. "We have been at this for hours, why don't we go take a bath and let our brains rest for a bit!"

Galad stood up from his chair and responded with a sly smile, "You don't have to ask me twice anytime it comes to seeing you naked!" He then picked Swan up in his muscular arms and said with a deep chuckle, "Let's go get clean!"

Several hours later as they lay in each other's arms in their giant bed Swan asked, "Galad do you believe in destiny or that we make our own way?" He rolled onto his side looking into her eyes with those golden eyes, "I believe we make our own destiny through the choices we make, good or bad. I made a bad choice years ago when I helped Ibis obtain the Divinity Stone that Jason now controls. I had to kill a noble giant to get it for Ibis. I have regretted it for many years. It now appears, that mistake is what allowed the Stone to fall into Jason's hands. He in turn used it to eliminate the volcano that was causing so much havoc. Ibis trapping me in a stasis spell was due to my own bad choice, that's what I got for trusting him. That bad choice led me in revenge against Ibis, thus finding you, trying to kill the same wicked guy. Which allowed me to know and fall in love with you. Our bond grows stronger as dragon and rider each day." Galad kissed Swan passionately and she returned his enthusiasm.

The next day Galad came across a section of text in an old manuscript that explained how the Dragon's Tear came about. The text claimed Argos, a Grand Wizard, captured

Aziris, the last green dragon. Argos demanded to know the whereabouts of Aziris' lair and hoard. The dragon swore he would never reveal his lair's location to the wizard and instead permanently transformed into the large emerald known as the Dragon's Tear. The Tear has a silver lined engraving in the likeness of Aziris on its face and contains all his magic. Galad laughed at the idea, thinking it absurd, but after further consideration, decided it was no more absurd than other recent events. That story was the only mention of the remarkable gem he came across.

That tale was as strange as a scroll he read earlier in the day describing the tools used in crafting the landscape of the world. Although at least that scroll mentioned the Moon Stone being used for setting the tides of the world's bodies of water. Unfortunately, the scroll did not say where to find it or where it was last seen.

After a week of searching the lair library, and not finding out much more, Swan and Galad decided to head back to Silverton. They decided to find Jason and see if they could use Galad's help in smelting the ore. After all dragon fire could melt anything.

Once they were in the air Swan reveled in the feeling of the freedom of flight that she so loved. Galad was finding he liked having this beautiful warrior as a rider and was proud to claim her. He thought the two of them made an exceptional pair, especially if they could help right the world and restore its beauty and magic.

The pair flew north, from Dragon's Claw Isle, quickly reaching the coast. It wasn't long before they flew over the Spine Mountains and Galad was banking right, turning to the east, as they spotted the colorful tents of the Sundowners camped around Mystery Waters. The green area had quadrupled its size since their last fly over. The area was becoming a lush oasis, with palm trees and tall grasses waving in the breeze. The area was attracting more of the tribe daily so there were many more tents visible than their last visit. As they flew east, they passed over the Spine Mountains again, flying over the lush, forested land of the Green Folk lands. Galad banked to the south, and they flew along the mountain chain until they spotted the town of Silverton on the horizon. Galad landed in a field just a short distance from the tinker coach that was parked next to Mikiel's large colorful tent.

As usual their arrival caused quite a stir in the encampment, until Galad transformed to his human form. He and Swan joined Nathan in Mikiel's tent.

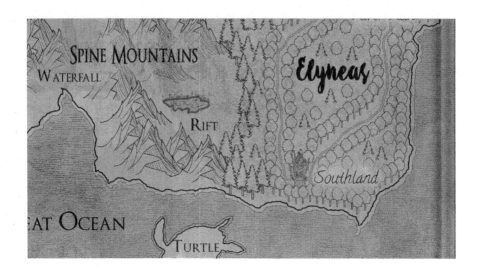

News of the Moon Stone

Azrador accompanied Leila and her party of elves out to the area where the wards had been set to keep the lizard creatures contained. The terrain changed from lush green forest and foliage to the brown and grey cracked ground that had been reported. They were attacked by three of the large lizardmen when they jumped the party's lead archers. Two of the archers were killed before they could get off a shot. Two others were paralyzed by the spitting lizards but were saved when Leila cast lightning on the monsters. Azrador tried to mind speak to the last lizard coming out from a behind a rock. It was standing on its hind legs and managed to spit on the lead horse. The horse dropped in its tracks almost instantly, throwing its rider to the ground. Azrador asked the creature why it was here attacking people. Its only response was, "Hungry, Hungry, kill, kill, you die!" After hearing that, Azrador knocked one of his deadly arrows and planted it between the creature's eyes. Dropping it to the ground, dead.

Impressed with what she just witnessed Leila commented, "That was impressive, so far only crossbows have been effective in killing those creatures! That is quite the bow you have there!"

Azrador puffed up his chest a little as he responded, "The creature would only answer with hungry, hungry, kill, kill. You die! I didn't want the creature to be correct. I thought mind speak might communicate with them." Azrador explained.

Leila shook her head as she replied. "Well at least you got a response from them, I have tried several times and got nothing. Killing them before they kill or paralyze someone is best!"

Azrador was fascinated with the change in the terrain as they neared the Rift. He could see the Temporal Rift that was from the underworld, spinning in the distance. There were mountains to its north and west, with the Great Ocean to the south. He thought it was at least trapped here for the time being. The group rode around the vicinity checking the wards that were containing the lizard creatures. Azrador could see many more of the creatures coming out of the ground as they got closer to the Temporal Rift. When Leila was satisfied with her inspection they headed back to the camp outside Silverton.

Azrador was quite taken with this elven beauty. She was smart and talented, and he couldn't get enough time with her. They bantered back and forth on the journey back to camp like they had known each other their whole lives.

When the party entered camp, a messenger was waiting for Lady Leila. She invited Azrador into her tent for refreshments while she read the message. Azrador was glad to see at least the elves used normal furniture; he wouldn't have to sit on the floor or a pillow. A lovely elf female brought wine, cheese, bread, and honey while Leila read the message.

She smiled after reading the message while taking a sip of the wine. "My grandfather knows of this Moon Stone we search for. He found a mention of it in an old script. It told of its use in setting the cycle of the tides that keep our land and waters stable. The last mention he found for it was in an incredibly old manuscript that gave its last known location as the Turtle Iles. However, he mentions that the Turtle Isles are but a ruin now and have been for over a hundred years. Grandfather doubts little would be found there but has no other clues. He will send more messages if he finds anything else of interest."

Azrador asked, "Where are these Turtle Iles located and how do we get there? I have never heard of them." He then took a piece of cheese and popped it into his mouth. "It's not a lot to go on, but that's all we have right now."

Leila took a bite of cheese before stating, "I have never been there, but it is in the southern Great Ocean. We can ride to the city of Southland and commandeer a ship to get us there. I have a writ from King Alwin that allows me to do whatever I deem necessary to end this anomaly. Do you think it is worth the trip? They are pretty skimpy clues?"

Azrador thought a moment before replying, "Nathan, Gunter, and I had pretty skimpy clues that led us to the tunnels under Ozgood's lighthouse. Those tunnels were created by giant worms that tunnel through rock and leave precious stones behind them as waste. We encountered several of the beasts on the trip, but it led us to a mist covered island that contained the Dragon Tear and this, the Ring of the Forest I wear. So sometimes you have to follow the clues you are given, no matter how small!" Azrador took a sip of his wine.

Lady Leila rose from her seat and approached Azrador. "It's decided then, in the morning we leave for Southland." Looking deep into his eyes she asked, "Azrador, would you like to stay and have dinner with me? I have so enjoyed your company today. I think we still have much to discover about each other."

Azrador felt that odd feeling in his stomach again when he answered. "I would be delighted to spend more time with you Leila. I too have enjoyed our day together! I will allow you to freshen up for dinner while I report our day to Nathan and Gunter. I will inform them of our decision to leave for the Turtle Isle in the morning and of our hope for finding the Moon Stone there."

As Azrador left her tent Leila found herself staring at the backside of this elf. She had not been attracted to a man in an awfully long time. She thought to herself, "This one is special!" She quickly ordered a bath drawn and clothes laid out for the evening. Leila instructed her handmaid what she wanted served for dinner before retreating to a relaxing hot bath. With magic, even in the wilds you could have some creature comforts. Leila melted into the fragrant bath, soothing her sore muscles after the day riding on horseback. She couldn't stop her thoughts from turning to the dashing young Ranger Mage and what the evening might bring.

When Azrador reached the tinker coach he found Nathan, Gunter, Swan and Galad sitting around the table talking. Jason, the giant, stood nearby looking imposing as always. He was holding a black staff that Azrador could feel pulsing with magic. He took notice of the blue aura surrounding the young giant.

The group was discussing the elements needed to construct the Celestial Rod that would close the Temporal Rift. Jason would be required to construct the actual rod, which would be made by combining iberium and palladium, to make adamantine. Once that task is complete, he will need to follow the specifications in the ancient scroll that Galad has provided. Fortunately, Jason still had some of both kinds of ore stashed in his magic pack. Once the rod was created, Nathan would use his enchanting and goldsmith talents to mount the artifacts on the rod, in the correct order and spacing. They were still missing the Moon Stone but had all the other needed artifacts. That is where Azrador jumped in and explained his day with the Lady Leila and her party of elves. He described their encounter with the lizard creatures and how powerful their paralyzing venom was. Gunter asked whether he had collected a sample and was not happy that Azrador had failed to obtain a sample. He did however mention one of the creatures had been returned on one of the horses for further inspection. Gunter thought he might find a way to reverse the venom if he had a sample and was anxious to examine the creature.

Azrador continued with his narration, he told them about the message from Leila's Grandfather, and about their planned departure for the Turtle Isle in the morning. Galad dismissed the idea and said he had flown over the area numerous times and all that was there was rubble. The conversation continued until Azrador realized he was late for dinner with Leila and hurried off to her tent.

When Azrador arrived, the table was set with fine China and linens. Candles were lit all around the large luxurious tent. Lady Leila was dressed in a shimmery silk gown of royal blue with matching slippers. Her hair was braided with small blue flowers threaded into it and she had donned an alluring perfume for the occasion. Azrador glanced at his ranger clothes and felt more than a little under dressed when he saw the lovely elf in her beautiful gown. He was wearing the same dark green leathers that a Ranger Mage usually wore. It had not occurred to him that he should have changed clothes for dinner, not that he had anything else to wear. Next time, if there is a next time, he will check with Nathan, maybe he has something more appropriate. At least he had left his bow and quiver behind, but still carried his Blazeguard in its sheath.

After complimenting Leila on her appearance Azrador was seated across from her while dinner was served. The main course was a delicious meat pie in heavy gravy with fresh dark bread that was still warm. Azrador chuckled when he saw the wine being served was a light white vintage bottled by the Heavenly Slope Vineyard. After the heavy meal they had a small cake with cinnamon and sugar crumbles on top, with coffee, as a dessert. The conversation had stayed light while the servants were present, but after they were left alone, with another bottle of the wine, they moved to a padded sofa. After Azrador was seated, Leila smiled into his eyes and took the bold move of sitting on his lap, wrapping her arms around his neck. "I have been wanting to do this all day." She whispered in a sexy voice, before kissing him firmly on the lips. The kiss stirred desires in Azrador that he had not had in many years, if ever. He returned the passion with much enthusiasm. Soon both their passions were lit, and they adjourned to Leila's private bedroom.

Turtle Isle

The next morning, when Azrador woke in a strange tent it took him a moment to realize he was still holding Leila in his arms, as she slept against his chest. What a night they had. Azrador did not want to wake the sleeping beauty, so he lay there reflecting on the particulars of the previous evening when he felt Leila stir. She kissed him passionately, before rising from the bed, naked. Azrador stayed in the bed and admired what a beautiful, graceful creature he was looking at. She casually slipped on a robe as she explained, "I will order our breakfast, it will be served after I bathe and dress."

He watched her walk out of the room, into another room of the huge tent. Azrador again replayed the highlights of the previous evening before rising. He dressed and returned to the table where they had dinner the night before. A servant brought him hot tea and sesame cakes with honey and butter for breakfast. There also was a plate of sausages already on the table. Leila joined him before he finished his first cup of tea.

This morning she was dressed in dark green leathers and boots, remarkably similar to what Azrador was wearing. She wore her long hair in a tight braid with several silver butterflies threaded through it. She was smiling broadly as she entered the room, kissing Azrador gently, before sitting down at the table next to him. Leila quickly loaded a plate with several sausages as the server brought a platter of fried potatoes. She added a large scoop of them to her plate and a cake smothered in honey. After the server left the room, she gave him a sly smile and said, "I seemed to have worked up an appetite last night, how about you?"

Azrador was so surprised at her directness he choked on the cake he had just taken a bite of. Quickly recovering he answered, "Yes, I do seem to be a bit famished!" He proceeded to load a plate of his own with the sausages and fried potatoes. After they both wolfed down their breakfast Leila ordered provisions be gathered for them and horses be saddled. She also requested four men as an escort to accompany them in case they ran into trouble along the way to Southland.

When they arrived at the stable a groom was holding the reins of Ebony, Leila's jet-black horse. She approached the proud stallion, giving him a pat on his neck as the tall black beauty nuzzled her in greeting. Azrador saw her sneak Ebony some lumps of sugar she had snatched from the breakfast table. It was obvious she had great affection for this noble steed. The silver embossed saddle was a work of art that also stated her rank if you didn't know her. Azrador was handed the reins of a good-looking quarter horse, tan with a white blaze on his forehead, appropriately, he was named Blaze.

Leila led the group out of camp and onto the paved road that led to Southland. Azrador had to give the elves credit, their roadways here were wide and smooth, and fairly straight. He thought the scenery was directly out of the elven legends of old. Huge trees, ten feet around and a hundred feet high were common. And most of the shrubs and bushes had blooms of many colors. He saw numerous deer on their trip, and a beaver that was the size of some pigs. Along the way, on their rest stops he communed with nature and the wildlife that was abundant. He was surprised to find everything at peace and in harmony.

Along the way they stopped at a small pond, to take a break and water the horses. Leila and Azrador decided to stretch their legs by taking a short hike into the forest. Looking at all the natural beauty and the life teaming around them Azrador had an idea. "I think this is a suitable place to try out the Ring of the Forest." He didn't have to look long before he spotted a small pine tree that looked like a good target. Walking up to the two-foot-tall sapling, he grasped a branch in each hand. Closing his eyes Azrador started to hum.

Azrador opened his eyes when the branches pulled out of his hands as the little tree started to grow. He stepped back and he and Leila watched as the little pine tree grew into a full-grown tree of eighty to one-hundred feet tall and eight feet in diameter.

Just as the trees growth came to a stop Azrador collapsed on the ground. Leila rushed to his side. He seemed to be breathing fine but was unconscious. Holding his head in her hands, she tried to bring him around by kissing him. When that failed Leila had a thought. She decided to try to mind speak with him, with more than a little concern Leila pleaded with him, "Azrador please wake up!"

Slowly Azrador started to come around. After he blinked a couple times, trying to get his bearings she kissed him again. This time he kissed her back and thanked her for waking him.

Leila sighed in relief before commenting, "I believe growing the tree drained all your energy, causing you to pass out."

Azrador looked at a huge tree where the little pine had stood just minutes before. Looking at the ring in awe he looked back at Leila, "I am impressed with this ring, but I will have to use it more sparingly, until I get the hang of it."

Taking one last look at the giant tree that minutes before had been a sapling he smiled at Leila before suggesting they get back on the road.

When they got to the town of Southland, Azrador was surprised by the size of the busy seaport. The smell of the salt air preceded the sight of the beautiful aqua blue water offshore and a harbor full of large ships with many sails. Leila led the way excitedly, "I have a cousin that owns several ships in this port. That should be our first stop."

She stopped the group in front of a large townhouse that had a fountain in the courtyard. Leila dismounted and requested Azrador to accompany her. She wanted to speak with her cousin Marshall. A butler showed them into a parlor while Marshall was made aware of their arrival. The butler returned with tea and cookies while they waited.

A short time later a tall, thin, older elf joined them in the parlor. He was dressed in an elegant robe of purple trimmed in silver scrollwork. The old elf moved with a grace rarely seen in one so old, as he glided across the room. He greeted Leila with a kiss on the cheek, welcoming her to his home. Leila introduced Azrador and went on to explain her mission from King Alwin.

Grateful for the warm welcome Leila explained their plan in more detail. "We need a fast ship to take us to Turtle Ilse, in the southeastern Great Ocean We need an ancient artifact known as the Moon Stone. We have hope of finding it there. Our research of the ancient scrolls tells us that at one time it was somewhere on that island. Have you ever heard of the Moon Stone Marshall?"

Marshall considered the question for a moment before answering, "No, I do not recall ever hearing of anything called a Moon Stone. I do recall my grandfather talking about needing to change the ocean tides one season. He spoke of an artifact that was required to do that, but I never heard any more on the subject. It was long ago, and I do not even know if they succeeded. The good news is I have a ship available that can drop you off on Turtle Isle. It will have to continue on to its next port of call but would pick you up on its return the following week. If one week is not enough time to explore the islands ruins it will return again the next week."

Leila briefly consulted with Azrador before deciding that should work.

The Great Ocean

Once aboard the ship, Azrador was sure he was not made for sea travel any more than he was cut out for flying. The nonstop motion of the waves aboard the ship started to get to his stomach not long after leaving port. He knew the voyage to Turtle Isle was going to be a long one. The constant rocking and rolling made his stomach do flip flops.

Leila was unaffected by the churning sea, in fact, she loved being top side in the prow of the ship. She was exhilarated by the spray and foam from the ocean wetting her face. She found the large ship was quite comfortable. The vessel had a crew of twenty elves manning the sails and two elves using magic to influence the winds. The elves had learned, many generations ago, how to use magic to control the wind. As a result, they made good time on the seas. Azrador was thankful to see they were only at sea for two days.

When they reached Turtle Ilse and disembarked, it did

not take Azrador long to recover. When the skiff brought them ashore it became obvious how the island got its name. Looking up and down the beach they could see large sea turtles laying eggs in the sand. Others had already laid their hatch and were covering it with sand, and some were done creating their nest and were headed back into the ocean. Azrador counted thirty or so within his sight, each weighing several hundred pounds. It made him think of the tasty turtle stew Gunter made for them on Misty Island months ago. He hoped Leila hadn't heard his stomach growl.

Soon Azrador, Leila and the four-soldier escort that had accompanied them removed their packs from the skiff. They stood watching the skiff as it returned to the ship.

Leila scanned the shoreline beyond the beach. This part of the island was hilly with a rather rocky landscape. Picking a path Leila started inland along an old path. It wasn't long before the landscape changed, and they started a steeper climb. Leila looked back towards the beach and commented on how many of the massive turtles there were. The terrain got less rocky as they climbed, with more scrub brush and eventually trees coming into view. Ahead Azrador could see the remnants of several ancient buildings, their foundations were all that was left of them. After exploring the area, they began to understand the lay out of the ruins. Eventually they found what had previously been a road. With Leila and Azrador in the lead the four soldiers fanned out, watching for any dangers along the ancient brick road.

After spending the day exploring, they decided to make camp on a plateau that overlooked the surrounding area. It was the highest elevation they had found on the island, so far. The plateau gave them a splendid view of most of the island. There was one area, to the south, where the view was blocked by a small mountain. They set up their camp and placed wards of protection around it in case there was dangerous night life they were not yet aware of.

They discussed their next step, while eating some travel

rations, and sitting around the campfire. It was decided that in the morning, since they couldn't see around it, they would explore the mountain. While they discussed their plan, they could hear sounds of unusual creatures, nearby. They also heard some howling, but Azrador claimed it was not the howl of a wolf. They also heard a loud, annoying clicking sound that continued all night. Sleep eventually caught up to all of them and they turned in for a restless night. Leila did not seem open to company, so Azrador slept in the tent with the soldiers. He was thinking of her when sleep finally overtook him.

The next day, they prepared to hike to the south end of the island. Leila came out of her tent and saw Azrador sitting next to the fire, in a lotus position with his eyes closed. He was humming while touching the ground. Leila watched with fascination as Azrador communed with nature. Ranger Mages are unusual in that they could sense things from their surroundings. Leila did not have that skill, but she greatly respected those that did.

Within a few moments Azrador opened his eyes and greeted her with a good morning and a smile. "Evidently, at low tide, there are some caves along the southern shore we should explore. That is if we don't find something more promising on the way there." Azrador also warned, "I also sensed that we are not alone on this island."

After they finished a light breakfast, the group packed up camp. The team was on its way early that morning. As they neared the mountain, they saw remnants of more buildings. These were still ruins but seemed to be in better shape than the ruins they had explored the day before. Some of the buildings still had walls and sections of roof on them. One of the soldiers exploring ahead of Leila walked into the building closest to the road. He had not been out of site for more than a moment when they heard a scream.

All of the elves, including Leila drew a weapon. They approached the building as a group. When they got to the doorway, they could see that the soldier had managed to get his sword out and cut the head off a huge rat. Unfortunately, he was quickly overtaken as more of the huge rats tore at his legs and arms. By the time Azrador reached the door the rats had already torn the man apart. Azrador quickly cast Kaminari, causing lightning to jump from one rat to another, killing them all before Leila even made it to the building.

She did arrive in time to smell the burnt hair from the rats and see the bloody mess that had been one of their guards. Looking around the room, it appeared at one time to have been an inn. They could still see a section of the bar that had once served drinks. Stepping outside to get some fresh air and empty her stomach Leila commented on the size of the vermin and how aggressive they had been. She felt terrible about the loss of the soldier and gave her condolences to the three guards left and promised to take care of his family. The soldier's gruesome death had put everyone on edge as they explored the two other buildings in the area. They found nothing promising but did hear some scurrying in the last building. Leila thought it may have been more rats, or worse yet, something else. Azrador told her it sounded like spiders to him. He did not tell her how much he hated spiders.

After a hard climb up and around the small mountain, they looked down, onto a beach on the southern tip of the island. It was close enough they could see several exceptionally large sand crabs scratching around some ship wreckage that must have recently washed ashore. The crabs were larger than a horse, with large pinchers, the size of a horse's saddle. Azrador watched as one of them speared an unlucky sailor that was stuck in the wreckage. Thankfully the sailor was already dead as the crab munched away at his arms first, then his legs, and finally the torso. They all watched from above as one of the other crabs grabbed the head and ate it, hat, and all.

Azrador turned to the group and stated, "It looks like we shall have to deal with those sand crabs before we can explore the caves, if there are any caves."

Leila drew Icicle, her short sword and shouted, "Let's go

kill those things! They should make a good supper don't you think?"

Azrador admired the woman for not being flustered by the monsters in the least. The crabs took notice of their decent and started to scramble towards them. The soldiers escorting them aimed and fired their crossbows, only to see their arrows bounce off the armored shells. Azrador grabbed his bow, selected a yellow feathered arrow from his quiver and fired it over the crabs as they reached where the beach and rocks meet. Golden sparkles fell from the arrow as it passed over the crustations, gently falling onto the trio of giant crabs. The crabs slowed down and then collapsed, sound asleep. Leila laughed, finding the sleeping crabs humorous. Turning to Azrador she asked him if he was hungry. Turning her attention back to the sleeping crabs, in a breathy voice she said the word "Freta" and a fireball formed in her hands. She threw the fireball, striking the three crabs as they slept. Turning her attention back to Azrador she stated, "I am not known for my cooking ability, but dinner should be done soon!" she quipped as she hopped down the rocky slope to the beach.

Azrador smiled at her comment on cooking and asked, "Did you bring butter for dipping?" He followed her down the slope, at a slower pace, watching as the fire went out. When he got close enough, he could smell cooked crab. It was then that he realized she was right, he was hungry. Leila walked over to one of the crabs, Azrador watched her use Icicle to chop off the huge claw. Another strike and the claw cracked open, still steaming. Using his dagger Azrador cut several pieces of the crab claw and offered one to Leila.

Leila smiled as she nodded her head, "Not bad but you are right it calls out for some dipping butter, and maybe some salt." As she wiped the juice from her mouth, she motioned for the rest of the team to join them.

Azrador scanned the area as they ate. A large span of beach was visible, so Azrador thought it must be close to low tide. Judging from where the sun was, it was also getting late in the day.

After everyone ate their fill of crab, they started to further explore the coastline. Where the sand met the rocks there were a lot of possibilities for caves. Azrador was discouraged by the lack of camping sites along the beach, not wanting to climb back up the way they had come. Not knowing how high the tides got, meant they could wake up wet, or worse underwater. There also was no way for them to know what other creatures might inhabit the island.

After spending some time searching, and not finding any caves, Azrador decided to commune with nature, in the hope of learning exactly where the caves might be. Sitting down in the sand, in a lotus position, he dug his fingers into the sand and quietly started to hum. He closed his eyes and focused on his surroundings. It was not long before he sensed that the caves were not far off. But he also felt a threatening presence. He had a strong feeling that there was much danger on this island. His intuition was telling him to beware! The strength of the feeling startled Azrador; he had never felt such a strong warning. They would have to proceed with caution.

He stood up and stretched his legs as he confided in Leila what nature had revealed to him. She smiled at him and told him to follow her, and not to worry she would protect him! Azrador was surprised at how casual she was about the danger they may be in, but he followed, since she was heading in the direction of the caves. Bringing up the rear of the party he lost sight of her and the three remaining guards as they went around a bend in the beach. Azrador didn't get why she would ignore his warning but hurried to catch up.

When he came around the bend, he saw Leila and the soldiers being attacked by a group of large snakes. One of the oversized snakes had already gotten a hold of one of the guards and was constricted around him. The large snake was also biting into the soldier's neck. Azrador, in quick succession, fired two silver arrows. The first arrow struck the snake closest to Leila, freezing it solid. The second arrow did the same to the snake that was wrapped around the soldier but was too late for him. Leila pulled a wand and cast a wall of flames at three others headed her way. One of the two remaining soldiers chopped the head off another as it attempted to spit poison at him. The last snake crawled into a hole in the rocks that had not looked big enough to accommodate a snake its size.

While the others recovered, Azrador examined the dead snakes. Each of them was at least ten feet long and a foot around. They were an odd iridescent green, and scaly with a diamond shape marking on their heads. Azrador had never seen this kind of snake before, and he thought he knew every snake type. Knowing Gunter would ask where his samples were when he heard the snake story, Azrador took samples of the poison gland and a portion of one skin. Gunter was a collector of oddities and even claimed to have found a dragon egg once. He always wanted a sample of anything rare or weird.

After the attack Azrador looked directly at Leila and asked, "Now will you trust me when I ask you to be more cautious? This is a dangerous place! Who knows what else we will find?"

Looking him in the eye Leila said, "I apologize for my arrogance Azrador, we will proceed with caution from here." Turning and pointing down the beach Leila informed him, "Before the snakes attacked, I saw a cave, just ahead, near that small green patch there." Leila said, pointing to a small dark opening just ahead, where the rocks met the beach.

When they reached the cave entrance it was larger than it had appeared. Part of it was below the surface of the beach and sloped downward probably flooding at high tide. Leila cast a floating light and the four of them entered the cave.

Once they were inside, they saw it was a large cavern. There was a pool of liquid in the center of the floor, but it did not appear to be water. The cavern had a strong ammonia smell that was getting stronger as they approached the edge of the pool of dark liquid. There were stalactites and stalagmites staggered here and there, some the size of wagons, some still dripped from the ceiling. They could hear a skittering sound that seemed to be coming from overhead, but they could not see anything. Azrador told them the most probable cause was bats, which did not make Leila feel any better about the creepy sound.

Azrador decided this would be a good time to reach out to nature and see if he was correct. Within seconds of him sitting in the lotus position he had his answer. Unexpectedly thousands of bats flew to the exit, leaving for their evening hunt. The four elves ducked as the flurry passed them by. Azrador thought these bats looked larger than most, but they were still insect eaters and no real threat to them.

Azrador soon learned of Leilas hatred of bats The swarm of bats had flustered Leila initially, but she rapidly recovered and cast a fireball at the last of the bats. She regretted the move almost immediately, when the flaming bats crashed into the pool of liquid bat poo. The pool ignited in a giant ball of fire, quickly raising the temperature in the cave, as smoke replaced the sea breeze. Since their exit was on fire their only choice was to push deeper into the cave system.

The cave turned into tunnels going down, deeper under the mountain. It wasn't long before the air cleared, and they could feel a breeze coming from ahead. The tunnel leveled off and eventually opened into a large cavern with a high ceiling. In the center of this cavern contained a large pool of water, and the walls were covered in white crystals of some type. Azrador scraped a sample of the crystals into a flask, for Gunter, and then approached the pool of water. Leila bent down and was about to taste the water when he stopped her.

"Wait, doesn't this pool of water seem out of place to you? Why, do you think, the bats don't use this space?" Azrador thought something didn't feel right but couldn't put his finger on it. One of the remaining guards had lost his canteen and was extremely thirsty so he disregarded Azrador's warning. The soldier took off his helmet and dunked it in the water, using it like a pitcher. Within seconds they watched as the helmet started to melt, as well as the guard's gloves. The elf was lucky to get them off before he was seriously injured. As it was, he suffered slight burns on his hands, that Leila quickly healed, but it could have been much worse.

After seeing the result Leila exclaimed, "This adventure gets more deadly by the step!" finally seeming to understand Azrador's caution.

There were two exits on the other side of the pool of liquid. After pausing for a moment Azrador chose the passage on the left, since he thought the fresh air was coming from that direction. The ball of light he cast, lit the tunnel as it started to slope upward. The air got fresher as they climbed the incline.

Eventually the tunnel opened to the outside, and they found themselves in a stone courtyard. It looked like a remnant of the past but was apparently intact. The courtyard faced a large stone temple, with ornate stonework lining the stairs that led up to the entrance. It was now deep into the night and a full moon shown down on them.

At the foot of the steps Leila asked, "Perhaps we should make camp here for the night? We could search the temple in the morning."

Azrador considered Leilas suggestion before responding, "That is a tough choice! Is there more danger out here or in there? This area appears to be surrounded by sheer rocks and it doesn't look like anything could scale the rock walls, but who knows what could fly in here from above. The place is hidden from view, or it wouldn't still be here. I vote for going inside, There are probably torches in there, to light the place up, and it is shelter compared to sleeping out here." Azrador said taking the first couple steps toward the entrance.

Leila took another wand from her pocket and said, "I agree, but let's do this slowly and with weapons at the ready."

Azrador nodded in agreement, proceeding forward slowly. He approached the entrance, which consisted of two large, eight-foot high, gold-plated doors, that were locked. The two guards pulled and pushed on each one but could not budge the doors.

Leila told the soldiers to stand aside. She then cast an unlock spell causing the two gold doors to swing open. As she stepped through the doors, torches lit down a long gallery that was built into the mountain side Temple.

Various statues lined the gallery walls. After examining them for a few moments Leila was the first to comment, "The architecture is elven for sure. What its purpose could be, hidden away like it is, remains to be learned." Stepping up to a carving of an elaborately dressed elf Leila exclaimed, "I recognize this statue! It is King Avelorn, the very first of the Elven Kings. I have seen statues like this one in the capitol city of River Run."

Azrador suggested they eat and get some rest. "Since the doors were locked its likely we are safe inside here for the night. Let's close the doors and make camp. Looking around I can see many rooms and chambers off this one, that we can explore tomorrow. It has been a long day and we all could use some rest." He then sat down and removed some travel rations and a flask of water from his pack.

Thinking that was a great idea Leila set out her bedroll, "Agreed, food, water, and rest. Who knows tomorrow may be equally trying!" She said as she stretched out chewing on a piece of jerky. "You know Azrador I am glad you are with me on this adventure. Even in these conditions I feel safe with you here." She whispered, as Azrador laid out his bedroll next to hers.

Azrador smiled into her eyes as he responded, "There is no where I would rather be than here with you my dear Leila! Even on this island!" Azrador said as he laid down next to the lovely elf, giving her a gentle kiss on the lips. "Sleep well." Azrador whispered as he lay down and closed his eyes. The foursome was soon sound asleep, but each had terrible nightmares of being threatened by creatures they had not yet faced.

The Elven Ruin

When morning light came through the windows mounted high up the walls, it woke the party. The night before they had not seen the windows, due to darkness, but now the morning light poured through them. The light lifted everyone's spirits, after suffering the previous day's losses. The sunlight lit the interior of the temple, showing just how impressive was. The windows were stained glass and depicted elven heroes fighting a variety of creatures. After spending some time studying the windows, Leila said they were a depiction of elven history. The first window displayed King Avelorn, doing battle against orcs, others showed three generations of kings fighting horned devils, trolls, and ogres.

The morning light coming through the stained-glass windows struck the gold plating on the statues and was almost blinding. Azrador wondered to himself if they were solid gold or just plated with it. After some morning travel rations and water the group was ready to explore the rest of the complex.

There was a large room to the left of the entrance, and they decided to explore it first. Judging by the number of books lining the walls it was a library. There were several large tables in the center of the room, with a few books scattered on them. Most of the books in the library were covered in cobwebs and dust but seemed to be well kept and in decent shape otherwise. Leila opened several and commented on them being history books. Azrador felt drawn to the last bookcase at the far end of the room. He allowed himself to be led by the feeling and stepped up to the last bookcase. At the last moment he decided to continue to trust his elven instincts and closed his eyes while selecting a book.

Taking the book from the shelf Azrador read the title. He almost dropped the heavy volume when he saw it was titled "Exodus." Flipping through the pages he soon discovered it described the exile of a group of enchanters that had broken the cardinal rule of enchanting. They had used black magic to create weapons. They then used those cursed weapons to conquer other lands. Some of their brethren even used them on the high seas, to sink ships and take the spoils. The tome also warned those that possessed these weapons would become corrupted souls. According to this book the elven leaders were able to defeat the rogue enchanters, exiling them from the elven lands. The book also claimed the rogues took some of the corrupted weapons with them into their exile, or they forged them over again, no one was certain. The elven leaders created and cast a powerful spell that had never been seen before. That spell went into effect when the exiles crossed over the border, out of the elven lands. It caused the outcasts to forget their history and their homeland. The punished were to roam the world forever in their shame, not even knowing why. Azrador wondered if this book spoke of the tinkers and the desert people. It almost had to.

The story seemed similar to the tales Nathan had told him over the years, he wished he was here to ask. The thought occurred to him that his people might be the enchanters in exile. Afterall, until recently he had no idea Elyneas even existed.

His concentration was abruptly broken by a loud noise coming from somewhere deeper in the complex. Azrador quickly placed the book in his pack, for later reading. Leila had not found anything worthwhile in the books, so they moved back to the gallery. Once there they chose a different hallway that led away from the gallery. This hallway had several other rooms off it and the group found several magic artifacts that Leila was able to identify as significant and placed in her pack, but no sign of the Moon Stone. The hallway stopped at the base of a spiral staircase. Following the stairs up to a large room that was a lot different than the first-floor gallery. The first thing to catch Azrador's eye was a large telescope sticking out of a window, on the south side of the room. Some shelves along that wall contained what looked to be models of worlds and their moons.

Large murals lined the other walls, some depicting cosmic events of either the past or future, there was no way to tell. The murals were all colorful works of art. Some depicted weather events, as well as meteor showers. One mural depicted a tsunami wave wiping out an elven city. Azrador thought they were similar to the murals behind the Mystery Waters waterfall. It was hard to say what they meant, if anything, or if they were just works of art. But when Azrador looked at them he felt like they might be getting closer to finding the Moon Stone.

Leila examined the telescope before looking through the eyepiece. It was to her surprise, not aimed at the sky. The telescope was aimed at and focused on an outcropping of rock, to the south. She could see what looked like a door on the outcropping. She could not see any way to reach it, but she speculated the door could be an exit not an entrance. Leila thought it odd that the telescope would be aimed at a part of the mountain, and not the sky. Her Grandfather Bretta had a small telescope he had shared with her when she was young. They always pointed it at the sky to see the moon and stars.

Leila took her eye away from the telescope long enough to ask Azrador to join her. "Azrador, come look at this please." Leila asked as she put her eye back to the eyepiece.

Azrador reluctantly left the murals to join her at the telescope. When he looked through the eyepiece, he was also surprised to see it was aimed at the mountain and not the sky. "I think it must be a clue, Leila. That door may be our destination even if we don't yet see a way to get there." She could hear the excitement in his voice.

Continuing to explore the room and its furnishings provided no more clues. So, after they were satisfied with their examination of the room, they back tracked down the spiral stairs, searching along the way, to see if they had missed any clues in the large temple complex.

Returning to the library Azrador brought out the Eye of Illusion. He looked through it, examining the whole room. On the far side of the room, he noticed two books that glowed and were colored in the magical spectrum. He kicked himself for not thinking to use the Eye the first time they were in this room. One of the books was green the other red. Azrador reached for the green book, but when he pulled on it the book merely tipped, it would not come off the shelf. A loud grinding noise ensued, and they soon watched as a section of wall opened. It led to another spiral staircase leading upward. Azrador and Leila tried to contain their excitement, not daring to hope they had found the path! No one gave a thought to the other book.

The spiral staircase went up several stories, before finally leading them into a large hall. In the center of the hall a huge replica of their world slowly turned with its moon revolving around it. The world turned slowly, but they could not tell if it was done mechanically or magically. Azrador spotted the part of the world he was familiar with from maps he had observed in the past. He was stunned to see his was such a small piece of the world they lived in. He had no idea the world was this large. So much of it was a mystery, and only a small portion had been explored, that he knew about. He recalled a conversation with Galad when he commented that the world was much bigger than any of them knew. At the time he thought it was just a dragon boasting, but now it seemed more likely he was telling the truth.

Leila was dumbfounded at the replica of the world and how small a portion they inhabited. "Azrador how can the world be so big? After all the centuries the elves have been alive why do we not know more about the other parts of the world? This is so much to absorb. I see now we are but children to the world outside of our lands. Why have we not been taught this?" Leila shook her head trying to absorb what all this meant. "It is obvious to me that elves built this temple long ago. Why has this secret been kept from us for so long?"

Azrador studied the spinning globe for a while before commenting, "Look at how much of the world is water and look at how many large islands there are." As the globe revolved, they began to realize that their lands had been sectioned off from the rest of the world. From the Emerald Sea south to the Great Ocean and east to the Cobalt Sea. Their peoples were separated from the rest of the world by enormous mountain chains and never-ending bodies of water. Watching the world turn, it became apparent for some reason, unknown to them, the people of the north were separated from the dwarfs and the dark skinned, as were the Green Folk. Azrador thought it almost looked intentional. He wondered, could it have been on purpose? A Plaque under the revolving world named it The Revised Realm.

Azrador again used the Eye of Illusion to finish looking around and exploring the room, looking for anything magical. A long marble counter lined the west wall and when he looked at it through the Eye, Azrador could see objects sitting on the counter that were not visible without it. It was almost too much to take in. Above each object a symbol floated, he assumed the symbol indicated the function of the object. There was a gold pyramid that had a mountain symbol hovering above it. There was also a silver goblet that had a lake symbol hovering over it. Another object, which looked to be a flute, had a tree above it and a whirlwind hovered over a copper snake. There were two empty spaces on the marble slab. Over the first empty space hovered a shining sun and over the other space hung a green teardrop. Azrador's attention finally came to rest upon a huge, half white half black pearl, with a large wave hovering over it.

Azrador gave a loud shout. "We have found it! We have found the Moon Stone!

It took several moments for Azrador to gather his thoughts before saying, "It is hard to believe but I can see objects on this counter. There are symbols hovering above them. After seeing the spinning globe and these artifacts I think we may have stumbled on to the tools that were used to create our world."

Looking through the Eye again, Azrador said, "they could use these items to make mountains, lakes and streams or grow plants. One artifact appears to affect the weather, and another seems tied to the change of the tides and for the oceans, breathing life into them. I wonder how long this has been here. Leila, you look through the Eye and tell me what you think."

Leila gasped as she looked through the Eye of Illusion and witnessed the items on the counter for herself. The symbols above the magical artifacts were elvish and Azrador was correct in his assessment. As a young elf Leila had been taught these symbols in an old book of fairy tales. They were called the Tools of the Creators. She had been taught that these ancient tools were used in the forming of their world. The mystery was not solved, but they had found what they had come for, the Moon Stone. Leila hugged Azrador and said, "These ruins are a mystery that needs more exploring when our current task is handled. Thank the gods for leaving the

Moon Stone here!" Leila kissed Azrador on the cheek and said, "Let's hope the ship is on time in picking us up. They are due back tomorrow."

As they made their way back out of the temple and were leaving, they again passed the library. It occurred to Azrador the two books in the magic spectrum he had seen there could be important. The green book had been the switch for the concealed door and could not be removed but he thought to grab the red book off the shelf putting it in his pack for later reading.

The Plan

Nathan was relieved to see Swan and Galad had returned from the lair without incident. He invited them into Mikiel's tent, offering them a seat on a nearby pillow. Mikiel's tent was large, but the main room was a little crowded. Jason sat on the floor beside Nathan, Mikiel sat to his right, at the head of the table. Amara and Gunter sat across from him. The group was totally engrossed in a discussion about the building of the rod, and who should be the one to use it.

After Swan was seated on the other side of Nathan, Galad pulled out the ancient scroll that contained the diagram of the rod. "I believe this scroll contains the measurements and specific size and shape of our device, as well as where each of the artifacts is to be attached. I have cast a stasis spell on the scroll, to preserve it, it is extremely old and delicate. I use a statis spell on all my ancient books, scrolls and artifacts, to preserve them."

An excited Jason leaned over the scroll, moving his finger across the diagram, taking in the required measurements, making notes on a scrap of parchment of the connections needed for each piece to be added. Jason looked at Galad and smiled, "This is exactly what I need to build the rod!"

Galad referred to the scroll as he explained to the group at the table, "According to this scroll, Jason is going to build us The Celestial Rod. That Rod is what will be used to close the rift."

Jason was examining the diagram closely, talking more to himself than the others at the table he mumbled "It looks like the rod itself is to be made of adamantine, a very specific blending of iberium and palladium. These two metals are exceedingly difficult to work with. Even though I was able to create the Divinity Staff and Blackstar, with these metals it is very difficult and tricky to get right." By now Jason had forgotten the others were even in the room as he went on. "This rod is to be tapered from the top, similar to the Divinity Staff, I can easily do that. The way I read this, the Dragon's Tear should be mounted first, at the top. That means the rod will need a depression for the Tear to sit in. Hmm.., then comes the Sacred Sun Medallion. Mounted below it will be the Eye of Illusion. The final addition will be the Moon Stone, if Azrador and Lady Leila are successful. At least the size of each of the required artifacts is listed, so I can anticipate how they would articulate."

Nathan, who had been quietly studying the scroll without much to say, tapped Jason on the shoulder. "That is where I come in Jason. The scroll dictates that each artifact is to be mounted using gold ore. Most of you here, other than Swan, don't know or have forgotten, I am a Master Goldsmith, and that is the metal that must be used to mount each item."

Jason turned and looked at the tinker before laughing out loud. "No, I did not know you were a goldsmith, let alone a master goldsmith. Nathan you never cease to amaze me. Of course, you should be the one to mount the four artifacts."

Amara waited for Nathan and Jason to finish their conversation before adding, "According to the Book of Blessings I will have to charge the Sacred Sun Medallion and the Moon Stone combining my magic and the blue mana stones."

Jason and Nathan continued to study the scroll as Galad further explained to the others, "I have not examined the shield that Swan and I recovered from Strongheim very closely yet, but according to this scroll the Celestial Rod will somehow attach to its backside until needed at the Rift."

Nathan interrupted Galad, explaining, "When Gunter, Azrador and I found the Shield of Torevir the Eye of Illusion was attached to its back."

Upon hearing that, Jason shook his head as he got up and retrieved the large shield, placing it in the center of the table. He then sat back down and went back to his review of the diagram, noting all the components needed to create the Celestial Rod.

Galad returned to thought, "After the rod is used, the Defender of Torevir will prove its worth by protecting the person carrying it."

Galad then turned to Gunter, "The way I read this, the person holding the Shield and the Rod will have to get close enough to the Temporal Rift to throw the rod into it. I would like your interpretation of it. I would feel better if you could verify its meaning before we go much further with the plan. The scroll's diagram is self-explanatory, but I have never seen this script before."

Gunter nodded and began the translations and soon confirmed Galad's appraisal of the document.

Turning back to the group at the table Galad continued, "I read some other ancient documents that verified that throwing the Celestial Rod into the Temporal Rift is the only way to close it."

Galad was interrupted by a commotion outside the tent as Azrador and Leila arrived from their mission. Mikiel rose to greet them. "Glad to see you two returned safely to us. How did your excursion to Turtle Isle go? You both look like your mission to Turtle Isle had been a little rough."

Amara rose, offering her seat to Lady Leila. "Rest here and I will bring you something to eat and drink. The two of you must be exhausted after sailing from Southland to Turtle Isle and back in a week. We heard the seas were rough during your return to Southland."

After Leila was seated Azrador grabbed a pillow to sit on, tossing it on the floor between Gunter and Leila. Rubbing his backside he said, "Six hours on horseback is more than I've seen in a while also.

Leila nodded as she glanced at Azrador, "Yes, the return trip was a little rough, but not enough to bother me. He may think otherwise." She stated as she pointed to Azrador.

Azrador shook his head, "You won't catch me at sea again if I can avoid it. I was a little uncomfortable when I flew with Swan and Galad, but I was never so sick in my life as I was at sea!"

Gunter had heard enough when he interrupted Azrador, "alright already, enough about you! Did you find what you went looking for or not?

Azrador looked down his nose at Gunter, as he pulled a huge pearl from his pack. Looking around the group at the table he grinned. "I believe you needed one Moon Stone." He said as he set the pearl on the table in front of Gunter." Reaching into a pocket inside his tunic he pulled out the Eye of Illusion. "You may also have the Eye of Illusion back as well. Since I accomplished my mission, I no longer have a use for it." Azrador said with more than a little pride in his voice as he returned it with a snap to where they had found it on the back of the shield.

A vigorous discussion and debate ensued over who should carry the shield. Mikiel was the first to speak. "I want to do it, even if it risks my life. It would be an honor to save our people after all their years of suffering."

Amara had returned with refreshments for everyone as Mikiel pleaded his case, she was not pleased with what she had just heard. She saw to it that everyone was served before turning her full attention on Mikiel. "Brother, I do not think that is a good idea at all. Let someone else be the hero. I have already lost one brother, don't ask me to condone the loss of another. Besides, you know Willem would not allow it, after all you are his heir apparent."

Mikiel looked at his sister a long moment before responding, "This is not a decision for Willem to make. It is mine and mine alone."

The gathering all turned and stared at Galad when he loudly cleared his throat, interrupting Mikiel, and Amara. "Isn't it obvious who should be the one? I have the knowledge and the magic required. Who among us would be a better choice?"

Swan had sat quietly listening to the conversations at the table before jumping up and exclaiming, "What's wrong with me doing it? I have been involved in this mission since it began. I was even there at the beginning when we went to Blessed Bluff. It was just the three of us back then, Nathan, Gunter, and me. In fact, that is where Nathan found the cursed weapons. That is also where I found the Trident Ring and Gunter found a huge rock, he likes to call a dragon egg. It just looked like a big rock to Nathan and me. I don't think..."

Galad turned to Swan, grabbing her by her shoulders as he roared, "What did you say!"

Hearing the anger in Galad's voice Nathan placed a hand on Galad's arm, attempting to calm him. "Calm down my friend, Gunter is the only one who believes it's a dragon egg. When Swan and I saw it, we told him that rock was not a dragon egg, but we were never able to convince Gunter of that. Of course, back then we didn't believe dragons were real." Nathan gazed into Galad's golden eyes and smiled as Galad released Swan.

Swan trying to reassure Galad turned to Gunter, "Last I

saw, you were putting that rock into that magic bag of yours. Do you still have it?"

All other conversation at the table had ceased when they heard Galad roar. He had the full attention of everyone in the room when he let go of Swan and turned his angry golden eyes on Gunter.

Swan looked at Gunter, anxiously telling him, "I would suggest, if you still have that pink rock that you're so proud of, you go get it and show it to Galad, now!"

At that declaration Galad looked from Swan to Gunter and back to Swan before asking, "Did you say pink? All dragon eggs are pink! They remain pink until fired by dragon's breath. Only then will the egg reflect what color the dragon will be."

Gunter, who was not enjoying the attention of the dragon, tried to sound casual as he responded to Galad's demand. "Yes, I still have it. I never mentioned it before now because it is petrified. I even had Henrick, my brother-in-law, the Master Alchemist examine and test it. He agreed with my conclusion that it was indeed a petrified dragon egg. I have hung onto it more as a keepsake than anything else. My pack is in Nathan's coach. I will go retrieve it." He hurriedly rose and left with Galad staring after him.

Trying to ease the tension in the room Leila turned their attention back to the task at hand. "Swan you were voicing your desire to be the one to close the Rift. Do you really think you can?"

Swan looked at Galad before answering, "I think Galad has forgotten what happened when we ventured too close to the Rift. None of our magic or enchantments worked. All we had was our physical ability. Lucky for us I was well trained, by Shaman Quesa. My skill with my Trident is the only reason we survived. Galad was helpless without his brawn, magic and dragon fire and would have been much more useful then, if he had been in dragon form. That is when he is at his strongest. A warrior carrying the shield and the rod will no doubt have to fight to get close to the rift and do so without magic.

Unfortunately, in dragon form you are too large for the shield to protect you. Besides, according to Mikiel, your strengths will be needed to protect the shield bearer's left flank."

Azrador had sat quietly listening, staring at the Shield of Torevir lying on the table as the argument went on. "I think Swan may be right about Galad. He has more strength and magic ability than all the rest of us combined. Besides, I think Lady Leila and the elves are correct in their concern about how much blowback will come when the Celestial Rod lands in the Temporal Rift. Galad is much too large for the shield to protect. I don't believe it is your task either Swan. You are the strongest woman I have ever met, but I fear the weight of the shield is too much, even for you." Looking to Leila for confirmation, he caught her trying to hide a huge yawn. Standing up and looking at the others around the table he suggested, "Everyone is exhausted from the looks of it. Why don't we call it a day?"

Mikiel looked at Azrador like he was crazy, "Are you kidding? There is no way I'm leaving until I see this pink dragon egg, or rock!"

Azrador looked at Leila and sat back down. One look at her and he knew there was no way she was moving from her spot at the table either.

Mikiel addressed Azrador directly, "I think you are right about us all being exhausted. We should sleep on who carries the shield tonight; we can make our decision tomorrow. I suggest we gather here in the morning for breakfast. Hopefully we will be able to decide the bearer of the Celestial Rod then."

Gunter interrupted Mikiel when he entered the tent, out of breath after the short run, he exclaimed, "I ran all the way to the coach and back." He dropped the pack on the floor and immediately started rooting around in it. Pulling out specimen jars, small vials, and a variety of other odd and ends from his collection. Looking nervously at Galad he stated, "Don't worry, I know it's in here. It has been quite a while since I had it out. Everyone was tired of me talking about it, so I put it away."

Galad stood staring at Gunter with his arms crossed, impatiently tapping his foot.

Gunter was shoulder deep in the pack when he grinned and exclaimed, "Ah ha! I found it!" Using both hands Gunter removed the large rock from the bag.

As Gunter removed the pink object from the bag Galad grabbed it, shoving Gunter to the side. Swan was going to scold Galad for his rough treatment of Gunter but decided not to when she saw him gazing reverently at what must really be a dragon egg, a pink dragon egg. She did not recall it being so large.

Galad tore his gaze away from the egg long enough to glance at all in the room and state, "This egg is not petrified. It appears that it is protected by a stasis spell, similar to the spell I use on my collection of ancient scrolls and books."

Lady Leila had always believed in dragons her whole life and was amazed at what she was seeing. "Galad, so you mean to say that egg could contain a baby dragon?"

He smiled at Leila before fixing his gaze back on the egg as he whispered something under his breath. Within seconds the pink egg began to pulse as it was surrounded by a purple glow. Several minutes passed and slowly the glow faded, and the egg returned to its original pink.

Galad stood proudly holding the egg out over the table and declared, "Behold this egg in my hands! It is going to be the first female dragon to be born in more than a hundred years! Thank you Gunter for keeping it safe all this time."

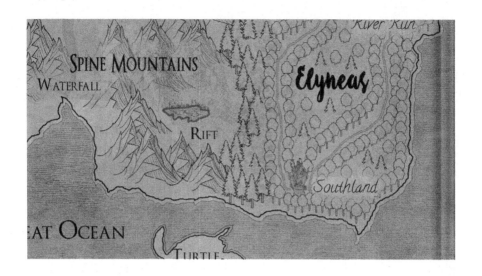

Dragon Egg

Not long after the dragon egg reveal, the group decided the day had been very eventful and that it was a good time to turn in, so everyone left for their respective quarters. Lady Leila and Azrador showed Galad and Swan to the tent Leila had ordered erected for their use, rather than the pair sleeping in Nathan's coach with the others. Once Galad and Swan were alone in their tent, she turned to him and looked in his golden eyes and asked, "Are you serious about the egg being a female dragon? Can it really hatch?"

Galad was still holding the pink egg as he stared back at Swan and replied, "The egg will remain in that state until I bathe it in dragon fire. Or so my tutor explained, when I was growing up and learned how to make baby dragons."

Swan looked around the tent until she found a large maroon pillow. She took the egg from Galad and placed it on the pillow. She then took his right hand and led him to two large pillows nearby.

Galad was a little confused by Swans actions. He thought to himself, "Doesn't she get it? Right now, all I care about is that egg."

Swan took notice of the look on Galad's face before she asked, "Galad, since we are on the subject of babies, I have a few questions I have been meaning to ask. Now seems like the right time. I'm quite curious, can you get me pregnant? And if you can what happens then? Will I have a human baby or a baby like you, a dragon that can be human when he chooses?" Swan asked with a grin, but with a note of concern in her voice.

Galad suddenly realized how the day's events were affecting Swan. Trying to reassure her he took both of her hands in his, he looked into her eyes and answered her as honestly has he could. "Yes Swan, it is in my power to make a child with you. The most likely outcome would be a human baby with strong magic." Galad said while thinking more seriously on it.

Swan gave Galad the best smile she could muster, "That still sounds fuzzy to me, how about spelling it out for me please." Swan said sweetly.

Galad, who had never anticipated having this conversation did his best to answer her. "For us to make a child I would have to use my magic as we couple. The magic is used to protect the child while in your womb. Otherwise, your body would reject my seed and not allow the pregnancy to go forward." Galad said with a bit of precision, almost like he was reciting a lesson."

Swan was a little more at ease after his reply and even more curious now, "How long does a pregnancy like that last? Have there been many children of dragons?"
Glancing over at the large egg she inquired, "I won't have to lay an egg, will I? Please, at least tell me the baby will come like all other human babies." She pleaded with Galad.

Thoughts of Swan laying an egg set Galad to laughing so hard he couldn't answer her for a moment. "Well, you are after all, named after a bird. Swan, a little irritated at Galad for his ambiguous answers, couldn't keep herself from laughing too.

Galad wiped tears from his eyes as he tried to give her a serious reply. "I have no experience in this area, but I have been told the pregnancy is the hard part, almost two years. As to your question about other dragon children, yes centuries ago many of the stronger elves were the children of dragons. They were known to have tremendous vitality, and to live longer than full blooded elves." Galad finished, as he stared in wonder and amazement at the pink egg.

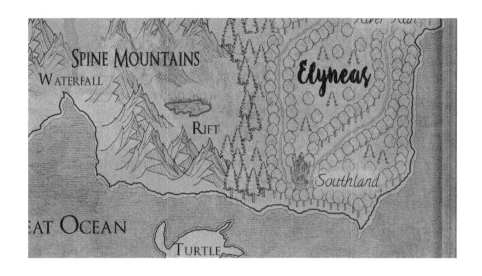

The Shield Carrier

After the meeting broke up Mikiel, Amara and Gunter continued to discuss the day's plans. Mikiel insisted he should be the one to carry the shield, while Amara was adamant, he not be the one. While the two of them argued, Gunter was carefully placing all the jars and objects of his collection back into his pack.

Having had enough of her argument with Mikiel, Amara stood and left the room without a word. Mikiel and Gunter looked at each other and shrugged, but it was only a few moments before she returned carrying a large thick tome.

Amara placed the book on the table in front of Gunter and smiled as she looked in his eyes. "Gunter, I can't believe you have been toting a dragon egg around for months and never even mentioned it. Galad sure got excited about it didn't he? I was interested in what you thought of the writings in this book. The dead High Priestess, Danica, and I, have communicated more than once. She is who guided Mikiel and I to travel to Drifting Sands, in the northern part of the Great Scarlet Desert.

That is where we discovered the pyramid that had been her home in the floating city of Bantez. Due to Danica's guidance, I knew where The Book of Blessings was hidden, before ever venturing there." Amara said as she placed the book in front of him.

Mikiel thought this might be a good time for him to bow out, but he had one more task before he did. Rising from his pillow he took a deep breath and reached for the Shield.

Gunter and Amara watched as Mikiel lifted the heavy shield. Setting the tip of the shield on the floor, where it was almost as tall as he was. He looked straight at Amara before stating, "I guess that eliminates your argument that the Shield of Torevir is too heavy for me to carry, doesn't it?" He then propped it up against the wall before turning back to Gunter and his sister. "And on that fine note I am calling it a day. I would suggest the two of you do the same. Goodnight."

Gunter and Amara, somewhat stunned by the display, watched Mikiel leave the room. Just before he moved out of sight Amara caught a glimpse of Mikiel rubbing his right shoulder.

Gunter looked at Amara, unsure of what to say. "I guess he really wants to be the one to throw that damn rod."

Amara looked at Gunter and decided to change the subject. "Back to the Book of Blessings. There is a substantial amount of info in it that may prove useful."

Gunter removed his ring of rainbow-colored glass and inspected the book's cover. "Wow, this thing lights up with a blue glow when viewing it with the purple section of glass." Out of the corner of his eye, to his left, he could see a glow. Turning the glass on Amara, Gunter couldn't believe what he was seeing. "Amara, now that I look at your tiara, I'm almost blinded. Wow, even your earrings are aglow!" Gunter continued to look at Amara through his magic glass. Her necklace had the most powerful, pulsing magic he had ever seen. He continued to look at her through the ring as he asked, "Amara, all your jewelry contains more powerful magic than I have ever seen, how did you come by it!"

Amara smiled and had that twinkle in her violet eyes,

that Gunter liked so much. "It was the property of Danica, the high priestess. I found her and her belongings while Mikiel and I were in the ruins of the pyramid. When she first saw me wearing her jewelry, she seemed angry, but after we spoke, her attitude toward me changed. Before I left the pyramid, she told me to wear her jewels and to use their magic wisely." Reaching up she lightly touched the tiara as she explained. "The Tiara of Knowledge is how I am able to read the Book of Blessings, without it I don't understand a word of it."

Pulling the book closer, she flipped it open to the pages containing the spell that powers the Sacred Sun Medallion. "I would like to read it to you, to see if you understand the book the same as I do." Pointing to a passage she read it aloud to Gunter. "I think this passage explains here how to cast the spell for The Ceremony of Renewal. That spell is how the Sacred Sun Medallion is powered. The spell will take all the magic and mana I can muster, plus it will require the additional mana from three mana stones. Danica communicated to me that she had to rest for two days after casting it. During recovery she was vulnerable, so guards protected her day and night, until her magic returned."

Gunter watched Amara's face as she read the book. It was all he could do, not to smile at the look of deep concentration on her face.

When she was done reading that spell to Gunter, she flipped past many pages until she came to the spell for powering the Moon Stone. "Here the book contains a similar spell for the Moon Stone. It also requires all of my magic and mana, plus three mana stones to cast it. At this point I only have three that I can use. We may have to wait for the three mana stones I have, to recharge, before we can renew the Moon Stone."

As Amara turned the pages, Gunter had viewed them using his many-colored pieces of glass. He noticed the aura on the two pages was different. "Amara, these two spells have a totally different aura from each other, even if they seem similar. You are right though; I can't read any of the script on the pages. What language are they written in?"

Amara touched the tiara and laughed, before answering Gunter. "I have to admit that before my hair wrapped itself around the tiara, I couldn't read a word of it either. I don't know what language it is called." They both laughed at that. "It requires my full concentration when I am reading it to understand it!"

Gunter hated to bring the evening to a close, but it was getting late when he suggested, "Let me sleep on it tonight! Perhaps tomorrow we will think of a way to recharge the mana stones, or maybe Galad has some in his lair. He seems to collect almost as much stuff as I do." Gunter offered before saying his goodnights to Amara.

Leila and Azrador

After seeing Galad and Swan to their quarters, Leila and Azrador walked to her teams' tents. As Azrador turned to say his goodnights to Leila she grabbed his hand and said, "Don't think you are going anywhere yet young man!" she grinned as she pulled him along, into her tent. Azrador was fatigued after their long journey and knew he smelled like the horse he had ridden for six hours earlier in the day. Yet he found he could not refuse this lovely elf.

Leila had red wine served by her handmaiden and some cheese and bread for a late-night snack. Turning to her maid, "Mirza, prepare a bath for two please."

Mirza gave a quick bow before replying, "Yes, my lady, it shall be ready soon!" Mirza hurried into another room in the tent complex that was Leila's home away from home.

Handing Azrador a glass of the fine red wine from a winery north of the Satin River, Leila said, "The possible hatching of a dragon egg is simply amazing don't you think! Galad acted like he was positive it was a female!"

Azrador shook his head as he chuckled, "Gunter has

been hauling that thing around all this time! We have just been humoring him. None of us other than him believed that it was a real dragon egg. Even if it was, after Henrick examined it and concluded it was a fossilized dragon egg, I didn't believe it could become a real dragon! Of course, none of us from north of the Shadow Mountains believed dragons existed!"

Taking a sip of the wine Azrador popped a piece of cheese into his mouth, realizing he was hungry after all. "It should really not be a surprise. The guy collects everything. I have known him for a long time, and I suspect he has some dwarf blood mixed in there. I have met his sister, Gretchen, and she looks more like a dwarf than an elf, for sure, but really nice lady. I have to admit though, he is a hell of an enchanter! He is who enchanted Swan's boots and bracers, giving her extra strength, endurance, and agility. In his travels he has collected some very interesting artifacts. He also carries some amazing wands that he created."

Leila was quiet for a moment before adding, "I think the dragon egg adds to the excitement of our mission, as if it isn't exciting enough as it is. You know a possible female dragon means that Galad could possibly mate with it. How exciting to imagine!" Leila took a sip of her wine and also tried the cheese squares. Azrador ripped a piece of bread off the loaf, buttered it and took a large bite.

With his mouth a bit full Azrador added, "I think Swan may have something to say about Galad mating with anyone but her, when it comes down to it. She is very headstrong and is used to getting her way if it's something she wants. She is also a hell of a warrior. I think she may be the one to lead us with the shield and rod. Her argument of Galad's assets when he is a dragon outweigh his benefits when in his human form, once magic stops being effective. Although, that shield is very heavy, I am not sure if she could carry it and fight. I know I wouldn't want to!"

Leila breathed a sigh of relief under breath, "Well, that's a relief! I was afraid you would insist on being the hero! I am just now getting used to having you around, and who ever faces the Rift may not survive the blow back I am expecting."

Leila took another long drink of her wine before confessing, "The other elves and I are still concerned with how much blow back will come from the collision of such powerful magics as the Celestial Rod and the Temporal Rift. Do you think it will cause a large explosion? Could it produce a whirlwind? There is a fear among my men that we might make matters worse. After all we are basing all this on a four-hundred-year-old scroll. Can we really trust a gold dragon?"

Before Azrador could answer her Mirza announced the bath was ready.

Leila stood, holding a hand out to Azrador. "Come Azrador, you smell worse than a spitting camel I met once, and that means I do too! We shall bathe and discuss this further. I had a message from King Alwin awaiting my return. He is sending an additional five hundred soldiers to lead our way to the Rift and help clear the lizard creatures." Desiring to change the subject, she looked deeply into Azrador's eyes as she said, "You know, if we survive this, I am going to want you to meet my mother!" Leila smiled and reached out for Azrador's hand. She removed her clothing as she led him into the next room, where a steaming bath was waiting. All Azrador could do was smile back, he was in wonder of this amazing woman. He also knew he was getting attached to her. The hot steamy water felt heavenly and so did Leila when he took her in his arms. He was thankful he wouldn't be sleeping with Nathan, Jason, and Gunter in the tinker coach this night!

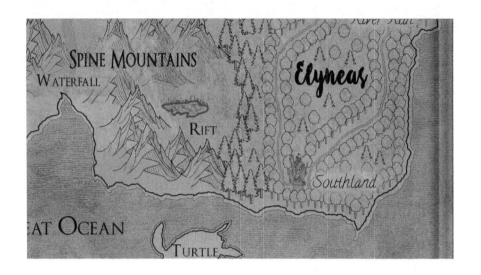

Breakfast Chatter

In the morning, at breakfast, the conversation picked up where it had left off. Lady Leila again vocalized the elves concern about the plan. "We have no idea how strong the blow back is going to be. Is there really no other way to close the Rift? I'm a little uncomfortable relying on an ancient scroll."

Galad turned to Leila to answer her concerns directly. "I understand your reluctance, Lady Leila. Let me reassure you, it is the best information we have been able to find. I have no alternate plan." Looking at each individual at the table he asked, "Have any of you come up with a better plan? I think we go all in on the strategy we have."

Leila was still finding it hard not to stare at Galad and his golden eyes when he was talking. Seeing no other options Leila agreed. "Alright, it does look like we have no other option. We still haven't discussed who will carry the shield and rod. I have no desire to be the one, neither does Azrador. So, who shall it be?" She asked as she scanned the room.

Amara took note of Mikiel drinking his coffee with his left hand. He seemed to be keeping his right arm close at his side. Setting down his coffee cup Mikiel addressed Lady Leila's question. "It looks to me like we are down to four candidates, myself, Swan, Jason and Galad." Looking Swan directly in the eye he stated, "Swan, after everyone left last night, I picked up the shield, to get it off the table. I was more than a little surprised at how much it weighs, and that's without the rod attached to it. Before we go any further, I would suggest you try it."

Swan put down the piece of bread she had been eating and stood. Walking over to the shield she realized for the first time just how large it was. She grasped it in both hands and lifted. The shield was only three or four inches off the ground when she set it back down with a thump. Looking around the table, she shrugged and sat back down as she exclaimed, "You can take my name off that list Mikiel. I hate to admit it, but there is no way I could do it."

Amara looked at her brother and pleaded, "Mikiel, please give up on carrying the shield, there must be a better choice!"

It was then that Mikiel confessed, with a chuckle, as he rubbed his right shoulder. "The reason I knew you couldn't carry it Swan is because after lifting it last night I can hardly lift my right arm this morning."

He then looked his sister in the eye and said, "You are right Amara I will be more help in the fight if I am protecting the shield bearer." Looking at Galad and Jason he said, "It looks like it will be up to one of you."

Amara tried no to show the relief she felt at her brother's honesty and his realization of how far he might have to carry the large. Looking first at Galad and then at Jason she asked, "Which of you shall carry the shield?"

Feeling everyone's eyes on him, Jason stood up and suggested, "Lets discuss who carries it once we have succeeded in creating the Celestial Rod, there are many steps to be done before we must decide!"

Galad agreed with Jason, "He's right we should work on the problem at hand first. Jason, I offer you the use of dragon fire when smelting the ore for the rod. I also offer my assistance in anyway needed in the making of the rod. I have always admired the skill required of a craftsman, like yourself, in the creation of difficult items. I see the making of this Celestial Rod as historic if it works. If we succeed, centuries from now people will know what we have done, because I will document it myself. After all, if the scroll is to be believed this has been done at least once before."

As Galad was speaking a messenger came in, "Lady Leila, forgive my interruption, but you told me to notify you when the supplies you requested from Silverton had arrived."

Jason smiled for the first time that morning. "Great news! I will have need of the arriving portable forge, anvil, tongs, and special reagents to make this rod." Galad, Jason and Mikiel woofed down the remainder of their breakfast, anxious to get to work.

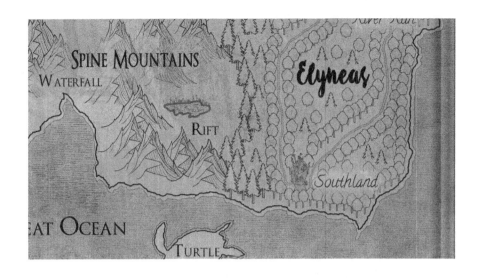

The Smithy

Several horse troughs were brought to where the portable smithy was to be set up and used. Galad and Mikiel went to work getting the smithy assembled and properly set up, while Jason emptied his pack.

After she finished eating, Amara left the servants to clean up the remains of breakfast and followed the men to the location of the forge.

As Jason removed the iberium and palladium from his pack Amara caught a glimpse of what looked like a mana stone.

Amara excitedly asked him, "Jason, do you realize what that blue stone you are carrying is? Let alone how rare they are?"

Jason looked up at Amara and grinned as he replied, "Yes, I do. They are mana stones. Jade and I mined them in the Sky Mountains, when we were searching for palladium and iberium ore." Reaching into his pack he removed three large blue stones and set them on the ground next to his feet.

Amara stared in awe at the size of them. "I had only seen mana stones in my dreams before venturing to the Bantez ruins. I obtained three of them myself while there. High Priestess Danica used them in the annual Ceremony of Renewal to power the Sacred Sun Medallion. The Sacred Sun Medallion was how they kept Bantez floating above the desert. While the city floated it also slowly turned, keeping the city high above the sandstorms of the region, for a season. So, you see the High Priestess and the mana stones she draws from must be very powerful." Amara took several steps, drawn to the Stones lying next to Jason.

Standing in front of Jason she went on to explain, "I will need at least six stones to power both the Sun Medallion and the Moon Stone, the larger the better." Pointing at the stones at Jason's feet she asked, "Jason, would you allow me to use those Mana Stones, to make that possible? I promise to return them when I'm done with them." Amara asked as she tried to sneak a peek into his pack.

Jason looked up, taking notice of the girl's violet eyes and the tiara she wore. He smiled before answering the unusual request. "Amara, you are welcome to anything I have if it helps save our world from this threat. So much has happened in this last two years it makes my head spin. Until a few months ago my people didn't even know your people existed. The same goes for the dwarfs, the elves and make sure you add dragons to that list too!"

Amara reached down and picked up one of the large blue stones. She was shocked at how large it was, when compared to the ones she already had. Looking directly at Jason she said, "These mana stones will turn white when drained of their power. It is a well-known fact among my people that ancient mages used them to store magic energy, to be used later. What is not so well known is that mana stones are also required for dragons to breed. I read, in the Book of Blessings, that a female dragon must ingest a mana stone before she can make an egg and create offspring. The book went on to explain, that is why dragons are magical."

Jason nodded, "I am aware they are quite rare, but are they any rarer than the other ancient magic relics? I have been thinking about this a lot the last couple of days. It seems to be more than coincidence that we have all come together in this single purpose. Look at our team. We have different people, from different lands, all coming together with the appropriate magical relics, to solve a problem affecting all our different lands. The fact that as a team we have the skills and materials that a four-hundred-year-old scroll dictates are required to close this Temporal Rift can't be by chance. This same evil seems to have appeared hundreds of years ago, at least someone wrote down how they managed to defeat it. Why the pieces were scattered is a question without an answer, but I am thankful for your help and knowledge Amara; from what I have heard we couldn't have gotten this far without your help and unique magic."

Amara looked away for a second, a little uncomfortable discussing her magic with a man she didn't know well, and declared, "My magic is quite different from the others, I hope it is not offensive to you that I speak to the dead. That is how I learned of the ancient floating city of Bantez. That is also how I communicate with their dead High Priestess, Danica. In a foretelling, she spoke of the Demon Tassarion. She claims he is the evil behind the Temporal Rift. According to Danica, Tassarion will continue draining our world of magic and life, using it to make a new land, of his own. Jason, I believe that we must succeed for our world survive!"

Jason paused to think about what he had just heard as he took several nuggets of iberium ore from his pack. Wanting to reassure Amare he stated honestly, "I feel it is our destiny to solve this. I am but a humble blacksmith, from a small village in the north, and here I am, playing a part in the mending of the land. I can think of nowhere I would rather be! And I can think of nothing more important to do!" Jason unrolled the fabric his magic smithing hammer was wrapped in. Picking it up he smiled as he declared, "Let's get to work shall we!"

∞ ∞ ∞

Shortly after her conversation with Jason, Amara joined Mikiel and Gunter at the small altar they had constructed for the ceremony. Amara reverently placed the Sacred Sun Medallion on the homemade alter. The Book of Blessings lay on the alter next to it, open to the appropriate spell for charging the artifact. Three large blue mana stones lay on a table nearby, waiting to be drained. Mikiel and Gunter silently looked on, as spectators, wondering what it would be like to handle so much magic at once. They were excited to be witnessing a ceremony that had not taken place for over a hundred years. Amara stood before the altar with a stoic expression on her face, until she fell into a type of trance and began reciting the incantations provided in the Book of Blessings. A soft golden glow surrounded her and the altar, growing brighter as the mana stones began to glow. Slowly the blue stones faded from blue to white, as the magic was transferred from them to the Sacred Sun Medallion. When the process was complete, the glow from the medallion was blinding. Amara turned from the altar, smiled at the spectators, before fainting from exhaustion. Gunter rushed to her side, as did Mikiel. After checking to make sure she was only sleeping he picked her up and carried her to her tent and made her comfortable. Gunter stayed at her side as she slept the rest of the day.

Dragon Fire

Meanwhile Jason's work with the ores went much more quickly than he had anticipated. With Galad breathing dragon fire, versus a coal fire, he was able to smelt the metals much more quickly. Several times Jason had to mind speak with Galad, to remind him to slow down. To blend iberium and palladium properly you must not hurry the process. Being a dragon, Galad thought more heat was better, but Jason assured him it was supposed to be a slow process.

Azrador and Lady Leila assisted by magically creating the clay mold for the rod, to the exact specifications contained in Galad's scroll. When Jason was satisfied the ore was well mixed in the crucible, he slowly, carefully poured the liquefied ore into the clay mold that was clamped to the table. Taking a well-deserved break from the hot task and pouring water from one of the horse troughs over his head he realized it was just himself and the dragon standing around the smithy. This was the first time Galad, and Jason had spent much time together, since flying from Strongheim.

Galad mind spoke to Jason, "Swan tells me you never knew your mother, but were raised by a midwife. It is unfortunate to not have known her, I am sure. Swan speaks very highly of you and considers you a dear friend. She told me you triggered the return of her memory when you created her trident. That may have never happened otherwise."

Jason was touched to hear Swan thought so highly of him. He knew the golden dragon to be a little jealous, so he tried to hide his pleasure in Swan's compliment. Uncomfortable discussing his and Swans friendship with the dragon, he changed the subject back to getting to know Galad, "Did you know your mother Galad? Do dragons raise their young worms or are you on your own after hatching?"

Galad chuckled through the mind link and answered, "Yes, I knew my beautiful mother, and yes, I suppose you could say she raised me. According to her, my father was an ancient gold dragon and left as soon as he heard she was with child. The colony of dragons I am from, is unusual, to say the least. Human tutors were provided to teach languages and mathematics to us younglings. Older dragons taught us our magic skills and the art of fighting other dragons. When there were more of my kind, we were a warring clan. Many powerful dragons fought among themselves, until they reduced our numbers significantly."

After several hours of cooling, Jason removed the rod from the clay cast. Closely examining it before carrying it to the anvil. Taking the magic hammer that Nathan had given him as a child, he began rounding the rod. Galad slowly reheated the rod as needed, as the hammering continued. Once he was satisfied with the adamantine rod's shape Jason submerged it, one at a time, into the various reagents that now filled the horse troughs. He continued his hammering late into the night as he and Galad found a rhythm to their work.

∞∞∞

After helping Jason with the rod all day and well into the night, it was late when Galad returned to their tent. Swan had dozed off while waiting for his return. She jumped up startled when she heard him enter. She was wide awake now, her warrior instincts and adrenaline boosted by the noise.

Galad apologized to Swan, "I'm so sorry Swan I didn't mean to wake you, I know it's late. Jason and I just finished with the firing of the rod." He poured himself a glass of wine from a carafe on a table near the bed. Jason is quite soft-spoken for a giant isn't he?" He inquired of Swan.

Swan rose and poured herself a glass, remembering the shy quiet young boy he had been when they first met. She nodded, "Yes, he was even sweeter before he met Jade, the enchanter that forced him to make the Divinity Staff!" Swan replied. She was wide awake now, after the adrenaline rush of an abrupt awakening in a war zone.

Surprised at Swan's tone when she spoke of Jade he continued. "Well thank the gods he did! That Staff contains the Divinity Stone! The Gods had given the giant, Bone Biter, the task of guarding it. But while I was enthralled to Ibis, I killed Bone Biter for it. The act has haunted me all these years since. I feel better about it now, knowing it played a key role in how we got to where we are. That Stone was used to make the world! Imagine if Ibis had been able to use it. How would your war at home have turned out? I bet it would have ended much differently." Galad took another sip of his wine when he noticed some cheese on a platter and popped a piece into his mouth.

Considering Galad's point Swan asked, "How was a half giant blacksmith able to use the magic in the staff? I thought Jason's magic had more to do with the magic hammer Nathan had given him in his youth. Do you think Jason has always had magic?" Swan asked, before grabbing the chunk of cheese Galad was about to put in his mouth.

Shaking his head at Swan, he snickered before answering her. "In order to blend iberium and palladium into adamantine it requires magic. In the past, only a smith with strong magic at his touch has been able to blend those two ores. Nathan must have sensed it in the young boy, before his mother's magic manifested and started to grow. All those years ago, when Nathan gave Jason the raw ore for your trident, he must have recognized his ability, even if he had no idea where it came from." Galad grabbed a couple grapes from the plate and tossed them both into his mouth.

Swan moved a step closer to Galad and asked, "So, did it go well in the smithy, with the rod then?" She asked as she kissed Galad on the cheek.

Finding it difficult to stay on topic he did his best to answer her. "Yes, the young giant is a real grandmaster at the forge, a delight to watch work. He also has a strong resolve and focus. When he approaches a task, and then sets his mind to it, it's like he hasn't considered failing as an option." Galad whispered while embracing Swan and nuzzling her neck. Thinking of a task of his own.

Breaking the embrace Swan smiled at him before turning their attention to the large pink egg nestled into a maroon pillow. Thinking for a moment, unsure if she really wanted to know, she asked Galad, "What have you decided on the dragon egg? Will you fire it before battle, or are you going to wait until after the battle, in the hope that at least you survive?" Finding the questions difficult, but necessary she continued, "Who could or would raise the baby if you don't survive?"

Galad grew somber before answering, "Those are very thorny questions, ones I have been contemplating since the egg was revealed." Not used to experiencing regret, he confessed to Swan, "I feel I treated Gunter rather badly for the surprise! Jason and I had plenty of time to talk while we worked. According to him Gunter has been hauling the precious thing around for months. He has taken a pretty good ribbing and harassment by Azrador for keeping it."

In an attempt to reassure Galad, Swan explained. "If

it wasn't the "pink rock" it would have been something else. They banter back and forth like that all the time. At times it makes me crazy. Besides, Gunter really does collect everything and anything. I've seen him stop and collect spider silk, mushrooms, mold, monster spit you name it, and he probably still has it in that pack of his, or his vest pockets!" Swan said as she approached the egg sitting next to it on the pillow. Turning to Galad she grinned, "You have to admit, it does look like a pink rock."

Not seeing the humor in Swans teasing he went on, "No, it is more than that. Gunter recognized the importance of keeping the egg safe, and he didn't share its existence with many folk. Those he did share the discovery with, joked about the importance of a rock, and yet he persevered." Galad was deep in thought as he added, "I have decided to entrust Gunter with the egg's safety if he will stay out of the battle. I know he, of all people will keep it safe. Should I not survive the battle there would be no one to raise the dragon properly. I have considered all the options, and for that reason, I will wait to fire the egg until after the battle." Galad said as he stroked the egg.

Swan put her arm around Galad and looked up into his golden eyes, "I believe you have made a wise and well-intentioned decision. Gunter is the perfect guardian for the egg! But you are going to have to make up with him, after your reaction when you found out about the egg."

Feeling good about his decision Galad replied, "Swan, I think you are right! Let's get some rest, there is still much more to be done before the battle!" Galad took Swan's hand and led her back to bed.

∞∞∞

The next day, after a brief night's sleep, Galad, now in human form watched as Jason focused on his work. It was not long before he could see the magic being used by the big man. Casually he asked Jason, "What magic do you have at your disposal Jason? I can see a blue aura around you as you concentrate on swinging your hammer." When Jason finished etching the metal for one of the connections, Galad handed him a large mug of cool water. He gladly drank the offered water, thanking Galad.

Speaking to Galad, he chuckled as he recalled Grand Master Throdon, "That's what an ancient dwarf Grand Master Mage was trying to convince me of, just a few weeks ago. That seems like a lifetime ago now. Throdon claimed I inherited magic from my mother, Rose Carron. Throdon believed my mother was what he called a "traveler". According to him a traveler has very powerful magic. The most powerful are said to have the ability to open portals to other lands, and step through them. I thought it sounded a little far-fetched, but Throdon insisted I listen and believe him. After Master Throdon activated the Divinity Stone in my staff, I was able, with the help of the Divinity Staff, and a dedicated team of dwarfs, to put an end to the volcano that was causing the sandworms to attack, plaguing the dwarfs in Torevir, and the Sundown Tribe in the Scarlet Desert."

Galad felt a deep relief in hearing the Divinity Stone had found the proper home in this humble blacksmith. He had carried the burden of killing Bone Biter for all these many years. It had served a purpose after all.

∞∞∞

It took Amara two days to recover from the Renewal Ceremony. During that time, Gunter never left her side. He was also able to provide a potion he carried in his pack that aided her in regaining her strength. The magic she had expended in the ceremony had taken a lot out of her, just as the High Priestess of the Da Nang had predicted.

When Amara felt she had fully recovered the third day after the Sun Medallion was charged. She prepared and moved on to the next ceremony. Everyone watched on as she opened The Book of Blessings and began the incantations for the Moon

Stone. It had to be done under a full moon. The spellcasting was somewhat different. Besides requiring three fully charged mana stones, a blood sacrifice was required. Amara did not hesitate when the time came for it. When the incantation called for blood, she pulled her dagger from her belt sheath and sliced her palm open! Allowing her blood to cover the large black and white pearl that was the Moon Stone. The blue glow from the large mana stones transferred much more quickly than it had with the Sun Medallion. Overhead the full moon turned red as the blood spilled over the pearl. When the magic transfer was complete the Moon Stone looked like a reflection of the full moon, glowing bright and white. After Amara completed the spell and turned from the altar, took two steps and collapsed. This time however, Gunter was close by and caught her before she hit the ground. He lovingly picked her up in his arms and carried her to her tent. After seeing how much the spells had taken out of Amara, Gunter was thankful her part of the magic was complete.

Now that the rod had been cast and rounded, Jason moved on to polishing the indentations and pockets where the artifacts were to be mounted. After dragon fire was no longer called for, Galad chose to remain in human form. He watched with fascination as Jason finished his part of the project. "You know Jason, I have been giving this a lot of thought. If your mother was indeed a traveler you may find you inherited her powerful magic, as you mature. The fact you were able to transform Jordan's Bane into Jordan's Blessing using the Divinity Staff signifies your powers are coming of age. I think **you** may be the right person to carry the rod and shield!"

Jason set down his polishing cloth and looked at Galad like he was speaking a foreign language. Before Jason could respond to Galad's ridiculous suggestion, Nathan joined the two. Jason shook his head no, to Galad, before taking the rod out of the vice. Not seeing the exchange between Jason and Galad, Nathan looked at the partially completed rod as he exclaimed, "Its looking like you two succeeded in your part of the process!" Nathan said with pride.

Nathan couldn't wait to use his Master Goldsmith skills as his part in the creation of the Celestial Rod. It would be his task to mount the magic relics on the Celestial Rod. He had not brought his goldsmith skills up much, because he disliked bragging. He also had some minor enchanting skills, but nothing like the tinkers of ages past.

Walking up to Jason, Nathan looked closely at the rod, as he explained, "The Eye of Illusion will be mounted in the center. The Sacred Sun Medallion is to be mounted above the Eye. The Moon Stone will be mounted, at the same distance, below the Eye. The large emerald known as the Dragon's Tear, will form the top of the rod. With the silver dragon inscribed on the Tear facing forward." Looking at Galad and Jason he asked, "Did you know Aziris, the last green dragon's magic is contained in that stone? At least that is what I read somewhere."

Galad nodded, "You are correct Nathan. A wizard captured her, demanding the location of her hoard, while holding her in an enchantment. She poured all her magic into the making of the Tear. That is why it bears her silhouette. A very powerful artifact in its own right." Galad said sadly.

Now that Jason had completed his portion of the task, he reverently handed the rod to Nathan and smiled, "Thank you again, Nathan. If not for you giving me the magic hammer, all those years ago I could not have done it! I believe you are the person to finish the Celestial Rod!"

Nathan accepted the newly forged rod and smiled back at Jason and said, "Even back then Jason, I sensed you were destined for greatness, you have certainly not disappointed me!"

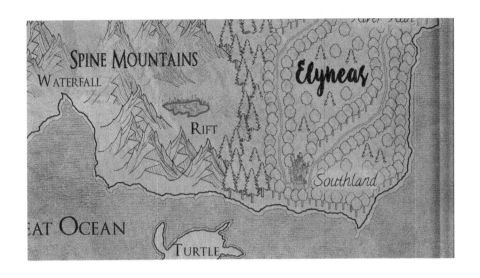

Checking the Wards

Azrador and Leila had watched Galad and Jason work on the rod until dinner time, finally returning to their tent when it became obvious, they would be working well into the night. When Azrador woke the next morning, he found Leila already dressed and giving orders to Mirza, her handmaid. Breakfast was waiting on a table across from the bed. After freshening up and having breakfast Azrador felt refreshed and full of vitality again. Leila joined him for a cup of coffee, smiling at him with a big grin.

Staring at her blue eyes and bright smile he said, "You look pleased this morning, and quite beautiful!"

Still grinning she joked, "I thought you might sleep all morning, the way you were snoring!" Leila said with a giggle. Turning to a more serious subject she noted, "We need to check the wards we have on the lizard men today. I have just received reports of their numbers growing rapidly and some are breaking out. I have thirty men standing by to leave as soon as you are ready." Finishing her coffee, she stood up and pulled on her gloves.

Azrador stood up and grabbed his gear from the corner. "I guess I'm ready then!" He took one more bite of breakfast and followed her out the door.

He caught up with Leila in time to catch her sneaking Ebony, her favorite horse, a small block of sugar. The large black stallion nuzzled her before she effortless mounted the black beauty. Azrador mounted Blaze and the two of them led the group of thirty elf soldiers to the boundary near the rift.

One of the first things Lady Leila noticed when they arrived at the perimeter of the ward barrier was that several markers were no longer active. They soon encountered a group of ten lizard creatures nearby. The lizardmen had taken down several horses and their riders before the group realized the lizardmen were hunting in groups now. Crossbows were brought out and four of the large creatures were down in the first few volleys. Azrador pulled two blue arrows from his quiver and quickly brought down two of the creatures. Leila cast lightning at another but only wounded it, as it continued to attack the lead rider. The captain of the guard took the head off that one in one mighty swipe of his elven sword. As four of the large lizardmen turned toward Azrador and Leila, they began spitting their foul poison. Leila cast a protect spell in front of them, while Azrador pulled a black and white fletched arrow from his quiver and shot. The arrow split into four projectiles, striking four separate targets. Taking the lizards off their feet with the impact.

Still trying to catch her breath Leila panted, "That was closer than I would have liked!" Leila said when she realized how close the monsters were getting. "There are so many more of them than the last time we were out here Azrador."

Azrador quickly scanned the lizard bodies, making sure they were dead. "I swear not only are they multiplying, but they are also getting bigger!" Let's see to the other wards. I hope the lizards are still contained." Thinking of Jason and Nathan, Azrador stated, "I think they better hurry with that magic rod and all. Not only is there a large increase in the population of the lizards, but the land is also much more barren than last time we were here." Azrador replied as they headed closer to the rift.

As they worked to restore the wards, they found more and more of the creatures were getting out. They had several more battles with the lizards roaming the land.

They did not have any luck getting close to the rift though. There were hundreds more of the lizard men packed in and around the rift itself. As they watched, from a distance, there was a steady flow of the monsters exiting the ground.

Leila, shocked at their increasing numbers, gave the order, "Let's get back to camp! I want to see what progress they have made on the Rod, as well as report what is happening out here. I don't believe we have much more time before they break out of our wards completely!" Leila said as she turned Ebony for the camp.

Nathan proceeded to roll out his tools on the worktable. He carefully assembled a horizontal vice, preparing his workstation. Earlier, when he had first arrived, he placed a small bellows that was attached to a metal box next to the worktable. The metal box already had coal burning in it. On top of the metal box was a crucible that he dropped four large gold nuggets into. Slowly pumping the foot bellows, he achieved the right temperature for the gold to melt into a puddle in the crucible. Placing a jeweler's eyepiece in his right eye, he began the tedious process of setting the artifacts into the indentations Jason had prepared.

He could feel the magic in the emerald pulsing in his hands as he placed the Dragon Tear. Nathan was using his best gold to attach the magic relics to the rod. Nathan could see that Jason had formed it perfectly, including the receptacles for each artifact to be placed. Nathan quietly worked on the rod the rest of the day.

Towards sunset Nathan rose from his seat at the workbench. He stretched, stiff from the hours of sitting. Galad and Jason had silently watched as Nathan applied his skill to the rod. Joining Nathan at the workbench the three men stood staring at what they had achieved. The Celestial Rod was complete! It was just shy of five feet tall and was a stunning masterpiece of jewelry. The setting sun reflected off the Celestial Rod, causing a rainbow on the horizon.

Galad slapped Nathan on the back and said, "You do beautiful work Nathan, let us all hope this works!"

When Swan woke the next morning, she found Galad had already left their quarters, even though the sun was just coming up. She assumed he was anxious to rejoin Jason and the making of the Rod. Swan took her time and freshened up, had breakfast, and finally wandered over to the smithy area, where she found Jason, Nathan, and Mikiel. She was surprised she hadn't seen Galad or Gunter anywhere nearby. She knew Gunter had been spending a lot of time with Amara, she was still resting from her spellcasting on the artifacts, she assumed he must be with her.

Swan addressed the group "Good morning fellas, have you seen Galad anywhere? I expected to find him here with the rest of you."

Nathan tore his eyes off of the Celestial Rod long enough to respond, "Galad came to the coach early, looking for Gunter, but he wasn't in the coach. I would think he is most likely with Amara." Nathan's attention returned to the rod immediately after he answered her.

Mikiel shook his head, "No, Galad woke me early this morning looking for Gunter in Amara's quarters. He hardly spoke but he did say he needed Gunter for the morning. The two of them left together right after that."

Not sure what to think of that Swan told Mikiel, "That seems quite odd on both their parts!" She headed to the stable area, to see if they were there.

∞∞∞

Galad chuckled as he soared over the Great Ocean with Gunter on his back, cursing as he held on for dear life. Gunter recalled how Azrador talked about his ride on the dragon. This was one of the few times he was inclined to agree with him. Galad had collected Gunter early that morning, with the promise of taking him on an amazing ride. It was all of that and more! Gunter managed to relax a little, as he watched the schools of fish changing direction in the ocean below them.

Galad mind spoke to Gunter for the first time, since transforming into his dragon form. "Are you enjoying the view from up here mage?"

Gunter thought for a moment before responding, "It's overwhelming at first, but I think I am getting used to it now! You promised an amazing ride and you are certainly delivering!"

The last contact before Galad broke off the mind link was, "You think this ride is amazing, wait until you see my lair if you want to be amazed!" They continued on to Dragon Claw Isle, in silence.

A short time later they landed through the giant hole in the mountain, entering the dragon's lair. Gunter dismounted from the dragon wobbly legged. It took him a couple of steps to get his bearing.

While Gunter oriented himself to walking again Galad took on his human form. Leading Gunter inside the cave. Gunter was quite surprised at what a richly furnished and decorated home the dragon had.

Galad ignored Gunter's surprise and stated, "Welcome to my home mage! Before we go any further, you should know few have ever seen it. Swan is the only other person that has been here and still lives." Galad smiled at Gunter as he commanded, "Follow me, to the library!" Galad turned and headed down a long hallway, leading Gunter into the dragon's huge library. The glitter of preservation spells covered the collection of books, scrolls and other odd documents. Galad walked to a section of books and pulled a large, leather-bound tome out of the row. Turning to Gunter, still smiling, Galad said, a little more sternly than intended, "You should know, it is rare for me to be wrong about anything. The few times that I have been, I admitted it. When I learned of the egg, I treated you harshly. After reflecting on my actions, it occurred to me without your perseverance there would be no egg. You carried it, keeping it safe, even after your comrades harassed you over it. I feel you should be rewarded for that perseverance. That is why I brought you here." Galad nodded at Gunter as he handed him the heavy book. "I gift you this rare book on enchanting. It is written in old elvish, but I have confidence you will find it more than interesting. Maybe your friend Azrador can help you translate it. I hear he is quite good at it."

Gunter looked at the golden eyed dragon, shocked at his words and the gift. Without saying a word Gunter accepted the tome, in awe of such a valuable gift. Gunter of all people knew just how rare books on enchanting were. Feeling he must say something, Gunter spoke, "Galad, you have nothing to apologize for. This tome is much too valuable for me to accept."

Shaking his head, Galad continued, "Now if you will follow me down the next corridor." Galad led the way out of the huge library and down another beautifully decorated hallway that was lined with paintings. Galad walked up to a blank wall and Gunter could hear him whisper something. Suddenly the wall swung open, revealing the dragon's treasure room. Gold, in any form imaginable, was piled to the ceiling of the massive room.

Gunter stood with his mouth hanging open for a few seconds before exclaiming, "By the god's Galad! Look at the gold you have accumulated! Your collection is massive! You have more treasure here than any of the three kingdoms!" Gunter said in awe as he stared at the display of wealth.

As Gunter gawked at the unimaginable amount of gold in the hidden room Galad went on, "You have been the caretaker of the unborn dragon that lays dormant in the egg. You are the first to know, I have decided not to fire the egg. With the battle in front of us, and not knowing who, if any of us, will survive. What I am about to ask of you is a heavy burden, not a reward like the book." Galad looked at Gunter, making sure he had the enchanter's full attention. "I ask you to continue to be the egg's caretaker. If we do not survive, I want you to take the Tinker's Coach as far away from here as you can. Perhaps in the future, fate will provide another dragon, to fire the egg. I show you my treasure room so you can provide for the youngling if it hatches. It is important for a dragon to have a hoard for their magic to grow. Its size determines how strong a dragon is."

Gunter watched, not knowing what to say, as Galad walked to the mound of gold and ran his hand through the many gold rings and coins. Selecting a gold ring with a clear stone he held it in front of Gunter. Galad made a motion with his other hand and a soft golden glow appeared, first surrounding the ring, then surrounding Gunter. Gunter felt a cold shiver run up his spine as the magic touched him. Galad handed the ring to Gunter. As Gunter put the ring on, Galad whispered the magic word for opening the vault in Gunter's ear. "The ring will always guide you to this location. If you encounter another dragon, be careful before revealing you have the egg. Some will try to trick you, to find my hoard. Hopefully none of this is necessary, but precautions are needed. Now, do you agree to be the caretaker of the egg? That includes staying out of the fight to protect it?"

Gunter was shocked at the suggestion he would not be with his friends when the time to fight came. "Wait a minute! You didn't mention the part about me staying out of the fight! I cannot stay behind and watch my friends go into battle!" Gunter was trying to remove the ring, but it would not come off.

Not surprised at Gunter's response Galad tried to reassure him, "Be calm mage, you are not a fighter, but an enchanter. The tome I gifted you will allow you to do enchantments that have not been seen in generations, surely you want to live long enough to use them."

Gunter hated to admit to Galad that Amara had made the same argument. He knew she would agree with the dragon, someone must keep the egg from danger.

Galad could see Gunter was considering his request, "Why don't you think on it during your return ride to camp. It is time for us to return!" Glad said leading the way back to the landing area.

Galad quickly took dragon form and Gunter placed the enchantment tome in his pack before he climbed aboard, dreading another "ride of his life". He considered what the dragon had said, on the ride back to camp.

When they arrived back at camp, Amara was still recovering in her quarters, so Gunter sat down next to her bed. He watched her sleep, impatiently waiting for those violet eyes to open again.

∞∞∞

While Galad, Nathan and Jason had worked to create the rod Amara was asleep, still in bed recovering from the Moon Stone Ceremony. While deep asleep she suddenly finds herself in the mist, without the protection of her shade amulet. Soon spirits began gathering around her, some appeared uninterested in her, but some felt more menacing. She felt a freezing cold sensation run up her spine, as Tassarion, the Demon, took shape in front of her.

Horned and red skinned with massive red, leathery, scaley wings he towered over her. The Demon had a deep red aura surrounding it and it held a large dark red trident in his right hand.

After looking her up and down Tassarion spoke with a booming voice, "Foolish girl! You have come here, unprepared! Bow down and swear allegiance to me now, and I may let you live as my personal slave. Soon I will command an empire and an army of the dead to do my bidding! Your puny magics have no effect here in my world!"

Before she could react, the demon reached out and grabbed her by the throat and squeezed. She could feel the burn of his touch as she tried to dispel him, with no effect. The burning escalated and she felt like she would burst into flames.

As her sight started to dim Amara could hear the High Priestess Danica whisper to her "use the frost amulet around your neck." As a last effort before she passed out, she reached up and touched it to Tassarion's hand around her neck.

Tassarion screamed out in anguish, releasing Amara's throat, retreating a few steps, with his hand smoking, before cursing her. "You will pay for that bitch!"

Amara awoke suddenly, her heart racing and breathing hard. She could still feel the creature's hands gripping her throat now that she was awake. Her sudden waking rousted Gunter from his dozing on an adjacent group of pillows, where he had been watching over her since the second transfer ceremony.

Concern for her marked Gunter's face. "Amara are you alright?" Seeing red, blistered skin where Tassarion's hand had been, he asked, "What has happened to your neck? You have burns all around it, let me get some salves from my pack." Gunter hurriedly searched for the right jar in his pack, as Amara glanced at the ring of burns around her neck in her dressing mirror.

Shocked by what she saw there she exclaimed, "By the gods it was real! I met the Demon Tassarion! He is immensely powerful and dangerous. Worse yet, he was able to enter my dreams. He almost killed me in my sleep Gunter!"

Gunter could hear the fear in Amara's voice. She was not calming down as Gunter administered the healing salve on her neck. Blisters in the shape of fingers had already formed all around her throat. After finishing applying the salve, Gunter produced a small vial and asked her to drink it.

Amara pushed the vial back at him as she shook her head. "No! I don't want to go back to sleep Gunter, he will be waiting for me!" Amara stated with fear in her voice. Looking Gunter in the eye she told him, only half-jokingly, "I may never sleep again!"

Gunter put an arm around her trying to comfort and calm her. "This won't put you to sleep. It will only relax you and help with the pain from the burns. You know I wouldn't risk harm to you Amara. Please drink it, you will feel better, and it will help you think straighter." Gunter handed her the vial, letting her decide to drink it. Amara tried to smile at the kind mage as she took the vial and downed it in one drink. In a few moments Amara began to feel much more relaxed. She felt the pulsing in her neck subside as Gunter's salve began to work.it and the salve began to soothe the burns.

Gunter patted the pillow next to him, "Come sit with me. I will help keep you awake as we wait for morning." Amara smiled at the mage. She was surprised that she had taken such a liking to him. If only life would slow down for a bit, she thought to herself, as she sat down on the pillow next to him. She leaned over and kissed Gunter. Taking him by surprise, but not for long. Embarrassed at her boldness she covered it by saying, "Thank you Gunter for being a friend. Since my twin, Dylan's death I find myself in need of one!" Amara said in a whisper as she kissed him again, more passionately this time. Morning was several hours away yet.

When Nathan had completed the Rod, he gave it a close inspection, hoping that he and Jason had gotten all the measurements right. It was then he recalled that the scroll stated if the Rod was built correctly, it would easily attach into position on the back side of the dwarven shield. Nathan was thinking about what the chances were that they would have found both the Shield of Torevir and the Eye of Illusion in Ruby Falls. None of this would be possible if the stone golem had killed Azrador and Gunter along with Nathan. The magic artifacts they found there had helped win the war against the Silver Tower and were about to lead them in their attempt to save mankind.

Galad, back in human form stated, "There is much more magic energy coming off it now that it is fully assembled, than what the individual pieces contained. I have rarely seen a more powerful magic item, and yet I know not what kind of magic it is. It is completely different than anything I have ever seen in the magic spectrum. I can also see the effect that Amara's charging has had on the Sun Medallion and the Moon Stone. A large amount of the rods magic is contained in them."

Jason sent a messenger with word of the Celestial Rods successful completion. The messenger also asked Swan to bring the Shield of Torevir to the forge. On getting word of the rod's completion, Swan informed Azrador and Lady Leila of the news as they arrived in camp from checking the wards. The three of them hurried to Mikiel and Amaras tent to retrieve it.

The three companions stood staring at the shield before Swan asked, "Azrador can you carry it? When I treated Mikiel's sore shoulder, he told me he hurt it just by picking that thing up."

Azrador, never one to admit failure, bent over. Intending to pick it up, by himself. At the same time, Leila bent over, sharing the weight of the shield between them. Smiling at Azrador she stated, as a matter of fact, "Let me help you. I saw how sore Mikiel was after lifting it. We are going to need all of us to be at our best, to close this thing."

Azrador looked Leila in the eye, looking to see if she was mocking him. "Alright, come on. I have no time to argue with you. Even though we all know I am strong enough to carry this shield on my own, I will humor you."

Behind Azrador's back Swan and Lady Leila exchanged grins. Happy not to have to argue with the stubborn elf.

When the trio arrived at the forge, carrying the large shield, Nathan motioned for them to place it on Jason's workbench. As they stood admiring Jason and Nathan's masterpiece, Azrador was nodding his head, as he examined the finished product.

Holding his hands over the Celestial Rod, Azrador closed his eyes and began to hum. After several minutes he opened his eyes and spoke, while still staring at the rod. "When the time comes, we should have all troops and personnel not required to do this task moved back a safe distance from the Temporal Rift. Lady Leila and the elves concerns are valid. I would expect a violent consequence when this strong magic strikes the anti-magic Temporal Rift, something similar to when Nathan threw the cursed weapons into Jordan's Bane only much more powerful. An explosion may be the least of it. We should take precautions."

Jason picked up the rod, taking a large amount of pride in the jeweled piece. Now that everyone, except Gunter and Amara, were present, he placed the rod in its place, on the back of the Defender of Torevir, feeling it snap into place. Suddenly the massive shield began to glow. They all watched as Torevir's Eye, on the front of the shield, turned green. The iris of the Eye now had an image of a dragon floating in it.

The group had been so focused on what they were doing they hadn't noticed a crowd had gathered. Apparently, after informing Swan, the messenger had continued to inform the whole camp of Jason and Nathan's success.

Proud to show off their fine work Jason held the shield aloft for all to see. The Elves and Sundowners gathered nearby all cheered their success!

Surprising even himself, Jason announced in a booming voice, "I will lead the way to the Temporal Rift! Who will join me!"

Galad thought Jason was the perfect choice and quickly followed with, "I will join you!"

Swan glanced at Galad before she piped in," We will join you!"

Azrador added, "I also will join you! I will not be left behind during such a momentous task"

Lady Leila spoke up next, "I will join you! As will all

my elf companions." Acknowledging the troop of solders King Alwin had sent.

Mikiel stood and said, "I too will join you! After the months of searching and preparing for this day I and my tribe are ready!"

Nathan, standing next to Jason slapped him on the back, "I too will come my friend! To glory, we all march together!"

Another cheer went up from the Sundowners and the soldiers.

Nathan stood considering what would come next. Soon, the much-anticipated battle would start, but would it be the end? Nathan worried that if they failed, he would never find the tinkers lost homeland. What choice did they have?

The Temporal Rift would swallow all life and magic. Eventually it would swallow their world if their plan failed. What good was a tinker homeland if all his friends were dead and the magic of the world was gone? Tomorrow they would have their answer. Nathan prayed it was the right one. Galad's scroll indicated the ancient artifacts would be redistributed again, after they used them, so using the Celestial Rod to close the Temporal Rift must not destroy the magic artifacts. Something Nathan was thankful for. Unfortunately, they will have to be found all over again if they are needed to find the homeland.

No one in camp slept well that night. Most lay awake while they thought of what they would be facing the next day, and what fate might bring!

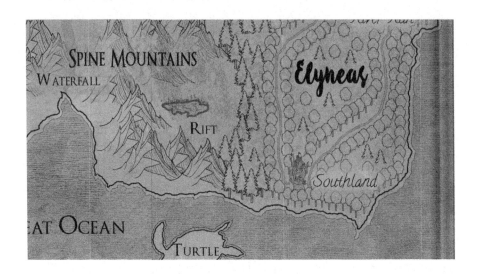

Dawn of Battle

Nathan woke as the first ray of sunlight filtered through the porthole in the front of the tinker coach. He hadn't sleep well, but was full of purpose, as he walked to a cabinet he rarely opened. The tinkers of old were a warring people, unlike todays friendly tinkers. They had smithed some of the best armor and weapons ever created. Unfortunately, the tinkers also created the cursed weapons as well. Their exile from their homeland was the price the tinkers paid for their lack of humility and humanity.

Nathan reverently dressed in his solid black adamantine chain link tunic and plate chest piece over it. Taking a moment, he studied his family sigil, proudly emblazed on the chest piece and matching plate helm, recalling the day so long ago, that his father presented it to him. Dressed in the battle armor of his kind he picked up Heart Crusher, his enchanted hammer, ready to meet his fate.

Mikiel was dressed in Sundowner Armor, a white tunic over silver chainmail before the sun rose, anxious for the day to begin. His family crest was also emblazed on his plate chest piece and headdress. He wore two curved swords strapped to his waist, awaiting his call.

Amara also wore silver chainmail and white tunic with their family crest on it. She also carried her twin brother Dylan's dagger, as a lucky charm. Her magic bow and a quiver of arrows were nearby, at the ready, along with her jewelry and magic.

Gunter had spent the night with Amara and had spent most of it trying to convince her to stay back from the main battle. He was extremely concerned for her safety after Tassarion's attack on her while she slept. She still had not fully recovered from the neck burns. Knowing how unhappy he was going to be about it, before she donned her battle armor Amara cast a sleep spell on Gunter, insuring he would be safe. Before waking she had witnessed a foretelling. In the foretelling she saw Gunter would not survive the battle. In her eyes, she was required to be there to face the Demon, not Gunter. Her chief wish was for the sweet mage to be safe back at camp.

Galad had convinced Jason to allow him to swallow three mana stones. He explained that if he swallowed the mana stones while in dragon form, he could protect their flank longer, using his magic and dragon breath. Afterall there still were over a thousand of the deadly lizard creatures between them and the Temporal Rift. Which was hard to imagine since everything around the town of Silverton was still green and had not yet been affected by the Temporal Rift.

Swan stood next to Galad, shimmering in the sunlight. Galad had presented her with a set of golden armor and helm, made from his golden dragon scales. The back plate displayed an etching of Galad, in dragon form. She spun her trident like a baton, impatient for the battle to commence.

Azrador and Lady Leila were both dressed in silver

mithril chainmail and matching shields, the only difference was their family crests. Azrador stood with Blazeguard in his hand. Leila stood ready, beside him with Icicle, her short sword at her waist. King Alwin's soldiers were lined up, ready to support them.

The time had finally come! Galad took the field as a golden dragon guarding the left flank of what could turn out to be the killing field. Swan was next to him with Nathan lined up to her right. Jason stood in the center, holding the Shield of Torevir in one hand and the Divinity Staff in the other. To Jason's right Mikiel stood, ready with two flaming swords, one in each hand. Amara, lined up to Mikiel's right, had an arrow knocked and ready to fire. Guarding the flank on the right were Azrador and Leila, their weapons drawn and shields at the ready. The elven guard and Sundowner soldiers were lined up in front of their line, waiting for the command to advance.

Taking one last look at his companions, checking to make sure all were ready, Jason removed the hood from the Divinity Staff. The radiant blue light of the staff blazed out ahead of them, shedding its light over the land. That was when the ground started to shake and the lizard creatures began lining up, like soldiers, in front of the spinning Temporal Rift.

The line of Elvin archers and Sundowner soldiers started to slowly move forward, marching in front of Jason's battle group. It was not long before the soldiers began to engage the lizard creatures with crossbows and ice wands.

Jason breathed in a deep cleansing breath and took a step forward, slamming the Divinity Staff into the ground. He then, in a loud clear voice declared, "Heal the land!"

A tremor went forth from the staff, rippling across the surface of the ground. The cracks in the ground nearest Jason started to close, healing the land, as the line marched forward.

Galad, breathing great fans of dragon fire, swept dozens of the large lizard creatures from the field. Nathan and Mikiel were focused on cutting down one lizard after another, as they got past the lead soldiers. Many of the lead fighters started to fall, either to the lizard's poisonous venom or to the bites from the scaly creatures. The lizard creatures were taller than a man when they stood on their hind legs. Word spread quickly when the soldiers learned that when the lizardmen took a standing position they spit their paralyzing venom, so the soldiers rapidly learned to avoid it.

Jason did his best to ignore the lizardmen, never taking his eyes off the spinning Temporal Rift that was their destination. Lizards seemed to avoid approaching anywhere near him. Jason could not see it, but he knew the Eye on the Shield protected him. The glow off the shield was repelling any lizardmen in his path. Every ten steps Jason would stop, plant the staff firmly in the ground, and loudly repeat the mantra, "Heal the land!" Each time, a tremor went out from the staff, undulating across the ground. Every time he repeated the chant the land around him healed its cracks, and green shoots began to appear under Jason's boots. What had been brown stubble minutes before was transformed into a green, vibrant land.

As the space between the front line and the spinning Temporal Rift shrank, the spinning of the rift increased in speed. Soon a harsh headwind began slowing their progress. Mikiel recalled a time, aboard Swift, when a huge windstorm caught him. To save the ship he had cast a whirlwind spell to counteract the winds. Hoping the spell worked as well on land as it had on the desert, he cast the most powerful whirlwind he could. The whirlwind spell was working well, until the Temporal Rift robbed Mikiel of his magic.

Their advance had taken them into the anti-magic zone, so everyone's magic was now dissipating. Galad could no longer cast spells or breath fire, but he still had his ferocious claws and teeth to use on the lizard creatures. After swallowing several he found them to taste like the ground they sprang from. The fight with the lizardmen was growing in intensity, and most of the elven and desert soldiers ahead of them were either injured or had fallen.

Since Jason had managed to close so many of the cracks in the ground, he had kept additional lizard reinforcements from surfacing.

Azrador's flaming sword, Blazeguard continued to work its magic when he struck with it, but Leila's Short sword, Icicle, failed when she tried to use its freeze spell. Even without its magic, Icicle was still effective enough to cut one of the lizards in half before it could bite her.

Azrador had his hands full fighting but was impressed with Leila's battle skills. He could see she handled her sword and shield exceptionally well.

Leila was the first of the team to fall. She was under attack by two of the nasty bastards, when one of them managed to bite her right arm, nearly severing her sword arm from her body.

Seeing Leila fall, Azrador rushed to her aid. With a strength he had never had before, he sliced off the two creatures' heads with one swing of Blazeguard, before tending to her wound.

Now, every time Jason slammed the Staff in the ground and repeated the mantra, "Heal the land," he could see the Temporal Rift moving away from them, toward the Spine Mountains.

Jason had slammed the Divinity Staff into the ground for the third time when he looked up and couldn't believe his eyes. There appeared to be a group of giants moving out of the mountains, behind the Temporal Rift.

Jason shouted at the top of his lungs, so all would hear him, "Reinforcements have arrived!" Shortly after that he caught sight of Hutch, wearing his beads, as he struck down one of the monsters with his spiked club.

Jason was starting to feel a little more optimistic about their chance of winning. As he healed the ground and closed the cracks the lizards were appearing less and less, so the numbers were beginning to turn in their favor.

Everyone was beginning to feel the fatigue of battle, as

well as the weakness caused by their life force being drained by the Temporal Rift. Everyone but Jason. He seemed to be immune to the draining life force. The Defender of Torevir provided a glow as it protected all around him, while the Divinity Staff was bathing the area in a blue light from above.

As the others felt their life force being drained, each time Jason struck the ground with the Divinity Staff he felt his strength increase. And each time he struck the ground with the staff the tremors sent ahead of him grew stronger. He could almost feel the Temporal Rift weakening, as it tried to drain the life from his comrades. The area of contaminated ground was shrinking, and they had eliminated most of the lizards.

Jason could see Mikiel and Nathan were finishing off two of the last lizard creatures. After patching up Leila, Azrador cut two more of the monsters in half with his flaming sword. He watched Nathan swing Heartcrusher, smashing into the snout of a beast before it could spit venom at him, just as Mikiel cut the head off the last one in front of him.

The spinning Temporal Rift was now rapidly changing colors as it continued to move west, ending up against the Spine Mountain range. When the Rift came up against the mountain it could not penetrate the stone of the rocky landscape, so it was blocked.

When the Rift stopped moving to the west, they all heard a loud groaning sound and a sickening voice scream "NO!"

Unexpectedly, Tassarion, the demon Amara had warned them of, appeared above the Temporal Rift. A hoard of skeletal warriors, wearing strange ancient armor and carrying swords of red, began to pour out of the rift. Jason watched as Hutch led the giants, moving forward to clash with the skeletal warriors.

Amara, spotting Tassarion above the Temporal Rift, shouted to her allies, "It is the demon, Tassarion! Shield yourselves, this battle is not over!" She was still able to use the Dragon's Ring fire to cut down a group of skeletons headed her way.

Hutch's giants, with their spiked clubs and shields, cleared a path through the smoking pile of bones, to meet the rest of the skeletons head on. The giants towered over the skeletons as their clubs were shattering their opponents into small pieces.

Jason watched closely as Tassarion was still floating above the spinning Temporal Rift, casting fireballs at the giants leading the attack. The giants shields deflected several fireballs before one of them was set on fire. He saw the red skinned, horned demon had a large snout, similar to one of Zella's pigs, and it held a large red trident in its right hand, while it flapped it's large, bat like, wings as it floated above the Rift. Tassarion was the size of two giants and blood dripped from its fangs.

The red blades the skeletons were using were fatal if you got struck by one. After the giants smashed some of the skeletons to bits, the remaining skeletons began to gang up on the giants. Three and four skeletons would attack a single giant. It wasn't long after the change in tactics that several more giants fell to the red blades of the summoned evil.

Amara, thanks to Danica's jewelry, was able to cast a Flying Daggers spell at a group of skeletons headed in her direction. She didn't realize she had already drawn the demon's attention, when she used the Dragon Fire ring on the previous group of skeletons. After that spell, the demon pointed his red trident at Amara, sending a huge black bolt into her chest, knocking her from her feet. Her armor and Danica's enchanted earrings protected her from some of the injury, but her chest was still smoldering, and her breathing was shallow when Mikiel reached her.

As Amara lay there she could not see, but she could hear her twin brother Dylan, telling her to get up, that her work is not yet done. As his voice faded it was replaced by the familiar voice of the ancient High Priestess, Danica, screaming at her, "Get up now girl, or you all will surely perish!"

Amara's vision was foggy, her head was pounding, and she could hear her heart beating loudly, but she took three deep breaths and forced herself to her feet. As her vision cleared Amara took stock of the battle. She saw her comrades were becoming fatigued, slowing their responses in battle. Remembering her foretelling of a few days ago, and the effect her necklace had on the demon in her sleep, she clasped Danica's Amulet of Frost and breathed the word "die" at the demon. Danica's necklace, like the other objects she had pilfered from the pyramid at Bantez, was immune to the Temporal Rifts leaching of magic. So, the temperature dropped at once, freezing the ground in front of her, all the way to the Demon thirty yards away.

Ten skeleton warriors froze in place between Amara and Tassarion. A dreadfully shrill scream erupted from the demon, before his image cracked and broke apart, exploding in front of their eyes.

Amara smiled when she saw the effect of the freeze spell on the demon. She was still smiling when Azrador saw the ground under her open up. He watched as numerous skeletons grabbed her, pulling her underground quicker than anyone could render aid. Leila watched in despair as the ground closed around Amara, immediately afterward she was gone.

Mikiel was standing less than four feet away when he helplessly watched as the skeletons dragged his sister underground. It had happened so fast, he was temporarily stunned, after witnessing his sister's disappearance. That moment nearly cost him his life, as a skeletal warrior swung its deadly red sword, aiming for his head. Fortunately, Nathan blocked the blow with Heartcrusher and then followed through, smashing the skeleton in the face.

Jason closed to within thirty paces of the spinning Temporal Rift when it began hurling black lightning bolts at them. One of the bolts struck Galad in the leg, knocking him down. Nathan deflected another bolt using his hammer as a shield.

Jason slammed the Divinity Staff into the ground with all his might, loudly repeating the mantra, "Heal the land!" The tremor that went forth this time was so strong it even turned the ground beneath the Temporal Rift green. They all watched as the Temporal Rift visibly shrank.

Jason signaled to his companions; it was time for them to retreat. They could all see the Temporal Rift was now rapidly changing colors as it spun even faster. Jason removed the Celestial Rod from its place on the Shield of Torevir, as his friends and allies moved further away. The glow coming off the magic artifacts was so blinding the skeletons had to look away from Jason and the rod. After confirming his allies had left the battlefield, Jason, with a mighty heave, threw the Celestial Rod as hard as he could over the heads of the few remaining skeletons.

Everyone else had halted their retreat and watched as the rod flew end over end, in what seemed like slow motion, toward the rapidly spinning Temporal Rift.

The Celestial Rod reached the Temporal Rift and landed in the center, causing a momentary flash of brilliant white light, followed by a thunderclap so loud, it hurt their ears. The ensuing blast took a moment but was so forceful it was felt in the chest of all present. Everyone except Jason, was knocked to the ground by either the blast or the rolling and pitching of the ground. The sounds of rumbling and the growling of the surrounding landscape went on for many minutes. The dust caused by the blast obscured everything from sight for several long moments after the ground finally quit moving.

When the debris started to settle, it began to sink in! Could the battle be over? The group of fighters and magicians were still trying to regain their footing, but still found it hard to believe when looking, the Temporal Rift was gone! As well as the remaining skeletons. More amazing yet, was the mountain that had been behind the Rift when the explosion began, was also gone.

Never more encouraged than at that very moment,

Jason again slammed the Divinity Staff into the ground and begged, "Heal the land!" He never meant it more than now. He closed his eyes, thinking of Jade and her importance in making this success. Just as a stiff breeze cleared the dust, blowing away the cloud that was covering the area. The stiff breeze had also helped carry away some of the smell of death that was all around them.

When Jason opened his eyes, he could not believe what he saw in front of him. He glanced back to see Nathan and Mikiel brushing themselves off, as they got up from the ground. Azrador rushed to the fallen Galad's side. Swan was already there, attempting to heal the black smoldering wound and stop the profuse bleeding caused by the black lightning strike. Galad's breathing was shallow, and a black burn had penetrated his golden scales. As Azrador felt his magic slowly returning, he added his healing to Swans, hoping for Galad's recovery. Slowly, Galad's breathing began to improve.

Jason, Nathan, Mikiel, Azrador, Leila, Swan, and Galad saw the killing field was covered in bodies. Some were their enemies like the lizardmen and skeletons. Others were their friends and allies that had given their lives, like the giants, elves, and Sundowners. Many had given their lives this day to ensure a future for their world.

Nathan's attention became focused straight ahead of them, as the dust continued to clear. Beyond where the Temporal Rift had been, the mountain behind it had disappeared. Just five-hundred paces beyond that, where the mountain had been, was a mature forest. Silver Oak trees reached three hundred feet into the air. Nathan was just able to make out what looked like fairies, flying around the tall, tasseled grasses ahead. The sunlight on their silver oak leaves made the whole forest shimmer. Nathan was so stunned, that for a few moments all he could do was stare with his mouth agape. He didn't even notice the blood running down his arm from a wound suffered in the battle.

Still not believing what he was seeing he asked Jason,

"Jason could it be real? After all we have been through! That looks like the land told of by my father, and his father before him, the lands of the old tinker stories! Could it really be, after all the centuries of searching for it?" Nathan seemed to be in a trance as he began walking towards the forest, picking his way through the bodies, his pace increasing with each step. After a few steps he was all but running. "I have to touch it! I have to know if it be real!" He exclaimed to no one in particular. For the moment, all Nathan could see or hear was what was ahead of him, all else in the world was gone.

One of the surviving elf healers was tending Lady Leila, but she was still woozy from the loss of blood she had suffered, when she asked Mikiel, confused, "Where has the mountain gone? It was there just a moment ago."

Azrador and Swan were finally able to revive Galad, now that the Temporal Rift wasn't sucking away any more of his life. The dragon was slowly returning to normal, but was still weak, a condition he hoped not to get used to.

As the group gathered around Galad they began to assess the situation. Azrador offered, "Could it be that the Temporal Rift was the last test of finding the lost tinker homeland? The stories claimed the relics would be needed to open the final door."

Nathan, still in shock, and afraid to believe it was real, stated, "None of us thought the Temporal Rift was that door, but it must have been. No wonder Tassarion was determined to stop us. If it wasn't for Amara I don't' think any of us would still be standing today. I don't know how I will find the strength to tell Gunter what has happened."

As they physically and mentally recovered from what they had been through each of them slowly walked toward the new wonders in front of them.

Past the first stand of shimmering Silver Oaks was a lagoon. There was evidence of a large harbor and a channel of water that continued from there into the Scarlet Desert now. It had merged with the Mystery River and lake in the distance.

From there they could see the colors from all the tents camped around the lake. A massive stone bridge crossed the waterway. On the other side of the bridge the forest and lush wildflowers continued. A wide paved road led on, into the forest as far as they could see.

Galad had recovered enough to transform to human form and had joined Swan. They walked hand in hand as they crossed the bridge into this fresh territory.

Mikiel had run to the spot he had seen Amara disappear, but there was no sign she had ever been there. His spirit was crushed at the loss of his sister, thinking it was too high a cost to putting down this evil. First Dylan and now Amara were gone, he had no idea how he would tell Willem they had lost the other twin.

It was while mourning his loss that he heard his sister's voice, coming from the beyond say, "Mourn not my passing dear brother, it was for a just cause, and contributed to your victory over the demon Tassarion and his minions. Worry not, I am here with Dylan, mother, and father and I am at peace. I need you to tell Gunter that my last thoughts were of him, and that I mourn the life we may have had together. As for you sweet brother, please settle down with one of those girls you like to visit so often and make me some nieces and nephews. We also want you to know mother, father, and Dylan and I are all so proud of you! You and Willem will go on to do great things together. Before I go, I have one request. Will you return the Book of Blessings to Danica? There is now no living person that can read it."

After agreeing to his sisters request Mikiel felt the sorrow lift from his heart, replaced by a joy he had never felt, as if by magic itself. Turning to observe the lagoon and former harbor in the distance, he could see Nathan dancing a jig on the other end of the large stone bridge. He felt the need to join him in the celebration. Mikiel's sorrow eased a little with each step towards his comrades on the other side of the bridge.

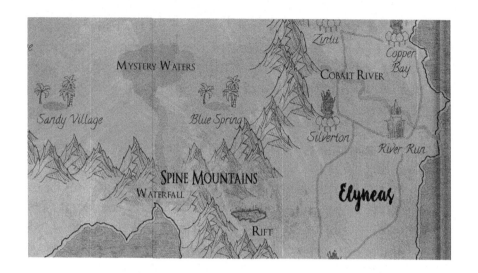

The Shimmering Forest

Gunter, driving Nathan's tinker coach, crossed the bridge into what they were calling The Shimmering Forest, parking in a clearing. He jumped out of the coach carrying brandy bottles and cups, anticipating the big celebration. When he saw the look on Mikiel and Nathan's faces, he knew bad news was coming. He quickly scanned the growing crowd of celebraters. He saw Azrador and Swan assisting Galad, headed in the direction of the coach. Starting to feel a sense of panic he continued to look around. He saw Jason, carrying the battered Shield of Torevir, in one hand and helping Lady Leila with the other. It was at that moment he understood why Mikiel and Nathan looked so distraught. Hoping beyond hope that the violet eyed beauty that had been Amara had survived, but knowing better, he approached the two men. Nathan took the brandy and glasses as Mikiel put an arm around Gunter, guiding him back inside the coach. Gunter broke down before

Mikiel could even tell him his love, Amara was gone.

Nathan took the glasses, heading toward the celebrating crowd, putting on a merry face, as he cried inside, knowing what his close friend was going through.

In the coach, Mikiel gave Gunter a full accounting of the battle. Telling him in graphic detail about how, when it looked like the battle was lost to Tassarion and his minions, Amara rallied from near death to save them all. Mikiel went on to describe Amaras last moments. He described how brave and courageous his sister was before she was taken by the skeletons.

He ended the conversation quoting Amaras wishes, "Mourn not my passing, dear Gunter, and know my last thoughts were of you, and that I mourn the life we may have had together. Worry not, I am here with my twin, Dylan, and my parents. I am finally at peace."

Gunter felt a calm of his own, consoled by her last thoughts being of him, and knowing she was at peace. He poured two tall glasses of brandy, handing one to Mikiel before toasting to "Amara! The bravest and most beautiful woman that ever lived!"

Mikiel went on to talk about their last conversation. "I believe my sister had an idea she might not survive the fight. As much as it broke my heart, Amara made me promise, if she was killed, I would return the Book of Blessings, and any of Danica's jewelry that remained after the battle, to the pyramid at Bantez. I cannot return what I do not have, but I can return the Book, as she wished." Looking Gunter in the eye he asked, "Would you join me, Gunter? You feel like a brother to me after what we have been through."

Gunter shook his head, as he replied. "No Mikiel as much as I would like to follow her wishes, my place now is beside Nathan as he goes forward in the tinker forest. I also feel close to you and your tribe and will always call you brother."

Mikiel nodded and raised his glass again, "To Amara!"

The two men continued their private celebration of

Amara and her heroism, sharing stories about her all night, before passing out from drinking too much brandy.

∞∞∞

Jason smiled at the outcome of the battle as he watched his friends start their well-deserved celebration. He waved back when he saw Hutch wave, as he watched the Giants of the Watch disappear up the mountain. The giants, like everyone else, had suffered many losses and were taking their dead home. Jason had no idea how Hutch and the giants knew to come to their aid, or where they had come from. All he knew was the Giants of the Watch had come to their aid, just in time. Without their help the skeletons may have overwhelmed them before Jason was able to complete the task.

When Jason reached the large stone bridge, he turned right and followed the inlet of water to the edge of what had been a desert a day ago. The Scarlet Desert was now connected to the ocean, by a waterway. From the looks of the harbor ruins, people had sailed from here, at one time.

Jason studied the ruins for several moments before walking out onto the sand. He closed his eyes and imagined a new landscape. It was at that moment that Jason had a vision of his own. Knowing what he needed to do, he opened his eyes, took two steps further into the desert and once again slammed the Staff of Divinity onto the ground, while repeating the mantra "Heal the land!" One last time the Divinity Staff emitted it's lovely, brilliant blue light. The blinding light went forth into the desert, instantly healing the land as it passed. Jason opened his eyes on what his imagination had thought of and saw the red sand steadily turn to a lush green grass, foliage spread like a pool of water. He could see streams sprouting up, in the distance. They could be seen as they flowed down the mountains, to the desert below, bringing a new beginning to the land. He watched the changing landscape cause two sand schooners to stop in their tracks, as the desert disappeared under them. He smiled, as he thought about how now the Sundowners would have an opportunity to return to the sea, if that was their choice.

As Jason watched the landscape changing in front of him, he felt a lessening of the power of the Divinity Staff. He saw Jade's blue stone no longer burned so brightly. He no longer needed a hood to shield his eyes from it.

As most of the battle's participants were rejoicing at being alive, Jason quietly reflected on the day's events. The Divinity staff had performed several miracles, all at once. The elven lands of Elyneas were now safe, and its magic felt strong again. The tinker homeland, that Nathan dreamed of and searched for all his life, had been found. Most surprising of the day's events was the Scarlet Desert had been healed of its lack of water.

He found it amazing that so many different peoples had come together in a unified task and succeeded in making a better world. What was even more amazing to Jason was that people that did not know each other existed, had worked together in a most unexpected way.

Galad and Swan spent the rest of the day helping with the funeral pyres of the dead from the battle. Galad's dragon fire ignited the pyres and sped up the smoky, smelly process and still gave the dead a good send off. Most of the remaining people watched with solemn faces saying their good-byes to fellow comrades.

The next day Mikiel, feeling hung over as never before, caught up to Jason, who was sitting on the ground watching the continuing greening of the desert before him. They both watched as the desert disappeared and a lush new land began to appear.

After several moments of silence between the two men, Jason spoke first. "I do not have the words to express my regrets and grief at the loss of your sister. I keep reviewing in my head what I could have done differently but have no answers. I did not know her well, but wish I had. I will always remember her bravery in the face of Tassarion, and her determination to not let him succeed. Without her actions I would not have succeeded."

Mikiel nodded in agreement, "Yes, Amara deserves a lot of credit, and it breaks my heart that she is gone, but she is content with where she is." Changing the conversation to an easier topic Mikiel stated, "My people are in your debt Jason; you have stopped the Temporal Rift and healed our land. My greatest hope now is that we all live in peace, enjoying future trade and cooperation. As my brother, Sultan Willem's representative what I say now is the same as if he said it himself. Jason Carron, if ever you need the aid of the Sundown Tribe all you need do is send word and we will be there! You are forever welcome; I hope you will consider staying with us and settling in these new lands. Amara was not the only beautiful woman in the Sundown Tribe." Mikiel proudly stated.

Turning to Mikiel, Jason smiled, "I appreciate the offer Mikiel but, I must return to Strongheim. I promised Clan Chief Brackus that I would return the Shield of Torevir. The first thing I have to do when I get there is to repair the damage done to it. Master Bluthe is old, and he says he has much yet to teach to me. I feel there is much more for me to do in this life." Jason said, with an insight he never had before. Mikiel spotted the two sand schooners that had come to a stop, now surrounded by grass.

Mikiel swiftly returned to his tent, to gather some tools and equipment. He hastily said his final goodbyes to the others, before trotting off to greet the stuck schooner captains.

Jason noticed a crowd gathering around the tinker coach, so he headed across the stone bridge to join them. When he approached, everyone gathered around him, giving out pats and heaping on the praise for doing an amazing job. Many also expressed how relieved they were that the Temporal Rift was closed. Everyone expressed their sadness at the loss of lives their victory had cost, especially Amara's.

Galad, in human form, greeted Jason, "Welcome Jason! I have been waiting for you to join us." Turning to his companions, Swan at his side, he announced, "Now that Jason has joined us, I will execute the fire ceremony, on our female dragon egg. When the firing is complete the color of the egg will tell us what color the dragon contained in it is."

Swan turned to Gunter, smiling at how hung over he was. "Gunter would you please fetch the egg from the coach?"

Gunter, feeling a little sluggish from the drinking with Mikiel the previous night, got up from the stool he was sitting on. He slowly made his way back to the coach.

Before fetching the pink egg that sat on a maroon pillow, on the main table, he helped himself to a small vial in his vest pocket. It was a sure-fire hangover remedy. He got the recipe from Henrick, years ago, after they had too much wine from the Heavenly Slopes Vineyard. He started to feel better right away, and thought to himself, too bad Mikiel left in such a hurry, he probably could have used a dose too.

Now with a little zip in his step, he stepped out of the coach, carrying the pillow with the egg firmly sitting on it.

Galad's attention was focused on the egg, as he addressed Gunter. "Ah Gunter, I must thank you again for keeping this egg safe during the battle. If you wouldn't mind, I would like your assistance in the ceremony!" Galad asked. Not waiting for an answer, because he assumed it would be yes, he spoke to the gathered crowd. "Please clear a wide area over here please!" he said, pointing to a clearing in the trees.

The spectators quickly moved out of the dragon's way. He then directed Gunter to carry the egg about thirty paces into the clearing.

Gunter counted out the thirty paces and turned to face Galad, asking "How's this?" He was a little uncertain about what was going on.

Galad's full attention was now on the egg when he answered. "That is perfect Gunter. Now, it will be your job to hold the egg, above your head, when I give you the word. I will transform and breath fire directly on the egg. It will levitate above you as I continue to fire it. When the fire ceases, the egg will drop to the ground, so you will have to catch it as it falls. After the firing, the egg will be fragile and must be handled carefully."

Gunter was beginning to wish he had never picked up the large pink rock. He could feel everyone's eyes on him as he held it in both hands, trying to think of a way out of his current situation. It only took one look at Galad for him to know there was no way out.

Looking at Gunter, holding the pink rock, it occurred to Galad, Gunter might not be strong enough to hold the huge egg above his head. He made note to keep a strength spell in mind, just in case.

A hush fell over the crowd when Galad transformed into a huge Gold Dragon. The dragon looked around the group, taking note of the number of witnesses to the ceremony. He thought it fitting, since the world thought dragons extinct, that they should now witness the color ceremony. Word that dragons live will spread rapidly after that.

Galad mind spoke to all in attendance. "Since time began there have been dragons, most lived far from your homes. To most alive today dragons are only myths and legends. You will all now bear witness to the majesty of the dragon's color ceremony!"

Galad mind spoke to Gunter. "Are you ready mage?"

Gunter mind spoke his reply. "I had waited a long time

to see if this really is a dragon egg. And I still would never have known if I had not met you. So yes, I am ready. Let us get on with it!"

Taking a deep breath and unfurling his wings, Galad mind spoke one last time to Gunter, "Raise the egg!"

Galad's words rang in Gunter's ears as he raised the egg high above him. Galad flapped his wings and left the ground, hovering in place, as he cast a levitation spell on the egg. The large egg slowly floated above Gunter's head, climbing higher than Gunter could reach. Showing his teeth and fangs to the crowd, in his version of a smile, Galad let loose a gout of dragon fire. The egg began to slowly rotate in the fire. Several moments passed as the dragon fire heated the entire area.

Galad continued to bathe the egg in fire for several moments before abruptly cutting off the dragon fire. The egg continued to rotate, turning slower and slower, changing to many colors as it did. Blue, red, black, green it continued to change color as Galad landed and transformed back into his human form.

He, along with the crowd of onlookers, watched as the rotating egg slowly came to a stop before dropping back into Gunter's waiting arms.

The audience broke into applause as Gunter caught the large egg. Gunter was so relieved to not be burnt to a crisp he didn't even notice how warm the egg felt.

Galad proudly addressed all attending, "We already knew the future dragon will be female, and now we know she will be a lunar white dragon, the rarest of all. Her white scales symbolize death and rebirth, so she will be associated with the moon god or mother goddess. Meaning she will have supernatural power and strength. We will get to meet her at the next full moon! She will be the first of her kind since Alabaster the Wise." Galad said with pride as if he was praising his own offspring.

Gunter carried the now snow-white egg on the maroon pillow, back to Galad and the group of spectators. He noticed the egg felt lighter than before and he swore he could feel vibrations coming from inside it.

As Galad and Swan approached him, Gunter stated in surprise, "This egg feels lighter now, and I swear the egg is vibrating inside!"

Galad reverently stroked the white egg as he spoke, "I am glad to hear that! It means she is beginning to wake up. Gunter, your next month will be spent watching over her and protecting her from harm. After all, you are her guardian, and will be until hatching! Swan and I must attend to some things on Dragon Isle, but we will return for the birth, at the next full moon. You did a good job here mage!" Galad said as he patted Gunter on the shoulder, before grabbing a mug and shouting, "A toast to Gunter! The man that found the dragon egg and kept it safe. Ensuring that dragons will live on!" The crowd roared Gunter's name and toasted a mug to him.

When the toasting to Gunter subsided Galad went on to shout, "A toast to the yet unborn dragon! She will be known as Amara!" The crowd again raised their glass and shouted, "To Amara!"

Gunter was stunned for a moment at the announcement of her name. He was so proud of the girl the dragon would be named for, that he could hardly contain himself. His mind went briefly to how proud Mikiel will be when he hears she will wear his sisters name. The celebration continued all day!

The next day the group started breaking up as people were anxious to be heading home.

Lady Leila was already mounted on Ebony. What was left of the elven contingent were mounted and lined up behind her. As her guard were saying their goodbyes Azrador rode up, mounted on Blaze. He stopped his horse when it was alongside Ebony. He cleared he throat and announced, "I have decided to stay here in Elyneas. I am going to River Run with Leila, to report our success to King Alwin of the Elves.

Jason, Swan, Galad and Nathan said their goodbyes, happy to see their friend among his own kind. Lots of hugs and "Safe Travels" were exchanged.

Gunter stood alone, off to the side, trying not to feel envious of the elf's happiness. He was trying to be happy for him but was having a tough time of it when Azrador, still mounted approached him. "We have had many adventures my friend. I will miss your company."

Gunter nodded his head, "As I will miss yours, my friend."

Azrador turned to Galad as he reached into his pack. He handed the object to Galad. "You have been a good friend Galad. As a heartfelt thank you for rescuing me from the cave, I would like you to have this. It is something special for your hoard!" Azrador said as he and Leila spurred their mounts forward, trotting north, toward the Elven Capitol.

They were not far along the road when Azrador pulled out the red book he had found on Turtle Ilse. He said to Leila, "According to this book, the island we found the Moon Stone on, was originally called Creation Ilse. In it there is a map to a place called Gemini, where all the people are only two feet tall. According to the book the people of Gemini were known for their crafting of magic gems. I was thinking after you give your report to your grandfather and King Alwin we should go exploring. What do you think?"

Leila smiling at him, while holding her injured arm, "I think we should rest for a few weeks, and enjoy each other's company, before we venture off again. Besides, I want you to meet my mother! I know you two are going hit it off!"

As they rode, for the first time, Azrador realized he might not get out of this one. It dawned on him he might be making a future life with another full bloodied elf! He thought to himself. "How bad can that be? She is beautiful, smart, tough as nails and a full-blooded elf! He decided, things were definitely looking up!"

After Lady Leila and Azrador rode off, Swan asked Galad what Azrador had handed him. Galad opened his large hand and there lay a solid gold pyramid, and a note. It read, "Makes a mountain out of a molehill!" It was one of the special artifacts he had taken from the Ruins on Turtle Isle. Galad smiled a big toothy grin, recognizing the magic aura around the pyramid. He thought this was a great addition to his ever-growing hoard.

Jason was examining the battered shield when Nathan approached, placing a hand on the big man's shoulder, "We couldn't have won without you Jason. Thank you for all you have done. The world is a safer, better place than you found it!" Nathan stated with sincerity. "What will you do now?"

Jason, leaning on the Divinity Staff, pointed at the shield, sitting on a bench in front of him. "I promised to return the shield to the dwarfs, and I have much yet to learn from Master Bluthe. So, I will repair and then return the shield." Jason got a faraway look in his eyes, as he recalled the entrance to Strongheim. He held the vision of the entrance in his mind. Unexpectedly, a portal opened in front of Jason.

Not sure of what he was seeing Jason looked through the portal. He could see the road that led into the dwarven stronghold. Apparently, Garth was right! His mother was a traveler. He was overjoyed to discover her traveling magic had manifested itself in him. Jason bent over and picked up the battered Shield of Torevir. He smiled and said farewell to Nathan. He shook hands with Galad and asked him to let him know when Amara arrived. He couldn't wait to see her. He stepped up to Swan, taking her hands in his, "I have known you a long time Swan and we have become good friends. I hope we meet again someday. He glanced at Galad, before bending down and giving Swan a kiss on the cheek before stepping through the portal and disappearing.

Nathan smiled at Gunter, Galad and Swan glad they had witnessed Jason's exit. Gunter didn't say anything, he just stood there, with his mouth agape.

Galad smiled, "That boy's magic is just beginning! The wonders he has already accomplished! Who knows what his future will bring?"

Swan picked up her mug, wanting to toast Jason Carron, the gentlest giant she knew, "Let's have another drink. Pour us one Nathan!"

Gunter and Swan had pulled out the stools and Galad started the fire ring. It wasn't long before Swan brought out her live wood flute. She played several of her favorite tunes as the three men drank and sang. As the sun came up over the Silver Oaks the four of them lifted their glasses, and Gunter made a toast, "Welcome Home Nathan!"

Nathan could only smile as The Shimmering Forest lay in front of them, just as it had in legend!

The End of this adventure!

But where does the road lead to?

Epilogue

It had been another wonderful winter vacation with the children, they were almost grown and wouldn't be coming as often or as long. They lost interest in magic and the tales about it. Tizzy expressed how she was glad that Swan hadn't died, and was in our story, again this time.

Alex said he wanted to hear more about Jason's next adventure. "A Giant Master Smith must make some amazing things!" He had said as he hugged Pawpaw goodbye. Pawpaw was glad to hear that. He knew this summer would probably be Alex's last one with him, until he had children of his own to bring to Pawpaw's. So, he would be sure to continue Jason's exploits next time. Especially since the Master Blacksmith does go on to many more adventures of his own. His mother's magic was just beginning to show and grow in the gentle giant.

Pawpaw had some great memories of the children, grandchildren and now greatgrandchildren. This winter holiday Odin was old enough that he got to cut down the spruce tree for decorating. They all laughed when Tizzy stuck her finger, threading the popcorn on needle and thread, for decoration on the tree. The teenagers had used the red toboggan, and went sledding down Moose Hill, and across the stream screaming, all the way. Now even the great grandchildren were almost grown. He had told them all many stories of the life of the Tinker and his travels over the years. As he thought back over the many vacations he had enjoyed with his children, Anita, Andrea, Kevin, and Chris. Their children Adria, Ross, Jamie, Shaun, Sara, Bridget, and Timmy. Which led to Tizzy, Alex, Odin, Payton, Paul, Dez, Craig, Debbie, DJ, Erin, Danny, David, Kate, Megan, Grace, Kaley, and Kristy. His heart was full as he thought back on all their visits.

Pawpaw enjoyed telling the stories, and like the kids, he almost felt like he was with the characters from those stories, when he told the tales. The children always brought him joy and laughter. Their vibrance and zest for life was contagious for Pawpaw. Their imaginations could see the wonders of life most vividly at that age. That light and vibrance seemed to dull when they became adults and became busy with adult life.

Pawpaw sat on the back porch of his country home, puffing on his favorite pipe, enjoying the sunset. Once the sun had set, he headed around the back of the barnyard. He walked past the barn, and into a small stand of trees that stood behind it.. He reached behind some brush that was covering something. He gave the rope that was hidden in the trees a yank. When he pulled the rope a large canvas, covered in snow, lifted off the Huge Multi-colored Coach. He climbed the steps and closed the door behind him. Pawpaw always slept better in the Tinker's Coach!

THE END

Cast of Characters-Book 3

*ArchMage Ibis / Autry-Head of the Silver Tower
Azrador / Sulan-Ranger Mage-Full Blood Elf
Brendal/ Green Folk-Daughter of Lord Bretta-Mother of Leila
Chancellor Graves / Autry- Chancellor to King Ferdinand
Clan Chief Brackus / Torevir-Chief of Clan Krackus
Gadna / Torevir-Assistant to Jason
Galad / Golden Dragon-Human
Garth / Sulan-Leader of the Giants of the Sky Rock Mountains & father to Jason
Grand Master Bluthe / Torevir-Grand Master Blacksmith-Grandfather to Kapo
Gretchen / Autry-Spouse of Henrick & sister of Gunter
*Gunter / Sulan-Mage friend of Nathan
Hanson / Green Folk-Butler to King Alwin
Henrick / Autry-Spouse of Gretchen-mage alchemist
Henrick / Autry-Spouse of Gretchen-mage alchemist
Jade / Autry-Mage enchanter of the Silver Tower-Twin of Mone'
*Jason Conner / Sulan-Master Blacksmith
King Alwin / Green Folk Land-King
King Charles / Green Folk-First elven King
King Ferdinand / Autry-Spouse of Queen Jennifer

King Gregory / Balzar-Descendant of Pirates

Lady Leila / Green Folk Land-Sorceress-Daughter of Brendal-Niece of Ruth & Ulrith-Granddaughter of Lord Bretta

*Lord Bretta / Father of Brendal-Grandfather of Leila

Marcus / Balzar-Captain of the Sky Rock Clan Flyers

Marshall / Green Folk-Lady Leilas cousin

*Mikiel /Scarlet Desert-Brother of Sultan Willem & Amara

*Nathan / Tinker

Olaf / Sulan-Blacksmith & Jason's foster parent

Princess Margaret /Sulan-Older daughter to Rudolf & Sofia-Sister of Queen Jennifer-Daughter of King Rudolf & Queen Sofia-Granddaughter of King Jordan

Princess Swan / Autry-Daughter of King Ferdinand & Queen Jennifer-Granddaughter of King Jordan

Queen Jennifer / Sulan-Wife of King Ferdinand-Daughter of Rudolf & Sofia-Sister to Princess Margaret-Granddaughter of King Jordan

Amara / Scarlet Desert-Sister of Sultan Willem & Mikiel-Mind speaker

*Rose Carron / Sulan-Jason Conner's mother

Simon / Green Folk-Butler to Lord Bretta

*Swan / Balzar-Warrior & Sky Rock Clan Flyer-Dragon Rider

*Throdon / Torevir-

Willem / Scarlet Desert-Sultan-Brother to Mikiel & Amara - Spouse to Eve

Zella / Sulan-Wife of Olaf & midwife to Rose

Magic terms
Cintelle-heal

Freta- Fire

Frezet- cold

Kaminari-Lightning Bolt

Guano-Personal protection
Gavno-Area of protection

Condors & Such

Prism-Swan
Firefly-Marcus
Dragonfly-Dohith
Swift-Mikiel's schooner
Beast-Jason's draft horse
Ebony-Leila's horse

Special metals, stones, and Items

Adamantine-Iberium and Palladium combined
Amulet of Frost
Book of Blessings
Eye of Illusion
Iberium
Mana stones
Palladium
Sacred Sun Medallion or Dominaca in dwarf
Dragon Tear
Moon Stone
Nightstone
Divinity Stone
Divinity Staff
Shade Amulet

About The Author

H. D. Bobb Jr.

About the Author
H. D. Bobb Jr. was born and raised in a small town in the Midwest. Retiring after 40 years of Chiropractic practice, he now writes books of fiction. Over his Chiropractic career he ran a multi-doctor practice and published professional articles and software manuals over his career. His wife of 30 years, Donna, also acts act as an advisor and editor of the book series. H.D. has always loved fantasy book series like the Wheel of Time and The Sword of Truth. When he retired from Chiropractic practice, he looked forward to the time required to develop a strong storyline and create rich characters you care about as the reader. He and Donna in their free time enjoy the great outdoors, hiking and gardening. They live in Port Byron, Illinois on two acres and love watching the wildlife there. The Trilogy of The Tales Told by a Tinker are now available as an E Book, paper back or hard cover on Amazon.
The Tinker, The Mage & The Princess
The Eye of Illusion
The Dragon & The Book of Blessings
Look for his previous publication Crystal Guardian of the Five Worlds.

Books In This Series

Tales Told by a Tinker

Follow the adventures of Nathan the Tinker and his mage allies in the search for magic artifacts that will lead to the lost lands. New lands open up and new tribes are discovered along with their secrets, and it may require a new cooperation of peoples to defeat the evil that threatens to consume their lands.

The Tinker The Mage & The Princess

Nathan the Tinker is searching the three kingdoms for clues to the lost lands. He is joined by several mages and a winged warrior in the quest. The Silver Tower is at war with the kingdom of Autry and is threatening to over throw the monarchy. Follow his amazing eight wheeled coach through the kingdoms and his search for ancient artifacts that will open the doors to the lost lands.

The Eye Of Illusion

The second book follows the discovery of the Eye of Illusion which will allow our adventurers to see clues to other artifacts needed for their quest. A Volcano has caused massive quakes and rockslides, which have opened a new pass south. Cave Spiders and Giant Sand Worms threaten the peace for the Dwarfs and the Sundown Tribe of the south. Explore the Great Scarlet Desert and the Dwarfs living under the Channel Moluntains.

The Dragon & The Book Of Blessings

This is the final book in the trilogy. A volcano has caused massive quakes and spooked the giant sand worms from their lairs. They are terrorizing the Sundown Tribe in the Scarlet Desert. The Elves of Elyneas have asked for help in solving a magic anomaly in the south of their lands. A Demon threatens to take magic from their world if not stopped.

Made in the USA
Monee, IL
22 May 2022

96835433R00184